ACCLAMATION FOR BOOKS OF VAN R. MAYHALL JR.

The Last Sicarius

For fans of the award-winning *Judas the Apostle* and newcomers to the Cloe Lejeune series, Mayhall once again delivers a smart, fast-paced thriller with exotic landscapes, a fascinating dose of biblical history, an intrepid heroine, conniving evildoers, twists and turns, and just the right touch of humor that will keep you turning the pages.

—Anne Dubuisson Anderson,
writing and publishing consultant

A rare opportunity to engross yourself in an historical thriller that takes you from New Orleans to the Vatican to the Holy Land … The action is often intense, and the characters leave you waiting to read about their next adventure. *The Last Sicarius* truly grabs you and doesn't let you go until the final page.

—Bill Profita, radio talk show host,
107.3 FM, Baton Rouge, Louisiana

Judas the Apostle

A thriller with theological underpinnings, set both in steamy south Louisiana and in the Old City of Jerusalem … a fascinating fictional exploration of the least understood and most maligned figure in the salvation story … this is the most original work of fiction I have edited.

Catherine L. Kadair, freelance editor

Most Christians and many religious scholars accept the story that Judas betrayed Jesus for money. But did he? The author offers the reader a religious mystery every bit as gripping as *The Da Vinci Code*. Set in south Louisiana and covering three continents, this crisply written debut novel is a page-turner full of suspense, with a fascinating look at the motives of one of history's most loathed villains. *Judas the Apostle* presents the possibility of alternative groundbreaking biblical history that is also a compelling read.

—Jim Brown, author and syndicated talk show host
(produced by Clear Channel Communications and syndicated by
Genesis Communications, Minneapolis, Minnesota)

An edge-of-the-chair thriller, a stunning history and geography lesson, and an unparalleled glimpse into the past of one of history's most maligned figures … *Judas the Apostle* tells a great and truly plausible story, against the rich and often diverse tapestry of Louisiana, America's most colorful and mysterious region.

—Bill Profita, radio talk show host,
107.3 FM, Baton Rouge, Louisiana

This is a page-turner with both mind and muscle. Its thrills and intrigue are offered up with an equal dose of historic heft. It carries you along as it makes you reconsider the well-worn stories you thought you understood.

—Anne Dubuisson Anderson,
writing and publishing consultant

Mayhall, a Baton Rouge attorney, has done the one thing in this book that is essential to keep a thriller thrilling: he has created a bad guy who is truly evil. The Kolektor lives in a bunker under a fake antiquity store in Jerusalem and he is without conscience. He cares only for what he wants. Mayhall has a clear and uncluttered writing style well-suited to the thriller genre. His plot is good. He does his homework on the history of his subject.

—Greg Langley,
"Judas Has Compelling Plot, Attractive Local Setting,"
The Advocate, October 9, 2012

"Louisiana Author Spins Thriller about Judas Iscariot"
—*The Hammond Daily Star*, November 9, 2012

The reader is transported to exotic locales throughout time, including ancient Masada, North Africa during World War II and modern-day Jerusalem and Lyon, France. South Louisiana readers will enjoy iconic venues in the book that include numerous scenes at LSU in Baton Rouge, Madisonville, Lake Pontchartrain and the Tchefuncte River.

—*The Point Coupee Banner*,
"Louisiana Author Examines the Role of Judas in New Thriller,"
November 22, 2012

Van R. Mayhall, Jr. has penned a fascinating thriller packed with twists and turns. Ancient language expert, Dr. Clotile LeJeune's quiet life is shaken when she learns her estranged father has been murdered. She travels to her home town to unlock the mysteries of a 2000-year-old oil jar inscribed with the name 'Judas Iscariot' that her father left her. The race for answers takes her on a dangerous quest across three continents in order to discover the identity of Judas Iscariot.

—*Legatus Magazine*, February 2013

Mayhall has spun a highly original, suspenseful and atmospheric thriller. It is a savvy story of academia, archeology and theology, but you can also taste the warm Louisiana thread that runs through it like a good flavor—the Tchefuncte River, the LSU Campus, the elements of close family ties and the influence of religion.

The story weaves a mystical spell in the timeless story of good against evil that is hard to resist; *Judas the Apostle* joins my personal rank of books that I call one-sitting reads.

—Jeanne Frois, "Worth Watching: *Judas the Apostle*," *Louisiana Life*, March–April 2013

A linguistics professor's inherited relic sets an arms dealer on her trail in Mayhall's debut religious thriller. The conversations are weighty but never burdensome thanks to thriller genre conventions: a formidable villain with a penchant for taking artifacts that aren't his; a murder, a kidnapping and a face-to-face showdown; and lots of suspense—indeed, simply opening the jar takes quite some time. The brilliantly open ending steers clear of definitive answers but provides adequate closure. A solid thriller with an invigorating religious theme.

—*Kirkus Reviews*, June 2013

Page after page, Mayhall's dialogue and crafting of suspense draw readers into the mystery of a two-thousand-year-old jar and the murders it has incited.

A fast-paced, changes-at-every-turn intellectual thriller, *Judas the Apostle* is a quality novel that grabs and won't let go until the final page is turned. From the first chapter, where protagonist Cloe Lejeune's elderly father is murdered, through the discovery of what lies in the two-thousand-year-old jar that has sat on her father's mantel her whole life, the novel takes the reader on a ride of discovery as each chapter unfolds.

—ForeWord Review, *Clarion Review*. Five Stars (out of five)

The Last Sicarius

VAN R. MAYHALL JR.

iUniverse LLC
Bloomington

THE LAST SICARIUS

iUniverse books may be ordered through booksellers or by contacting:

iUniverse
1663 Liberty Drive
Bloomington, IN 47403
www.iuniverse.com
1-800-Authors (1-800-288-4677)

ISBN: 978-1-4917-2106-3 (sc)
ISBN: 978-1-4917-2108-7 (hc)
ISBN: 978-1-4917-2107-0 (e)

Library of Congress Control Number: 2014900764

Printed in the United States of America.

iUniverse rev. date: 02/03/2014

This book is dedicated to Mama Lo, now and forever.

PROLOGUE

AD 70

Elazar ben Yair, leader of the Sicarii, stood on the battle ramparts of the Fortress Antoina in Jerusalem, gazing out at the chaotic scene below. Fire, smoke, and ruin lay all around him outside the wall. The fortress, which had been built by Herod the Great and named for Herod's patron, Mark Antony, still stood, ironically, against the Roman legions attacking the sacred city. The outer areas of the city had been overrun by Titus and his men. The fierce hand-to-hand fighting was now all within the old defensive walls of the city. The Romans had breached the outermost third wall and were working with their battering rams on the second one. It was only a matter of time.

Elazar turned away from the mayhem and saw his lifelong friend and second-in-command, Jacob, studying the soldiers below. Jacob was a student at heart, but he was also a warrior and had fought bravely the first time the Romans assaulted the fortress. The key to conquering the Jews was the temple, the path to which ran through the fortress. The Romans wanted the fortress because it overlooked the temple complex and would make a superb platform from which to assault the heavily fortified temple. The Jews had fought valiantly to defend it. Elazar knew a last stand would be made by the Zealots in the temple complex itself.

"Damn the Zealots," Elazar muttered.

"What's that, Elazar?" called Jacob.

"I was just looking at what's become of Jerusalem and thinking, but for the Zealots, this did not have to happen," replied Elazar.

"But the Zealots have fought courageously at every engagement, and without them we would not have been able to hold out so long," observed Jacob.

"Yes, but the Romans sent Josephus to us to negotiate an end to this madness. What did the Zealots do? They wounded him with an arrow and sent him away. We might have talked our way out of this."

"You are correct," said Jacob. "But now the Romans have begun to burn everything and to spare no one. The rumor is that Titus has lost control of his troops, and without discipline, they will burn and kill until there is nothing left."

"The city is lost, and God forgive me, so is the temple. Nothing can save us absent a miracle," said Elazar.

"What do we do?" asked Jacob. "The Zealots will insist on some sort of final stand and a glorious death for themselves, which, unfortunately, will also include us."

"Gather our people tonight," said Elazar. "Have them bring only food and water. We must travel lightly and swiftly. We will take the secret tunnel out of the city."

"Elazar, that's almost a thousand men, women, and children. Can we possibly escape with all of them?" asked Jacob. "The Romans will surely follow."

"All our people go. Anyone left behind will be tortured by the Romans and then killed or made slaves," responded Elazar.

"But nowhere will be safe. The Romans will only catch us in the open and make a quick end to us," said Jacob.

"The Romans will be tied up here for days or weeks with the Zealots and the others, finishing their killing and looting. We will have some time," responded Elazar.

"The Romans have come this far to put down the rebellion. They will follow us no matter where we go," concluded Jacob.

"There is one place where the Romans cannot follow," said Elazar.

"Where? Where is this place?"

Elazar turned back to view the fighting below. For a moment the heat of the flames pressed against his face. "The stronghold! It will be safe," he said at last.

PART I

THE KOLEKTOR

There is no calamity greater than lavish desires. There is no greater guilt than discontentment. And there is no greater disaster than greed.

—Lao Tzu, *The Way of Lao Tzu*

CHAPTER 1

AD 2ø13

JERUSALEM

In a wooded area near the Hinnom Valley, the servant watched as the priest and his Swiss retainers slammed into the Kolektor's defensive position in the parking area outside Hakeldama, shouting and shooting, assaulting the defenders with automatic weapons. This could only be a rescue party led by the monsignor's friends along with the Swiss Guard, personal bodyguards to the pope. His master, the Kolektor, had said they would come sooner or later. He knew the Kolektor's rear guard would fight like trapped rats. Each fighter understood the only choice was victory or death. The Kolektor tolerated nothing in between.

The servant, unarmed, was at the laptop computer in the rear of the panel truck when the cleric and his forces first struck. He had no alternative but to try to hide, so he cowered on the floor, wriggling under a tarp apparently left behind by a work crew. A fusillade of bullets began to splatter and ping against the vehicle's hollow metal walls. He could hear the answering fire of the weapons of the men who had been left to guard the Kolektor's flank while the Kolektor himself took care of his deadly business in Hakeldama, the Bloody

Acre. In a final overwhelming assault, the attackers launched such a volley of bullets that all the windows in the rear and the side of the truck exploded inward, showering the coarse tarp in broken glass. Only the heavy covering protected him from being severely wounded by the ricocheting pellets of broken safety glass. The Kolektor's men had been cut down where they stood. The way to Hakeldama and to the Kolektor, his master, was open.

Suddenly, there was silence. The servant peeked from below the tarp to see gun smoke and smell gunpowder all around him. Then he heard shouts from the assault team and their hurried footsteps as they converged on the truck and its duplicate next to it. He cowered under the cover again, trying to make himself invisible.

A voice shouted, "Check them!"

"They are all dead, Reverend Father," a man replied.

"Check the trucks!" someone else yelled.

The servant's heart pounded in his chest as the door opened and he felt the presence of someone in the truck with him, smelled the stink of the man's body, and heard boots crunch on broken glass. He held his breath.

"Nothing!" a voice cried out.

Then the man was gone, and footsteps moved away at a rapid pace. The servant slid out from beneath the broken glass–covered tarp and crawled to the front of the truck, where the windshield was still largely intact. Carefully, he peeked over the dash and saw the priest and his Swiss soldiers heading toward the pathway into Hakeldama—*after the Kolektor.* The Kolektor had told him this was the Bloody Acre that had been purchased by Judas Iscariot himself— the Bloody Acre where the Kolektor had decided to dispose of his hostages, the accursed monsignor, the lady scholar, and her son and uncle.

The servant then saw the monsignor himself, apparently no longer a hostage, speaking briefly to the cleric in charge of the Swiss assault force. Plainly, the Kolektor's plan to dispose of all of the hostages had not succeeded. The two priests joined their troops, hurrying on into Hakeldama.

The servant was unsure of what to do. Should he attempt to go to the aid of his master? The sound of a single shot in the distance from the interior of the Bloody Acre galvanized his attention. It was followed by a long, keening scream. He had never before heard such a shriek, imbued as it was with equal parts horror and despair, but he knew in an instant that it came from his master. For a moment, he wanted to cover his head and ears. The screech devolved into a bawling and then abruptly cut off. Electrified by his terror, he jumped behind the wheel of the truck and turned the key, hoping that somehow the engine and other essential parts had not been seriously damaged in the gunfight. The engine fired up immediately, and he backed the vehicle out of the space and drove deliberately off to the south. In the rearview mirror he saw the other truck and his dead comrades framed like stick men in their death throes, but as he watched, no one followed.

The servant had not survived in the Kolektor's employ for so many years without being able to figure out what was happening. The master was surely in terrible trouble, if not already dead. But plans had been laid for such contingencies. The servant knew exactly what he had to do. He hurried back to the Kolektor's bunker below the Jewish quarter of the Old City in Jerusalem.

CHAPTER 2

TURKISH-ARMENIAN BORDER

The servant gazed out over the ice-capped peaks framed by the floor-to-ceiling windows in the rear wall of the dacha. This place, the Kolektor's most sacred retreat, was near the small village where the Kolektor had been born. The village had been looted and burned by the Turks in World War II. The Kolektor's parents had been murdered and his sister transformed into a babbling idiot by the atrocities. The Kolektor's father had beseeched the local priest to help them get out. But the church either could not or would not help. His master had vowed vengeance.

Years later, the Kolektor had returned and purchased land and built this sweeping sanctuary overlooking the mountains bordering Turkey and Armenia. In his most trying times, the Kolektor would return, reconnect with his roots, and be renewed. He spoke Armenian, as did his servant, and he had often visited with the surviving villagers, some of whom still remembered his family. The servant knew that the Kolektor would return no more.

Head hung low, he sat and wondered what he should do now. The plan the master had laid out had been followed explicitly. After the fiasco at Hakeldama, he had retrieved the contents of the Kolektor's personal safe. Upon arriving at the simple antiquities shop that was the facade for the underground bunker, he had seen that the door had been forced and the security system bypassed. The servant feared that the Israeli authorities had arrived before him and that he would be arrested. But everything was deathly quiet.

The servant had gone directly to the master's inner office and accessed his private safe, which had not been disturbed. Apparently, whoever had been there before him was after something else. There he found the master's computer and account codes and a personal letter handwritten by the Kolektor. The envelope was not addressed to the servant, but when he saw the name on the envelope, he opened it anyway:

> Dearest One,
>
> Since you are reading this, I must be dead. I have lived long and well. Even so my life is not over. You have been lately in my most intimate thoughts. It is right that you should carry on in my absence. We are, and always have been, one in our cause.
>
> You will have the computer and bank codes to the vast riches I have amassed. You are my heir. To you I leave everything. You are my successor. You shall become the Kolektor. Find the rarest things and make them yours. Let nothing stand in your way. This is your destiny.

The letter was signed by the master.

The servant knew the rest of the master's plan by heart. As he departed the bunker perhaps for the last time, he had noted that the jar and the manuscript were gone. Nothing else seemed to have been disturbed. Initially, he wondered who could have taken the relics. Who would have taken them but left all the other treasures untouched? Whatever had happened to the master at Hakeldama must somehow be connected with the break-in and theft of the manuscript and the old oil jar, he concluded. He would have to consider that when there was time.

On the way to the airport, he had phoned the pilots. One of the Kolektor's private jets was warming on the tarmac when the servant arrived at the general aviation depot of the airport. In a matter of minutes, he was on his way at five hundred miles an hour to this retreat. The servant studied the Kolektor's final message over and over. Tears of rage came to his eyes as he thought of the years he had served his master. Should the servant not be the Kolektor's rightful successor? He had been with him since their university days. He had earned this, had he not? Still, he was sworn to his master under his native ways. The servant had little choice but to begin to contemplate his destiny.

A few hours later, the servant had landed at the nearest airport that could accommodate the jet. Here the servant switched to the Kolektor's helicopter and was ferried to the chalet. He arrived to find the chalet freshly cleaned and provisioned as usual. A bevy of loyal servants had always attended to the master's needs. He called them all together, greeted them, and told them the Kolektor would never return. He could barely control his grief—his anger!

The servant had then finally retired to the master's lounge and seated himself in his master's favorite chair. He was accustomed to taking orders, not giving them, not making decisions for himself. He was shocked to think of the riches represented by the computer and account codes. The Kolektor had amassed billions, and now it was all up for grabs. The note left everything to the Kolektor's heir. But who better to continue the master's work than his most trusted servant? Had he served the Kolektor all these years to come to nothing? Still, what of his oath and his lifetime of devotion to his master? What of the old ways? The servant was sorely conflicted, and soon doubt began to worm its way into his mind. Could he even do it? What if something happened to the heir? What if the heir was dead? Even so, and even if he had the master's blessing, was he up to stepping into the Kolektor's shoes?

The Kolektor had been after the Judas jar and the manuscript, items reputedly of incalculable value. He had captured the scholar, Dr. Clotile Lejeune, and her cohorts along with the jar, the manuscript, and all of her research. But something had gone terribly wrong at Hakeldama, and they had somehow thwarted the master and all his forces. The master was dead. *The Kolektor dead?* He could barely hold on to the thought. Now it seemed the Lejeune woman once again had the jar and the manuscript of the Judas Gospel. Somehow she or her allies must have been behind the break-in at the bunker.

The Kolektor himself thought she had discovered something far more important than the Judas Gospel. There were whispers about a journal. Some said a diary had been kept by one of the Apostles, perhaps Judas, of the three-year ministry of Jesus Christ. The very idea had inflamed the Kolektor. Such a thing would have value beyond thought or calculation. It could upend the world's religions or confirm them. The master had been mad to learn the truth and to possess its proof. It had resulted in his end.

Shaking his head, the servant realized that the day had gotten away from him while he was lost in his thoughts. A fire crackled in the nearby fireplace. It was all very comfortable and familiar. He looked up as a servant slipped silently into the room.

He approached with a tray of sweet meats and condiments and a carafe of wine.

"You must be hungry," the servant Noosh said in Armenian. "Would you consider some refreshment … master?"

After a moment he replied, sharply, "The master is dead. I cannot be your master. I am your leader, your Karik."

CHAPTER 3

RIO DE JANEIRO

TWO MONTHS LATER

Miguel jumped into the Land Rover next to his wife of fifteen years and his two boys, ten and twelve years old. Miguel's eyes lit up every time he saw them. Their baggage had been loaded by his men, and all was ready for them to go into the city for a weekend holiday.

His men, ex-soldiers, had positioned themselves strategically around the vehicle and the walkway from his mountainside home. Their weapons were at the ready. He hated that he and his family required such a high level of security no matter where they went. These were the wages of his business and the enemies he had made over his almost five decades of life.

Both boys were going to be tall and thin but well muscled like their father. But unlike their dad, both boys had their mother's deep brown eyes and high cheekbones. With some Spanish and some native Brazilian heritage, she had finely sculptured features and long black hair. Her father was a high-ranking patron in the Brazilian social hierarchy.

As the boys fidgeted in the large backseat next to him, he felt his satellite phone buzz. He had told his office no calls, but this was his personal, secure phone, and only a few people had the number. Holding up the sat phone, he looked at his wife and said, "I have to take this in the open."

She glanced at him, smiled, and said, "Hurry, then."

"Come on out, boys, for a last stretch before the long ride," said Miguel.

Miguel stepped out of the Land Rover and glanced at his chief of security. In response to his unspoken question, the man nodded that all was okay. With the two boys trailing him, Miguel walked back toward the house, away from the trees lining the driveway, while looking at the tiny screen on the phone. The boys were kicking a ball back and forth. He noted out of the corner of his eye that the security chief was walking up the driveway toward the rear gardens. The man was very thorough.

As he mounted the steps, tiered landscaping on either side, he began to enter the call-back number. When he had entered all the digits, he checked them against the number on his screen.

Just as he hit the green "send" button, one of the boys kicked the ball back toward the car, and they both turned and ran after it. Almost immediately, the Land Rover erupted into a massive explosion of fire, glass, and metal. Miguel was blown against the heavy front door of the mansion, and all went black.

***

Searing pain tore through his body as he sought consciousness. At the edges, he began to perceive light. The agony doubled. Miguel blinked and began to take in some of his surroundings. A nurse sat in a chair in one corner of the room, reading a magazine. One of his men, fully armed, stood at the foot of the bed facing the door. He had no doubt there were others outside. The light faded, and Miguel once again found the refuge of unconsciousness.

Time swirled around him. He knew there was something he had to do, but he was so tired. Still, it would not let him alone, so he began swimming toward the light. Struggling, he opened his eyes and saw the hospital room again. There were doctors, nurses, a couple of his bodyguards, and his number one, Tomás.

"Water," he croaked.

One of the nurses put a straw between his lips, and he drank deeply. Nothing had ever tasted so good.

He looked at Tomás and asked, "My family?"

Tomás shook his head and said, "They were buried two days ago. You have been gone for five days."

Miguel closed his eyes. Why had the two boys run back toward the vehicle? He began to sob—deep, heaving, inconsolable sobs.

"Tomás, who?" asked Miguel after he began to collect himself.

"We don't know yet, boss," replied Tomás. "We have feelers out but no hits. We have checked on the most likely suspects. Right now, it does not look business-related. From what we have been able to find out, this seems to have been personal."

"Personal?" Miguel let the word roll on his tongue. "I need to get out of here."

The doctor stepped forward and said, "Out of the question. You must rest. Although you have no broken bones, you have suffered a severe concussion. It was necessary to keep you in an induced coma for a while to make sure there was no swelling in the brain. Now that you are awake, we will want you here for several more days for extensive tests."

"Doctor, I am tired. Please have the room cleared so I can rest," said Miguel.

When all save Tomás had gone, Miguel said, "Tomás, put our people on the street. Money is no object. There will be a trail or path. Find the people who killed my family."

CHAPTER 4

MADISONVILLE, LOUISIANA

TWO MONTHS LATER

"Cloe, something has happened, and I must ask you to come to Rome to speak with me and some of my colleagues," the monsignor said with some urgency when Cloe answered his transatlantic call.

"Albert, that's impossible," Cloe responded, even though she knew the monsignor worked directly for the pope and would not make the request lightly. "I'm in the midst of the translation of the journal, and it's not going very well. I cannot leave now. What can you tell me?"

"I can't talk about it on the phone," he replied. "You must come. I would not ask if it were not important. I need J.E. as well."

"Well, that's it then … J.E. isn't here, and I can't leave what I'm doing. I'm so sorry, Albert," said Cloe firmly, feeling somewhat perturbed at the mysterious request.

"Then I will come to you," he said.

***

Though Cloe was in Madisonville, Louisiana, they made plans to meet in the French Quarter at the Criollo Restaurant in the Hotel

13

Monteleone two days hence for lunch. In a way, she felt relieved for the break. She was immersed in the journal the Sicarii had given her after Hakeldama, which she believed had been written by one of the Apostles and chronicled Christ's three-year public ministry. It had been such a happenstance discovery. She had been translating the Judas manuscript from the jar her father had found in Tunisia during World War II. His unit had been detailed to knock out an Italian fortification in the Atlas Mountains that protected the Gafsa Pass for the Germans. During this mission, he had fallen into a cavern and had come out of this cave of jars with the Judas jar, which then sat on his mantelpiece for sixty years and had come to Cloe when he was murdered in his Madisonville home. Cloe had inferred the existence of the journal from her translation of the Judas manuscript.

The Kolektor had learned of the existence of the Judas manuscript and the possibility of the journal. His determination to possess them had resulted in the murder of her father, the kidnapping of her uncle, the battle at the Church of St. John in Lyon, France, and eventually the showdown at Hakeldama, the very field where Judas may have died. Only the appearance of the mysterious guardians of the jars, the Sicarii, had saved them and caused the death of the Kolektor and the destruction of his criminal organization. The Sicarii had entrusted her with the second jar, which she believed might contain the journal.

If this were such a journal, it would predate the earliest of the Gospels by at least two decades and, as a contemporaneous record, could have enormous influence on the Jesus story. It might end up *being* the Jesus story. Currently, she was stuck on a particularly tricky translation of the Greek text. She felt the weight of the Church on her shoulders. Such a journal might rewrite religious history.

While she was in New Orleans to meet the monsignor, she would take the opportunity to visit the library at the Ursuline Convent, which was said to be filled with ancient documents. She knew there was a relationship between the order of nuns that owned the convent and Lyon, France, where the Church of St. John was located. There were many connections between Lyon and the Gospel of Judas Iscariot and, maybe, the journal that had been referenced in that Gospel.

As Cloe dressed that morning in her small bungalow-style home in the riverside village, she wondered what the monsignor could possibly want with her. She was an ancient languages expert formerly in residence at the University of Washington in Seattle. After the recent harrowing series of events, including the murder of her father and the kidnapping of her uncle by the Kolektor, all leading to the discovery of the journal, she was back to her quiet academic life, except now she was in Louisiana, living in her childhood home, and connected with Louisiana State University. No matter what, she simply could not leave this critical part of the translation at this time. The monsignor had led her to this work, and it had almost cost her life and the life of her son, J.E. What could he possibly ask of her now?

When she had finished dressing, she packed her handbag and drove off. Since coming back to Madisonville, she had learned how to drive and had bought a car. She had never needed one before, but in Louisiana she did.

As she gazed in the rearview mirror, she saw the neat home with its row of magnolias. She thought briefly about her long-dead mother, Marie Louise. Even now she could see her mother in the swing on the front porch in her apron shelling peas for dinner. She could not think of her mother without her thoughts shifting to her father, Thib. He had died violently at the hands of the Kolektor, defending his home and the Judas jar. As she remembered the last few days with her mother and her father's death, her heart hurt.

Pressing on, she turned off Water Street and crossed the swing bridge spanning the Tchefuncte River. Soon, she was on the Lake Pontchartrain Causeway, headed for New Orleans.

The lake was turbulent with the short, choppy waves for which it was infamous with area mariners. Cloe couldn't help but wonder whether the stormy conditions were not some sort of portent for her meeting with the monsignor. She shivered despite the car's warmth as she remembered the Kolektor's plan to crucify her and her cohorts at Hakeldama for interfering with his plans to possess the jar and the journal.

Forty minutes later, Cloe entered the French Quarter from North Peters Street. This route ran along the Mississippi River, which sliced New Orleans neatly in half.

The streets of New Orleans were filled with the human gumbo that inhabited or visited the city, from men in business suits to the homeless and lost and every kind of person in between. As she drove slowly along the crowded street, she looked up through the moonroof and saw that the weather was worsening. It looked like it might pour down any minute. She thought she heard the distant rumbling of thunder. Cloe pulled abreast of the automobile entrance to the Monteleone Hotel and saw that the "full" sign was not posted. She smiled at her good luck and turned into the hotel garage. The attendant, a young man whose badge gave his name as Etienne, took her keys and moved quickly to park the car.

"I'll be here only an hour or two," said Cloe.

"Fine, ma'am; I'll keep her close," said the young man.

Cloe passed through the automatic door and began to weave her way from the garage onto the main floor of the old hotel. It had been family-owned for goodness only knew how many years, but with the recent refurbishment and upgrades, Cloe thought it was spectacular. Criollo was a product of the makeover. Cloe had read that it was one of the best new restaurants in New Orleans.

Once inside the foyer of the restaurant, she immediately saw Marco, the food and beverage manager. Before this, Marco had been a legendary, thirty-year veteran of another French Quarter landmark—one of Cloe and J.E.'s favorites. Marco knew everything and everybody.

"Hello, Dr. Lejeune," said Marco with a wry smile. "I believe there is a distinguished-looking gentleman awaiting you in the restaurant."

He led her to the table she had reserved, and there sat the monsignor.

"Hello, Albert," she said and gave him a warm, friendly hug as he stood to greet her. Cloe saw that her friend might have aged just a bit from the fight with the Kolektor, but on him it was just a touch more gray in his hair and a deeper wrinkle here and there. *"Distinguished" truly was the right word,* she thought.

"Cloe, it's good to see you," he replied.

They sat down and ordered drinks. Without request, Marco brought the house specialty, a gulf shrimp, blue crab, and avocado appetizer. Hot French bread pistolettes and an assortment of other homemade breads with three types of butter followed.

The monsignor did not waste time on pleasantries. "Cloe, we need your help. A crisis is brewing that may affect everything you are doing. I need you to come to Rome and meet with key people there."

"You said that on the phone. You know I can't go. I've told you that," responded Cloe. "I've got too much to do on the journal."

"I can't go into any detail here, but I would not have flown so far to make this personal entreaty if it were not critical," replied the monsignor.

"Albert, you have to tell me *something*," said Cloe, conflicted by her work and her friendship with the monsignor.

Marco returned, and they ordered. Cloe's favorite dish was the pan-seared scallops, with a side of creamed spinach. It was always perfect. The monsignor ordered the soft-shell crab BLT. He also chose a nice white wine for them.

They relaxed into lighter conversation, mainly about J.E. and all that had happened since their near-death brush with the Kolektor and his minions. She told him J.E. had been appointed to an elite intelligence course at the military college and was close to finishing. She spoke briefly of her struggle with the translation of a Jesus conversation with someone she thought might be St. John.

The meal came and went, and over coffee, the monsignor leaned in close to Cloe. "I know this is difficult, but it could be a matter of life and death. The pope himself considers this to be of the utmost importance. Please come to Rome."

Cloe knew this was not an idle statement by the monsignor. She had been through enough with him to know this was serious. Still, she had her work on the journal. "Albert, come back to Madisonville with me, and we will talk further. I want to show you what I have done on the translation. I'll keep an open mind."

"Fair enough," said the cleric. "Do you have a car? I took a taxi from the airport."

"Yes, it's down in the garage," she said as a bright bolt of lightning appeared in the restaurant's window, followed immediately by a terrible crash of thunder. The lights flickered but held.

The monsignor paid the bill, and they went to the valet area of the garage, where rain was pouring down so hard that it was beginning to back up in the street. The hotel now had several young valets fetching customer cars. Cloe gave Etienne her ticket. He grabbed his yellow slicker and ran off into the maelstrom, no doubt thinking of a handsome tip. Cloe and the monsignor watched as the young man ran to the car in the lot just across the street, opened the door, and jumped inside. Five seconds later, as he apparently turned the ignition switch, the car exploded with a blast so mighty it drowned out the lightning and thunder. Pieces of the ruined vehicle sailed through the air in all directions. The blast knocked Cloe and the monsignor flat as debris rained down around them.

Cloe looked up and screamed in horror. Her hair hung down over her face in soggy strings; she was soaking wet from the rainwater blown over them by the explosion. She rolled toward the monsignor and saw the look of shock on his face. Both of them were covered with debris.

"Albert … what's happened?" she yelled after a moment, when she could speak. "My God! What about the poor valet … Etienne?"

"I'm afraid no one could have survived that blast," he said, apparently beginning to come to grips with what had just happened and checking himself for injuries.

He studied Cloe, saw the frightened look on her face, and said, "Are you hurt?"

"No … Albert, are *you* hurt?" she cried out.

"I think I'm unhurt, but I'm afraid our past has reached out to us," he said miserably, getting to his feet and helping Cloe up.

She considered this and said, "I have to go to Rome, don't I?"

The monsignor responded quietly. "Yes."

CHAPTER 5

Less than forty-eight hours after the horrific explosion and its aftermath with the police, the carnage, and all of the questions, Cloe now focused on the fact that she was in the presence of the direct successor to St. Peter. In the rush to get to Rome, she had had little time to understand the ramifications of the bomb in New Orleans. That would come later. Right now she intuitively knew she had to be here.

"Here" was the pope's personal study in the papal apartment. These were not sumptuous quarters by modern standards. In fact, they had undergone an upgrade only a few years earlier when Pope Benedict XVI brought everything up to what Americans would call "code." The electrical and plumbing had been completely inadequate, not to mention the heating and air-conditioning. Plus, a large library space had been added to house Benedict's enormous personal collection of books. After Pope Benedict's almost unprecedented resignation, the library had been moved to Castle Gandolfo along with the pope emeritus.

Although Pope Francis had elected to reside in a more modest apartment, the pope's quarters continued to serve much the same business function as the White House in Washington, DC, but on a considerably smaller scale. The political center of the Vatican was here, and this was where the pope conducted the most important and private aspects of his business.

Clotile Lejeune studied the face of Pope Francis as he entered the room. Many said that his predecessor, Benedict XVI, glowed with the light of scholarship. Francis's face showed … what? *Humility,* she thought, that and fatigue. Cloe worried that it was too early in his tenure for the newly elected Pope Francis to seem so tired. Although he smiled slightly, Cloe could see dark shadows under his eyes and deep wrinkles of age. This was undoubtedly a result of his newfound responsibilities. Pope Francis was not only the head of state of the Vatican, an independent though small country, but also the leader of the billion-plus-member Roman Catholic Church.

Observing Francis, Cloe now felt her own weariness after the day's long flight and the events leading up to this trip. Her thoughts went back to the scene at the hotel in New Orleans where poor Etienne lost his young life because of a bomb meant for her. There seemed to be no end to the violence that had swirled around her since her father had bequeathed the jar to her. Here she was again, this time meeting with the pope himself, on the verge of goodness only knew what. Of course, she had not known that she would be personally meeting with the pope. The monsignor had not told her about this until they were en route to the Vatican.

"Dr. Lejeune, welcome to the residence," said Francis in English with a tired but sincere smile.

The monsignor had given her a rudimentary lesson in papal etiquette on the flight to Rome. Cloe bowed slightly and said, "Holiness, thank you." She kissed the ring of St. Peter on the pope's extended hand. Likewise, the monsignor made his greetings to the pope, who then ushered them to a small conference area in the study.

When they were seated, a nun from the order that serves the papal residence brought fresh, hot coffee, which Cloe thought was as tasty as any in Louisiana. Somewhat refreshed, Cloe looked expectantly at Francis and then at the monsignor.

"Albert has told me a little of your ordeal in Jerusalem at Hakeldama," said the pontiff. "How are you and your son, J.E., doing in its wake?"

"J.E.'s fine. He's actually on detached, short-term duty at one of the intelligence schools in the United States. I expect him home at any time. We have talked about what happened in New Orleans and about this trip. If necessary, he will join me here later. My wounds have all but healed," responded Cloe, unconsciously flexing and rotating her right shoulder near where she had been shot in the chest by the Kolektor.

The Kolektor—even now she could hear his screams as he was crucified by the Sicarii at Hakeldama. Just desserts for a man—a monster—who had murdered her father, kidnapped her ninety-year-old uncle, and stolen an ancient relic of incalculable value. In a matter of a few weeks, this Kolektor had entered her life, totally changed its course, and almost succeeded in killing her entire family. All this was in the pursuit of his monstrous greed and lust for ancient things. Somehow the pope's characterization of the experience as an "ordeal" seemed inadequate.

The pope turned to the fourth occupant of the small study. "Dr. Lejeune, this is Father Sergio Canti. Father Sergio is the assistant camerlengo. Are you familiar with the office of camerlengo?"

"Yes," responded Cloe, studying the young man carefully. He was about J.E.'s age of twenty-six but with more of a doughboy physique. His eyes were sharp and betrayed an intense intelligence and something else, something she could not quite identify. Cloe thought there might be some steel under the soft exterior. "When Pope Benedict's predecessor died, there were pieces in the American press on the camerlengo," she continued. "If I understand correctly, the camerlengo has certain nondelegable duties to perform upon the passing of a pope."

"Yes, my child, while the office of camerlengo has meant different things at different times in the history of the Church, in this context the camerlengo is an officer of the papal household. Among the duties of this office is the formal determination of the demise of a pope. If the pope has passed, the camerlengo will strike the pope's head gently three times with a small silver hammer used only for this purpose and call out his name, inquiring, 'Are you sleeping?'"

"Fascinating," whispered Cloe.

"Once the pope is declared dead, the camerlengo takes possession of the Ring of the Fisherman and cuts it in the presence of the cardinals to signify the end of the pope's reign," continued Francis.

"He then notifies the Curia and the College of Cardinals and assists in the funeral preparations and in the convening of the all-important meeting of the cardinals to choose a successor."

"Such a tradition; it takes my breath away," uttered Cloe, although she wondered how these duties would be relevant now.

"Father Sergio is one of the clerks in the office of the camerlengo," stated the monsignor. "In time, with experience and wisdom, he may aspire to become camerlengo, should that be God's will. But every candidate who would hold an office so close to the pope must be tested and found worthy. He is trained in many things, and His Holiness has asked him to be here in case he can be of service in our efforts."

"What efforts are those, Monsignor?" asked Cloe, wondering if they were getting close to the punch line in this story.

"Perhaps we should begin with what you have learned about the second jar the Sicarii left you after the firefight at Jerusalem," suggested the pontiff.

"Yes, the Sicarii," Cloe responded, looking inward. "Holiness, as you may know, the mysterious appearance of the Sicarii saved us from certain, terrible death at the hands of the Kolektor at Hakeldama. He wanted to destroy anyone who had any knowledge of the oil jar found by my father, Thib, in Tunisia during World War II."

Cloe shuddered. If the Sicarii had not intervened, she, J.E., and Uncle Sonny would have died, crucified on those trees. As it was, the Kolektor's men had been killed by the short blades of the Sicarii, and the Kolektor had himself suffered the excruciating death of crucifixion on an ancient oak. The Sicarii had decreed an eye for an eye, and the Kolektor that night reaped what he had sowed.

Cloe lowered her head as she stepped through these only months-old events in her memory. She had not spoken of them to anyone but J.E. since Jerusalem. It had all begun when she received that ill-fated phone call from her Uncle Sonny notifying her that her father, Thibodeaux Lejeune, had died suddenly. She and J.E. had gone back to Madisonville for the funeral and had discovered her father had been murdered in his home as a result of a break-in. In due course, the police had determined that the murderer was a professional thief and sometimes killer who died from a shotgun blast from Thib as the older man sat bleeding to death in his bedroom.

She had done what was necessary to bury her father and to take care of his affairs. At her father's lawyer's office, she had learned that Thib had bequeathed to her the old oil jar he had found in World War II. Tears came to her eyes as she thought about the will and the personal letter from her father.

"Cloe, are you all right?" questioned the monsignor.

"Albert, it's still hard to believe that I, a simple languages professor in Seattle, became enmeshed in an international conflict with a billionaire ex-arms dealer over possibly the most important relic to be found since the birth of Christ. Now the jar has cost another life ... the poor valet at the hotel."

"Time may prove the contents of the oil jar to be just that, earth-shakingly important," replied the monsignor.

"Perhaps. We have already discovered the earliest version of the Gospel of Judas Iscariot known to exist," continued Cloe, "but it's damaged. As we speak, experts are trying to restore the smudged interior pages of that manuscript so that it can be translated and understood."

"That is extremely interesting," said Francis as he offered more coffee. "However, the true revelation may be about the journal. Dr. Lejeune, think of it—the possibility of a writing by one of the Apostles chronicling the daily details of the three years of Christ's life before his death. Can you tell me what you have learned?"

"Holiness, you realize such a diary, a firsthand contemporary account, if authentic, might refute what is written in whole or in part in the Gospels. The synoptic Gospels were not written until decades after Christ's death, and the Gospel of St. John, the last to be written, was authored at the very end of the first century." Cloe realized immediately that she had been impertinent, lecturing the successor to St. Peter on scripture. Hand to her mouth, she rose slightly to apologize profusely.

Francis gestured to her to keep her seat and indicated that he knew no insult was intended. It seemed he had some experience with American frankness.

"Cloe, the pope is well aware of the implications of such a writing," said the monsignor, "but he also believes the document will only confirm and, more importantly, enrich what we already know. While only the pope, his private secretary, and a few others with need to know are aware of these developments, great excitement has been generated."

"Holy Father, I'm not able to say much about it as I have only just started on the reconstruction and translation of the snippets of paper that might eventually prove to be this journal. Right now I can't say what we have is even a cohesive writing, much less a testament to Christ's public ministry. It's all just in pieces and scraps. I'm nowhere near being able to provide any sound scientific analysis of the document. I'm just not ready."

"I understand, my child," responded Francis kindly. "But that is not why I asked you to come here with such urgency."

"Cloe, there has been a development," whispered the monsignor.

"What is it?" she said sharply, suddenly on guard once again.

"It may be only a rumor, but if true, it affects the timing of everything."

"For goodness' sake, Albert, what is it?"

"We don't know for sure, but the Vatican has ears in even the most remote places."

"Albert," Cloe said more shrilly than she intended, "what do you know, or what do you think you know?"

The pope turned to her and said, "Our sources tell us the Kolektor is risen."

CHAPTER 6

"Holiness, the Kolektor … alive? It can't be. I saw him crucified at the Bloody Acre," Cloe spewed out in shock. "There can be no doubt. The monsignor was there. He saw the man nailed to the tree by the Sicarii as justice for his unforgivable offenses."

"Cloe, this is true, and His Holiness does not literally mean that the Kolektor himself lives. Surely, he died of his wounds," responded the monsignor quickly.

"Well … what does he mean?"

"We are not sure, but we think the Kolektor's organization, or at least some substantial part of it, may still be intact," summarized the monsignor.

"But how can that be? They were all killed at Hakeldama, except for a few who were captured later," asserted Cloe.

"True enough," agreed the monsignor. "But the Kolektor's organization was much larger and more pervasive than we suspected. Even though we cut off the head, some parts seem to have survived. His riches may fuel some sort of continuing enterprise."

"Enterprise?" Cloe said hoarsely, fear for herself and for J.E. welling up inside her. "You speak as if this were some sort of business being transferred from one generation to another. The Kolektor and his forces almost cost me my life and that of my son. Monsignor, I remind you that you were tied to the tree as well and in line for execution."

"Child, this must have been such a terrible experience for you and your son," the pontiff interjected. "I'm also aware that your aged

Uncle Sonny was in dreadful jeopardy as well. The weight of these things on your shoulders must even now be overwhelming."

Cloe heard the genuineness of the pope's concern as he spoke. She had indeed often, in honoring her promise to her dead father to find the origins of the jar, felt the weight of the world on her shoulders. But she had come through that and thought the Kolektor and his evil organization dead and gone. *Now this.*

"Holy Father, how can this be?" she asked. "Does this have anything to do with what happened in New Orleans?"

The young camerlengo-in-waiting found his voice. "We don't yet know the origin of the bomb, Dr. Lejeune, but our intelligence sources tell us not all the Kolektor's men were killed or captured. One, in particular, is unaccounted for. The Israelis report that the Kolektor's personal safe was emptied by someone with the combination, and one of his planes departed the Jerusalem airport not long after the incident at Hakeldama."

Cloe turned to her friend and asked more sharply than she had intended, "Monsignor, who is it?"

"The missing man's name and identity are not clear," replied the monsignor. "But from the Israeli intelligence, we have surmised he was at the very top of the Kolektor's organization and trusted implicitly."

"I had very little opportunity to learn the names of any of the Kolektor's men," Cloe responded. "The monsignor, J.E., and I were kept isolated from everyone in that bunker in Jerusalem except the Kolektor and his servant, Dadash. But he seemed to be just a humble manservant. I doubt we have anything to fear from him even if he survived."

"Hmmm … Dadash; in Armenian it means 'brother,'" replied the monsignor.

"He was initially kind to me, providing food and a place to rest," said Cloe. "But he had Uncle Sonny, J.E., and the monsignor locked up under terrible circumstances and kept them trussed up even when the Kolektor finally allowed them to come to his office. I don't remember him being at the little clearing at Hakeldama. But of course, in my condition, I could have missed him."

"I tend to think you are correct. He was a simple house servant and is probably a dead end in our search," stated the monsignor.

Father Sergio added, "The person who emptied the Kolektor's personal safe probably took with him the most valuable materials and information the Kolektor had secreted. More than likely this included account codes, bank locations, and other information, putting the vast wealth of the Kolektor under that person's control."

"My God," Cloe whispered. "It's not over, is it? In some ways it's only just begun."

"Cloe, I'm afraid you may be right," said the monsignor. "Someone has all of the Kolektor's knowledge and his incredible resources, and that someone may have helped carry out the Kolektor's most ruthless orders. The only remaining question is what the person's motives will be. Will he be driven by a covetousness similar to the Kolektor's? Will he seek revenge?"

"Father Sergio, what do we know of where this person may be?" asked the pontiff.

"Holy Father," replied the assistant camerlengo. "Our intelligence people are working on this, but as of now we know relatively little. The Kolektor is thought to have had some sort of retreat in the mountains on the Turkish-Armenian border, but no one knows where. Given the direction and trajectory the plane took leaving the Jerusalem airport and where it dropped from radar and satellite detection, it's a good bet that is where this person went after Hakeldama. That's probably his base of operations."

"Operations?" queried Cloe. "What operations? Holiness, why am I here? You haven't brought me all this way just to hear these things. You have something in mind for me. What is it?" Cloe worried that she was getting sucked into another quest and that this time, it might not end so well for her and J.E.

"No, my child," said the pope. "You are quite right. There is more—matters of great concern to me and to the Church. I need your help." He turned to the monsignor and said, "Albert, if you please."

"Cloe, we have reports from several different areas that retainers in the service of unknown persons are making inquiries about the cache of oil jars your father found in Tunisia during the El Guettar raid in World War II. Although he brought only the single jar back to his home, he reported that there were scores, if not hundreds, of jars in the cave. A lot of money is being spread around in the effort to find the jars. Isolated intelligence from Lyon, France, and Jerusalem and Tunis normally would not have attracted much attention, but the monks manning our special operations intelligence center have put two and two together."

Cloe knew from prior experience that the Vatican had an order of monks in its ops center who had access to most of the world's intelligence agencies plus their own resources. Eyes and ears were everywhere, but it was a matter of connecting the dots. These monks were as good as anyone at that.

"But Albert, the Vatican tried to find the cave of jars years ago and failed," she responded. "Why should we believe this person could find what the Vatican's experts could not find?"

"Cloe, a number of things have changed since that expedition thirty years ago," the monsignor began. "First, modern exploration techniques and equipment are far superior to what was available to the original Vatican team. With ground-penetrating radar, infrared, and other aids, we cannot rely solely on the hope this new search will fail.

"Moreover, there is the matter of the Sicarii," continued the monsignor. "Not only we but also perhaps the remnants of the Kolektor's forces know the link between the Sicarii and the cave where the treasure of oil jars rests."

"Yes," commented Cloe, tendrils of concern beginning to swirl around her. "The survivors of the Sicarii massacre at Masada changed the group's mission from violent rebellion against the Romans to destruction of the Roman Empire through the propagation of Christianity. With early Church leaders, they fostered religious writings and expansion of the Catholic Church until, in the third or fourth century, Constantine converted to Christianity and the pagan juggernaut that had been the Roman Empire was finished. The Sicarii told me while I was with them right after Hakeldama that many of these writings, some thought lost for all time, were preserved by them and placed in the cave my father found."

"Quite so," whispered the monsignor, looking directly at Cloe. "The Sicarii know where the cave is located. The Kolektor's successors are not only looking for the cave; they are looking for the Sicarii."

***

Cloe sat absorbing the apparent fact that someone had taken over and was running the Kolektor's organization and that the same person was after the Sicarii. After they had meted out justice to the Kolektor at Hakeldama, the Sicarii had cared for her. Cloe had been shot by the Kolektor and had lost a lot of blood. She spent a full day with them while they made arrangements for her to be treated confidentially at a private sanatorium outside Jerusalem. She had made deep friendships with the women of the Sicarii who had saved her and her son. Though they had had only a short time together, the bond had been forged. Now the Sicarii, her comrades, were the quarry. And judging from the events in New Orleans, so was she.

"Whoever these people are, they will never find the Sicarii," said Cloe with hope in her voice. "They have lived in the shadows for almost two thousand years. No Armenian thugs will be able to uncover their secrets."

"Perhaps," said the monsignor, pausing.

Cloe knew a bucket of cold water was headed her way. The monsignor had that irritating talent. Still, she cared deeply for him, like a member of her family. They had been through a lot together.

"As we sit here tonight, whoever is looking for the Sicarii has been in Jerusalem and at the sanatorium where you were hospitalized. We think the Sicarii arranged for you to be brought to the sanatorium after the fight at the Bloody Acre. Your care was set, and all was paid in advance. These operatives will follow the money wherever it leads.

Let us hope the Sicarii are not at the end of the trail," concluded the monsignor.

"Albert, I know you well now, and I can see that this is not all," said Cloe, bracing herself. "You would not have interrupted my research and brought me here just for this."

"Dr. Lejeune, it's only a rumor," whispered the pontiff. "But we had to bring you here to tell you what we have heard."

"What is it?" pleaded Cloe.

"Well, there is talk of … another," said the monsignor. "One who may be more ruthless than the Kolektor, one who springs from the Kolektor himself."

"From the Kolektor?" queried Cloe, a chill running up her spine. "You already said someone has succeeded to the operations of the Kolektor's empire. Is that who you mean?"

"No," replied the monsignor. "We think this is someone else— perhaps blood-related. Internally, we refer to him only as 'Q,' after the Armenian word *dwnwuq*."

"Q? *Dwnwuq*? What does this all mean?" Cloe inquired, dreading the answer.

"Cloe, the Armenian word *dwnwuq* means 'heir,'" replied the monsignor. "Heir!"

"Heir?" repeated Cloe disbelievingly, struggling to accept that not only had the Kolektor's organization arisen but that the Kolektor also might have a blood heir.

CHAPTER 7

"Dr. Lejeune, nothing less than Christianity itself needs your help," pressed the pope. "I do not say this to be dramatic or to overstate the matter. Our situation is critical. Not only must your work not fall into the hands of whoever is operating the Kolektor's organization, whether it be this supposed heir or one of the Kolektor's former lieutenants, but you must find the Sicarii's cache of jars before the Kolektor's thugs find them. In the wrong hands, the knowledge that may be contained in the jars could be corrupted into a tool of the evil forces bent on the complete destruction of Christianity. This was the goal of the Kolektor, and it may also be the goal of his successor. This cannot be allowed. The cave of jars must be found, and the information put in the hands of scholars to be translated and given freely to all."

"Cloe, His Holiness and I have discussed this in detail, and you are the only one who can do this," added the monsignor. "You are already working on assembling and translating what may be the rumored journal itself, or at least a path to it, if it exists. This is clearly why the Sicarii left the second jar with you."

The young camerlengo noted, "You have engaged the Kolektor's forces and have come out victorious with the help of your friends, the Sicarii. You have as much knowledge of these people as anyone alive. This would be a huge advantage."

Cloe, beginning to get angry at what they were suggesting, responded, "Yes, and my son, my uncle, and I only barely survived our last encounter with the Kolektor. This is a job for the police or the army, not me."

"I know your concerns. We all share them. The problem is that you and J.E. are already involved in this. The Kolektor's people know you have the first jar and the earliest version of the Judas Gospel. It is possible they know the Sicarii gave you a second jar. Certainly, the Kolektor was aware of the cave your father found in Tunisia containing possibly hundreds of such jars, and we have to assume his people know as well. They know where you are and where your family is. They have proved themselves beyond any civilized, human restraint in seeking what they want. Possibly, you could avoid them by giving up both jars, the manuscripts, and all of your work to the authorities in the United States or even to the Vatican. Could you do that?"

Cloe reflected on this and knew she could not give up her life's work. Even if she did, this might not help because stored in her brain was research and information that would be invaluable to the Kolektor's organization. She was stuck, and she knew it. "Why not turn your suspicions over to the authorities?" she asked in a quiet voice.

"Which authorities?" asked Father Sergio.

Cloe considered this and realized she was beginning to not like this cleric with the biting tongue.

"This is a problem," said the monsignor. "There is no overarching jurisdiction that we could use. Evidence of the Kolektor's activities has been found in Turkey, Armenia, Israel, France, and the United States, and the cave, we believe, is in Tunisia. Also, the police authorities are generally, by nature, reactive. If a crime has been committed, their resources are dedicated to finding and punishing the guilty parties. It's unlikely they could be convinced to search for a supposed treasure trove of ancient texts."

"Besides," observed the now annoying camerlengo, "most of the governments who might get interested in this would confiscate anything that may be found. It could be years before competent scholars could have access to study the materials—or never."

"Do you mean a situation like the Shroud of Turin, where the Church, for hundreds of years, prevented scholarly inquiry, until very recently?" asked Cloe.

"Precisely," said the cleric, apparently not seeing the irony.

"Dr. Lejeune," said the pope, "it is our duty to try to safeguard you and your family since we helped you get in this predicament in the first place, plus you have done a great service to your faith with your work to date. You and J.E. will not be alone. Swiss Guards will be assigned to protect your uncle back in your hometown. Do you remember Father Anton?"

"Yes, certainly, Holiness," replied Cloe. "He is the director of Vatican field operations—the ones J.E. refers to as your special operations personnel. He was crucial to our survival."

"Yes, my child. Father Anton and a suitable contingent of the Swiss Guard will be at your service, as will Father Sergio and the monsignor. The monks in the operations center will provide intelligence. You will have transportation and all the equipment you need. I pray you will agree to put the journal translation aside for a bit and find your father's cave of jars," concluded the pope.

The walls of the pope's now-empty library drew in around her, seeming to squeeze the breath from her body. The pope and the others said nothing, waiting.

She looked up and said with a hoarse voice and courage that came from the seventeen-year-old runaway she had once been, "This time we make an end to the Kolektor!"

CHAPTER 8

In his office in a skyscraper high above Rio, Miguel sat at his desk shuffling papers and, more than occasionally, staring out the window. His desk was a series of tables bridging the two huge windows in the corner office. It was more like an architect's office than a … a what? He wondered now what he really was. He had called himself a businessman, but much of what he did was above and beyond the law. A specialist in black-market commodities, he filled a niche for unusual goods, from illegal guns to stolen Picassos.

He reflected on what had happened since his release from the hospital weeks ago. He had fully recovered from the explosion that had taken the lives of his wife and two boys. At least, he was physically whole again. Even so, he had spent most of his time dwelling on the loss of his boys.

The door to his office suite opened, and Tomás quietly entered the room. He and Tomás had been together for many years, and Miguel had come to depend on him, trusting him completely.

"Boss, I have some news," said Tomás.

"I've had enough business for today," said Miguel. "I think I'll head to the gym." He knew he had not put in a full day at the office since he had come back from his wounds. He had all but abandoned the hillside villa where the family had lived and had moved into an apartment in the office building.

"Our people have located Juan," Tomás said softly.

Miguel spun his chair away from the window, eyes now locked on Tomás. Juan was his former security chief. "Where? Where is he now?" queried Miguel.

"He is dead," replied Tomás. "He was killed in the firefight with our men when they tried to capture him. They had tracked him to a remote mountain village where he had some kin. Our people had to fight their way out of it."

"How?" asked Miguel.

"We found him by means of cell-phone tracking and other technology, along with good detective work," Tomás continued.

Miguel knew that Tomás had never completely trusted Juan for reasons that were more dependent on intuition than fact. Still, it must seem to Tomás that he had been proven correct.

"Well done, my friend," said Miguel, "but with him dead, the chain is broken, and there is no one to lead us to whoever killed my family and tried to kill me." He hung his head as the memory of that day washed over him.

"Not entirely true, boss," replied Tomás. "We got his computer and his cell phone. Actually, he had two phones—one he was issued when he worked for you and the other, a satellite phone, with a private account that we have been able to penetrate."

Miguel reflected on this. Statistically, almost every crime was either planned using a cell phone or talked about on a cell phone during or after commission. A satellite phone was just as good a lead. Of course, Juan, his former chief of security, would have known that.

"A private phone account like this may suggest that somebody got to him, boss," said Tomás. "Why would he need it unless he was doing something he didn't want known? Here's a printout of the list of numbers that called or were dialed from the satellite phone account for the thirty-day period before the bomb went off. This cost you plenty to get."

"I'm not concerned with the cost," said Miguel, scanning the list. After a minute or two of studying the numbers, he sat bolt upright. "Tomás, what connections do we have in France?" Miguel asked with urgency.

"We have import/export partners in Marseilles," replied Tomás. "Why? What do you see?"

"Unless my guess is wrong, I see the answer to who tried to kill me and did kill my family," said Miguel. "I know this number. I have used it before. It's on here several times."

"Then it's someone you know," said Tomás.

"No, the person I knew is dead. This is someone else, but this may lead me to him," Miguel concluded. "Contact our people in Marseilles and get someone to the Church of St. Irenaeus in Lyon. He is to wait there unobtrusively until I say otherwise. I don't care how long it takes. He is to observe the church."

"What are we looking for?" asked Tomás.

"Anything," said the boss. "After you make the call, I'll tell you a story, and then it will be payback time."

CHAPTER 9

The papal jet flew northwest, chasing the setting sun on its port side. The airplane was a version of the small commuter jets that served minor population centers, but it was big enough to carry the Swiss Guard and Cloe, J.E., and the two religious in comfort. The crew included a pilot, copilot, and engineer.

The group seated around the small conference table in the center of the papal jet had grown in size and skills. J.E. had joined Cloe in Rome and had been briefed on everything that was known. Cloe smiled with pride as she watched her son. He stood over six feet and had dark wavy hair and a solid physique like his grandfather Thib. He had many skills, including tactics, intelligence, and ranger hand-to-hand training, and he was a master at several weapons systems. J.E. had earned a theater ribbon and the Silver Star in Iraq. He was quite at home with the squad of fifteen Swiss Guards who now provided their security.

Their leader was Vicar General Antonio Sigliori, who had also joined the little group. Father Anton had been with them at Hakeldama and was the Vatican military ordinariate, controlling papal field operations. He was about J.E.'s height but leaner and maybe fifteen years older. His gaze said he had seen many things.

Cloe considered the magnitude of the task at hand. From her father's letter, she knew the cave containing the jars was somewhere in North Africa near the Gafsa Pass in the Atlas Mountains, but this could cover hundreds of square miles. It was critical to somehow pare the search area down to something manageable. They had the field notes from the first search the Vatican had commissioned after initial interviews with Thib thirty years earlier. However, that expedition might have walked right over the site and not have known it. So everything had to be searched. Cloe wondered if the task was hopeless.

The monsignor, seeming to have read her mind, said, "Cloe, this is a monumental job without a map or, at least, a direction. Where do we start?"

"Albert, all of our resources won't find the cave unless we have some sort of advantage," Cloe responded.

"But what could that be? Have you found anything from the second jar that helps us?" queried the camerlengo-in-waiting.

"No, thus far there have been no clues from the text in the second jar, and I wouldn't expect there to be any," said Cloe.

"Why not?" asked the young priest.

"Because the timing is all wrong. If the contents of the second jar originated during the three years of Christ's public ministry, that would have been years before the Sicarii were supposedly wiped out at Masada. Still more years would have passed before the survivors began their campaign to collect ancient religious works and store them in the cave," concluded Cloe.

"We have to contact the Sicarii and convince them to lead us to the cave," said J.E.

"When we parted company in Jerusalem, the Sicarii left no means for me to contact them," said Cloe. "As you know, they are few in number and have survived all these centuries by living in the shadows, in secret. The Vatican ops center has put out feelers, but it will be easier for them to find us, if they want to do so, than for us to find them."

"Fine, but that still leaves us looking for clues. Where do we start?" asked the monsignor.

"Why, Albert, I thought you might remember," responded Cloe. "We start where we left off … at the library of St. John."

CHAPTER 10

"The library of St. John?" repeated the monsignor as they flew on. "But, Cloe, we learned when we fought the Kolektor in Lyon that there was no such library, or if there ever was, it had been destroyed with the razing of the church centuries earlier."

"Whoa, I don't follow any of this," said Father Sergio, throwing his hands up. "Lyon, Kolektor, Church of St. John, library? What's this all about?"

"I thought you were fully briefed on our battle with the Kolektor," said J.E.

"I read everything we had on the final fight at Hakeldama near Jerusalem, but there wasn't time to go behind that," replied the young cleric.

"Well, here's the fifty-cent version," said J.E. with a smile, before turning serious. "During World War II, my grandfather found a cave with this strange jar in it. The jar was very special to him, and he brought it back to Madisonville, Louisiana, his home. The Kolektor hired a thief to steal the jar, and Thib walked in on him. He shot Thib, but Thib blasted him with his old shotgun. Upon Thib's death, Mom received her odd inheritance—the old oil jar. We took it to the university—LSU—in Baton Rouge, and it was carefully opened."

"Yes, and it contained the oldest known version of the Gospel of Judas Iscariot, the now so-called Lejeune Manuscript," Cloe added. "The monsignor and I were in the midst of beginning to translate it from ancient Greek to English when the Kolektor contacted us demanding the manuscript. The man tried and failed to kill J.E. and me at the university. We believe he did have our friend Father

39

Aloysius from Madisonville killed. But we laid a trap for him at the lab where the jar was being studied. Our people, including the Swiss Guard plus local authorities, killed or captured all of the Kolektor's men. We even found and seized his multimillion-dollar airplane. It looked like he was finished, so when he called again demanding the jar and the manuscript, we ignored him. But we underestimated him, and he had the last laugh when we learned he had kidnapped Uncle Sonny and was holding him hostage."

"The Kolektor proposed a swap: Uncle Sonny for the jar, the manuscript, and all of our research to date," continued the monsignor.

Even now, months later, Cloe could feel her anger rising, and her face began to flush. The monster had taken ninety-year-old Uncle Sonny and made him a pawn in his quest to satisfy, however temporally, his lust for old relics. She had promised her father she would find out why the jar was special, and she had promised herself she would find Thib's murderer. She and J.E. had sworn a terrible oath that they would get Uncle Sonny back.

"The exchange was arranged for Lyon at the Church of St. John, now the Church of St. Irenaeus," finished the monsignor.

"Why there?" asked the priest over the sounds of the engines.

"Because when we translated language from the Lejeune Manuscript, it indicated that the Bishop of Lyon, St. Irenaeus, may have been involved in commissioning the Judas Gospel," said Cloe.

"That's ridiculous," responded the assistant camerlengo. "Everyone knows Irenaeus was a devoted apostolic and fought heresy at every front. He published the last word on such things in a second-century work popularly known as *Against Heresies*. He never would have supported a gospel by someone he would have considered the betrayer of Christ."

"And yet our research suggests that he did," stated the monsignor.

"There is little question that text translated from the Lejeune Manuscript, the original Greek version of the Gospel of Judas, implicates Irenaeus as being involved," said Cloe. "The evidence suggests that Irenaeus saw something, a writing of some kind, that caused him to reevaluate the motives of Judas as told in the Jesus story."

"Oh my God," cried the young priest, jumping up. "The journal! You believe he saw the journal the pope spoke of. This is what changed Irenaeus's mind."

"Bingo," said J.E. "Now you have some idea what's been going on."

Cloe watched as Father Sergio settled back into his seat and looked down as if examining the palms of his hands in close detail. She knew he was trying to absorb the enormity of what he had just heard. She still had trouble getting her mind around the possibilities.

"I don't know what to say," Father Sergio continued softly. "This is unprecedented. This could change everything."

"Hold up there, Serge," remarked J.E. "Believe me, we have been through all the highs and lows. We have suggestions and implications from what we have uncovered. But although Mom is working hard on what may end up being this journal, it remains to be proven. And we still don't know who wrote it and why."

Cloe chuckled to herself to hear J.E. give the young cleric a nickname and to hear them communicating in a youthful vernacular. He might be the assistant camerlengo, and J.E. might be an officer and a gentleman, but they were both twentysomethings. Just then Cloe felt the airplane roll to port and begin its descent into Lyon, France.

Twenty minutes later, after the plane had landed, Cloe looked around and shivered upon remembering that the last time she was here on the tarmac, she was outbound as the Kolektor's captive. As she walked toward the terminal in the gathering darkness, she asked the monsignor, "Do you think the Kolektor's people are here?"

"Cloe, the Kolektor is most assuredly dead, so he can't have anybody here," responded the monsignor. "If you mean, could our newfound enemies be here, I think we would have to say yes. But they are under control of someone else, either the high-ranking associate of the Kolektor or this 'other,' this Q, of whom people whisper."

"I'm not sure the distinction helps, Albert," said Cloe. "You think our enemies are here, don't you?"

"They could be, but they would not know we are here. I think we probably have the element of surprise. We need to take care of our business and get out," said the monsignor as they walked along.

Cloe reflected on this, glanced over her shoulder, and said, "Yes, and we thought we had the element of surprise the last time we were here, and we ended up the Kolektor's prisoners." Cloe looked around feeling very small and vulnerable as a wind much too cool for this time of year blew across the tarmac.

CHAPTER 11

As much as Cloe liked the little inn at which they had stayed the last time in Lyon, the group elected to go to a different hotel on the off chance that the Kolektor's thugs might be waiting for them at the first place. She was hard-pressed not to think of them as the Kolektor's people. She accepted the fact that the Kolektor himself was dead, but these were his minions financed with his wealth. Someone had taken up the dark mantle of leadership of the Kolektor's organization and was now the Kolektor's standard-bearer. It really was as if he were still alive. Certainly, the evil that was within him still existed and had been somehow passed on.

As they ate dinner in the dining room of the small hotel, they discussed the plans for the next day. The room was cozy, furnished with antiques. The tourist season had not yet begun, so they had the place pretty much to themselves. Candles were in abundance, giving the area a warm atmosphere. Cloe wondered, not for the first time, whether this was just the eye of the hurricane.

Father Anton—or Tony, as he had insisted on being called— had taken most of their Swiss Guard directly to the church. He had detailed three of them to go to the hotel to watch after Cloe. The church had been decommissioned and was closed. It would not reopen until the tourist season.

As they ate, J.E.'s cell phone rang. He listened for a few seconds and then said, "Mom, it's Tony. He says they have thoroughly swept the church grounds, and everything is quiet. He says it's almost deserted."

"J.E., ask Father Anton … Tony … if he has checked the tunnel under the church," said Cloe.

J.E. whispered into the receiver, waited, and then responded, "Mom, the exit side of the tunnel is clear. That's the first thing they checked, and guards are posted there."

The phone conversation over, J.E. turned back to the group now sitting in silence.

"Well, everything seems secure," said the monsignor, finally. "The Swiss are very thorough and will be there all night to keep things secure for when you arrive tomorrow."

***

Later, in her room, Cloe reflected on the message from Father Anton. *Secure.* How could she be sure? The Kolektor and his henchmen had been so clever that first time. Preparing for bed, Cloe couldn't help but flash back to her last trip to the Church of St. Irenaeus. They had found themselves hostages, at the mercy of the Kolektor and his armed mercenaries, with their Swiss friends and protectors locked outside the church. Cloe remembered thinking that it was only a matter of time before the Swiss broke in and rescued them. But the Kolektor had activated a hidden lever behind the altar, and a trap door and spiral staircase had appeared. The Kolektor, his men, and his hostages had all escaped into a tunnel under the church. They were out and headed to the airport before the Swiss even knew they were gone. Everything had seemed so well planned and executed by the Kolektor, Cloe had almost lost hope for being rescued. Now, as she climbed into bed, she felt a terrible trepidation, as if she was on the eve of reentering the lions' den.

CHAPTER 12

The Karik sat at his massive desk in the study overlooking the mountains rising from the opposite rim of the valley. The Kolektor had used a more intimate area in the remote chalet for his office and work space. That had been a terrible waste of this wonderful view. One of the first things the Karik had required of the staff was that they get rid of all of the Kolektor's furniture and personal items. Everything not related to the work was burned in the rear garden. The Karik knew these actions would tell everyone that the era of the Kolektor was over.

Once that was done, the Karik had taken as his own the large central room with the cathedral ceiling and the floor-to-ceiling windows across the rear. He had had a raised platform built across the rear half of this area to house his office. The rest was made into a smaller, more intimate living room. Even now the large fireplace crackled with the warm glow of a natural fire.

The Karik smiled as he surveyed what he had wrought. The Kolektor was dead and gone, and all that had been his was now in the Karik's hands. This was by right of possession if not by right of law. He had taken care of the few who had raised questions. They would never be heard from again. Now he had the undying loyalty of everyone who remained a part of the organization. He smiled to himself. To paraphrase the English, the Kolektor was dead; long live the Karik.

The house satellite phone jangled, arousing him from his reverie.

"Yes," he said into the device.

"Karik," said the distant voice. "It is as you said. They have arrived."

"Elaborate," the Karik said curtly into the phone.

"Our people have been waiting near the airport for some time, as you know," responded the voice. "Last evening a large private plane arrived with no markings beyond the required tail numbers. From the descriptions you provided, we can be sure the woman, her son, and the priest are all here now."

Although he had teams in other cities looking for them as well, the Karik had suspected they might go to Lyon. From what the woman had been forced to divulge to the Kolektor on the night of Hakeldama, he knew that she and her colleagues had gone to the church a day earlier than the rendezvous date agreed to with the Kolektor to pursue some research. He knew some discoveries had been made, but apparently she was not finished.

"Karik, there's more," continued the man. "There are two more priests with them and at least a dozen men who look like soldiers of some sort."

"Well, they have come prepared for something," the Karik said, smiling to himself. "This is the Vatican's work, maybe that of Francis himself. One would think the new pontiff would have better things to do. This proves that the woman and the Vatican believe there's still something worth seeing at the church."

"We searched the church and grounds very thoroughly. We found nothing," the field operative replied.

"The woman found something before. She is very resourceful," said the Karik.

"What are your instructions, Karik?" asked the operative.

"Observe. Do not engage them," he ordered. "Let's see what they find."

"A wise decision, Karik," the employee said.

But the Karik was not finished. "As to our bomber, he has now failed twice. See to him and his family with the usual punishment."

***

Later the Karik sat alone in the darkness in his new study, contemplating the conversation with his servant. He had been present on many occasions when the Kolektor had instructed his agents and had been present not a few times when he had ordered swift and terrible retribution on those who had not met his standards. The words had just seemed to roll off the Kolektor's lips. It was just business. Had he acted as the Kolektor would have acted? He thought so, but how could he be sure? Had he given the orders the servant would expect? He did not want anyone to sense that he was unsure about what to do. Indecision and uncertainty could be fatal in his business. Still, when he thought about the instructions he had given for the bomber's family, his hands shook, and he hung his head.

CHAPTER 13

Cloe looked up as they approached the entrance to the church. Though old by modern standards, the church was a nineteenth-century replacement of the ancient structure, dating from the first or second century, that had once been on this site. It had been the primary place of worship of those known as the Lyon martyrs, the second-century Christian martyrs in Gaul, now France. Cloe knew that Irenaeus himself had been buried in the church. She wondered what else was there.

Father Anton and the Swiss Guard had deployed throughout the church complex. Cloe, the monsignor, and Father Sergio climbed the steps to the church's porch. J.E. had arrived earlier and was inside, according to Father Anton.

Cloe noticed that the door to the church had been replaced. The Swiss had shot and chopped through the old door after the Kolektor had locked all the doors and taken them hostage. Cloe thought it eerie as she approached the door that it swung open at the monsignor's touch as if nothing had happened. It bore no witness to the deadly fight that had taken place here only a few months earlier.

As Cloe entered into the interior gloom, she stumbled, and Albert steadied her with his arm. One look in his eyes told her he fully understood. The church was beautiful in spite of the sacrilege that had taken place there at the Kolektor's hands. Full-size icons of various saints adorned the walls overlooking the church. Irenaeus himself was there. Cloe remembered seeing his face with its rounded beard, so different from his death mask in the tomb. This was the place of the monumental discovery she and Albert had made the last time:

two simple ancient Phoenician letters hidden in the death mask of Irenaeus. They were the link, she had thought then, between Irenaeus and Judas that would help them understand the Judas Gospel, but the link later proved to be something else altogether. There was a connection between them all right, but not in the way she had expected.

J.E., standing near the altar rail, waved. "Hey, Mom, it's like old home week, back in the Church of St. John where we first encountered the Kolektor and his thugs."

With the help of his crack, Cloe pushed these memories away and tapped into her scientist persona. She would not let the frightening past keep her from carefully examining what she had come to see. "Okay, let's all spread out and see if there is anything on this level," she said. "I really want to go into the tunnel, but I don't want to miss anything that might be up here."

"What are we looking for?" asked J.E.

"Our real focus is something your mother saw," answered the monsignor, "maybe a door, when we were hustled through the tunnel under the Kolektor's guard. But if you see anything out of place here, call out." The group fanned out, with each of them studying a different section of the old church. As they proceeded toward the altar, Cloe burned with scientific curiosity about what had happened to them and how the Kolektor had made his escape with them as his hostages. It was all about the altar.

"J.E., can you see the mechanism the Kolektor used to pull up the trap door?" asked Cloe after they had studied everything on the main floor of the church.

J.E. turned and walked up the steps to the dais on which the altar rested. He circled the altar as Cloe and the others approached. When Cloe joined him, he was on his hands and knees, studying the floor behind the altar. She stooped down, and both of them continued running their hands over the floor area, looking for the trigger that would reveal the door and spiral staircase. The ancient floor was still cold as ice from the winter.

The monsignor joined them, and after a bit he said, "What's this?"

Cloe looked carefully and saw what at first appeared to be a bit of an irregularity in the tile that formed the flooring directly behind the altar.

"Try flicking it up," she said. "Does it move?"

The monsignor took his key ring from his pocket and used a small key to raise the very end of the irregularity, which, once extended, turned out to be a small bar hidden in a very cleverly crafted slot in the floor. The end came up and the monsignor seized it and gave the handle a tug.

Cloe gasped and jumped aside as a trap door cleverly built into the floor fell away and a spiral staircase appeared. Had Cloe not jumped, she might have taken a nasty fall.

"My, my," said J.E., chuckling. "It's a good thing the ancients never heard of IEDs. Otherwise, we would all be toast."

"Well, there it is," said the monsignor. "Irenaeus himself may have used this in his day."

"Surely, the martyrs must have built this avenue to escape in the event of an attack by their persecutors," added the young priest. "I've studied a lot of church history, but this is living history."

"But how can that be?" asked J.E. "I thought you said the original church that the martyrs would have used was destroyed."

"True enough, but not everything was ruined," responded the monsignor. "Background I have read on the original church tells us that parts of the old walls and much of the stone flooring survived. We know from our last visit here that some of the underground features still exist."

"Let's hope there is more church history somewhere below," responded Cloe. She turned to J.E. to lead the way.

J.E. pulled out small but powerful LED flashlights from his oversized pockets and handed them out to everyone. Cloe noticed that he was carrying a box about the size of a large toolbox. *Good,* she thought, they may have need of tools.

"All right, let's move carefully. Everything is very old and may not be entirely sound," said J.E. "One at a time. I'll go first. Mom, you come next with Father Sergio, and then the monsignor can protect our flank. With Father Anton and the Swiss outside, we don't need to leave anyone in the church."

A dankness floated up to Cloe's nostrils as she waited at the top of the stairwell for J.E. to give her the okay. She watched as J.E.'s light seemed to inch down the stairwell steps. She could hear his boots scraping on the stairs, but she could not see J.E. himself at all in the stygian blackness. About twenty feet down, Cloe saw his light suddenly stop and go out.

"J.E.," Cloe called, holding her breath, "what's happened?"

"Light's out is all," responded J.E. after a few seconds. Cloe could hear him banging the flashlight case against the tunnel wall. After a moment the light winked back on. "Come on down. All clear," he said.

Cloe flicked her light on and headed into the abyss, wondering what lay ahead.

CHAPTER 14

At the bottom of the stairs, Cloe shone her light and looked around carefully at the tunnel. When she had come through here as the Kolektor's prisoner, she had been forced to run to stay ahead of their Swiss pursuers. There had been little time for observation in the rush to escape.

The tunnel was narrower than she recalled. Barely wide enough for two people to walk abreast, it headed almost immediately downward. Many of the spider webs that had been broken with their prior passage had been rebuilt by their engineer occupants.

Cloe remembered the passageway as rather straight and short. Doubtless this was a product of her predicament and the haste with which they had come through here. She looked at the monsignor and saw he was studying one side of the tunnel. "Albert, what do you see?" Cloe asked, shivering and moving to him.

"It's just the shoring for the walls and the ceiling," replied the monsignor. "It's very old, not decaying, but hardening almost like stone. I've been in my share of old archeological digs, but I've never seen anything quite like this. This tunnel has been here for an exceedingly long period of time. It may be the oldest thing remaining on this campus."

J.E. had moved ahead, and Cloe heard him whisper almost to himself, "Hello. What do we have here?"

They converged on him, and Cloe could see he was standing in front of a section of the passage that turned left and then, a few feet later, right. It was so narrow only one person at a time could pass.

"Albert, I don't remember this part at all," Cloe mused.

"I'm not surprised. We came through here so quickly, and at that point, J.E. was unconscious from the blow to his head and was being carried. You and I were being half-dragged in the Kolektor's haste to escape. I vaguely remember this section because I was thrown against the wall by one of the Kolektor's thugs," replied the monsignor. "Apparently, I was not moving briskly enough for his tastes."

"I don't recall it, but I sure know what it is," said J.E. "It's a defensive position, sort of a man-made defile. With this, only a few defenders could hold off a large number of attackers because the attackers would be forced to go single file through that section. Archers and spearman could easily pick them off. The short sword would finish any who got through."

"Oh," said the young camerlengo. "That's how three hundred Spartans under King Leonides held off the entire Persian army at Thermopylae a half a millennium before the birth of Christ."

"Bingo!" cried J.E., smiling. "Serge, you might actually end up being useful for something."

"Yes, I might surprise you before this thing is over … jarhead," responded the young priest.

J.E. doubled over with laughter. "Jarhead? That's the worst insult I've ever heard," he said between gasps for breath. "You got me mixed up. Ground-pounder, yes. Meathead, yes. 'Jarhead' is reserved for our leatherneck friends in the Marines."

"From what I've seen thus far, I think it's an apt description," responded the camerlengo with disdain.

Now J.E. was howling and drawing chuckles from Cloe and the monsignor.

"Serge," he said after a while, wiping tears from his eyes, "I think I'm going to like you."

***

The uproar had died down, and Cloe was once again walking along the wall searching, for exactly what, she wasn't sure. Certainly, they were looking for possible clues as to where the Sicarii's cave full of ancient jars that Thib had seen was located. But Cloe was unsure how to distinguish such clues from anything else—that is, if the Sicarii had even left any. Still, she had seen something the last time through, which was why they had come here first. There was something here.

As they passed through the defile, J.E. remarked, "Mom, this passageway is protected on both ends. No one could have accessed it from the church without knowing it was there and about the secret lever. On the other hand, you couldn't get through it from the outside because of the defile, if it were guarded."

Cloe saw a light ahead indicating the end of the tunnel. She had discovered nothing.

"J.E.'s right," said the monsignor. "The tunnel was an escape route, but it was more. Why fortify the exit side of the secret tunnel? Why arrange it so guards could prevent anyone from entering from the outside?"

"Maybe this was done to protect whoever was inside the church from enemies using the tunnel for access," observed Father Sergio.

"Unnecessary," replied J.E., studying the walls. "The trap door only opens from inside the church by means of the hidden lever. This was designed to be able to defend the interior of the tunnel."

"You would only do that if there were something to protect inside the tunnel itself," reasoned Cloe. "We've missed whatever it is."

Cloe turned and led them back toward the church. In the area where the defile began, she scrutinized the walls, and within a slightly concave area she noticed what might be the very faint outline of a doorframe.

"Here's something," she said, now remembering thinking that she had seen a door, maybe two, the last time through. As she stepped back and studied the wall, the outline of the door became more apparent. The door itself was covered with mold and looked very much like the earth that surrounded it. It was quite old and appeared not to have been opened in an exceedingly long time. Smallish by modern standards, it probably had been built at a time when people, on average, were much shorter, Cloe surmised. It was maybe five and a half feet by three and a half feet.

"What do we have here?" asked the monsignor, coming up to look.

"Don't know, yet," responded Cloe, totally focused on the portal. She began scraping the mold and dirt from the frame.

The camerlengo jumped in to help. Pretty soon the door and its frame were plainly visible. There were no markings on it at all. It was an extremely stout, hard wooden door, but its surface had been planed almost smooth. Cloe could see no doorknob or latch. A keyhole as large as a quarter was the only feature on the door.

J.E. put his shoulder to the door, but it would not budge. He hit it several times, and the monsignor pitched in. There was no give in it at all. Indeed, the last time they hit it, there was a low rumble from above.

"Careful ... force does not seem to be the answer," said Cloe. She knelt down and tried to peer through the keyhole but could see only darkness. When she used one of the little flashlights, she could see a little farther, but the keyhole channel narrowed somewhat an inch or so from the opening. She could not see beyond that point. "Interesting," she said under her breath. In the stillness they all heard her.

"What's interesting, Mom?" asked J.E., rubbing his shoulder and staring at the door.

"The interior of the lock is not made of metal but of what looks like some type of gemstone, maybe jade," Cloe replied, amazed and wondering if this could be right.

"Jade?" mused the monsignor as each man took a look at the interior of the lock.

J.E. took his cell phone from his hip holster and carefully photographed the keyhole.

"Not only is the interior formed of some gemstone substance such as jade, but there are also mechanical gears in there made of the same substance," continued the monsignor.

"What does all that mean?" asked the camerlengo.

"It means the lock was built of a material that would long outlast metals, particularly those of the ancients. Whoever built this wanted this lock to be here a long time," answered Cloe. "It also means that this mechanism was added later because the first- or second-century Christians would not have had this technology."

"I agree," stated the monsignor, standing up after his examination of the lock's interior. "I think we have to consider the possibility that the builders of the tunnel were the early Christians who founded the Church of St. John. That would have been Irenaeus and the early Christian martyrs. If so, this tunnel dates from a time within a couple hundred years of Christ's death. This door and this lock are something else altogether and could have been added later. Somehow, circumstances changed, and maybe even the whole purpose of the tunnel changed."

"The metals of that early era were rather crude, but this lock is more like a piece of art at which the makers were very adept, at least a few hundred years later," said Cloe, picking up the thread. "The key must mesh with these fine gears to open the door."

"True, and this also means there is likely only a single unique key that can connect properly with the gears and open the lock," noted the monsignor. "Given the detail in the interior of the lock, I'm guessing that trying to open this door without the correct key may also cause unpleasant consequences."

J.E.'s head jerked up. "Monsignor, are you saying you think this door is booby-trapped?"

CHAPTER 15

"Almost certainly, young sir," replied the monsignor. "I don't see the builders going to the trouble of making the tunnel almost assault-proof and later creating a lock with a Jules Verne–like mechanism and then neglecting to penalize anyone who attempts to circumvent their handiwork."

Cloe smiled at the monsignor's understatement, another talent of his she had come to appreciate.

"We're going to need the key," J.E. said, slumping back against the wall.

Cloe was bent over, studying the keyhole as if she might open it by force of mental effort. "I have seen that peculiar shape before," she said at last.

The monsignor stooped and examined the area very carefully. Standing again, he said, "You are right. There's something familiar about it. We need to think of it less as a key and more as a special tool that is designed to open this specific door."

"It's got to be in the church," said Father Sergio. "Doesn't it? Where else could it be?"

"Right, Serge, if the ancients needed the key, they would want it to be close at hand," said J.E. "It's got to be nearby, but where?"

"All right," said Cloe. "Let's check the walls of the tunnel very carefully to see if we have missed anything. I thought I saw a second door the first time through."

After another thirty minutes of searching, even Cloe had to agree there was nothing further to be found. If she had seen a second door, it most certainly had been in her imagination.

They rallied back at the door, and Cloe said, "We need to go upstairs and search the church again carefully, this time with an eye toward finding something that will open this door. We need that key!"

Cloe led the group back the way they had come, up the spiral staircase and into the church. "J.E., you and Father Sergio search the back of the church from about the midway point to the door. The monsignor and I will look forward and into the altar area. When we are all finished, if we have found nothing, we'll meet at the niche where St. Irenaeus is buried."

Cloe looked around the old church. Even though it had been decommissioned as a house of worship, it was still filled with niches, alcoves, and icons, any one of which could conceal a hundred such keys. Without any more information, Cloe worried they wouldn't find anything, even though it might be in plain sight.

"Plain sight," said Cloe out loud, "just like the clues in Irenaeus's death mask."

"What?" asked the monsignor, having heard her but not seeming to understand.

"Albert, you remember when we searched Irenaeus's tomb for clues relating to the library of St. John?"

"Yes, the day before our meeting with the Kolektor, we searched the niche and tomb area and found the ancient Phoenician letters *yuhd* and *shin* embedded in the death mask, roughly the equivalents of the English *I* and *S*. At that point, we thought they referred to 'IS' for Iscariot, proving that Irenaeus was connected with the Greek version of the Gospel of Judas. Of course, later events proved that to be incorrect."

"Right, but the clues were in plain sight. We did not need to find them; we just needed to understand them," Cloe continued. "What if the key is hidden the same way?"

"There are only two such obvious places in the church," the monsignor said. "One is the tomb, which we have searched in detail, and the other is the full-size statue of Irenaeus we observed on our way out of the church."

Both turned toward the figure of Irenaeus that stood on the right ascending side of the church near the altar rail. Cloe studied the icon of the saint as she slowly walked toward it. It seemed completely unremarkable, but as she got closer, she could see from the style and detail that the statue was very old, much older than this nineteenth-century church. The porcelain figure was garbed in a ceramic robe-like cassock that replicated the coarse cloth of the day. A large rosary surrounded his waist like a sash or belt. He had a staff with a crook at the top that reminded Cloe of a shepherd's walking stick.

They both studied the staff closely. Finally, the monsignor straightened and said, "I think we may have found our key."

CHAPTER 16

Cloe called to the others, and soon J.E. and the camerlengo were also closely examining the staff. It extended from above the head of the life-size statue to near his left foot on the base of the work.

"I don't see any breaks in the rod," said the monsignor. "It seems to be made of one piece. Surely the whole thing is not the key."

"Mom, the keyhole in the tunnel had a unique shape to it," said J.E. "Look at the end of the shepherd's crook. That's the only place we can clearly see the cross section. It's close, but it's not the same as the keyhole."

"J.E., can you show us the picture you took?" asked Cloe.

Cloe stood back as J.E. pulled out his cell phone and pulled up the picture of the keyhole. They all stared at it and at the end of the staff.

The monsignor said, "The staff is solid stone or very hard wood. Even if we could get a section from it, I do not believe it is a match for our keyhole. It seemed promising at first, but it's not the key."

"Well then, where is the key?" questioned Father Sergio.

Cloe had continued examining the statue as they discussed the rod. Her eyes now fixed upon the large cross at the end of the heavy rosary around the saint's waist. It also seemed to have been constructed of porcelain or some similar ceramic material. It had been painted in incredible detail.

"Hmmm," she said. "What's that writing at the foot of the cross? Are those numbers? I haven't seen that before."

The monsignor peered at it and said, "It's Greek, which is a little unusual itself here in a Roman province. Cloe, what does it say?"

Cloe looked closer, studying the inscription. "It's a number, 177," she said. "There does not seem to be any punctuation. Could that be a year?"

"Perhaps," said the monsignor, considering the possibilities. "That would be about the right time for the creation of the original church, plus or minus."

"But where does that take us?" asked J.E. "What else happened in 177 AD?"

"Nothing comes immediately to mind," said the monsignor dejectedly. "Wait a minute. Some of the early martyrs of the new Church were executed here about that time. In fact, one of the most famous, Blandina, was martyred in about 177."

"I don't see how that connects to anything," said Cloe.

"Hold on," said the young camerlengo. "What if it is not a year? What if it is 1-77 or 17-7 or 1-7-7? Could that mean something?"

"The ancients didn't use the month, date, and year convention as we do," responded Cloe. "I don't see what the others could mean."

"First-rate thinking," said the monsignor. "But in ancient times the number one was sometimes code for the first book of the Gospels—Matthew. This code was used for the first three hundred years or so of Christianity because of the Roman persecutors. Early Christians needed to be able to cite the Gospels in a way that was not immediately obvious. Perhaps it is a reference to scripture."

"That would make sense, but what might it mean?" asked Cloe.

"It may be a reference to the seventh chapter of Matthew, line seven," said the monsignor.

"But what does it say?" queried J.E.

"It says, 'Knock and the door will be opened to you,' or words to that effect," whispered the young camerlengo, fingering but not opening his pocket Bible.

"Okay, then we have found our key," replied J.E. "We just have to figure out exactly where it is. The cross is square, so it's not the key."

The monsignor examined the boxy crucifix carefully and said, "Perhaps there is something inside the cross. It may be like a Chinese puzzle, possibly sliding open if we can find the trigger."

"Possibly, but would it even still work after so many years?" asked the camerlengo.

Cloe moved forward and took off one of her shoes. "I have an idea," she said. With that she smacked the cross with a wicked blow with the heel of the shoe. Both priests grimaced at the smiting of the religious relic.

The cross shattered, and everyone but Cloe gasped as the strange object that had been concealed within its hollow interior was revealed. The gray-green article gleamed in the low light of the church.

"Gentlemen," said Cloe. "I think I can say that we have now found our key."

CHAPTER 17

"Wow, Mom ... how did you know?" questioned J.E. excitedly.

"I didn't know. It was just a guess," responded Cloe, grateful she had not damaged the statue for nothing. "But with the message on the cross itself, I had a good feeling it might be a sort of container for our key, based on the process of elimination. As someone once said, when you eliminate the likely possibilities, whatever is left, no matter how improbable, must be the answer."

The monsignor chuckled. "Or words to that effect," he said, recognizing the loose reference to one of the favorite sayings of literature's greatest detective.

"Whatever," said Cloe, smiling. She knelt on one knee and studied the instrument in what remained of the crucifix. It was large, about the size of an old-fashioned jailhouse key. But it seemed to be made of the same material as the interior of the lock in the tunnel. "If I'm not mistaken, this is jade, just like the lock mechanism," said Cloe. "Look at the pattern of the key. It's designed to mesh with the interior gears of the lock."

She removed the key from what was left of its hiding place and held it to the light. Though it gleamed only faintly in the low light of the church, it mesmerized its onlookers as surely as if they had found the lost cache of Solomon's gold.

Cloe ran her fingers over the oddly shaped device. "J.E., shine your flashlight on the very bottom of the key."

He pulled the light out and shone it where directed, and there, Cloe clearly saw two marks that she had seen before. *"Yuhd* and *shin,"* she said with growing excitement.

"Sorry, but what's that mean?" asked the young camerlengo.

Cloe, the dead languages expert, assumed her professorial role and said, "These are ancient Phoenician letters roughly translating into English as *I* and *S*. No one speaks this language anymore, so it was put here hundreds, perhaps thousands, of years ago."

"Well, it's obviously the sign of our friends the Sicarii," interjected J.E. "It's the same as you found in Irenaeus's death mask the last time here."

"Imagine," said the monsignor, "once again, we are following the trail they left, perhaps almost two thousand years ago."

***

Soon they were back in the tunnel facing the ancient door. Cloe held the key they had extricated from the cross of St. Irenaeus. "How shall we do this?" she asked.

J.E. responded, "Let me have the key. Everyone else needs to go up the tunnel shaft a ways, just to be safe in case something unexpected happens."

But what about you? Cloe thought.

Reading her face, J.E. said, "Mom, I'm as fit as anyone here and, if something bad goes down, best able to get out of the way."

She couldn't refute that, so she handed him the key and slowly moved up the tunnel, calling out, "Be careful, J.E." She wanted to add something about how much she loved him, just in case, but she knew this would embarrass him. When everyone was clear, J.E. moved to the door. As Cloe watched intently, he bent down and inserted the key into the mechanism.

He turned to Cloe and flashed her a great Lejeune smile. Her heart almost burst. She continued watching closely as he exerted a bit of pressure on the handle of the key. Cloe saw it rotate. "J.E., it's turning," she whispered.

Gears began to grind, slowly, reluctantly, after all these years. The area over the shaft where J.E. now stood began rumbling and vibrating, softly at first but then more violently. The ceiling above him appeared to ripple.

"Run!" cried the camerlengo. "It's coming down! It's a trap!"

Dust and spoil poured out of the overhead space, but it held. The noise abated, and the tunnel became as quiet as a grave. Then there was a click.

"What was that?" asked Cloe.

The monsignor peered into the gloom and said, "I think the door has been opened unto us."

CHAPTER 18

Cloe stepped forward and studied the portal. The lock had given up its secrets, and the door was now ajar.

"Careful," cried the camerlengo. "Everything could still come down."

"I don't think so," said the monsignor. "If it was going to collapse, it would have done so when the key was turned."

J.E. grasped the edge of the door and began to pull it open. They all looked inside.

"It's just a wall," said Cloe, disappointed. "The door opens to a wall."

J.E. had his light on the mass behind the door. "It's made of mud or something like that."

"Very old mud," said Father Sergio. "These are mud bricks that were common for building purposes many, many years ago."

"So if there was anything here, it has been sealed," concluded Cloe.

They all gathered dejectedly and sat down in front of the brick wall that sealed off whatever lay behind the Sicarii door.

"Now what?" asked the camerlengo.

"Well, now it's time for some modern military technology," said J.E. He grabbed the toolbox-size container he had brought into the tunnel and snapped the clasps on it. Soon, he had in hand a device that looked a little like a portable x-ray machine from a dentist's office.

"J.E., what is that?" asked Cloe. "I thought that was a toolbox."

"If I could hazard a guess, I would say that is a ground-penetrating radar machine," interjected the monsignor, smiling and reading the large warning label pasted on the side of the device.

"Right you are, Padre," replied J.E. "We'll warm this baby up and see what we are dealing with here. It can tell us what's back there and about how far."

Cloe watched as J.E. activated the battery pack and pressed what looked like a very large bore barrel against the wall. He studied a screen at the back of the machine.

After a few minutes, J.E. had completed his examination. "The wall is only inches deep, maybe twelve to fifteen inches. There's definitely a space or passageway behind it," he concluded.

Excitement was again building in Cloe. "Now what?" she asked.

"Well, we don't have any tools, so I have to go back up to the van and get the rest of the stuff I brought."

"Why not just call Father Anton and get one of the Swiss to bring the tools here?" asked Father Sergio.

"I haven't been able to get a cell-phone signal since we entered the tunnel, Serge. Anyway, I want to check on our security," responded J.E.

***

A few minutes later, J.E. returned with two pickaxes and a shovel. He also had a small toolbox. "We're being watched," he said.

"What do you know?" asked the monsignor.

"I spoke with Father Anton," replied J.E. "He and the Swiss have sighted at least two people observing the compound and our activities."

"They might be agents of the Kolektor's forces or of this new stranger, the heir," replied the monsignor.

"Either way, I think we can count on them knowing who we are and what we are about," concluded Father Sergio. "Perhaps we should consider leaving and coming back another time."

"No," said Cloe. "We have come too far, and we are too close. But we must hurry."

They all turned to the wall, and with one of the pickaxes, J.E. struck it with a mighty blow. The barrier absorbed the strike with little apparent damage.

"Well, I think we have our work cut out for us," said Cloe.

Each of them took turns with the picks and shovel. After about twenty minutes, they had cleared a hole large enough for them to enter. J.E. stepped up to it.

"Whoa, J.E.," Cloe said. "Remember, the exterior of this passage was booby-trapped. Let's see what our lights can reveal."

All four of them shone their powerful little lights into the gloom on the other side of the barrier.

"There's not too much here," said the camerlengo. "It's just a short hallway framed up with wooden timbers like the tunnel."

"The walls are earthen like the tunnel," added the monsignor. "They appear to have been excavated about the same time. I don't see anything that looks like a trigger for a trap."

"The ancients were tricky," said Cloe. "They seem to have spent a good deal of time thinking about keeping intruders out of their tombs and other secret places or making them pay the ultimate penalty if they did gain access. Let's proceed very carefully, one at a time, and stay close to the walls. If there is some kind of pressure switch for a trap, it will be in the middle of the passage where people could be expected to walk and step on it."

She turned to enter, but J.E. said, "Mom, I'll go first."

"You have the radar, and you are the only one who knows how to operate it," she replied. "I got this."

Cloe entered the short tunnel, and the others followed. She pressed against the dirt wall and crab-walked sideways along the passage. With each step she worried she would spring some hidden latch, causing disaster. The light was bad and the air increasingly hard to breathe. Sweat broke out on her brow even though it was cool here underground. She realized she had so tensed her shoulders that her neck had begun to ache. How could walking such a seemingly short length of passageway take so long? But after a few more paces, she reached the end.

"Thank God," she said. She felt she had finished a marathon.

"Well, there's nothing here," said Father Sergio. "It's a dead end."

J.E. trained the radar on the left-hand wall. He repeated the procedure on the right-hand wall and then on the wall at the end of the tunnel. After a thorough examination he said, "Nothing."

"Could it be we have missed something?" asked the camerlengo.

"I don't see how," said J.E. "The radar shows nothing within its range, which is considerable. Perhaps there was a cave-in that filled completely in if this area was once the library."

"Remember," commented the monsignor, "when the possible fails us, what is left must be the answer. Try the floor."

Cloe watched as J.E. scanned the radar over the floor of the small cavity. His shoulders slumped as he studied the readout on the machine.

"Nothing!" he said. "It's a dead end."

CHAPTER 19

"We are not quite finished," said the monsignor.

"Albert, we have carefully examined the walls, the end of the tunnel, and now the floor," responded Cloe. "We're done … Wait!"

"Mom, what?" quizzed J.E.

"The monsignor is right … No matter how unlikely, whatever is left must be the answer," replied Cloe. "J.E., scan the ceiling."

J.E. worked the instrument against the ceiling, and a few minutes later, he nodded. "There's something up there."

"How could that be? The ceiling is a good eight to nine feet from the floor. Still, if we have learned anything about the ancients, it is to expect the unexpected," commented the camerlengo.

"It's the last place anyone would look," said Cloe. "Without the ground-penetrating radar, we would not have had a clue."

"Okay, everyone spread out and look for some sort of trigger or access," said J.E. "Something's up there, and we are going to find it."

Twenty minutes later, they had examined every inch of the space.

"I couldn't find anything," said the camerlengo.

Cloe realized none of them had found anything. It was a mystery, just like the keyhole. *Could it be?* she wondered. "J.E., where's the key we used to get in here?" she asked.

"Here," he said, patting his pocket, "but I don't see anyplace to use it."

"Oh my God," the monsignor whispered.

"Look at the door we entered," Cloe mused. "We used the key on the outside to get in. What do you see?"

J.E. and Father Sergio rushed to the door and examined it carefully. The monsignor grinned at Cloe.

Father Sergio said simply, "There's a keyhole on the inside of the door."

The short shaft was absolutely silent while its occupants considered the implications.

"Why would there be a keyhole on the inside?" asked the camerlengo.

"Yes … exactly!" said J.E.

"J.E., close the door and engage the mechanism," said Cloe.

"Wait a minute," suggested the camerlengo. "If you close the door, what if we can't get out?"

"I don't think that's going to be the problem. There's a latch on the inside, so this was not meant to trap people in here, but to prevent them from entering—and then even if they did enter, they would find nothing. Ingenious!" concluded Cloe.

J.E. swung the door closed, and everyone heard a click.

"Now, J.E., I suggest you insert the key and turn it," said the monsignor.

J.E. shone his light on the door and then on the keyhole. He withdrew the key from his pocket and inserted it in the door.

Cloe saw him try to turn it clockwise as he had on the outside of the door. Nothing happened. It was as if the lock had frozen.

J.E. tried the same motion a few more times, and then he grunted and flicked his wrist to the left. Cloe saw the key twist and turn. Once again the lock clicked open, and the sound of ancient gears filled the space, grinding their mechanical song.

The earthen ceiling over them began to shake and crumble. Small fragments fell, and then larger chunks joined in what looked like the early stages of a cave-in. Dust and debris began to rain down, and Cloe found she could hardly breathe. Rocks pummeled them, and she saw the monsignor stumble.

"Against the walls!" Cloe screamed. Earth, rocks, and dust flooded into the small area. "Cover your face and head. For God's sake, don't look up!" In a minute or so it was over. Dust filled the air, but four small lights still shone. As the silt settled, Cloe looked around and could hardly believe her eyes. Where there had been nothing but open space in the small corridor, a stairway was now descending from the ceiling.

CHAPTER 20

"Boss, there's something going on at the church," said the man who had been posted by Tomás to watch the Church of St. Irenaeus.

Miguel listened to the small voice on the satellite phone. His man had been there waiting for some time. "What is it?" asked Miguel.

"Well, nothing has happened at all for a good while because the church is no longer active. I have seen a few tourists here and there, but that's been it for days," replied his retainer.

"Yes?" nudged Miguel.

"This morning that all changed," said the voice. "A van pulled up, and a number of people unloaded. There were two priests—one old, one younger—a woman, and a young man."

"Describe them," said Miguel.

After listening carefully to the descriptions, Miguel thought the woman had to be Dr. Lejeune, expert in old languages from the United States. He had been able to learn a good deal about her online. He knew she was the key. The older priest must be the monsignor with whom she was friendly, and the young man surely was the woman's soldier son. He had no idea who the young priest was.

"Well, that's very interesting," mused Miguel.

"There's more, boss," said the man on the phone. "Late last night, there was some activity at the church compound, but we could not see well enough in the dark to know what it was. This new group this morning was met by two men who must have already been at the church. They had a decidedly military look to them. I think there may be others, but I do not know for sure how many."

"I see," considered Miguel, thinking they might be the leaders of a detachment of the Swiss Guard. He had not expected the Vatican to mobilize such resources around the woman. He wondered how many soldiers they had with them.

"It would appear that these people are not tourists but have some serious business at the church," concluded the lookout in Lyon.

"What happened after they arrived and unloaded?" asked Miguel.

"The military-looking group spoke to the newcomers, occasionally pointing to different areas of the church complex. After a bit, the conversation apparently over, the woman and her companions walked up the steps of the church and entered."

"Obviously, the soldiers arrived last night, reconnoitered the compound, and then set up some sort of perimeter protection," said Miguel. "What's happened to the woman and her group?"

"They have been in the church for hours—virtually the whole day. The young man originally carried a box about the size of a large toolbox into the church and later returned to the van once for what looked like a smaller toolbox, a shovel, and a couple of pickaxes."

"A very thorough report," said Miguel as he prepared to ring off. "You and your employers have my thanks."

"Boss, that's not all," replied the man.

"Oh, what else?" inquired Miguel.

There was silence on the phone for a few seconds before the voice came back. "This morning's arrivals are not alone. There's a second group here watching them."

CHAPTER 21

The stairs had descended as if on pistons, slowly and without much noise. Cloe guessed that if she could find the mechanism that controlled the stairs, its works would look like the interior of a fine watch with a jeweled movement.

Quiet had now once again fallen over them as the stairway locked down with a clunk. The last of the dust settled, and everyone approached the stairs and looked up.

"Is it safe?" the camerlengo asked.

"This would be the perfect place for a secondary booby trap. In the IED world, the first explosion is often just the attention-getter that lures the real targets in to investigate or to help anyone injured," J.E. responded.

The monsignor walked around the staircase, examining it closely. "I don't see anything," he said. "If it were a trap, it would be triggered by weight on the steps. They are all solid. I think we are good."

With that he jumped onto the second step and began to move upward. Cloe gasped, but the monsignor was already halfway up. The steps creaked a bit but held firm, as the monsignor had predicted.

"J.E., I'll go up next," said Cloe. "Father Sergio should follow, and you come last, but the two of you bring our tools. Who knows what we will find."

Cloe headed up the stairway, and the others followed. When she reached the top, she could not see the monsignor, who had apparently moved out into the now dust-filled space above. "Albert," she called, reluctantly breaking the long silence of the hidden room.

"Here," he replied softly, almost reverently.

Cloe shone her light toward the sound of his voice and saw that the sizable space was partitioned by a sort of walkway down the middle. He was standing a good way down the aisle in the open hall, looking forward with his back to her. That and the dust were why she hadn't seen his light in the first place. The room was larger than she had expected, and the ceiling was higher. The floor was constructed of stone of some type, perhaps slate. It had been so finely crafted that no mortar was visible between the plates.

The monsignor was now only a few paces ahead. As she caught up to him, she could see he was studying the surroundings. There was a look of amazement on his face.

"Albert, are you all right?" Cloe asked, taking in more of the chamber. In the murky darkness, she could see what looked like the shapes of a number of bunks or beds. Perhaps this had been the sleeping quarters of some of the early religious of the church.

Just then, J.E. and the camerlengo reached them. As they set the tools down, they too began to gawk about at the mysterious space.

"I'm fine," the monsignor said.

"What is this place?" asked Cloe, suppressing a chill.

"Cloe, I believe we are looking at the long-lost library of St. John the Apostle, author of the last of the orthodox Gospels."

***

"Library?" questioned J.E. "Where are the books?"

"We need to carefully search this chamber," Cloe said. "But we need to do it together so we can see."

"That might not be necessary," said the monsignor. "I saw wall sconces with torches or candles in them when I first walked down the main aisle. Let's see if any of them still work."

A few minutes later, they had circumnavigated the room and lit the candles in the sconces with matches J.E. had in his toolbox. These were not dainty little modern candles but large candles meant to facilitate reading, Cloe realized. Some of the wicks were a quarter inch or more in diameter. Although they still did not produce bright light by electric values, they were sufficient to illuminate the larger area. Cloe and the monsignor stood almost back-to-back as they rotated 360 degrees, taking in everything. The most significant features of the room were two rows of rectangular objects, flanking the center corridor. While Cloe had initially thought these might be beds, she could now see that whatever they were, they were clearly not for sleeping. They appeared to be stone boxes about the size of a child's bunk bed. She would have to look more closely at those.

"If this is the library, where are the books?" asked Cloe, echoing J.E.'s query.

"Gone. But this was indeed at one time a library," the monsignor replied, pointing to the walls with their shelves and niches.

"Mom," yelled J.E., "come see!"

Cloe and the monsignor moved toward J.E., who was examining the wall of the chamber that was closest to the church, if Cloe had her bearings correct.

As they approached, J.E. turned to face them. "This end of the room has been sealed," he said. "Look—see the mud bricks, like downstairs? There was once an opening here. The way we came in was not the only access to this area. The entrance we used must have been added later."

"The young sir is correct," said the monsignor after studying the area. "I think if we excavated the area, we would find that this room once connected with the basement or a subbasement of the church—not the existing church, of course, but a much, much older one. Maybe as old as the second-century church that was the worship place of the original Christian community in Lyon."

"My goodness," said Father Sergio. "If true, this is a remarkable discovery. No, it's an astounding discovery! Think of it … the early Christian leaders may have studied in this very room. Pothinus, the first bishop of Lyon, then Lugdunum; Blandina; and perhaps Irenaeus himself. These people are all saints now. We may be walking in their ancient footsteps."

"The first church building was largely destroyed centuries ago. The current church is only about two hundred years old," added the monsignor. "This room, the tunnel, and a few remnants upstairs may be the only things left from those earliest days."

"But why is it still here?" queried J.E. "If most everything was destroyed, why was this spared?"

"Well, the books, codices, and scrolls were obviously moved or destroyed," said Cloe. "Still, this room was somehow sealed off and secreted away for these many years. The people who sacked the church apparently never found this chamber."

"There must have been something else here that was valuable to the early protectors of the church that could not be easily or, perhaps, quickly moved," posited the monsignor. "Therefore, they sealed off this chamber in such a clever manner that no one has ever found it … until now."

"What could it be?" asked the young camerlengo. "Everything was destroyed. Even the tombs of the martyrs of Lyon were ransacked and ruined."

"All I can say is this is not supposed to exist," mused J.E. "What else do we think we know about the destruction of the Church of St. John that may not be true?"

"J.E.'s right," said Cloe. "Throw out whatever we have read or believed about this church and its history. It's our job to write a new story." She turned and headed back into the center of the chamber. "Let's start with figuring out what was left hidden here and why."

CHAPTER 22

Cloe walked among what she had originally thought might be beds or cots in a sleeping chamber. As she played her tiny light over the objects, she realized they were solid stone. As she looked more closely, they reminded her of something. "Oh my God!" she exclaimed, amazed. "It's a graveyard."

The monsignor approached her and said, "Not a graveyard per se, but we may be looking at ancient tombs, a sort of catacomb, almost two thousand years old."

"But if so, how did the library of St. John become a mausoleum?" questioned J.E. "What the hell happened here?"

"A good question, J.E.," said the monsignor. "Given the signature of the Sicarii—SI—on the key that got us into this place, I'm guessing they had something to do with the removal of the contents of the library. If we find Thib's cave, there may be something there that could shed light on this place."

"Tombs in the attic," said Father Sergio shaking his head. "This is amazing."

"In all likelihood, the books were removed when the library was sealed off, and this secret room was used as refuge for the remains of whoever is here," added Cloe.

"But why," asked the camerlengo, "would the remains be secreted like this?"

"Had to be some special people," said J.E.

Cloe moved toward the first sarcophagus. It was smaller than she would have expected, probably because of the smaller stature of the ancients. There looked to be eight to ten of these stone coffins. She passed from one to another until she had carefully viewed all of them. The others followed her through the room.

"Well, there is little to distinguish the individual tombs. They are all completely plain and obviously very old," Cloe said. "The only thing is the inscription on each."

"Yes, what do you notice about them?" whispered the monsignor.

The young camerlengo straightened from looking at one of the stone dedications on a tomb near him and said, "They are written in Latin, which was the official language of the day. Each appears to bear a name and a few words, probably some brief description."

Cloe said, "Father Sergio and Albert, walk with me and help with the names. I'm fluent in Greek, Phoenician, and ancient Aramaic, but my Latin is a little rusty."

Studying the first inscription, Father Sergio said, "This one says 'Ponticus.'"

On they went down the line of stone sarcophagi, Father Sergio or the monsignor struggling with the worn scratches that made up the Latin inscriptions, in turn calling out the names: Maturus, Sanctus, Attalus, Alexander. Finally, they were nearing the far end of the chamber. Only three stone tombs were left. But the clerics had gone strangely quiet, whispering between themselves, as they leaned down examining one of them.

Finally, the monsignor stood and asked Father Sergio, "Are you sure?"

"It's what I think," he said simply.

"What is it? What does it say?" asked J.E. Cloe leaned in, looking at the inscription.

"It says 'Blandina,'" said the young priest, softly.

"My God," said Cloe, her excitement rising. "These must be the martyrs of Lyon. Lyon was one of the centers of Christianity in the second century, and the martyrs were among its most famous advocates."

"The next one reads 'Pothinus,' who we know was the first bishop of Lyon," stated the monsignor. "These are the best known of the identified martyrs of Lyon. All were martyred for their refusal to renounce their faith toward the end of the second century."

They stepped to the next tomb. Cloe bent to examine the inscription, wondering aloud, "Could Irenaeus himself actually be here instead of upstairs in the church where his tomb is supposed to be?"

"Not in this one … it says Polycarp," the young priest replied.

J.E. piped up and said, "Monsignor, wasn't that the guy you say bridged the gap between St. John and St. Irenaeus?"

"Yes, the young sir correctly remembers that John mentored Polycarp in Christianity, and Polycarp taught Irenaeus," responded the cleric. "This *is* astounding."

"Perhaps the last stone coffin contains Irenaeus," speculated J.E.

Moving to the last sarcophagus, the monsignor visibly strained to read the dedication. He was silent for a moment, and then he straightened, turned to Cloe, and said, "It's not Latin; it's written in ancient Greek."

CHAPTER 23

"Karik, we have been to the hospital in Jerusalem where the son of the Lejeune woman was treated for the wound to his arm," said the functionary, facing his master. He had flown back to the retreat from Jerusalem to report in person.

"Yes, an oversize nail from a large-bore nail gun will leave a mark," said the Karik as he observed his servant. "Too bad my predecessor was not more accurate with his shot."

"The young man had surgery to correct nerve damage and was released after a few days," continued the man. "We could find no records that could lead us to anyone connected to the Sicarii."

"Is that what you have come all this way to tell me—that you have failed?" questioned the Karik, his voice rising with anger.

"No, Karik," said the man quickly, beginning to sweat under his clothes. "We then went to the private sanatorium where the woman, the lady doctor, was brought after Hakeldama. It is most likely that they saved her life since she was close to death due to loss of blood."

"Yes, yes … I know all that," replied the Karik harshly. "Do you have anything new for me?"

"The private hospital keeps scrupulously exacting records. We could not identify who brought her in, but after studying the financial records, we learned who paid for the treatment. Payment was made by a number of computer transfers among various accounts through several banks in different countries. The transferor thought this was untraceable, and it would have been for most people."

"Yes, but my people are experts in this regard. I always have to know with whom I'm dealing," said the Karik with a smirk.

"That is so, Karik. We employed your experts, and we have a name and location. As we speak, I have people searching out this individual who may have paid for the doctor's treatment and who may be our link to the Sicarii," the servant said. "We will find her and earnestly seek her cooperation."

"Very good, my faithful friend," replied the Karik, softening. "Do use the full measure of our capabilities to convince her of our requirements of her. Time *is* of the essence."

"I understand fully, Karik," said the man, beginning to calm down somewhat. "We will get from her the location of the cave, if she knows, and if not, the names of others who do know. We will find the location."

"Excellent. Keep me closely advised. When you do find the location of the cave, I will no longer have any need for the Lejeune group now at Lyon."

"Understood, sir," replied the underling.

"Remember, do not disappoint me. I have studied my predecessor's methods and have found him overly lenient with those who failed him. I shall not make the same mistake," concluded the Karik, his left arm beginning to shake slightly.

The servant crept toward the door, now sweating furiously again. As he exited he looked over his shoulder and heard the Karik say softly, "Do not fail me!"

CHAPTER 24

"Greek?" Cloe questioned. "Everything else has been written in Latin. Are you sure?"

"See for yourself, signorina," said the monsignor a little stiffly.

Cloe stooped to read the inscription.

"Is it Irenaeus in Greek?" asked J.E.

Cloe knew Irenaeus, the second bishop of Lyon, had played a pivotal role in the Judas story found in Thib's jar. It could be very important if he were here because it might show another link between Irenaeus and the Sicarii. But she and the monsignor had already carefully examined his supposed crypt upstairs in the church itself. It seemed completely authentic. So she knew Irenaeus was not likely to be here. Still, a number of these saints were also supposed to be buried elsewhere, some with their own churches dedicated to them.

Cloe studied the scratches on the end of the stone coffin. "Hmmm ... it says 'Speratus,'" she said.

"Speratus, Speratus ... who the hell is Speratus?" asked J.E.

"I don't know," replied the monsignor.

"Nor I," said Father Sergio.

"Well, it seems we have some research to do," concluded Cloe.

"Is there anything else?" asked the monsignor. "This seems completely out of character with everything else we have seen here. The others are reasonably well-known martyrs from Lyon, and all of their inscriptions are in Latin."

Cloe looked closer. Was that something else under the name? "Let me have some more light," she asked. She ran her fingers over the now well-illuminated markings. She paused, turned, and looked at her friends.

"What is it?" asked J.E.

"There is something more. It's a number … 2119."

The monsignor turned to them and said, "Surely this is another clue left behind by whoever did all this, likely the Sicarii themselves."

"Yes," she agreed, "but what can it mean?"

"The book of Mark, eleventh chapter, line nine. I don't know that one offhand. Father Sergio, can you help?"

"As a matter of fact, I can," said the young cleric with a smile, drawing the small, well-thumbed Bible from his inside jacket pocket. "The context is Jesus's entry into Jerusalem on Palm Sunday," he said a moment later. "The sentence beginning in the ninth line says, 'And those who went in front and those who followed were all shouting, *Hosanna! Blessings on him who comes in the name of the Lord!*'"

"How in the world can that be a clue?" asked J.E.

"I don't know," said Cloe, beginning to feel some fatigue. "Albert, any ideas?"

"Perhaps the words and letters form some sort of anagram or code with an embedded message in them," suggested the cleric.

"That would not be in keeping with the clue to the key on the cross of St. Irenaeus. It was direct once we understood the reference. There's something wrong here," said Cloe, "but I don't know what it is."

"Maybe the thing for us to do is to wrap it up here and head back to the hotel where I can use my computer," added J.E. "I'm betting there is some connection between Speratus and, maybe, Jerusalem or something else in the quote from St. Mark's Gospel that will be our clue."

"J.E., you're right. We've been here all day, and I'm getting tired," responded Cloe, stretching her back. "Albert, I think we should carefully photograph everything and exit the way we came in."

"We'll close the trap door and the outer door to the tunnel. We'll lock both and take the key with us so that no one can follow this trail," suggested J.E.

As the monsignor began to photograph everything and J.E. packed away his equipment, Cloe wondered whether they had hit a dead end. The clue was there, so it must lead somewhere, but where?

The monsignor looked at Cloe, and reading her dejection, he said with a smile, "The good Lord never gives us a challenge that he does not also give us the means to overcome. We will find the answer."

Cloe smiled a bit, her spirits lifted a little, but she was not so sure. No, she was not sure at all.

CHAPTER 25

That evening, Cloe, the monsignor, J.E., and Father Sergio met in the dining room, now joined by Father Anton. It was small by hotel standards, perhaps a half-dozen tables. The menu was brief, but Cloe thought she had never had a better meal. The foie gras appetizer and endive salad were to die for. The grilled hen garnished with shallots, walnuts, and oyster dressing was perfect. All was complemented by wines from the area. The friends sat fulfilled while coffee and chocolate were served.

"We've had quite a day," said Cloe. "We may not have gotten any further with our search for the jars, but the discoveries we have made will keep a gaggle of experts busy for a good while."

"Quite right," said the monsignor. "I have notified the Vatican through the pope's personal secretary, and they are sending their best forensic team to carefully investigate the secret chamber. They will probably have to enter through the back wall since we have the key to the trap door, but they will have the equipment to do so."

"Why not leave the key for them?" asked J.E.

"Because if we left it there, whoever is outside might use it to discover what we have learned," replied the monsignor. "We have no time to wait for the Vatican team; we have to find the cave of jars before the Kolektor's men do."

"I'm sure that in a few weeks or months we will know a great deal about the chamber and its contents," said Father Sergio. "Still, that leaves us here and now."

"Right you are, Serge," replied J.E. "I've been able to do some research on our mystery martyr, Speratus. He was not one of the Lyon martyrs at all. Most of the Lyon martyrs were from Gaul or from areas to the east, such as Armenia."

"And Speratus?" asked Father Sergio.

"That's the weird thing. He was the principal martyr of the Scillium martyrs in the second century. This was another persecution, but in North Africa."

"My goodness, what are the remains of a North African martyr doing in a hidden chamber in the Church of St. John in Lyon, France?" asked Father Sergio, bewildered.

"Good question," commented Cloe. "Did you learn anything more specific about where the Scillium martyrs were killed or where they lived?"

"Yes," replied J.E. "Scillium was a small town or province that existed two millennia ago. There are variations on the name, such as Scili, but I don't think that's important right now."

Cloe sensed something was coming. J.E. had found something. "Where would Scillium or Scili be located now, if it still existed?" she asked softly.

"The authorities are not completely sure," J.E. responded. "It was such an ancient place and small and rural ..."

"Where, J.E.?"

There was a moment of silence before J.E. answered. "Tunisia," he said.

***

The monsignor had been oddly quiet during the conversation. The group turned toward him now, sensing that he was pondering something that he would explain to them in due course. He paused and looked around at them, as he had done so many times before. Finally, he said, "The circle is closing. Our God *does* work in strange and miraculous ways." And then he became quiet once again.

The friends drank their coffee, stared at their napkins, and considered.

Finally, Cloe said, "It's the jar, isn't it? It's about my father's jar."

"Yes," said the monsignor as if from a distance. "Your father fell into a cave in the Atlas Mountains in Tunisia just before the Battle of El Guettar during World War II. There, he found the jar containing the Judas Gospel. That's Thib's cave. There were scores of jars in that cave. Can any of you today tell me that you do not believe that Thib's cave contains the library of St. John from Lyon and perhaps much more?"

"How can we be sure?" queried J.E.

"You are correct," responded the monsignor. "This is all speculation. But I think our working theory of what happened must be that the Sicarii were involved in the removal of the library contents and probably took them to the cave. The cave, the jars, the Sicarii, Speratus, and somehow, the Church of St. John are all bound together. Although this is something of an intuitive jump, I think we are on our way to Tunisia. And we must get there and find the cave before the Kolektor's men find it. If we are wrong … so be it. My faith tells me this is the right direction."

"Monsignor, I have been thinking about the number inscribed on the Speratus coffin, the one that may correspond to Mark 11:9," said the young camerlengo.

"Yes?" responded the monsignor.

"Well, the only thing I can say is that the second and third books of the New Testament were written about the same time," said Father Sergio.

"Yes, yes!" replied the monsignor. "That might be it."

"What?" pressed J.E.

"J.E., there is confusion and debate in some quarters as to whether the Gospel of Mark or the Gospel of Luke was actually the second book written," said the monsignor. "In ancient times it was probably even more confusing which one was the second book."

"You mean someone could have left a clue referring to the second book when he really meant the third book, the Gospel of Luke?" queried Cloe. "Is that possible?"

"Very possible," said the monsignor. "Scholars are aware of this confusion and make allowances for it."

"If the book of Luke is the actual reference, what does the clue mean?" asked J.E.

There was silence, and a smile came over Father Sergio's face. But it was more than a smile. It was the look of a person who had just glimpsed the face of God.

"What does it say?" asked Cloe, softly.

"This is so amazing," he replied. "I know we are on the right path."

"Just tell us," blurted out J.E.

Sergio looked at all of them in turn and said, "Search, and you will find."

PART II

THE CAVE OF JARS

"Shadow," said he,
"Where can it be—
This land of Eldorado?"
"Over the Mountains of the Moon,
Down the Valley of the Shadow,
Ride, boldly ride,"
The Shade replied—
"If you seek for Eldorado!"
                    —Edgar Allan Poe, "Eldorado" (1849)

CHAPTER 26

At thirty-seven thousand feet over the Mediterranean, the world looked beautiful and tranquil. The clouds were fleecy, and all seemed to be in harmony. Cloe imagined that there were no conflicts and no mysteries to be solved as she gazed out the window on the flight to Tunis. Cloe wished this moment of peace would last. She thought about her father, Thib. She remembered the terrible fight they'd had on the night she ran away so many years ago, a pregnant teenager. They had not spoken in the twenty-five years in which she had lived in Seattle. Still, she had missed him and now was sometimes consumed with regret over her stubbornness and pride. In some small way, she thought she was making amends through her efforts to locate the cave where Thib had found the jars. Cloe thought he would be pleased.

Once they understood the clue, Cloe and the monsignor had realized that they needed to do more research into Speratus and his origins. J.E. had researched Speratus and the martyrs of Scillium both online and through the Vatican ops center, but there was not much there. What he found was that in about AD 180 the Romans beheaded six martyrs in Scillium because of their faith. Oddly, beheading, as a form of execution, was thought to be humane and was reserved for Roman citizens. The leader of the group was Speratus, and he alone spoke in defense of the martyrs. He may have been a teacher. The one thing J.E. learned that could help was that Speratus was from a small village in the Atlas Mountains.

"J.E., can you pin down any more information on the location of Speratus's hometown?" asked Cloe.

"No, I can't find anything more," said J.E. "Eighteen hundred years is a long time."

"Yes, can you imagine how many small villages may have come and gone in that time?" added the monsignor, twisting in his seat to face J.E. "This may be an impossible task."

"Still, it's our only lead," said Father Sergio. "We are guided by God's hand. You said so yourself in Lyon."

Chastened, the monsignor said, "Sergio, you are correct. We must have faith."

***

Leaning close to his mother, J.E. whispered in her ear, "Do you think the priests are right that we are somehow guided by God's hand?"

Cloe heard the sliver of wonder in his voice and thought about their prior brushes with death and the amazing progress they had made to get to this point. "Someone is watching over us, and in my book that someone is God. Too many things have happened for all this to be merely random. I thought I had somehow lost my faith, but when we went back to Madisonville to bury Thib, I found it was not lost but only misplaced," said Cloe. "It came rushing to me like an old friend."

"I've seen things on the battlefield in Iraq that no one can explain," responded J.E. "Some of what we have seen with the jars is like that. I can't say for sure we're going to find the cave, but I've got a pretty good feeling about it."

"We have some damned determined foes who will do anything to find the jars and to keep them away from us," said Cloe. "I think they tried to kill me and, maybe, the monsignor in New Orleans. I don't think they are finished."

"No. I think we have to expect that the closer we get, the more desperate and violent things will get," observed J.E. "They'll hit us again."

As Cloe listened to her son's frank appraisal, doubt whispered in her ear, and she feared for J.E. She could not lose him. Yet she knew they were all in harm's way.

Gathering herself, she said, perhaps more to herself than to her son, "J.E. ... you are right. We will find the cave."

CHAPTER 27

"Karik, we have the location of the cave," said the servant into the phone.

"Are you sure?" asked the Karik.

"We used the information from the sanatorium and tracked down the woman who paid for the medical care of the Lejeune woman."

"Yes?"

"She knew nothing about the cave, and she died poorly," said the servant. "But before she did, she revealed the name of her contact. We then located the contact, and our people employed the usual methods to question her. The contact has been persuaded to give us the information we seek."

"How can we be sure you have the correct location?" asked the Karik, knowing the techniques that would have been used on both women. He recognized that under such pressure, people would sometimes say anything. He had witnessed that many times with the Kolektor. He knew he had to put the torture out of his mind, or his shakes might begin again. He had to stay focused.

"The woman has drawn a map to the cave. She did so with the last strength she had before she died. Only then did she do so because we told her we knew her family, and they would pay for her lies. This is why I believe her map to be true."

"Well done, my loyal servant," said the Karik, pausing and wondering what the Kolektor would do now if he were here. In the brief hiatus, he felt the servant studying his words carefully. Deciding on his course of action, he said, "Now that I know the location of the cave, it seems I have no further need for the Lejeune woman and her friends. I owe them a debt that I'm very happy to repay."

"Karik, we have implemented the plans you required. All is ready for you. Here is the code, which can be activated from any cell phone," responded the servant before reciting the numbers.

The Karik smiled, took down the code, and said, "I will be in Tunis shortly, and we will claim the contents of the cave. And then there will be no limit to my power."

CHAPTER 28

Cloe had dozed a bit on the flight but now was fully awake, looking at her watch. She realized they were about an hour and an half out of Tunis. She didn't know exactly how they would find Thib's cave, but she believed if they could find the true burial site of Speratus, this would at least lead them to the current site of the library of St. John and, perhaps, to the cave of jars. She wondered, once again, were they the same?

She looked around at her fellow travelers. Some of the Swiss were sound asleep, and others were engaged in card games or letter writing. J.E. and the monsignor were collaborating on goodness only knew what strategies. Father Sergio was asleep. All was quiet.

Suddenly, the plane bucked slightly and then started to wander side to side. Almost immediately, the cockpit was filled with shrill alarms. Cloe could hear the crew yelling and could sense their ordered panic.

The pilot came on the intercom and said, "Everybody buckle up. We are experiencing some difficulty with the controls."

Cloe glanced out the window. The weather was perfect. Not a cloud in the sky. Whatever was happening was internal to the aircraft.

J.E. and the monsignor were now quiet, focused on the pilot's comments. Father Sergio had awoken. Tension worked its way through all the inhabitants of the plane like a highly contagious virus. Cloe saw shoulders tense, heard muted, anxious voices, and smelled the beginnings of fear. Cloe's concern spiraled up, and she worried for herself and for J.E.

The plane strayed back and forth and then began to lose altitude rapidly. To Cloe it felt like the jet was in a dive, headed toward the water far below. The dizzying motion began to sicken her stomach. She thought she might throw up.

The pilot now said over the intercom, "Our hydraulics are out, and the backup system is not responding. We have no control over the airplane except for the throttles. We are going down. Prepare yourselves to ditch at sea."

Fear spiked through Cloe, threatening to blot out her reason and steal her ability to react correctly to the crisis. "J.E.!" she screamed. And suddenly, somehow, J.E. was in the seat next to her, tightening down his seat belt.

"Mom," he yelled over the increasing din in the cabin from the plunging plane, "strap your seat belt down as tightly as you can. In this jet, there are life jackets apart from the seat bottoms." He had grabbed two of them, and he wedged them between the seats as he tightened his belt.

The jet continued its fall toward the earth. The speed increased, and the angle became sharper. Cloe looked about wildly, but she knew at this rate and pace, no one could possibly survive the crash. The plane would be demolished on contact.

J.E. leaned over and pushed a life jacket to Cloe. She unwrapped it and began to put it on, seeing that J.E. was already wearing his. She struggled with the fasteners, and finally J.E. closed her up in the jacket. When she looked back from her seat near the cockpit door, she saw grim but determined faces all about her. Everyone had a flotation device on and was hunkered down. The priests had begun to lead prayers. Cloe joined them.

Through the door to the cockpit, which was now open, Cloe could hear the Mayday calls from the copilot as the captain fought the controls of the doomed craft. The flight engineer was on his hands and knees, trying to tear removable panels out of the cockpit floor. Cloe could feel the early tendrils of shock beginning to set in. She wasn't sure she could move even if she knew what to do.

Suddenly, J.E. looked at her and said, "I love you, Mom." Then he tore his seat belt off and dove to the floor of the plane, toward the cockpit. Almost weightless due to the free fall, he flew forward and slammed into the bulkhead near where the engineer was trying to dismantle the floor. He shrugged off the contact with the metal wall, rolled toward the engineer, and began to work furiously to tear off the panels to reveal whatever was beneath.

As he and the engineer got the first section off, thick smoke roiled out of the small opening, pushing them back. Both of them began to cough, and the captain donned his oxygen mask. The engineer reached back and under his seat and produced two small oxygen bottles and masks. J.E. and the engineer put them on and went back to opening the deck.

The acrid smoke now entered the cabin as the airplane continued its fall. *Oh my God, we can't have more than a minute or two before we hit the water like hitting a concrete wall*, thought Cloe.

As the smoke filled the cabin, Cloe could smell burning hydraulic fluid and could taste an acidic rotten egg stench in her mouth. She could hardly breathe and began gasping and coughing. Suddenly, the overhead opened, and an orange mask dropped into Cloe's lap. She pulled the mask on and breathed deeply. She felt reprieved if not paroled.

J.E. and his cohort had gotten a couple more panels up and were hanging over the edge of the now-open cockpit floor, looking at something beneath. The engineer had removed a flashlight from his nearby tool kit. Both of them reached deeply into the hidden area. Cloe surmised that the control lines were there, and whatever the damage was, it was there as well. The noise of the falling plane was beginning to sound like a rushing freight train.

The pilot screamed, "Hurry, the water is coming up!"

J.E. and the engineer were saying something to each other, but Cloe couldn't hear. The engineer grabbed a fire extinguisher and sprayed it into the cavity. Smoke went everywhere, but when he was finished, there was less of it.

"Forty-five seconds to impact!" cried the captain.

The copilot left the controls where he had been assisting the pilot in trying to right the plane and dropped to the floor to see if he could help with the repairs. J.E. reached into the toolbox, pulled out a silver tool, and fell over headfirst into the cavity.

As he did, the engineer yelled to the captain, "Give us some slack on the yoke!"

A half dozen heartbeats later, J.E. jumped up from the hole and roared, "*Now!*" Then he ducked back into the space below.

The pilot grabbed the steering yoke, put both feet on the console, and began to pull back with all his strength. Nothing happened.

Cloe's heart hammered in her chest. She could hardly breathe.

"I need help!" the pilot screamed.

He strained against all the g-forces aligned against him, and the copilot struggled up and climbed into his seat. He too gripped the steering mechanism and tore it back from the grip of gravity.

"Deploy the airbrakes," called the captain.

"Capitan, at this speed the wings will be torn off!" cried the copilot.

"If we don't slow this plane, we will be just a grease spot on the sea," he yelled. "Airbrakes!"

The plane shook violently, and Cloe braced for the wings to come off. But the hurtling missile that the plane had become began to slow. Hope rang a small bell in her heart. Cloe could now see out the cockpit windows. The sea was rushing toward them like some massive tsunami.

"Full flaps … we need lift!" the pilot cried.

"Captain, the plane will come apart," screamed the copilot.

"We're dead anyway," yelled the pilot. "We need to slow this monster!"

The flaps, apparently on a different hydraulic system, came down, and if it were possible for there to be more turbulence, there was. The jet shook violently and felt as if it would surely disintegrate. Still, the water rushed up.

"Brace for crash!" screamed the pilot into the intercom.

The jet began to pull up, slightly at first and then more, but it was too late. It hit the water hard, but it glanced and did not tumble. Again and again like a flat stone, it skipped across the water at a terrible speed. Finally, it stopped, and there was an eerie silence.

And then it started to sink.

CHAPTER 29

Miguel heard the knock at his door from what felt like a great distance. He had been in a dead sleep, sweating and tangled in the bed covers, dreaming of the boys as he had last seen them. The two boys, gangly and laughing, had rushed back to the car, now forever in slow motion in his dreams. Their smiling faces haunted him. Tears had washed down his cheeks.

He rolled over, turned on the lights, and said, "Come."

Tomás strode into the room and whispered, "Sorry to disturb your rest, boss, but there is news. You said to let you know immediately, no matter the time."

"Yes, what is it?" Miguel responded, shaking off the sleep and the dream.

"Yesterday, the group with the Lejeune woman and the priests finished whatever they were doing in the church and went back to their hotel," said Tomás.

"You woke me for that?" said Miguel in a flash of anger.

"No, boss, the interesting thing was that this morning they all rushed to the airport, boarded a private Vatican jet, and flew out," replied Tomás.

"Right, perhaps headed back to Vatican City to report to the pope on whatever they found, if anything," said Miguel.

"Not unless they are going to the Vatican via Tunis," responded the retainer.

"What? Tell me what you know," said the boss.

"Our man on the scene is very resourceful. He bribed the clerk at the general aviation station, and we have the flight plan dutifully filed by the pilot of the plane," said Tomás with a smile. "Sometimes, it does not pay to follow the rules."

"And you are sure that Tunis is the destination?" asked Miguel.

"No doubt about it. Not only is that what the flight plan states, but we tracked the plane on radar and by satellite, and it is clearly headed for North Africa, most likely Tunis," Tomás replied.

"Then that will be where we will find the one I seek."

Tomás started to say something, but Miguel cut him off.

"Pull our people together. We are headed for Tunis … right now."

CHAPTER 30

Cloe dreamt of her mother and father. It was a simple dream, really. She was at the breakfast table in the Water Street house, and her mother was frying eggs and bacon. Cloe could smell biscuits and fresh dark-roast coffee. They were all together. But the color began to run out of the dream, and everything became darker until she could hardly see her parents. They were going, fading, and Cloe realized she was cold. She should not have been cold.

"J.E.!" she screamed, suddenly coming awake and realizing where she was.

The water rose up over her shins. Fear grabbed her heart. She looked around and saw that the plane had been virtually destroyed. Debris and wiring hung over her, sparks flashed in the water, and smoke filled what was left of the cabin. She looked back, and beyond a few seats, there was no airplane at all. It looked like the tail had been sheared off in the crash. Where there had formerly been the resolute faces of the Swiss, there was nothing. Where was J.E.?

The water continued to rise. Some of the windows had burst. The plane was sinking back end first, creating an air bubble toward the front of the jet where she was. She knew it would not last long. Sea water gushed in. She had to get out.

She fumbled with her seat belt, but it would not open. Cloe tugged on it and pounded on it, but the belt held fast. She struggled violently against the strap. The water rose and was now chest high. Soon she would not be able to breathe and would drown strapped to her seat. How deep were they? Could she make it to the surface even if she could get out of the seat belt?

"J.E.!" she screamed one last time before the rising water rushed over her. The water ran up her body and rolled over her face. She knew it was the end. Cloe prayed to God to help her and her son. She asked her mother to pray to the Virgin to save her and J.E.

As the cold water engulfed her, she felt someone tugging at her seat belt. The water sought to drag her down, and the force at her waist countered to lift her up. The battle was close and in doubt. But suddenly, she was free of her seat. A strong arm grabbed her, and they fought the hanging wires and debris for freedom.

Cloe kicked for all she was worth, but the world began to go black just before she and J.E. burst through the surface of the water and gasped for breath.

They hugged each other and thanked God for their deliverance. A life raft had automatically deployed and bobbed to the surface not too far from them. They swam for it.

After falling into the raft, Cloe said, "J.E. we have to look for other survivors."

J.E. secured the oars from the craft, and they paddled around the crash site. "Helloooo!" they heard someone yell. Paddling in that direction, they soon came upon a survivor clinging to some wreckage.

"J.E., Cloe, your faces are like heaven to behold," said the monsignor as he bobbed in the sea. They helped him into their raft and continued to search but found no other survivors.

"But what about Father Sergio, Father Anton, and the Swiss?" asked Cloe, scanning the surrounding sea. "Surely, we haven't lost them all!"

"We may not know for a while," responded the monsignor. "It looks like the tail broke off a distance from here on the second or third time we hit the water. There may be survivors there."

"But right now, it looks like we are it," concluded J.E., studying the horizon. "Our friends may take more time to be rescued."

The monsignor removed his shoes and stood in the raft, reconnoitering 360 degrees around them. The day was bright and clear. Sitting back down, he said, "Nothing. I don't see anything. Visibility is good for a long way, but there's nothing out here but us."

The monsignor bowed his head, and Cloe knew he was praying for their friends. She watched J.E. join in, and she did likewise.

"Mom, help is on its way," said J.E. after a bit. "When I was helping the engineer rip up the floor to get at the control lines, I could hear the copilot calling Mayday and our position. The Mediterranean is not the Pacific. We'll be found before you know it."

Cloe took heart from this, collected her thoughts, and asked, "J.E., what were you and the engineer doing?"

"We were trying to see why the jet had no control with either the main hydraulic system or the backup mechanical system," he replied. "The hydraulic system was hopeless—the lines were damaged, and all the fluid had leaked out."

Cloe shivered as she listened and then realized that she, J.E., and the monsignor were not only all wet but also covered in jet fuel. The smell of the fuel was overwhelming, and she thought she might be sick. Her stomach turned over but then settled down. As the adrenaline began to wear off, she became more uncomfortable and more tired. She now realized why she had been so cold in her dream. Wide awake now, she was trembling from cold and the fright of the near-death experience.

"How did you fix it?" asked the monsignor.

"We didn't. We focused on the mechanical system, which consisted of control cables. They had been severed, but I used a locking wrench to overlap the cables and clamp them. The orientation of the pilot's yoke was off, but it worked to get the nose up enough so we hit the water with only a glancing blow. That's it ... saved by a wrench in the engineer's tool kit."

"Saved by the quick thinking, improvisation, and heroics of J.E. and the crew is more like it to me," said the monsignor with a smile.

"It's strange for both the primary system and the backup system to fail like that," suggested Cloe. "It had to take a rare series of accidents to put us here."

J.E. scoffed. "Accidents? That was no accident! Someone rigged and then triggered, probably by cell phone, a small container of acid near the control lines. When it detonated, it showered the lines with acid, which ate them through and almost killed us all. This was intentional. Someone tried to kill us."

"Is there no end to this?" cried Cloe, now sick from grief, salt water, and fear. Cloe huddled in the bottom of the raft as J.E. put his arm around her.

"Albert, it had to be someone in the Kolektor's organization," said J.E.

"Yes, but it's strange," said the monsignor thoughtfully. "They were watching us in Lyon to see what we would do and where we would go. They must have thought we were at least one link to the cave. Now they don't care. Sabotaging the plane means whoever this is thinks we no longer have anything to add to the search for Thib's cave. We have somehow become expendable."

CHAPTER 31

The Karik lifted his satellite phone as he flew toward Tunis. "Yes?" he said.

"Karik, the Lejeune woman and her cohorts are all dead," reported his servant Noosh. "As you directed, we triggered the acid bomb, and they must have hit the water at over five hundred miles an hour. No one could have survived."

"Are you sure?" asked the Karik, realizing his plan had come off perfectly and beginning to enjoy his success.

"We heard the distress call from the plane's captain. There is no question he had lost control of the aircraft, and they were preparing to crash," replied the servant. "We followed the doomed jet until it fell below our radar capability. A search has been organized, but nothing has been found. They are gone."

"Well, this is a fine moment. The obdurate woman and her pesky friends who saw the end of the Kolektor and who have bedeviled me are finally finished," responded the Karik, smiling with satisfaction. As he reflected on his success, he realized that he felt less conflicted than he had been before. The rush of power ran through his veins.

"We have our forces prepared to follow the Sicarii map to the cave," said Noosh.

"Tell them to await my arrival. I want to be there when we enter the cave and retrieve the biblical riches that must lie there," ordered the Karik. "This will be a great day of glory and one to be feared by all the world's religions."

CHAPTER 32

Miguel sat on the terrace of the Les Berges Du Lac Concorde hotel. The view of Lake Tunis was magnificent. The old hotel had more stars than most galaxies. Service like this simply did not exist except here in Tunis, the jewel of the Mediterranean. He sipped a frozen vodka, straight up in a crystal stem. It was rather warm here, but there was a gorgeous breeze off the lake. "Boss," said Tomás, entering the terrace, "we have some news."

"What is it?" asked Miguel somewhat reluctantly.

"You told us to stake out the airports and look for inbound private jets that might be suspicious," replied his number one. "Our men at the Tunis airport report that a plane inbound from the east, maybe Turkey or Armenia, has landed."

"Yes?" asked Miguel. "Was there something special about it?"

"Well, boss, we have seen a lot of inbound pleasure planes, but this was all business," said Tomás. "First, it was larger than the usual private jet, and the men who got off had a military look to them. They had rucksacks, duffels, and backpacks rather than suitcases and briefcases. They were all dressed in black in spite of the heat. Their leader was a small man dressed in traditional Bedouin robes and headdress. He looked like something out of *Lawrence of Arabia*."

"Yes, of course, that would be the servant who has become the master," replied Miguel. "I have heard he has always had a secret flair for the dramatic. I look forward to meeting him. Where are they now?"

"Boss, they rented a couple of vans and traveled across town to the old Maison Blanche hotel," replied Tomás. "They have checked in and, from what we can tell, are seeking local guides for an expedition into the mountains."

"Very interesting. I know the Maison Blanche well. Traditional, but without the breeze of the Les Berges. Tomás, you have done well. Please keep up our surveillance, but make sure they do not know we are watching," ordered Miguel as the sun began to set behind the hotel.

"That we can do, boss," replied the retainer. "What's our next move?"

"Right now they are our best lead to find the cave. We wait. We watch, and at the right time, we even the score."

CHAPTER 33

The Tunisian coastal police vessel located the three survivors only a few hours after they had gone into the raft. The sea cops had heard the Mayday calls and had homed in on the GPS locator signal from the raft. After the group had been picked up, given blankets, and served strong coffee, the vessel continued for some time to search the debris field. But darkness had temporarily halted the search, and Cloe, J.E., and the monsignor were the only survivors found thus far.

The three were questioned closely by the Tunisian authorities about what they were doing and what had brought the plane down, but they simply responded that they were doing historical work on ancient Christian martyrs from the region and had no idea why the jet had crashed. After a while, they were dismissed, and the monsignor contacted a local hotel and made arrangements for them.

The prefect of the police, Captain Reynaud, said, "Mademoiselle, there is nothing for you to do here at our headquarters. We will search again tomorrow, and doubtless, we will find your colleagues."

A while later, a cab deposited them at the Les Berges Hotel. As tired and as worried as they were, it was necessary to get some clothes and supplies. Cloe went to the ladies' shop and quickly replenished her wardrobe and toiletries. J.E. and the monsignor were attended at the gentlemen's store. When she saw them later for dinner, Cloe wondered whether she could ever get used to seeing the monsignor without his priestly garb.

"Albert, you look … different," she said, observing his smartly tailored, Western suit.

"Yes, signorina," he replied sheepishly. "Unfortunately, there were none of my usual clothes for sale in the hotel's shops."

"From my point of view, that's probably best," said J.E., looking around warily. "At least for today, until we get the lay of the land, the less attention we attract, the better. There are likely fewer Catholic priests here than religious of other types. You would stand out like a neon light."

The mood among them was one of fatigue from the day's events and cautious optimism about the whereabouts of their colleagues.

"I'm tired and sunburned, but I'm also hungry," said Cloe.

They ordered wine and the Tunisian lake bass special as Cloe looked around at their surroundings. They were seated on the hotel's open-air terrace overlooking the lake. The sun had set, and a near-full moon was rising in the east. Cloe sipped her wine, perhaps a little more quickly than she had intended, but she remained concerned for Father Sergio and the others.

"J.E., I think the moonrise over the river at home would give this place a run for its money," mused Cloe, beginning to feel the effects of the wine and getting a bit homesick. "Still, it's absolutely gorgeous." She turned to the monsignor. "Albert, I was thinking of Father Sergio. When we were introduced in the pope's quarters, you said something about the need for a person close to the pope to be found worthy … something about a test. What did that mean?"

"Yes, Father Sergio aspires to be camerlengo, an important officer of the pope's household," replied the monsignor. "Such candidates must prove themselves by satisfactorily completing tasks assigned by the pope."

Cloe smiled at the monsignor's optimism in using the present tense for Father Sergio and asked, "This was his test? He was assigned to our team to prove himself?"

"Yes, the pope feels he has great promise and is ready," said the monsignor. "He certainly helped us in France."

"Yes, I am becoming quite attached to him," said Cloe.

J.E. grunted and said, his voice rising a bit, "They're going to find Serge. He was amazing at Lyon. We need him."

Just then, Cloe heard a band—an orchestra, really—begin to play. They were situated at the end of the terrace. The sweet notes of the strings and the low song of the brass rolled over Cloe in an almost enchanting way. She stared at the moon, listened to the music, and wished to forget that someone had tried to kill them all earlier.

She was swaying in her chair when she opened her eyes and saw a man about her age standing in front of her, bending at the waist. He was garbed in a summer tuxedo, white jacket, black trousers, and black bow tie. A red rosebud adorned his lapel.

"Señorita, my name is Miguel," said the man, "and if I do not presume too much, my American friends call me Michael. May I request the honor of a dance?"

Swept away momentarily by the need to escape from the ugly reality of the day's events, Cloe looked at J.E. and then at the monsignor, and seeing no objection, she nodded and smiled. "Michael, I am Clotile. My American friends call me Cloe, and … I accept."

As they danced, J.E. studied Miguel closely, doing the civilian version of a threat assessment. After a few moments, he relaxed, but he kept his antennae tuned for any cause for concern for his mother with this newcomer. "Seems okay," commented J.E. after a while, to no one in particular.

On the dance floor, thoughts of the horror of the last few months, including her near death at Hakeldama and in New Orleans, the plane crash, and the whereabouts of her colleagues, had all fled as Cloe and Michael danced to the strings and horns under the stars and the moon.

CHAPTER 34

"Karik, the woman and some of her cohorts are alive," said the servant Noosh when he entered the hotel suite.

"What? I thought you said they were all dead, that they could not have survived the crash," responded the Karik, turning his back on the man to hide his bitter disappointment and growing anger that somehow his men had failed to properly execute his perfect plan.

"It cannot be explained," said the servant. "The airplane's controls were destroyed, and it should have hit the water at a fatal speed. Somehow they thwarted our efforts. They were rescued and have now checked into the Les Berges Hotel here in Tunis."

"Do you mean that you failed the Karik?" asked the Karik directly, rounding on the servant. This was not the Karik's fault. Someone else had failed.

Noosh, visibly shaking with fear, said, "Yes, Karik, I do not know what went wrong, but I did not achieve the result desired." The servant hung his head and awaited his fate. He knew the Karik could not abide failure and could be expected to punish it severely, even unto death.

The Karik paused and studied his servant. Complex emotions washed over him. He knew the Kolektor would have made an example of Noosh. A slight tremor passed through his left hand. Sometimes a near brush with fate was a more effective management tool, rationalized the Karik. In this, he was different from his predecessor. "What else do you have to say?" he asked.

"Sir, we have retained local guides to lead us into the mountains to search for the cave," he responded. "They are provisioned and prepared to depart at first light tomorrow."

"Have they seen the map?" asked the Karik, testing him.

"No, sir, as you instructed, they only know we wish to enter the Atlas Mountains in search of archeological ruins," replied the servant. "You were very clear they were not to see the map or know our destination for fear they would talk about these things among their friends."

"Yes," said the Karik. "Except for the fortunate doctor and her friends, all seems to be in order. Soon we will have the treasures from the cave."

"What shall we do about the woman and her group?" questioned the servant, eager to correct his near-fatal mistake.

"Patience, my friend," said the Karik. "Tunisia is still a wilderness. If they choose to follow us or to look for the cave on their own, some terrible accident may yet be visited upon them. Only death awaits them in the Atlas Mountains."

CHAPTER 35

The casino in the hotel was small and intimate. Gambling in Tunisia was like the other vices, tolerated for those with the right resources. Unlike the American casinos, this was a black-tie affair. One had to dress to gamble. Only four games were licensed: craps, blackjack, roulette, and baccarat. Cloe looked around at the crowded tables. *So many people with so much money*, she thought.

She and Michael had danced until the band could or would play no more. Although Cloe still felt a deep sense of concern for her colleagues, the wine and Michael had pushed the worry back a bit. She had needed this release. Now, in the early morning hours, she should feel dead tired from the day's events, but she felt uplifted. Indeed, Cloe felt marvelous. As she thought about it, she could not remember ever having felt *marvelous*, except with J.E. But that was a different kind of marvelous. She had felt good before, even great! But had she ever felt this kind of marvelous? She couldn't say. But she did know the reason for this feeling: Michael.

"Cloe, do you like to gamble?" Michael asked.

"I've never been in a casino," she whispered. "I have no idea whether I would like it or not."

She gazed at his handsome profile, but her thoughts returned to her friends. A deep sense of guilt rolled over Cloe. Still, she suspected that if Father Sergio were here, he would say "marvelous" only comes along once in a while, so why not enjoy? She smiled as she thought of the young camerlengo's probable reaction.

Michael led her to the roulette wheel and said, "What's your lucky number?"

She stammered and thought about the first clue—Matthew chapter seven, line seven— and said, "Seven."

"Okay, we'll put a hundred dollars on number seven, and we'll hedge it with lower odds, line bets, and an odd/even bet," Michael said, his brow furrowed in concentration.

As she watched the wheel spin and the ball drop, Cloe was mesmerized by the money, by the risk, and by Michael.

"Number seven," called the croupier. "We have a winner!"

They raked in the number bet at odds of thirty-five to one. *Thirty-five hundred dollars won on one bet*, thought Cloe. And Michael said that was before the winnings on either the line or the odd/even bets. They played on and won more.

After a while, Michael said, "Let's try our luck at something else." He wrapped his arm around her waist like they had been lovers for years. Cloe was more afraid of herself than of Michael. But she moved easily toward a game of higher risk and, perhaps, higher reward.

"This is baccarat ... the chemin de fer version," Michael told her. "It's the prince of games. It's a combination of poker and blackjack but not like either. The object is to make an eight- or nine-point hand and to beat the banker's hand. It sounds complicated, but you'll quickly catch on."

Cloe sat at the immaculate green-felted table and watched the croupier deal cards from a shoe. She and Michael ordered drinks. After thirty minutes she and Michael had, somehow, won a considerable pile of thousand-dollar chips. Cloe studied the stack and knew the total was several times her academician's annual salary. Although she had put nothing up, she somehow felt she had already risked much this day and had lost. Or had she won? Conflict rippled through her.

Cloe leaned over and whispered in Michael's ear, "Michael, let's have a final nightcap on the terrace."

"Excellent," he said, gathering the winnings. As he stood, he tossed five one-hundred-dollar chips to the dealer and led Cloe to the terrace.

The air had cooled a bit, and Cloe shivered. Michael wrapped his arm around her, and when he had seated her, he removed his jacket and put it around her shoulders. The waiter brought a brandy for Michael and a B&B for Cloe. They sipped silently and smiled at each other.

"Michael, this has been wonderful," said Cloe. "This has been a day of such highs and lows. I have never had an experience like this. I don't know what to say. Thank you for tonight."

"Cloe, the pleasure is all mine. Thank you," he replied graciously. "What now?"

"It's very late, and I must meet my son and our friends tomorrow. We have urgent business we must complete," said Cloe. "I have to reluctantly call it a night."

As they arrived outside the door to her suite, Michael turned to her and said, "Cloe, I must see you again. Perhaps after your business is finished tomorrow, we can have dinner. Your son and the monsignor would be welcome."

The monsignor? Cloe blinked at this, but before she could think about it, Michael took her into his arms and kissed her. *Marvelous,* thought Cloe, and she kissed him back for all she was worth.

CHAPTER 36

Cloe sat bolt upright in her bed. *Monsignor*, she thought. What was that about? How did he know about Albert? Trying to orient herself, she shook her head and studied the curtained window. She knew from the color of the light that it was not early. Looking at the clock by the bed, she saw it was midmorning. J.E. and the monsignor had cut her some slack. Now she needed to get herself together and find them.

Forty-five minutes later, J.E. and the monsignor were seated with late-morning coffee in the living area of her suite. Cloe had showered and dressed and now felt pretty good in spite of the lack of sleep.

She sat with them, swallowed the black coffee with steamed milk, and said, "J.E., I don't know what came over me last night. I'm so sorry to have pushed you and Albert off like that. It's just that …"

"Mom, don't worry about it. Miguel was very courteous and proper. You needed a respite after all that had happened. We knew you would be fine here in the hotel. I hope you had the time of your life," replied her son.

"Well, I guess I did," said Cloe, smiling. "What of Father Sergio and the others?"

"Captain Reynaud called earlier and said the search began again at dawn, but there's nothing yet," replied J.E. "I left all our contact information with him."

"Signorina, we have some good news," said the monsignor, now properly dressed in his freshly laundered and pressed black cassock with scarlet piping.

"Wait a minute, Albert," Cloe said with some urgency. "When Michael and I returned to the table after that first dance, do you remember how I introduced you?"

J.E. responded before the monsignor could. "Well, you introduced me as your son J.E., and you introduced the monsignor as Albert Roques."

"That's correct," confirmed the monsignor.

Cloe then related to them what Miguel had said about dinner the next night when they parted—that her son and the "monsignor" would be welcome. "How could he have known you were a cleric, much less your rank as a monsignor?" asked Cloe, beginning to feel distressed. "You were dressed in civilian clothes."

"I have never seen the man before," replied the monsignor quietly. "I think we have to assume Miguel has some foreknowledge of us."

Cloe lowered her head. Her heart hurt like never before, except on that fateful night when she had learned that Evan, J.E.'s father, had been killed in an accident aboard a dredge in Lake Pontchartrain. She had screamed then, a black scream from deep within her breast. She wanted to scream now. How could she have let herself be taken in like this?

"Oh, Mom, I'm so sorry," said J.E., coming to her side and putting his arm about her.

"J.E., for a while, I felt like Cinderella with her prince. But it seems my prince had a bit of a different agenda. I wonder who he really is," Cloe said sadly, tears filling her eyes.

The monsignor said, "J.E., let's give your mother a few minutes."

"No!" responded Cloe sharply. "We have important business to complete. I'll worry about the prince later. Now we have to focus on our clues and find the cave. We've got to find Speratus. Remember, if we seek him, we shall find the cave. As the pope said, we have to find the cave before anyone else."

"I quite agree," said the monsignor. "Our research indicates that the hometown of Speratus was in the Atlas Mountains, but it probably no longer exists independently as an entity. It was a small village outside of a Roman installation of the time."

"Right," said J.E. "The name of the Roman fort might seem familiar—Fort Roumain a Elgucttar. It's high in the mountains overlooking the village, now town, of El Guettar, which is the very place mentioned in Thib's letter as the site of the battle during which he came upon the cave. We are really hot here. The cave has to be in the vicinity of the fort."

"Makes sense," said Cloe. "Where is it, and how do we get there?"

"Hmmm," said the monsignor.

"What's that, Albert?" asked Cloe.

"I was just thinking that whoever knocked our plane down must be after the same thing we are after—the cave. Could this be the successor to the Kolektor, this 'leader' as they call him?"

"Well, we have known since the meeting with the pope that he was after the cave because he was searching for the Sicarii to lead him to it," said Cloe. "What we didn't know was that he was aware of us and that we were going after Thib's cave."

"Yes," said J.E., "his people were probably watching us in Lyon. If so, I suspect the plan was to follow us to the cave. He was covering all bases, searching for the Sicarii but also keeping an eye out for our team. One way or the other, he would have the cave and its treasures."

"Quite so," replied the monsignor. "But if he thought he might need us to lead him to the cave, why sabotage the jet? Something has changed."

"Oh my God," said Cloe, gasping. "This 'leader' and his forces have some other source of information as to the cave's location."

"Yes," said J.E. thoughtfully. "That makes us excess baggage and has turned what has always been a race to find the jars into one of life or death."

CHAPTER 37

The Karik stood, robes flowing, on a promontory overlooking El Guettar in the far distance. Only a smoky miniature of the city was visible. It had taken three days to get here, but one of those days was spent addressing equipment problems. *A curse on this place*, thought the Karik. *Nothing works properly.*

"Karik, the landmarks on the map don't match the detail here on the ground," said Noosh. "We are unsure of the location of the cave."

"You mean you do not know where it is," responded the Karik, sensing once again that the plans he had laid might be delayed, if not thwarted. He tried to consider what the Kolektor might have done in a similar situation. Fuming, he began to reconsider his long-suffering relationship with his too-often-fumbling servant.

"We know we are in the correct vicinity, but the details on the map don't coincide with what we are seeing here," replied the servant. "Our local guides have gotten us this far, but they can take us no further with this map."

The Karik turned and surveyed the incredibly coarse texture of the mountainous terrain. Before him was a series of interconnected hills and slopes interspersed with cliffs and mountainous jags. Although the sky was clear blue, everything below it seemed to be a shade of gray. The air was filled with sand and pumice. Even after a mere one day of actual searching, the Karik and his men were miserable for the experience. The only thing remotely in the vicinity was the shell of an ancient Roman fortress. Some said the Italians had used the ruins as a base to guard the Gafsa Pass during World War II.

"Do you believe the woman you tortured to get the map deliberately obscured the final location to thwart us?" asked the Karik.

"Yes, Karik," responded the man. "Either she did it deliberately, or she was out of her head with pain when she drew in these final details."

"Fanatics!" said the Karik. "These Sicarii bear watching carefully. You tortured her to draw the map betraying her sisters and their secret order, but she has, in death, had the last laugh as we wander these mountains with a faulty map."

"So it would seem, my Karik," said the servant. "What are your orders?"

"Our water is almost finished," observed the Karik after a few moments' hesitation. "We have to go back to El Guettar for supplies. Leave three men with what water and provisions we have left. Give them one of the satellite phones. Their task will be to look for Dr. Lejeune and her colleagues. I suspect they will be along."

"Perhaps it is good that they survived the crash," ventured the servant.

"Don't tempt my tolerance for your incompetence," responded the Karik. "Only your honesty keeps you alive. I have so few I can trust."

"Thank you, Karik," responded Noosh.

"If you had gotten an accurate map, and if the doctor and her friends had perished, we would have our treasures by now," railed the Karik. He paced back and forth, anxiously, knowing the Kolektor would have terminated the servant right then and there. But if he did that, what was he to do out in this wilderness without help? "As it is, we are reduced to scouring this godforsaken terrain looking for less than a needle in a haystack."

"Forgive me, my Karik," replied the servant. "It shall all be as you have decreed."

CHAPTER 38

Cloe studied the town of El Guettar as they entered in the rented Land Rover. They had checked again with Captain Reynaud, but there was no news and thus nothing to do but continue with their urgent mission.

El Guettar was relatively small, somewhat primitive and isolated. Thib had written about it, a key venue of the World War II African campaign, in his final letter to her. Here the combined British/American forces under General George Patton and others had beaten the Afrika Korps led by Rommel. Germany had been defeated in North Africa right here, Cloe realized. Her father had been an important part of it.

She looked at J.E. and saw that he was as quiet as a church mouse, taking it all in as they drove slowly down the main street.

"Gosh, Mom, my grandfather was a hero here," said J.E. solemnly, as if reading her mind. "Look at this terrain. A night drop into the mountains overlooking this pass would have been nearly impossible. Yet he made it in with all of his men intact and knocked out the Italian fortress in the mountains that was protecting the pass."

"I have always known that what he did was very special, but being here and hearing you describe the details of what must have happened brings it all home," replied Cloe, pushing a tear from the corner of her eye. "It makes me very proud of Thib and everything he did."

"It wasn't just special; it would have been amazing by any standard," added J.E. "And to think, somewhere up there is Thib's cave filled with artifacts. We're gonna need some pretty good intel to find it. I suspect you could wander around for years in those mountains looking for it if you didn't know pretty closely where it was."

"The young sir is correct," chimed in the monsignor. "We have to find a place to stay and then seek Speratus. That's our clue. We should carefully reexamine our notes to make sure we have not missed anything."

"Notes … oh my gosh," said J.E., reaching into his bag. "I completely forgot. When I went to the front desk to check out in Tunis, there was an envelope for you, Mom. Sorry. Here it is."

Cloe reached for the packet. It was a business-size envelope with the hotel's name and logo on it, and her name and room number had been typed plainly on the front.

"Looks like it's from the hotel," said Father Sergio. "It might be some sort of survey or perhaps a corporate thank-you note."

"You're probably right," she said. Just as she was disinterestedly turning the envelope over to open it, something caught her eye. Looking down the street, she saw a small open area filled with camels and men. There was a lot of commotion, with the men yelling and camels braying. "What is that?" she asked.

"Well, it looks like a good old-fashioned camel auction," responded the monsignor, smiling.

As they passed, Cloe looked more closely. Sure enough, men were inspecting the camels and yelling bids, trying to attract the attention of the auctioneer. The whole place was filled with dust and noise.

"All good," said Cloe, absently slipping the unopened envelope into her purse. "Let's find a place to stay."

***

As they drove down the central highway through the town, Cloe saw mainly one- and two-story residences interspersed with a few businesses. The homes were what Cloe thought of as early "biblical"—that is, constructed of handmade brick covered by plaster or something similar. Typically, the upper story was open, presumably due to the heat. She knew from J.E.'s research that El Guettar was chiefly distinguished by its pistachio crop—that and the fact that it had been for hundreds, perhaps thousands, of years an oasis on the east–west journey of commercial caravans. El Guettar had no commercial airport and, as far as they had been able to determine, no hotels. The occasional pilgrim and pistachios seemed to be the order of the day.

"We may have some difficulty finding accommodations," said the monsignor. "I suggest we stop at one of the shops and see if we can get a recommendation."

After trying several of the pottery and souvenir shops, they finally found someone who spoke a bit of English. After much hand waving and yelling, they finally understood they were being directed to a nearby dwelling. It was considerably larger than those around it and had an interior courtyard for parking, which was accessed by means of a gate in the large exterior wall.

"Hey," said J.E. as they drove into the parking area of the building, which surrounded the interior courtyard on three sides. "This is probably the oldest known tourist court motel."

"Tourist court?" asked the monsignor with a puzzled look on his face.

"Yes," said Cloe. "They were everywhere in the United States in the decades before and after World War II. They were mainly mom-and-pop motor hotels where you could drive in and get a cheap room for the night."

"I see," responded the cleric. "I guess in Europe we had bed and breakfasts before the great hotels were built."

"Well, that certainly sounds a lot more charming," observed Cloe.

Cloe noted that theirs was the only car in the courtyard. As they began to exit the vehicle, a small, much-tanned old man in an impeccably pressed white cotton suit appeared. *This must be the proprietor*, thought Cloe. She braced for the communications problems that were sure to follow.

The old gentleman straightened his starched collar and tie, bowed from the waist, and said in perfect English, "Welcome to my humble lodging. My name is Achmed. How may I be of service?"

Cloe smiled brightly and said, "We are touring ruins in the mountains, and we need quarters for the night. Can you help us?"

"Most certainly," replied Achmed. Their host clapped his hands together sharply, twice, and two boys sprang from the shadows at the edge of the courtyard and began unloading the group's gear. "Follow me, if you please."

He led them to a tiny lobby with a desk and an old-fashioned pen-and-ink registration book. They signed in, and he then escorted them to three separate but adjoining rooms on the second floor. Though small, they were clean and well kept. The furnishings were simple and obviously very old, but lovingly maintained. *Treasured*, thought Cloe. The bed in her room was draped in mosquito netting and had a wash basin with a pitcher of water and towels.

"Where's the bath?" asked Cloe, noting J.E.'s amused smile.

"My apologies, madam," said Achmed. "The bath is at the end of the hall, but you are our only guests. Our business generally picks up later in the year."

"Thank you, Achmed; I'm sure these will do nicely," replied Cloe.

"The evening meal draws near; please be my guests for dinner," said Achmed, smiling. "El Guettar is mainly a farming and subsistence community. There is a definite lack of fine-dining options."

Cloe looked at her son and the monsignor and read that they were as famished as she was. It had been a long day getting here. "Certainly," she replied. "We would be delighted."

"Excellent," said Achmed. "Please join us on the roof after the evening prayer."

Alone in her room, Cloe heard the solemn call to prayer drift throughout the community. She sighed at the peacefulness of the evening. Cloe considered everything they had been though to get here and finally felt a little at ease for the first time in a long time, even as she wondered whether the feeling would last.

CHAPTER 39

Cloe, J.E., and the monsignor climbed the sandstone steps to the roof of the three-story building. She knew the locals frequently took meals and indeed often slept on the roofs of these dwellings due to the heat. As they reached the top of the stairs and looked out, they were greeted by the sight of a rising moon of impossible size and deep orange color. Cloe stepped back in surprise and might have fallen back down the stairwell but for J.E. behind her. He grabbed her, and together they looked agape at the amazing sight.

As usual, the monsignor was clinical in his appreciation. "Extraordinary, how the light bends at the horizon in the heat of the evening at this latitude. This is what gives the moon the color and the optical illusion of larger-than-usual size."

"How romantic," said Cloe, smiling.

"Welcome, my friends," cried Achmed from across the roof. The trio approached the table and saw it was a heavy wooden affair that had probably been assembled on the roof. That it had been there awhile was clear from the deep fissures in the chair arms, caused by the expansion and contraction of the wood during the heat of the day and the cool of the night. Still, the table and chairs were sturdy things and would likely be there for many more years.

The table was candlelit and covered with a beautiful linen tablecloth. It was the kind of cloth that families handed down generation after generation. Doubtless, it was kept in a special cabinet or trunk for the most special of guests.

"Achmed, my friends and I are greatly honored by your invitation and these special preparations," said Cloe.

"Please, please, sit," said Achmed, obviously delighted, offering his guests the seats with the most wonderful views.

Achmed sat at the head of the table, and the woman introduced as his wife sat next to him. Two young girls, whom Cloe took to be granddaughters, acted as servers. They stood silently awaiting the proper cue from the host.

"My friends, it is our custom to bless our food, but our culture recognizes different customs and blessings from other religions. Would any of you like to bless our meal as your tradition may dictate?" he asked.

The monsignor looked at both Cloe and J.E., and Cloe could tell he was trying to gauge their reaction.

"Achmed," he said, "we all pray to the same One Spirit, and we would be pleased if you, our host, would bless our meal with the traditional Islamic grace."

Achmed smiled, bowed his head, and said the brief blessing. He next made an almost imperceptible sign to the young girls, who then descended on the table with a variety of local foods. Homemade flat bread with goat cheese was served along with cups of lablabi, a thick soup of chickpeas and garlic. Cloe was so hungry, she thought she had never tasted anything better.

As they ate, they took turns introducing themselves and giving some background. Cloe talked about her position as a dead languages professor and her interest in ancient artifacts. After everyone had spoken, the host inquired, "Dr. Lejeune, we are indeed honored to have such a distinguished scholar here in our humble country. What ruins do you seek to study in Tunisia?"

Cloe looked at J.E. and at the monsignor, weighing their level of caution with Achmed, and said, "Achmed, we are interested in a Christian martyr of the first century. His name is Speratus. We think he may have come from around here. Have you ever heard of him?"

"Hmmm, Speratus … yes, yes," he mused as the dishes were removed. "Certainly, I have heard of the legend of Speratus."

The young servers were now presenting the main dish, a couscous spiced with lamb and fresh vegetables. The conversation paused as everyone dug into the wonderful entrée.

"I believe couscous is something of a national food in Tunisia," suggested the monsignor.

"Quite right," replied Achmed. "For hundreds if not thousands of years, it has been a core food here. My thanks to my lovely and thoughtful wife for this kindness."

"Here, here!" exclaimed the diners all around the table, expressing their appreciation. Even in the moonlight, Cloe could see the wife of Achmed blush with happiness.

"Delightful," said Achmed. "Our couscous is prepared using a special two-chambered utensil, where the couscous is cooked in the upper chamber and the vegetables and meat in the lower chamber."

"Sounds like a thousand-year-old crock pot," said J.E. with a laugh.

"What is this crock pot?" asked Achmed, smiling, sensing a joke.

"Nothing, my friend," said the monsignor. "Let's get back to Speratus. What do you know of him?"

"Well, as you say, he was a first-century martyr of the Christian faith. He was the leader of the Scillium martyrs who were beheaded by the Romans for refusing to deny their faith. Although they were Christians, Tunisians have always respected and honored persons of such resolve in their faith."

"What do you know of Scillium? Is it located near here?" asked Cloe.

"There is little to be known of it. If it was ever a real location, it cannot now be found in this area," replied Achmed.

"But our research reveals Speratus was some sort of teacher, a professor, in Scillium," said J.E.

"This is all possible, but in the two thousand years since, the location of Scillium, if it ever existed as such, has been lost," replied Achmed. "It may have been another village or a portion of a town or city or something where the name has simply been corrupted. I cannot help you with that."

"Well, that can't be too surprising," said J.E. "In less than four hundred years we have lost the location of one of our earliest settlements, Roanoke."

"Okay, but you have heard of Speratus," summarized Cloe. "It's just that the location of Scillium is not known."

"That is correct," replied Achmed.

"Well, we have come to know that Speratus was buried in Lyon, France, and we have reason to believe he may be a clue to the ruins we would like to study," said the monsignor.

Achmed paused and looked at his guests. After a bit he said, "You may continue your story as you wish, but I will tell you two things that are true. The first is that I don't know much more about Speratus than I have told you, but I know who does know more about him."

At that point, the servers brought coffee and removed the dishes from the main course. The moon had risen, losing its abnormal size and returning to its usual color. Cloe sipped the brew and found it strong and full of flavor.

"And the second thing?" pressed the monsignor.

"The second thing … yes," said the old man. "The second thing is, most assuredly, Speratus is *not* buried in Lyon, France."

CHAPTER 40

"He could not be in Lyon," said Achmed. "The legend of Speratus has forever been that he rests in the Atlas Mountains above El Guettar."

"We did not actually see his remains in Lyon," said J.E., pondering the information. "We left that for the forensic scientists of the Church, which we notified of the discovery before we left."

"If he is not interred in Lyon, this gives more credence to the theory that the inscription we found was intended as a message," said the monsignor.

Cloe saw a shadow cross Achmed's face, and she wondered if they had said too much.

"Pardon," said Achmed, "I do not wish to be forward. Although we have visitors who seek various objectives here and in the mountains, we do not have many who inquire about Speratus."

"We believe Speratus may have some connection with ruins we wish to tour," said Cloe vaguely.

"Very well; it is your business," responded Achmed. "He is buried in the mountains above our city."

"But where in the Atlas Mountains is he then?" asked J.E.

"I cannot say for sure, but I can tell you who might know," replied Achmed.

Cloe turned to Achmed, studying him carefully, and said, "Anything you can tell us that might help would be so appreciated."

Achmed smiled and said, "In El Guettar, as I have said, the people respect the martyrs no matter whether they were Christian, Muslim, or otherwise. Indeed, on your way into town, you passed a wooded area known as the Jardin des Martyrs. There, you will find a man named Kais. He is the curator of the garden and is a Muslim holy man. He may be able to help you."

"Thank you so much for your hospitality and this information," replied Cloe, pushing her chair back and standing.

"I only hope you will find what you seek," finished Achmed.

***

Later in her room, Cloe pondered his last words: "find what you seek," the inverse of the very clue that had driven them to Tunisia: "seek and you shall find." She wondered whether somehow this was a clue within a clue, or was it merely a random remark? Could Achmed know more than he was telling them? And if so, why had he held back? As she prepared for bed, she took the cosmetics she had purchased at the hotel out of her purse, and the message from the hotel fell out. Cloe picked it up and turned it over. She slipped her finger under the seal and broke open the envelope. A single sheet of unlined paper slipped out. Cloe unfolded the message and saw that it was not a survey, nor was it from the hotel.

She read it over quickly and then started over slowly.

> Dearest Cloe,
>
> From your reaction at our good-bye, I know two things. You are aware that I was not completely honest with you. Although it was not a good start on my behalf, nothing was what I expected. I apologize for this and can only say there is an explanation. The second thing is I never thought I could care about another person, but you showed me it is possible. Can you understand that I was dead and now I'm alive again? You brought this to me. Let me talk to you.
>
> Michael

Cloe sat for a long time rereading the letter. She knew she too had been emotionally dead for a long time, before coming back to Madisonville to bury her father, after which she had ended up rediscovering her faith, her roots, and meaning in her life. She had felt reborn. Michael's words hit a chord with her. In this way, they were kindred spirits.

If his words are true, she reminded herself. She had been swept away once, and she vowed this would not happen again. She was much too sensible for this sort of thing. Still, she studied the note. The date and time were inscribed at the top. It had been written and, apparently, delivered to the front desk early this morning shortly before they had left. Why hadn't he called her room? *Probably off to something or someone else,* she thought. But somehow that didn't seem right. Maybe he had tried to call, but after they had left. She had no answers.

Cloe sat on the mosquito-netted bed and looked at the note. The only thing she knew for sure was that she had a mystery to solve and a cave to find. Perhaps this was just some romantic BS that she was not used to. Still …

CHAPTER 41

Cloe heard a seemingly faraway knocking. She turned in the bed, annoyed, and then started becoming angry.

"Cloe … signorina?" called the monsignor as he continued rapping on the door. "Are you all right?"

Cloe slowly opened her eyes but could not immediately make out her surroundings. She looked around tentatively and then recognized her room in Achmed's bed and breakfast. Had she overslept again? She could almost hear her long-dead mother chiding her to get up: "You're burning daylight, Clotile."

"Give me a moment, Albert," she replied. She had been dead asleep. As she began to sit up, Michael's note rolled out of her hand. She must have been reading it when she crashed. *Now what?* she wondered.

"Cloe, it's midmorning," the monsignor said through the door. "You said you wanted to get an early start."

"Yes, yes, Albert, I'll be down in twenty minutes," she replied.

Still feeling groggy, Cloe went to the basin and began to wash. What in the world was she to make of the note from Michael? And what about Achmed? She was unsure of whether he was friend or potential foe. He seemed warm and helpful, but was he even now looking for an opportunity to sell them out? Perhaps they needed to be more circumspect in their inquiries. Cloe wondered whether she had reached the point where everyone appeared to be against them.

***

Twenty minutes later, she met J.E. and the monsignor in the small parlor in the lodge. Achmed's wife had put together some bread, fruit, and fried couscous for breakfast. She ate and drank the wonderful black coffee. Only then did she really begin to come out of the fog she knew she had been in because of Michael's note. Even so, the note was so personal that she did not want to talk about it yet.

"All right," she began, turning to J.E. and the monsignor, "what do we know, and where shall we begin?"

J.E. said, "I think we start with the Garden of Martyrs and the holy man, Kais. We should see what he knows."

"Agreed," responded Cloe.

"Cloe, before we go, you should know something else has happened this morning, which is partially why I thought to disturb you," said the monsignor.

Cloe's gut clenched as she absorbed this, afraid she was about to hear more bad news or learn about some other challenge to their quest. "What is it, Albert?" she asked in a whisper.

"As you know, our cell phones are virtually worthless here, and the coverage is spotty, at best, for the satellite phone," said the monsignor.

"Yes," responded Cloe hesitantly.

"Well, even so, I was able to make contact with the Vatican intelligence center, our special ops center, this morning," replied the monsignor.

Cloe, not in the best of moods to begin with, was starting to lose patience. "Albert, for God's sake, what calamity has overtaken us now? Out with it!" she exclaimed.

"Calamity?" he responded. "No, it's not that. We have learned that some people have been pulled from the sea not too far from where our plane crashed."

"Oh my God!" Cloe almost screamed in delight and relief. "How can it be? What happened? Is it our friends? Father Sergio?"

"We don't know anything more than this. Some people, number unknown, were found earlier today, adrift, clinging to some wreckage," replied the monsignor. "We do not have any news of identification yet."

"It has to be them!" declared J.E.

"Or not," replied the monsignor.

"What we do know is, whoever they are, they all have injuries of various types and degrees, ranging from broken bones to exposure from being on the open sea," said the monsignor. "Even so, special ops believes they will all survive. All are in a hospital in Tunis and are being well cared for. We should know who they are within a few hours."

"If they are our people, it's a miracle," said Cloe. "The way the tail of the plane broke off, I can't believe anyone could have survived."

"Perhaps it is a miracle and God's will," said the monsignor. "We will soon know."

Cloe's heart lifted with hope. "God is good," she said at last.

CHAPTER 42

As they approached the Garden of Martyrs, Cloe reflected on the possible rescue of their friends. Her spirits were very high, and she was beginning once again to be excited about their search for the cave. No matter what, it seemed, they would somehow prevail.

They entered the parking area of the garden and pulled up close to a low, flat-roofed building typical of the others in the city. The difference was the greenery that made up the gardens. It was lush with cedars and ferns. Here and there, even from the parking area, they could also spot date trees and lemon bushes. A water source must have been engineered for irrigation.

They entered the building, which appeared to be deserted. "Hello," called Cloe, but there was no answer.

After a bit they went outside to the rear and into the garden. The silence was like a veil covering this cherished place and protecting it from the intrusions of the outside world. The atmosphere was truly holy.

Wandering through the garden, they found a number of alcoves where plaques had been dedicated to people who had died for their faiths. Although most were Muslim, a few were Christian. Here and there, one or two people were studying the inscriptions or lighting candles or incense in honor of the dead.

Finally, they came upon an old gentleman dressed in traditional robes who was working the soil in one of the martyr's niches.

"Good morning, teacher," said the monsignor. "Are you Kais?"

The man paused, seemingly pleased, wiped the sweat from his brow, and said, "I am. May I know who inquires?" he responded.

"Ah, learned sir," added Cloe, "we are pilgrims in search of the burial place of one of the martyrs. Our new friend, Achmed, has sent us to you."

"Achmed, that old fool," responded the holy man with a smile. "With what nonsense has he filled your heads?"

"Only that if anyone might know the burial place of Speratus, it is Kais of the Jardin des Martyrs," said Cloe. "Did Achmed speak incorrectly?"

"Achmed often speaks incorrectly, but he has a good heart. Why do you seek this obscure Speratus, who has been dead some eighteen hundred years?" asked Kais.

Cloe was ready for this and said, "Our work caused us to excavate hidden areas of the Church of St. John in Lyon, France, and we found indications that Speratus was interred there in the church. This seemed strange, so we seek the truth."

"Well, whatever you found was false if it said Speratus was buried in France," replied the holy man as he lifted his gaze toward the distant mountains. "Speratus lies there, in the Atlas Mountains. There is no doubt."

Cloe looked at J.E. and the monsignor and pressed a little further. "Sir, may we be allowed to ask you more about this? It's quite important."

"Certainly," the old man replied, his strong voice belying his apparent age. "It is time for my tea. Would you be my guests?"

Rather than return to the house, he led them deeper into the garden. In a few minutes, they reached a tiny clearing, the focal point of which was a small spring. It bubbled up into a fountain, which then disbursed the water through a series of pipes and drains. A copper pot of water was warming over a bed of coals next to the water source. A delightful breeze swept through the clearing.

"Please, be my guests," said Kais, motioning for them to be seated on the blanket that had been laid next to the fountain. He sat cross-legged adjacent to the small fire that was heating the water. The whole effect was like a Bedouin campsite in the desert.

"Kais, if I may, I'd like to make introductions," said Cloe, proceeding to explain who she, J.E., and the monsignor were.

"I am indeed honored to be in the company of a distinguished languages professor and her son, not to mention an esteemed representative of the Vatican," responded Kais. "It certainly excites my curiosity as to how you came to be here and, more importantly, why."

Cloe thought about this and felt like she was about to be boxed in as she had been with Achmed. She didn't want to lie to this man but felt cautious about revealing the full truth.

The small kettle began to boil, and Kais removed it from the heat. He opened the top and from a small box beside him took out what appeared to be a metal egg. The egg had numerous minute holes in it. He added several small spoons of tea to the egg and then let it slip into the heated water, holding it by a tiny chain. As the tea steeped, he set out four small clear glasses.

"Perhaps, my friends, we should start again," said the holy man, looking back at Cloe and the others. "I may live in a small, rural community in a mountain pass, but I'm hesitant to believe that such an august group has come here to confirm Speratus is or is not buried in Lyon. As you know, forensics and carbon dating could make this determination without you lifting a finger. Why do you seek Speratus?"

The monsignor, J.E., and Cloe all looked in amazement at each other.

"Well, it's not exactly Speratus we're looking for," said J.E. "However, finding him may lead us to our destination."

"More riddles, young sir?" asked the old man pleasantly. "My experience and intuition tell me you may be treasure hunters, perhaps even seeking the Cave of the Sicarii itself? Do you think you are the first? There have been many, many expeditions seeking relics and other treasures that are reputedly buried in the mountains. One such expedition, apparently looking for the cave, left here just three days ago."

Cloe's mouth fell open at Kais's revelations. She had thought they were being so circumspect, but of course, the holy man had to be correct. El Guettar did not get that many visitors, and certainly some would be looking for the cave or other treasures that might be hidden in the mountains.

"Our apologies for the deception, and yes, we seek the Cave of the Sicarii," responded Cloe directly.

"Then you have wasted your time," said the holy man.

"Why?" asked J.E. "Has it been found by this other group?"

"Certainly not," replied Kais. "Even now the bulk of that expedition is on its way back here to resupply. They have found nothing."

"Then why are we wasting our time?" pressed Cloe.

"Because," said the holy man, "the Cave of the Sicarii is like your El Dorado, a myth … it does not exist."

CHAPTER 43

A myth? Cloe asked herself. She knew something, at last, that the old man did not know. Her father had fallen into the cave during World War II and had brought back a jar containing evidence of the cave. The old man did not know that. He did not know about Jerusalem or Hakeldama, and he did not know about the Kolektor. She had herself been with the Sicarii. She knew many things the holy man did not know.

"Perhaps you are correct," she said, aware that she could not tell him what she knew. "But we have a map, and the burial place of Speratus is an important landmark."

"A map," said the old man with a chuckle. "There have been many maps. Indeed, the hunters who are up there now have a map. Their map is useless. Your map is useless. There is no cave."

"All right," said the monsignor, picking up on Cloe's approach. "But at least tell us what you know of the burial site of Speratus. What harm can that do? If our map is false, it can do no harm."

"You are correct. If you wish to scour the mountains in search of treasure, of what concern is that to me?" he responded finally. "You have been respectful, and I will tell you of Speratus."

Cloe sipped her strong tea and leaned in to listen to the old man.

"Speratus was a teacher and a martyr," said Kais. "You probably know this. But one thing you may not know is that Speratus, because of his position, came into contact with early Christian writers and their works. He had the opportunity to advise them and to work with certain groups who were interested in propagating the faith through the preservation and distribution of these writings. This was the

143

crime, in the eyes of the Romans, that was committed by the Scillium martyrs."

"We wondered about that because the Romans typically allowed the indigenous population to practice whatever religion they wished as long as they did not proselytize others," commented the monsignor.

"That is so," said Kais. "The Romans gave him and the others the opportunity to stop and recant. But they all remained steadfast in their faith. Finally, they were each put to death for it."

"Yes, it seemed they welcomed death in their faith," responded the monsignor.

"I think that's the common thread among the martyrs. They believed so resolutely that their conviction was stronger than their love of life. They beckoned death if it meant upholding their faith," said the holy man with admiration. "Can you imagine? Inviting the termination of one's existence because of the strength of one's faith. It has been my life in my latter years to dwell on these matters and to honor such souls."

"Extraordinary," said the monsignor. "They are without peer."

"Yes," said Kais. "And Speratus was among the greatest. Do you know the term 'marabout'?"

"Hmmm, marabout?" mused the monsignor. "I have heard the word somewhere."

"I know the term," said J.E. "It means little white house or some such. They are all over North Africa. They're monuments of some sort."

"Indeed," said Kais. "That is where Speratus lies. In the mountains near the old Roman fort there is a marabout dedicated to him. Perhaps there you will find the answers you seek."

***

Although they had lingered a bit with Kais and had finished the tea, the meeting was over when he told them of the marabout for Speratus. On the way back to their lodging, J.E. was already lining out the supplies they would need for their expedition into the mountains. They decided they would find the needed provisions and equipment and put everything together today and leave first thing the next morning.

"Hello, Dr. Lejeune," said Achmed when they finally returned to the guesthouse.

"Good evening, Achmed," responded Cloe.

"How was your visit with Kais? I hope it was instructive," he replied.

"Indeed it was," said the monsignor. "Do you know of an old Roman fort in the mountains near here?"

"Certainly. The only such installation in this area is the Fort Romain a Elguettar, which is located on a rock jutting from the mountains above El Guettar. I will show you the location later after you have rested. It can be seen with binoculars very easily."

Later, on the roof, as they enjoyed coffee in the now-waning sunlight, they all studied the location of the fort on a high peak above them. Achmed had given them directions to it. It would be about a six-hour drive up into the mountains.

"Achmed, have you heard of another group using El Guettar as a base to search the mountains for treasure?" asked Cloe.

"Oh, yes," he replied. "We have these expeditions from time to time. Everyone knows about them. This one left here about three days ago, and from their radio traffic, people say they seem to be headed back for provisions."

"Do you know where they are staying?" asked J.E.

"Certainly," Achmed said cheerily. "They are in a private lodging house to the northeast of the center of town. The place where they stay is quite similar to my home."

"May we assume then that pretty much everyone in El Guettar knows we are here staying with you?" asked J.E. guardedly.

"Oh, yes," said Achmed. "There are no secrets in El Guettar."

"Well, do you know when the other group will return to El Guettar?" asked Cloe quietly.

"By all accounts, they are due back tonight," said their host.

***

145

Later in Cloe's room, as they discussed what they had learned, there was a collective sense of concern.

"This group of so-called treasure hunters could be the one commanded by the Kolektor's successor," observed Cloe.

"I agree," said the monsignor. "If true, and if our presence in El Guettar is common knowledge, this leader—or Karik, as he is probably known in Armenian—will soon learn we are here."

"Without our Swiss Guard, it could be very unhealthy for us if that happens," said J.E. as he sorted and packed the provisions and equipment.

"Quite so," added the monsignor. "He may have been involved in the bombing in New Orleans. He has no regard for collateral damage or casualties. I still believe it is likely he was responsible for the sabotage of our airplane and the possible deaths of some of our colleagues. Although his people must have observed us at Lyon, for some reason they decided we were no longer needed to lead them to the cave."

"Kais said they had a map," said Cloe, sitting up straight in her chair. "I wonder where it came from and if the map could be the reason the leader, or Karik as you say, figured he no longer needed us."

"Very possible," responded the monsignor. "If the Karik believed such a map were genuine, he could only have obtained it from the people who truly know the location of the cave—the Sicarii or someone working with them."

"Yes, the Karik would have known of the Sicarii from Hakeldama. He has had his minions searching for them. Oh my God," cried Cloe. "Those poor people."

"They took care of themselves pretty well at Hakeldama," pointed out J.E.

"Certainly, but they had the element of surprise, and they outnumbered the Kolektor's men at least two to one," said the monsignor. "Here, the Karik only needed one of them. He must have hunted them until he was able to isolate one and get what he wanted."

The room grew quiet as everyone contemplated the fate of the poor, wretched individual who must have fallen into the Karik's clutches with information he wanted.

After a while, Cloe resumed the conversation. "So if they had a map to take them to the cave, why are they returning to town for supplies after three days of searching?"

"There's only one answer to that," asserted the monsignor. "And it suggests the need for immediate action on our part."

"Yes," said Cloe. "There's something wrong with the map, and they have not found the cave. They are still looking."

"And when they get here, they will find us," said J.E.

"Not if I can help it," said Cloe with determination. "Get all our gear loaded. We are leaving for the mountains tonight!"

CHAPTER 44

Miguel had flown in directly from Tunis earlier and was now awaiting Tomás at the bar at the Hotel Jugurtha Palace in Gafsa, Tunisia. The Palace was the best of the few hotels in Gafsa and was self-rated as a five-star hotel. Still, it was comfortable and clean and had a bar along with five restaurants serving different foods in various atmospheres. *Not bad, all in all,* he thought.

He looked up from his scotch, served neat, and saw Tomás striding toward him. "Sorry about the dust, sand, and grime, boss," Tomás said. "We've been in the mountains scouting the opposition led by a man known as the Karik. Our spies in El Guettar reported to us that he is referred to by his men as the leader, or the Karik in their language, and that he and his men had gone into the mountains near the old fort. I have come straight to you to report."

Miguel waved this away and said, "Tell me what you have learned."

"We have had several positions overlooking the various campsites of Karik and his men and have been able to follow pretty much all their movements," replied Tomás. "From what we can see, there has been a lot of activity but no results."

"Hmmm," mused Miguel.

"Karik's men have moved their camp several times, but all with the same result," Tomás continued. "They have found nothing. Earlier, we could see the Karik, pacing back and forth, cursing his men, presumably, for their incompetence."

"What are they doing now?" asked Miguel.

"Late this afternoon, the Karik's expedition began to pack up to leave except for a handful of men they have left behind."

"Do you think they are giving up?" asked Miguel.

"Probably not," replied Tomás. "If they were finished, I don't believe Karik would have left his spies in the mountains. I think they went into the mountains thinking it would be a rather quick trip to find the cave. After three days, our observations tell us they are out of water and other supplies. I may be wrong, but I believe they have gone to El Guettar to resupply."

"Your thinking is sound," stated Miguel. "Why would the Karik leave men behind?"

"Possibly, they're guarding the camp," suggested Tomás. "It does tell us the Karik plans to return."

"True, but what's to guard? They haven't found anything," said Miguel. "No, it's something else or someone else they're watching for."

"Well, we have stayed out of El Guettar, and my men in the mountains were very careful. I do not believe the Karik has any idea we are here," said Tomás.

"If not us, who?" asked Miguel, fully knowing the answer.

"Boss, it's the Lejeune group ... Dr. Lejeune and her two colleagues. Our intel from Tunis tells us it's just the three of them now. Dr. Lejeune, her son, and the monsignor are virtually unprotected."

"Where are they?" asked Miguel.

"They are in El Guettar, according to our local informants, who are very well paid for their information and their silence. Dr. Lejeune's group has purchased the supplies necessary to go into the mountains, probably in the morning."

"Can you say if the Karik knows Dr. Lejeune is in El Guettar?" asked Miguel.

"My spies tell me that he will learn of this when he returns to his lodge tonight. It seems El Guettar is porous with its secrets," responded Tomás.

"Something has happened to the Karik's plans. His supposed map may be faulty. He has men waiting for someone in the mountains," observed Michael. "He is expecting Dr. Lejeune, and he may now be counting on her leading him to the cave."

"You may be right, boss, but then it will be bad for them, very bad. The Karik is one ruthless patron," responded Tomás. "But really, of what concern is that to us? We will have ample opportunity to find the best time for payback to Karik while he watches the Lejeune group. This is falling into place very nicely."

"Yes, so it seems," whispered Miguel.

CHAPTER 45

J.E. drove and Cloe road shotgun as the Land Rover made its way up the mountain's winding highway filled with snake-like S curves and switchbacks. Soon what Cloe had thought of as a two-lane highway of sorts degenerated into a sometimes one-lane affair with blind curves. Often the edge of the road surface dropped off steeply into some unseen abyss. As they ascended, the paved track became less asphalt and more rock. Progress slowed to ten to fifteen miles an hour at best. Visibility was limited by the darkness, and the night gusts of wind off the mountain hammered the vehicle.

"J.E., I think we should find a place to stop until morning," said Cloe above the howl of the mountain drafts.

J.E. looked down at his watch. "Mom, it's late, and we've been rolling steadily for about four hours," he responded, assessing their situation. "But you're right. If we can find a safe place to stop, we would be better off."

Cloe looked above and saw a place in the next switchback where there was an observation area.

"There, J.E.," she said, pointing. "The road crosses back and has created a point where we can stop out of harm's way."

J.E. eased the Land Rover into the observation area and cut the engine. He momentarily slumped over the steering wheel in exhaustion. The monsignor, who had been napping in the backseat as if they were on a Sunday drive, snapped awake and alert. "What … where are we?" he asked, on guard.

"We are about three-quarters of the way up the mountain on the way to the fort," responded J.E. "This is as far as we go tonight. I'm beat, and it would be too dangerous in the darkness even if I was 100 percent."

Although J.E. had brought a tent and other camping gear, it was decided that spending the night in the solid vehicle made sense. J.E. deployed an alcohol stove in the lee of the truck and soon had a pot of coffee brewing.

Cloe and the monsignor joined J.E. around the stove and sipped the strong black coffee thankfully. They nibbled on cold lamb and dates packed by Achmed's wife.

"I see El Guettar down and to our left," said Cloe, looking at the beautiful, lit valley. "But what are those lights to the right?"

"That's Gafsa," responded the monsignor.

Cloe nodded and continued to gaze down on the valley, dimly lit with lights from homes and possibly a few businesses still open at this time of night. As she watched, the lights began to blink out one by one. Long ago, Thib might have looked down on this very sight after his forces knocked out the Italian positions that guarded the pass from above. Of course, there would have been a blackout in effect and far fewer lights sixty years ago, but still, he could have seen something on the valley floor in the darkness. Cloe felt close to her long-lost father, knowing they shared this sight and maybe this feeling.

She thought about what Thib might have felt, having just won a great victory but also having lost his ward, Bobby Morrow, to Italian mortar fire. Still, he had discovered the cave and the jar that Bobby had said might be more important than the whole mission. She could hardly imagine the emotional roller coaster he might have felt.

Cloe knew this was one of those rare, hallowed moments. Her blood had done something heroic here, and they were pursuing that legacy. "Destiny" was a word worn out by overuse, but she felt a sense that this was her fate. Whatever good or bad happened from here on, she would honor Thib's legacy and uncover the cave. She would find and protect its secrets.

***

Dawn crept over the ridge behind their camp. When Cloe blinked, her eyes felt a little like sandpaper from lack of sleep. They had talked into the night about the upcoming day's efforts. After their plans had been set, Cloe, J.E., and the monsignor had slept as best they could in the Land Rover, with each taking two-hour watches.

Cloe rolled out of the passenger seat, which she had set back in a full reclining position. She lit the cookstove and made preparations for coffee and breakfast. As the water percolated through the dark, roughly ground coffee beans, Cloe thought again of her father. She could almost picture him squatting here, maybe drinking his coffee out of his mess kit. Soon, her son and the monsignor would awake and join her. But right now she owned this space and this time.

"Morning, Mom," said J.E. softly a few minutes later.

"Hello, son," she said in reply.

"Good morning, all," said the monsignor as he stretched his muscles, sore from the cramped backseat.

The sun had risen a bit but had not cleared the promontory above them, which cast a wide and deep shadow on the valley below. El Guettar was bathed in early sunlight, but Gafsa was hidden within the deep shade of the mountain. Cloe almost gasped at the beauty of the landscape.

As they gathered around the stove and sipped coffee, J.E. said, "We probably have another hour or two to get to the old Roman fort. From there, we look for the marabout of Speratus that Kais told us about."

Cloe looked at them both and said, "Okay, that's it … let's go find Thib's cave."

CHAPTER 46

It was late morning by the time Cloe stood on the highest point of the Roman fort and gazed around toward the pass and then down the backside of the mountain. The valley below was even more beautiful from this vantage point than it had been at breakfast. She had no doubt that Thib had walked this space.

J.E. joined her and began to scan the area opposite the pass with his high-powered binoculars. He swept back and forth as Cloe watched. After a bit, he stopped scanning and seemed to focus on a point.

"Mom, there's something white out there, but I can't make it out," said J.E. "You can't see it without binoculars, and then it's only a speck."

Cloe took the glasses and studied the landscape. Sure enough there was something white among the sandy gray terrain.

"J.E.," she said, "that's our objective." She handed the field glasses to the monsignor, who, after studying the area, concurred.

The terrain was too rough even for the Land Rover, so they made up backpacks and headed toward the white speck. Their surroundings looked a lot like a gray moonscape but with numerous boulders and stone slabs at all angles, requiring them to constantly switch back and retrace their steps. A light dust hung in the air, clogging their nostrils and making breathing difficult.

By midafternoon, sweating and close to exhaustion under the heavy packs, they neared the marabout. Upon viewing the structure more closely, Cloe was reminded of the aboveground mausoleums in New Orleans cemeteries. Because parts of the city were below sea level, many families had built aboveground structures for the repose of their dead. About two hundred yards from the marabout, Cloe said, "Let's rest a bit so we can be a little fresher when we get there."

Lying in the shade of a large rock with his head on his pack, J.E. asked, "What do you think we'll find?"

"I don't know," said the monsignor. "What I do know is that this may not be the end of our search but only another beginning. Speratus may be merely a figurative portal of some sort to the cave. This may be only the source of another clue. We must hope and pray time has not obliterated whatever Speratus was meant to tell us."

Just another clue? wondered Cloe. She sincerely hoped they were nearing the cave. The biblical references they were following, the clues, were not inexhaustible. They gathered themselves, and after J.E. reconnoitered for anyone who might be on their trail, they pushed toward the marabout. As they neared it, they could see that it was a stone structure more round than square or rectangular. A low rock wall enclosed a small courtyard, which was centered around a temple-like round structure. It looked a little like a tiny, oddly shaped church. The small building in the middle was whitewashed by the eons in the dry desert.

Entering the courtyard, Cloe saw an entry to the tomb. "Here, this is the way in," she said, laying down her pack. There was an ancient doorframe around the portal. On the massive old beam over the door was written a single word in stick-like figures, in ancient Greek.

"What's it say, Mom?" queried J.E.

Cloe studied the word carefully and announced, "It says 'Speratus.'"

CHAPTER 47

The Karik sat in the front passenger seat of the rented van, gazing out the window at the bleak surroundings. They had been on the road from El Guettar into the mountains for several hours. He had dozed a bit, but now that he was awake, his thoughts had turned to his early days at university in Eastern Europe, where he had first met the Kolektor. They had become friends almost immediately, and he had eventually been drawn into the Kolektor's larcenous schemes. The Karik once again wondered what his life might have been had he and the Kolektor never met. He had lived in the man's shadow all these years, eventually becoming little more than his trusted servant.

Now he was the leader. He was on the verge of discoveries of which the Kolektor had only dreamed, even if getting here had entailed life-and-death decisions and orders. He began to sweat slightly as he considered the lives sacrificed in his pursuit of the cave.

Shaken from his ruminations by the vibration of the satellite phone in his inside pocket, he put his ear to the instrument and listened.

"Sir, they are here," said the servant to the Karik. "We were watching near the old fort this morning when the woman and two men arrived in their Land Rover. They studied the area of the old fort, but they were truly focused on the rear approach to it. After searching the back of the mountainside with binoculars for some time, they became excited about something they saw."

"Yes, yes," said the Karik impatiently.

"Following some discussion among themselves, they abandoned the vehicle and prepared packs for an overland trek," responded the servant. "Since that time, we have carefully tracked them hiking off to the northwest. It seems they have now come to some sort of edifice in the distance."

"Excellent," replied the Karik, shaking off his memories. "Maintain your observations, but do not approach them. We should be there in an hour or so."

"Yes, sir, we will keep them under observation. But I fear they may try to enter the structure, in which case we may lose them," said the servant.

"Do not let them see you," ordered the Karik. "Whatever they do and wherever they go, their time on this earth is very limited. Once they have led me to what I want, they will rest in these mountains for all eternity."

CHAPTER 48

Could this at long last be the actual tomb of Speratus the martyr? A deep sense of history enveloped Cloe as she studied the mausoleum. She considered the passion of Speratus and his young pupils when faced with the choice of repudiation of their new faith or death. Amazing!

Cloe watched as the monsignor and J.E. put their shoulders to the stone door to try to push it open. Nothing happened.

"Does it open inward?" asked Cloe, examining it carefully.

"I don't know," said J.E. "But it won't budge. It's obviously not a tourist attraction."

"All right, we've been here before," said Cloe, continuing to study the entrance. "Brute force won't do it. What we need is a lever, a key."

"Signorina, a key?" queried the monsignor, excited. "Could it be?"

"The key from the Church of St. John?" pondered Cloe. "J.E., do we still have it after the plane crash?"

"Right here," said J.E., patting his pack. "Other than the clothes on my back and what I had in my pockets, it's about the only thing I could save. It's in my new backpack."

"Okay, but how do we use it, if we do at all?" queried Cloe.

They all studied the marabout more closely. Cloe could see that whereas it had looked to be round from a distance, it actually had more of a horseshoe shape. The door was located on the flat side. The monsignor and J.E. crouched down on their hands and knees to carefully examine the doorway.

The monsignor stood, straightened, and turned to her.

"Cloe, this stone door is actually round. It overlaps the doorway on both sides and at the top and bottom. Thus, it makes a solid seal," said the monsignor.

Suddenly, a voice behind them boomed, "Yes, it reminds one of what is written of the tomb of Joseph of Arimathaea, the very tomb where Christ our Lord was buried."

Cloe, J.E., and the monsignor spun around, and there standing a few yards away were Father Sergio and two of the Swiss Guard.

"Oh my God! Sergio!" cried Cloe. She ran to the young priest and hugged him fiercely.

J.E. and the monsignor joined Cloe in the reunion and slapped Father Sergio on the back and clasped hands with the soldiers.

"Well, Serge, you do have a way of growing on people," said J.E. as they moved to the shade of the marabout to catch up.

The Swiss set up a tiny burner and began to brew coffee as they talked.

"Father Sergio," said Cloe with tears in her eyes, "we are so happy to see you. We heard some people were rescued, but we didn't know who. How could you possibly be here?"

"It is wonderful to see you and to be here," said the young camerlengo. "We three were the least injured in the plane crash. Father Anton and the rest of the Swiss who survived are still in the hospital in Tunis. We were released yesterday and followed you to El Guettar and then here. It seems there are no secrets in El Guettar. You were so engrossed in what you were doing that you did not hear our approach."

"Quite so," said the monsignor. "But we also were not expecting anyone from the direction from which you came."

"It was necessary to swing well to the north because you are being followed by someone," replied the young camerlengo.

"Followed?" questioned J.E., now looking to the south.

"Yes, from the fort we could see several people following you but taking pains to remain hidden from you," said Father Sergio.

"Either the Karik has returned more quickly than we thought possible, or he left men to watch for us," surmised J.E. "Either way, we should hustle to get into the marabout. It won't be too long before it's dark."

"J.E., we do have to get inside, but we are all exhausted," said Cloe. "Let's take five minutes to think through our options."

The Swiss served the coffee, and someone produced honey and chocolate. Cloe realized that they had skipped lunch, and she thought she had never had a better break. She stirred the honey into her coffee and munched on a bit of chocolate.

"Well, I'm sure you have had quite an adventure as well, but you can bring me up to date on that later. What do we have here?" asked Father Sergio.

Cloe briefly explained to Father Sergio what they had learned in El Guettar about Speratus and the marabout and then concluded, gesturing toward the structure, "The problem is we can't get in."

The camerlengo's sudden appearance had injected new energy into the group. "Well, let's take a look," he said.

They all went back to the doorway. Father Sergio examined it carefully, as did J.E. and the monsignor, once again.

"This part of the wall is almost straight," said the monsignor. "Still, no amount of effort will push the stone open."

"If I'm correct and this is like other tombs of its time, such as the tomb where Christ lay for three days after his crucifixion, it does not push or slide. It rolls," said the priest. "The stone door is itself round."

"Bingo, Serge," said J.E. from where he was crouched on the ground, looking at the bottom of the stone. "There's some sort of track that it is fitted into here at the bottom. It's like a closet door. Somehow it rolls open in the track."

"But how?" asked Cloe. "We haven't been able to budge it."

As they talked, the monsignor was scraping the sand away from the bottom of the door. Once he had finished, the track in which the door was mounted became obvious. "There's a small, oddly shaped hole here on the right side of the door," he said. "If the stone is to roll away, this would be the downhill side. But there's something blocking the track."

"What about our key?" asked Cloe. "Hurry, it's beginning to get dark."

"I'm not sure how that would work," responded J.E., now looking closely at the hole. "Maybe it would push a rod or other obstruction—whatever is blocking the stone door from rolling back—out of the way."

J.E. took the jade key out of his backpack and inserted it into the small hole on the downhill side of the door. Nothing happened.

"Okay, so that didn't work," Cloe said, disappointed.

"Hang on," said J.E. as he twisted the key in the shaft. "Hmmm, it won't give."

"It seems like the keyhole has been cut to accept our key, but it won't work," said J.E. "Maybe we have this all wrong."

"Wait a minute," said the monsignor. "It's been a long time since anyone has tried to enter this tomb. Perhaps we have to relieve the pressure on the mechanism to make it work."

Cloe watched as the monsignor and the Swiss Guards went to the stone door and, instead of trying to open it, put their backs to it. They were able to roll it upward slightly, as if they were trying to close it more tightly. The stone door gave a little as they struggled with it.

J.E. worked the jade key, and as the door moved up, he was able to push the key forward, and whatever had been blocking the door gave way.

"Okay," said J.E. "Let it come back, but gently."

The monsignor and the Swiss relaxed and let the stone door move downward. At first nothing happened, but then slowly the door moved along the track down and to the right. As it picked up speed, Cloe feared it might tear through the marabout and roll over the wall into the desert. But it came to rest at the bottom of the track with an audible thud.

The doorway to the tomb stood wide open.

CHAPTER 49

"Sir, we are about three hundred meters from the landmark where Dr. Lejeune and her party are located. We have been tracking and watching them most of the day, and now dusk is upon us. All but one of them have entered the structure," said the servant. "Also, another priest and two others have joined the Lejeune group."

"Where did the newcomers come from?" questioned the Karik.

"From the north, sir," replied the servant. "We don't know who they are."

"What of the one outside?" asked the Karik.

"He seems to have been left as a sentry," responded the servant. "We believe him to be one of the Swiss soldiers, but he appears to be unarmed."

"Yes, that would fit. They would have lost their equipment in the plane crash, and resupply of arms is not so easy in a foreign country," mused the Karik.

"They appear to be completely vulnerable," observed the servant.

"Appearances can be deceiving, especially in the darkness," replied the Karik, but he wondered if Noosh actually was suggesting action.

"Perhaps we should camp in place here and await the dawn," suggested the servant.

The Karik mulled this over and said, "We don't know why Dr. Lejeune has chosen to come here. Is this some sort of clue? Is it a landmark on some map she might have? Can this be the entrance to the cave itself?" The Karik was angry with his own indecision.

"We may not know the answers to those questions until she leads us to the cave," said the servant.

"Yes, and if we interrupt her prematurely, we might not learn of its location at all," said the Karik, thinking of the Sicarii woman who had sabotaged his map.

The servant knew the Karik had made his mind up. "What are your orders, sir?"

"Tell our men to make camp here, but no fires and no noise. Sound carries very well in the desert at night," ordered the Karik. "We will see what tomorrow brings."

CHAPTER 50

Once inside the marabout, Cloe studied the surroundings in the failing light from the open doorway. The structure was not large, hardly bigger than the niche in the Church of St. John where the sarcophagus of St. Irenaeus was situated. Once again, J.E. handed out small but powerful LED flashlights, which he had been able to buy when they had resupplied in El Guettar. Soon, other details of the chamber began to reveal themselves.

"If this is a tomb, where is the coffin?" queried J.E.

Sure enough, as Cloe looked around, she saw no stone casket like the ones they had seen at the Church of St. John for the other martyrs. The middle of the floor in the chamber was completely open.

"Amazing," said the monsignor as he studied the door mechanism. "There's a system of pulleys and wire ropes here that would overcome the inertia of the stone and pull it upward in the track to close. But how do you do that from outside? We must have missed something."

J.E. followed the wire from the block and tackle toward the floor, where some gears and shafts were visible. "Whoa," he said. "There must be a place outside to insert a tool like a crank. Turning the crank spins the gears and shafts in here, drawing the wire rope taut and eventually lugging the stone back up to the closed position. You have to have our key, or its mate, to knock the stone pin out of the door's path to open it, but a crank is needed to close the door from the outside. Ingenious!"

"But the ancients didn't have this technology or these materials," said the young camerlengo. "How is this possible?"

"Yes and no," said the monsignor. "The ancients were certainly aware of pulleys, blocks and tackle, and the like. They knew about mechanical advantage. However, their gears, shafts, and pulleys ordinarily would have been made of wood. This is not withstanding the jade construction of the mechanism in Lyon. That was very special, perhaps unique. They also would have used regular rope or leather thongs."

"So the ancients could have built this, but it would have been with different materials?" asked Cloe.

"Quite right," said the monsignor. "What I'm beginning to think is that the ancients did build this marabout with this ingenious mechanism centuries ago, and when the materials gave out, someone—I suspect the Sicarii—replaced them with modern materials, eventually resulting in what you see here tonight."

"If true, I think that tells us we are in the right place," observed Cloe, turning her light back toward the open central room in the marabout. "Let's see what else we can find."

"Mom," said J.E.

Cloe turned and saw her son standing in the doorway looking outward. It was now full dark, but the moon had not yet risen.

"J.E.?" she asked.

"The Karik and his men have had time to get to El Guettar and back. They could be out there watching us at this very moment," said J.E. "All of our weapons were lost in the plane crash. The Karik could walk in here right now and do whatever he wanted."

"But what can we do?" replied Cloe. "You said yourself we have no weapons. All we can do is press on and hope to find the cave before he catches up to us."

"Well, there's at least one more thing we can do," replied J.E.

"What are you thinking, J.E.?" asked the monsignor.

"We can close this door," he responded.

"Close the door?" asked Cloe. "What are you saying?"

"This marabout is built of stone and has survived for hundreds of years," said her son. "It's very solid and will act like a small fort. The door should be easy to close from the inside. All we have to do is use the block and tackle to pull the door to the closed position and then insert the doorstop pin to jam it from opening."

"Yes," said the monsignor. "The Karik won't have the key, and even if he could fashion a crank, it would do no good once the door is closed and jammed."

"Correct, they can beat on the door all they want, but without the key, that door will not open," said J.E.

"The roof of the marabout is vented, so we can actually set up our cookstove in here," said Cloe, catching the drift.

"What's the downside?" asked Father Sergio.

"The downside is that we will be trapped," said J.E.

This hushed the group as everyone considered the situation. J.E. stood in the center of the party and said, "But that's no different from where we are now. If the Karik's out there, we're trapped anyway. If he's not out there, it won't matter. The only difference is that although we can't get out without encountering him, he can get in. Closing the door makes it a standoff. We have enough supplies to last for quite a while."

"Yes, and I know Father Anton and the rest of the Swiss will come for us as soon as they are fit," said the monsignor.

"What do we do, Cloe?" asked the young camerlengo.

All eyes turned to Cloe. She so admired J.E.'s command of the tactical issues. But what could she say? Cloe was a dead languages professor. She belonged in a classroom teaching or in a lab translating the journal. Making life-and-death decisions had to be someone else's responsibility. Still, it had been thrust upon her.

She walked away from the group to consider the options. She paused in thought and then turned on her heels and said, "Bring the packs and equipment inside. Ask our Swiss sentry to come in and close the damn door."

CHAPTER 51

"Sir, the structure has gone dark," reported the servant.

The Karik's men had set up a small tent for their leader, and he now sat on a carpet in the mouth of the tent, facing outward. The only thing he lacked for his comfort was hot food. Still, the fruit and cold lamb had been exquisite. The white wine with which it had been served was also actually quite good. The moonrise in the east promised to be spectacular. The air was clear and clean. Life was good. He thought he might be able to get used to roughing it like this.

The servant continued, "Our sentries have been observing them for some time. They are inside the structure, and the doorway has been alight with lamps or flashlights."

"And now there is nothing?" pressed the Karik.

"Nothing but blackness," responded the servant.

"Can they know of our presence? Have our men followed my orders, or have we been revealed?" queried the Karik, his voice rising.

"Your orders have been followed to the letter. They cannot know of our presence by any act of ours tonight," responded the servant, starting to sweat even though the desert night was turning cool.

"Still, they have done something to quash the light, which suggests a defensive strategy. It is too early for them to turn in. A defensive action would only be called for if they thought someone was out here."

"A wise analysis, sir," said Noosh. "May I suggest, those dogs in El Guettar may have told Dr. Lejeune that you were in the area in the same manner by which they told us that the Lejeune party was near."

"Yes, yes," said the Karik, jumping up and beginning to pace. "So they know we may be here as opposed to knowing that we are here. Thus, they have taken a defensible position in case we are about. That's the Lejeune woman's accursed son who has that mentality. His tactics helped overcome the Kolektor. I owe him a special ending!"

The servant apparently did not know what to say and so kept quiet.

Calming himself, the Karik lifted the small goblet in which his wine had been served and drank deeply, emptying the glass. The servant scrambled to refill the stem.

"I grow impatient with this lack of action," said the Karik, his balance restored. "Tomorrow we will roll over them, and I will have my treasures. I will have the Kolektor's treasures."

CHAPTER 52

Now inside the marabout with the door sealed, Cloe took stock of her surroundings. The Swiss had set up the small cookstove and were once again brewing the ever-present coffee. She thought they must have coffee in their veins. The scene within, regardless of what lay without, was clubby. Tins of food were being heated on the grill. They would have coffee and hot food shortly.

Cloe joined the others sitting around the stove and wondered where they would go from here.

"The problem is still the same," said J.E. "We need to find the clue if there is one here. There is no sarcophagus, so how do we really know that Speratus is buried here? The holy man in El Guettar was positive, but he was also positive that the Cave of the Sicarii was a myth."

The food soon was ready, and all used their personal mess kits to serve themselves some kind of stew with canned peaches on the side. Cloe was amazed at what the Swiss could do with a small camp stove and a few tins of food.

After they had finished, they cleaned up the kits and put them away. The Swiss poured the strong coffee. Cloe sipped her brew while thinking about the "problem," as J.E. had put it.

Although their initial examination of the interior of the marabout had focused primarily on the door mechanism and the group's security, Cloe now stood and began to walk around the marabout, looking at each feature and fixture. There were sconces that at one time would have held torches. The most curious object was a shelf in the very back of the structure. On it was a small box.

The monsignor joined her, and together they studied the box. It was made of stone and was rather plain. There were some Greek letters on it and Greek numbers as well.

"Is it what I think it may be?" Cloe asked the monsignor.

"A reliquary is what I'm thinking," responded the monsignor.

By this time the others had joined them, and J.E. asked, "What's a reliquary?"

"It's not exactly a coffin, but it is a box where the last remains of a saint or martyr can be placed. Usually, there are just a few bones," said the monsignor.

"So this may be the final resting place of Speratus after all," said Father Sergio, crossing himself.

"Perhaps. Let me look at the inscription," said Cloe. She moved closer to the box and began to study the writing. She then turned, went to her pack, and took out a small notebook. Satisfied, she returned to the reliquary and began to make notes of the writings. Once she had done this, she settled back on her tiny camp chair at the stove. She studied her notes carefully.

"Mom, come on. You're killing us," said J.E.

"J.E., this box is very old, and the writing has been made indistinct by the ages," she responded.

"Can you guess what it says?" asked the camerlengo.

"My best guess is that it says 'Speratus the Martyr,'" said Cloe, smiling. "I think we have indeed found the tomb of Speratus."

"Is that it?" asked J.E., seemingly disappointed.

"No, there's one other thing," replied Cloe. "It's a number in Greek."

"A number," whispered the monsignor.

"Yes, it's the number 177," said Cloe. *There it was,* thought Cloe. She could see the expressions on the faces of her comrades in the flickering light of the camp stove. She could read what they were thinking. It was the same number that had been inscribed on the supposed Speratus tomb in the secret hall of martyrs at the Church of St. John. This very code had led them here.

"What can it mean?" asked Father Sergio. "We already used that reference to get here. Is there nothing more?"

"No, that's it," said Cloe.

"Then we are finished here because that's just a loop. It could even be interpreted to take us back to Lyon," said Father Sergio.

"I don't think so," said the monsignor. "You all remember that we believe the number 177 refers to the first of the Gospels, Matthew, chapter 7, verse 7."

"Sure, but what does that add?" asked J.E.

"Well, there are several clauses to that verse, all of which we have used thus far as clues to get here, all except one," said the monsignor.

"Yes, Albert, you are correct," said the camerlengo, becoming excited.

"Well, what does it say?" asked J.E.

"Ah, young sir, ever the direct approach," said the monsignor with a smile. "The part of the clue we have not yet used says, 'Ask and it will be given to you.'"

The room was very quiet as everyone considered the possible implications.

"Who do we ask? How do we do this?" asked J.E., growing impatient.

"Well, we are here in the tomb of Speratus the Martyr, so the situation suggests we should ask him," responded the camerlengo.

J.E. laughed and said, "Serge, Speratus is a pile of bones in that box. Whatever he knows, I don't think he's saying."

"What's your idea, jarhead?" quipped Father Sergio. "I'm only speaking conceptually. Of course, we can't ask Speratus himself. But somewhere in this room, the answer has been left. We just have to find and understand it."

"Father Sergio may be right," said Cloe. "Our guide, whoever he, she, or they are, perhaps the Sicarii themselves, did not bring us all this way to hit a dead-end wall."

Cloe went back to examining the reliquary and the niche in which it sat. But for these objects, the sconces, and the door mechanism, there was absolutely nothing else in the chamber. She found nothing else on Speratus's reliquary even after running her fingers across it and studying it closely with the flashlight. She moved on to the niche. "Hmmm, what's this?" she muttered half to herself.

The monsignor came over, and together they examined the niche in which the box holding the remains of Speratus sat.

"Albert, see that just above the niche?" asked Cloe. "It's a detail of some sort."

The monsignor studied the area, nodded, and said, "That's a small indentation with a familiar pattern. What are those markings above the notch?"

"I don't know. It's not Greek or any language I know," responded Cloe. "It looks to be a small circle with a horizontal line through its top quadrant."

The monsignor took a tiny tool from his pack and cleaned out the small hollow in the stone above the reliquary. Once he was finished, Cloe saw it was actually a small hole about the diameter of a quarter and was maybe a half inch deep.

"What in the world?" she asked.

"It's the same pattern as the hole outside the marabout that contained the doorstop pin," observed J.E.

"It's the keyhole!" cried Cloe. "Albert, where's the key?"

"Here," he said, slipping the jade key neatly into the hole.

Everyone stood silently looking at the key inserted firmly in the notch above the reliquary. It stood out almost horizontally from the wall. Cloe backed off and sat on her small camp chair, continuing to study the niche, the wall, and the key. The soldiers refilled everyone's coffee mugs. J.E. attempted to turn the key. He tried several different positions and angles. He tried to drive it deeper into the hole. Nothing worked.

"The key is static in this location. It does not itself drive the action as in the hall of martyrs in Lyon or as with the pin outside. Something has to act upon it in this location," analyzed Father Sergio.

Astounded, they all turned to look at the young priest.

"Well, Serge, sometimes you just take my breath away," said J.E. "But I think you may be right."

"Assuming that's correct, what's the actor?" asked Cloe.

The monsignor stood, walked over to the wall, and then turned to them. "To know that, we will have to figure out what the hieroglyph means."

CHAPTER 53

"Of course," said Cloe, "a hieroglyph."

"I know that hieroglyphs were used by the ancient Egyptians, but what's the relevance here?" asked J.E.

"Not just Egyptians, J.E., but also Chinese and almost all other civilizations have used and still do use hieroglyphs to communicate," said Cloe.

"Hieroglyphs are just pictures of something that form a sort of visual word," added the monsignor.

"But what do you mean we are still using hieroglyphs?" asked the camerlengo.

"They're everywhere," said Cloe. "The dashboard of your car contains many—ciphers for the lights, windshield wipers, and so forth. They are just little picture symbols that stand for a word or even a phrase."

"Okay, we have a little picture that stands for something but what?" asked J.E. "What does that tell us about the key and the cave? What can a circle with a line drawn through it near the top mean?"

"Well, I think we should get some rest. I don't think there's much more we can do tonight," said the monsignor.

Cloe's pulse quickened slightly. She had heard this tone from the monsignor before. She knew he had solved the mystery. "Albert, I think you have something to tell us," said Cloe.

Everyone turned to the monsignor. Cloe watched as he considered his words, riveting the attention of the room to himself. *He certainly knew how to seize the moment,* she thought. Even the Swiss paused in their card game to watch.

"Dawn," he said simply.

CHAPTER 54

Before the first light, Cloe and the others had awoken and made their breakfast. Locked as they were inside the marabout, the matter of their toilet was a little challenging, but they managed with a hole dug in the sandy floor as the latrine and blankets for privacy.

"Extinguish your lamps," ordered the monsignor suddenly.

In the now-faltering darkness they waited. The night retreated, and slowly light permeated the chamber from the vented area at the roof line. As it did, the jade key began to glow. A low hum was audible.

"Look, the key is absorbing the light!" cried Cloe.

As it did, an ink-black shadow was cast on the floor of the marabout. It started near the reliquary and extended outward as the light grew stronger.

"That's amazing," said J.E. "Such a dark shadow should not be possible in this faint light, but somehow the key is emptying all light from the area of the shadow. I've never seen anything like it."

The camerlengo stepped forward and scratched an X over the shadow on the earthen floor of the room. No sooner had he done this than the sun rose a bit, and the light changed entirely.

"The key has stopped its absorption of the light," observed J.E.

"Yes, and the dark shadow is gone," said the monsignor. "The dawn has passed."

The hum was gone now, but an acrid smell such as that of ozone lingered faintly in the closed air.

"Wow," Cloe said. She was at a loss for words, but in her heart she knew that somehow they were being guided by the hand of God.

A jade key absorbing the faint early morning rays of the sun and then creating a stygian shadow that should not exist was probably explicable with modern science, but how would the ancients have known and been able to use such a thing? Once again their ingenuity was amazing. Clearly, it was another sign, this time a physical one. But what did it mean?

"Well, I would say that unless someone has a better idea, X marks the spot," said the camerlengo with a smile.

"Serge, you have to be right for a change," retorted J.E.

J.E. went to his backpack and withdrew a short folded spade. When he returned to the former location of the shadow, he unfolded the short shovel and put the point of the spade into the center of the X drawn by Father Sergio on the floor. He put one foot on the blade and stomped down. The monsignor retrieved his spade and also began digging at the indicated point. Together they dug for twenty minutes or so and at the end had cleared out a space about two feet deep, two feet wide, and two feet long.

"This looks to be a dry hole," said J.E., sweating from the exertion.

"I don't understand; how could we have misunderstood the sign?" said Father Sergio. "It seemed so clear."

"Now what?" asked Cloe.

At that moment, a booming voice from outside the marabout yelled, "Dr. Lejeune, you and your associates have no place to go! Come out now and tell us what you know."

Almost immediately, with the new arrivals apparently not waiting for an answer, rifle and machine-gun fire began to strafe the door and other areas of the marabout. Dust was everywhere, but the stone door and walls held strong. The soldiers all hit the floor and reflexively reached for weapons they did not have. J.E. grabbed Cloe, pushed her down, and covered her with his body. Only the monsignor stood where he had been before.

When the fire relented, while the men outside were likely changing magazines, the monsignor said, "They can't get at us yet, but this old building won't hold forever. We have to find where this clue leads."

"Is that the Karik?" asked Cloe.

"I don't know for sure, but that's my best guess," said J.E. "They will do what they have to do to get in. We have no weapons to fight them off. We need to solve this problem. Serge, you are the big science brain here. What did we do wrong?"

Everyone looked at Father Sergio. He studied the floor for a few seconds and then looked at the roof.

"We didn't adjust for the fact that so many years have gone by, and even the sun's position in relation to the earth has changed," muttered the camerlengo. He took a giant step off where he had marked the floor with an X before the dig and yelled, "Here!"

J.E. and the monsignor fell on the new place and dug like their lives depended on it. As the machine-gun fire ate away at the stone door, they could barely hear the monsignor's shovel hit something solid.

Excited, the cleric jumped back and said, "That's something."

Quickly, he and J.E. struggled to clear the spot. In the newly bared place they all saw it.

"My God," said Cloe. "It's a door."

CHAPTER 55

J.E. jumped down into the shallow hole and grabbed the ring at the end of the trap door. He gave a mighty tug, and the portal popped open. As Cloe stared down into the ink-black pit into which the door opened, she thought she had never seen anything so uninviting. But then the machine-gun fire against the door and walls of the marabout intensified, and she realized whatever was down there had to be better than the Karik's guns up here.

The monsignor shone his light into the abyss beneath, but little was visible except the beginnings of a rock stairwell.

"Grab our gear and let's go!" shouted J.E.

The Swiss had long since packed everything up to make ready for whatever was ahead. Everyone grabbed a pack and headed for the hatch in the floor of Speratus's marabout. J.E. led the way down, but his pace quickly fell off as he entered the darkness. There was an absolute and total absence of light. This was even worse than the staircase and tunnel beneath the Church of St. John in Lyon. J.E. used his flashlight, but the tar-like dark swallowed the beam. Cloe could barely see the steps of the stairs before her.

"J.E., we have to slow down. I can't see a thing," she said.

Progress slowed to a crawl. Cloe looked back and saw that the monsignor and the Swiss had closed the trap door.

"Albert, can you lock it behind us?" yelled Cloe.

"We are using the handle of one of the shovels to try to bar it. I think we can rig something," he responded. "I don't know how long it will last, but it will give us a little time."

"All right, everyone, carefully," pressed Cloe.

The descent began again with J.E. on point. It seemed to be a circular stone staircase that ran along the walls of a tubular shaft. Around they went, each footstep echoing off the stone walls.

Cloe was beginning to become disoriented with the circular movement in the blackness.

"We're down," shouted J.E.

"Thank God," said Cloe breathlessly, relieved.

Father Sergio, J.E., and Cloe gathered at the bottom of the stairwell. Shortly, the monsignor and the Swiss caught up. The Swiss had lit their lamps, and everyone had turned on their flashlights.

The group fanned out back to back and shone the lights outward. This part of the chamber was fairly large. At least it did not have a claustrophobic, low ceiling. But Cloe could see no jars, or much of anything else for that matter.

BLAM! From above them came a huge explosion, and Cloe felt the concussion.

"Sounds like they have blown open the outer door to the marabout," said J.E. matter-of-factly. "If they have that kind of ordnance, they won't be long getting in here."

"J.E., what do we do?" cried Cloe.

"Well, as best I can determine from the reports the Vatican had on the battle of El Guettar, Thib's paratroopers landed and approached the Italian positions from the northwest," said J.E. "That's where Thib and Bobby Morrow fell into what we think might have been some part of this very cave."

"J.E., are you saying we should try to reverse that course?" pressed the monsignor.

"Exactly," said J.E., pulling his compass from his shirt pocket. "Thib was proceeding southeast, so we head northwest." J.E. studied the compass and then pointed obliquely away from the stairwell. "That way," he said.

They crept along in the direction J.E. led, moving through what looked to be a series of rooms. In each of the rooms, they paused, but there was nothing. Some of them contained niches as had been described by Thib, but there was nothing on them. Cloe could not be sure they were even in Thib's cave. After a few minutes, they reached the end of the series of chambers. It was a dead end.

"Are there any offshoots?" queried the camerlengo. "Did we miss anything?"

"I did not see anything we missed," said the monsignor. "This is it."

"But it's all empty," said Cloe. "This can't be Thib's cave. Where are the jars? He said there were scores or hundreds of them."

"Maybe it's not the right cave," agreed the monsignor. "There must be many caves under these mountains."

At that point, they all heard a second, smaller explosion.

"That's the trap door," said J.E. "They didn't bother trying to clear the rigging we used to block it; they just blew it. You know, if we had had just a few choice items from my bag on the plane, we would have booby-trapped that door, and the bad guys would be roasting in hell right now."

As J.E. spoke, the monsignor was studying the walls, apparently looking for some way out of the trap. "Jesus, Mary, and Joseph," he said reverently.

"What is it, Albert?" asked Cloe, moving to him.

When she reached him, all he could do was point to the wall. Cloe shone her light at the area and saw a shelf-like niche. Her light went higher, and she froze.

There above the niche was a single word scratched in the stone in stick-like ancient Greek letters: IOUDAS.

CHAPTER 56

"Oh my God," cried Cloe. "This *must* be Thib's cave. This is the very niche the jar he brought back from the war came from. It's exactly as he described it in his letter to me, with the word *IOUDAS* inscribed in the stone over the niche."

"We can't be entirely sure," said the monsignor. "There must be many caves."

"Albert, what more do you want?" asked Cloe. "You read Thib's letter. This is the cave, and it's empty."

Terribly disappointed, Cloe wandered away from the wall and flopped down on the sandy floor in the middle of the room. She wasn't sure whether she had willingly sat down or her legs had just given way. Had she come this far only to fail? What had happened?

Wait a minute, she thought. One thing and one thing only would prove this was the right cave. She got on her hands and knees and began to rummage around in the sand, shining her light here and there.

"Is that it?" she asked herself aloud.

The monsignor had joined her and was watching, as were the rest. "Cloe, what are you doing?" he asked.

She looked up. "Remember Thib's letter? Do you remember what he said he did with his flashlight?"

Smiling, the monsignor dropped to his knees and joined the search. Cloe shone her light on something that gave back a red reflection. She crawled to it, picked it up, and turned triumphantly to the others.

The monsignor gasped. "Well, my goodness, there can be no doubt now. No doubt at all."

"What is it?" asked Father Sergio.

"It's the red lens from Thib's flashlight," said the monsignor. "His letter states he took it off after he and Morrow fell into the cave so he could see better. At that point, he no longer had any need for the red low-light lens."

"So there is no question that this is Thib's cave where there are supposed to be scores or hundreds of jars," said Cloe. "Where are they?"

"Where, indeed?" blasted a new voice from the darkness of the corridor, in the direction from which they had come. "Come, Doctor, surely you have some idea."

Cloe turned and saw the man she assumed was the Karik. She could not see his face well in the darkness. He stepped into the room with six well-armed thugs. Their guns were leveled at J.E. and the other men. She saw J.E. assess the situation, but it was clear there could be neither flight nor fight right now.

The newcomers were garbed traditionally like the residents of this area, with robes and headdresses. Their weapons, however, were completely modern and, Cloe knew, lethal.

"Well, Doctor, what have you to say for yourself?" asked the leader of the group.

Something about the way he said this triggered a memory in Cloe, and she said, "Karik, I presume, or do you not have the courage to tell me your name?"

"Karik will do," said the man.

"Oh, come now, Karik. No need to be modest. Your fame goes before you, in the form of death and destruction," said Cloe directly.

The man began to fidget as if she might have struck a nerve.

"But we have met before, and I know your true name. You're Dadash, previously the servant of the Kolektor," asserted Cloe. "You're nothing more than the Kolektor's house mouse."

The monsignor snickered, and the Karik's eyes burned with hatred at Cloe.

Knowing she had seized the conversation and that the Karik was on the defensive, Cloe pressed on. "I'm assuming that you used your position of trust with the Kolektor to somehow take over his organization after his death at Hakeldama. How did you do it?"

The Karik's men, who apparently understood some English or at least the body language, began to shuffle nervously. The Karik himself seemed unsure.

"You must have gotten control of the Kolektor's money somehow. That's it, isn't it? You have stolen the Kolektor's fortune and assumed his identity," asserted Cloe.

The Karik swiftly stepped forward and backhanded her across the face. She landed on her backside and saw stars. J.E. jumped forward toward the Karik, but the monsignor grabbed him before he could get himself shot.

"Stop!" screamed Cloe. Shaking the cobwebs from her head and rubbing her swelling cheek, she dragged herself to her feet. She stepped toward the Karik. Saying nothing, she smiled at him.

Furious, the Karik hoarsely croaked in his own defense, "I am completing the mission the master gave me. When you have told me where the jars have been taken, I will finish the plans the master laid out for you and your colleagues at Hakeldama."

"If that's your plan, why should we help you at all?" queried Father Sergio.

The Karik tore his hate-filled eyes from Cloe and studied the young camerlengo. "I have met the doctor, her son, and this accursed priest, the monsignor, but I do not believe I know you," said the Karik, moving toward Father Sergio.

The Karik pulled an ugly handgun from under his robes and pointed it at Father Sergio. "Tell me where the jars have been taken, or I'll put a bullet in your new priest's head," said the Karik dryly, his voice cracking.

"We don't know," said the monsignor. "We found the cave just as you see it."

"That's right," cried Cloe. "We're as surprised as you are that this part of the cave is empty. Perhaps the jars have been moved to another area of this series of caverns."

"Perhaps … Noosh, take two men and search everything thoroughly," replied the Karik. "We shall see, Doctor. If this is another tactic to stall for time, it will go hard on your friend."

CHAPTER 57

"Karik, we have searched everywhere. There are no jars," said Noosh. "There's nothing at all in the cavern."

The Karik turned slowly and faced Cloe and the other members of her party, who had now been securely bound. He approached leisurely, seemingly lost in thought, perhaps debating courses of action. Cloe could only wonder what was going on in that wicked, twisted brain.

"Dr. Lejeune, what can you add to help us with our predicament?" he asked mildly. "The treasure we have both sought seems to have eluded us. I am not pleased."

Cloe stood, only her arms having been bound, and considered the situation. Once again she and her comrades were on the brink of ignominious death at the hands of the Kolektor's organization embodied in this shallow imposter. What could she add, and who would save them even if she could prolong things? Hope fled like a shadow away from the morning sunrise.

But Cloe was able to recenter herself. The seventeen-year-old unwed mother and street fighter she had once been surfaced. "Karik, it seems someone else has bested us," she said.

"Yes," he replied collegially. "Still, we were the only ones who knew of the cave and were searching for it."

"Is that so?" Cloe queried. "Was there no one else? Where did you get your map?"

"How did you know of the map?" he asked.

"It was common knowledge in El Guettar," she responded. "Who could know of the cave so as to make a map?"

"Perhaps the Vatican," the Karik said offhandedly.

"But the Vatican representatives are right here in the cave. Why would they remove the jars and then come here to fall into your trap?" she asked, realizing the Karik was no Kolektor. "No, there is another player on this board. Where did you get the map?"

"The Sicarii," he said. "I knew from Hakeldama that they were the guardians of the cave. I simply put out the necessary forces and money until we found people connected to them. In the era of modern communications and computers, not much can be hidden."

"So what did you do?" Cloe continued. "Did you torture some poor soul to get your blasted map?"

"Of course," said the Karik. "But the woman tricked us somehow even in her death throes, mucking up the landmarks. The map was useless. Her family will pay for her deceit."

Cloe smiled at her Sicarii sister's courage, but it was not a smile of happiness. It was a smile of resolution. It was a smile of iron will.

"Well, Karik, it's plain that your incompetence has put you and us here in an empty cave," she whispered. "Your torture of the Sicarii woman somehow tipped the clan off that you might know where their most precious treasures were located. They didn't know that your victim had misled you or couldn't take the chance that she hadn't."

The Karik considered this and said, "I see now how you got the best of the Kolektor. Your reasoning is sound. But I shall not make his mistake."

"What will you do?" queried Cloe.

"That is not for you to know, as you and your pesky friends will die here," said the Karik.

"But the Sicarii are now on the alert," observed Cloe. "You have no chance of finding them or where they have taken the jars. You are finished."

"I found them once, and I will find them again," finished the Karik. "I will have the jars."

CHAPTER 58

Cloe was trussed up and thrown next to the others. At least, it seemed, they were not going to be shot, though that only meant the Karik probably had something worse in mind for them. The Karik and his men had headed out of the entrance tunnel that opened into this section of the cavern. They were gone, leaving Cloe and the others in overwhelming darkness deep within the earth.

Cloe struggled with her bindings but in doing so only seemed to tighten them. She could barely breathe after her exertions. Suddenly, she felt someone behind her working her fastenings. It was absolutely pitch-black in the cave.

"It's me, Mom," whispered J.E. Somehow he had gotten loose.

He quickly untied her, and as they freed the others, Cloe asked, "How?"

"When they tied me, I flexed the muscles in my arms and wrists. After they left, I relaxed the muscles, leaving me enough slack in the ropes to eventually wriggle out of them. Not very original but effective. We have to be very careful and get out of here," said J.E. "They have not left the cave yet; I can still hear footsteps in the distance."

"Where are our flashlights?" questioned the monsignor. "Do we still have our equipment?"

They spread out and searched by hand in the blackness, but their lights and most of their equipment had been taken. The only thing left was some camping gear.

"J.E., can you lead us out of here? We can't see a thing," said the monsignor.

"I'm not sure," replied the young soldier. "But hurry, join hands and let's move to the sound."

They linked arms and followed the diminishing footfalls of the Karik's men. Soon, they were completely lost. They could no longer hear anything from the Karik's soldiers. It was absolutely silent, with no point of reference whatsoever.

"Okay," said Cloe, "let's sit for a minute and think. There must be some way out of here."

"Ack …" said the young camerlengo.

"What is it?" asked Cloe.

"I just butted my head on something," he replied.

The monsignor moved forward and felt the wall near where he had heard Father Sergio's cry. "Wait a minute," he said.

"What?" asked Cloe.

"It's a sconce. We've seen several since we entered the marabout," replied the monsignor. "There's a torch in it. Does anyone have matches?"

"Here," said Father Sergio sheepishly. "I smoke occasionally. I don't have matches, but I have an old Zippo. It might be a little waterlogged, but they are supposed to light every time."

"A Zippo—what's a Zippo?" asked J.E.

"Just the finest lighter you have never seen," responded the monsignor, his tone of voice implying that he might be smiling in the darkness.

The camerlengo popped the top on the lighter, and it made its trademark *zilk* sound. Almost immediately there was a flame. The monsignor lowered the torch and lit it, and the area brightened enough that they could discern their surroundings.

"Wow," said Cloe, very quietly. "I have never really known true darkness until tonight. This is such a relief."

"We have no time to lose," said J.E. "We have to get out of here."

"But, J.E., the Karik is gone, and we are alive," responded Cloe.

"Yes, and do you wonder why we are alive?" asked J.E. "We were at the Karik's complete mercy, yet he let us live."

"The young sir is correct," said the monsignor. "The Karik has something else in mind. J.E., take the lead and get us out of here."

J.E. grabbed the torch and quickly led them toward what they hoped would be the entrance to the marabout. But while wandering around blind, it seemed they had lost their way. After a while Cloe noticed they had only returned to the place where the Judas niche was located.

"Gosh, we are back where we started," said the camerlengo. "Now what?"

"We keep going," said J.E.

CHAPTER 59

Cloe and the rest of the party moved out as the torch began to sputter a bit. They had looked for more torches as they went along, but the few additional sconces they had encountered had been empty.

"J.E., we need to get back to the marabout," said the monsignor. "I think this is the tunnel that we came through to get here."

"Albert, I think that's right," J.E. replied, "but that's the same way we went a while ago that got us back here. We have to be careful not to reenter that loop."

As they entered the tunnel, the torch flickered, smoldered, and looked like it might go out. But then it brightened again, popped, crackled, and continued to light their way.

They moved cautiously but as quickly as they could. After about ten minutes, the torch sputtered again, and this time it went out. Father Sergio tried to relight it but without success. It was done.

"Okay," said J.E. "This won't be easy, but we can still get out. Serge, let me have the Zippo. I'll get us free of this hole." J.E. snapped the lighter open and fingered the flint wheel that brought the flame. They continued to move in the now diminished flickering light. The shadows stalked them at every turn.

After a short time, J.E. dropped the stainless-steel lighter. "Damn," he said as everything went dark once again. "It got hot."

"Yes, that lighter always lights, but it is not meant to be a beacon," explained the camerlengo.

The whole group dropped to their hands and knees and searched for the lighter. After a minute, the monsignor said, "I have it."

"What we will have to do is light it for a couple of minutes and then close it to cool. We will have to wait in the darkness to proceed," said Father Sergio.

"Here, J.E., take it and we'll time it so we can make progress as best we can," said the monsignor.

Cloe thought about this and silently thanked God she was among these people. They were in a terrible way, having been abandoned deep underground by the Karik in the pitch-black, perhaps to wander until exhausted and to wait for death to overcome them. But that was not in the hearts of her friends. While there was breath, there was hope. She loved these men.

They went along in this manner until they reached a place where the tunnel split off in two directions. At that point they had to shut off the lighter so it could cool down.

There, in the dark, Cloe said, "This must be where we went wrong the first time."

"I think that's right. The problem is I'm not sure which way we went," said J.E. "This time, we have to choose the correct fork because I doubt our lighter has another circuit in it."

"Which way do you think, J.E.?" asked Cloe.

"I think we went left the first time around, but I'm not sure. Let's try the right," said the young soldier.

"We are all with you, young sir," said the monsignor.

They sat in the darkness while the lighter cooled, contemplating the terrible choice before them. One way could mean life, and the other could spell ignominious death in the rat trap in which the Karik had left them. Cloe began to burn with anger. She would get out of here, and she would see the end of the Kolektor's organization.

"What's that?" whispered the camerlengo.

Cloe strained to hear.

"Men," she said, answering so softly that she wasn't sure anyone heard her. "The Karik has come back to finish us."

Sure enough, they all could now hear the approaching footsteps of a group of people. Soon flashlight beams were bouncing off the walls and ceiling of the tunnel. There was nowhere to hide. The passage here was straight without transepts.

Cloe was as miserable as she had been while totally and completely under the Kolektor's power in Jerusalem. The men approached.

"Dr. Lejeune ... Cloe?" one of them called softly.

Cloe jumped up and cried, "Oh my God ... Michael?"

CHAPTER 60

BLAM! An enormous explosion ripped through the cavern. Sand and dust blew down the narrow passageway, and Cloe could do nothing but hug the floor of the tunnel as the near-hurricane-force wind blew over her. Debris tumbled along the stone tube in which they were hunkered down. Possibly, it lasted only a few seconds, but it felt much longer.

Just at the point when Cloe thought she could hold on no longer, the vortex began to abate. A minute or two later, the howl of the wind was gone, but the cave was filled with sand and dirt.

"I can't breathe," cried Cloe.

"Mom, take your scarf and put it over your mouth and nose," yelled J.E.

Cloe followed his suggestion, and soon she had caught her breath, even though her mouth and eyes felt like they were still filled with dust and sand.

Then someone next to her handed her a handkerchief, dampened with water from a canteen. She took it and was able to wash the dirt from her face and eyes. She felt so much better. Her vision began to clear, and she could see a bit in the light of the newcomer's flashlight. "Thanks," she said, handing the handkerchief back to him.

"You are welcome," said Michael.

"Michael, what are *you* doing here?" queried Cloe.

"Well, I thought I might be coming to your rescue, but now I'm not sure," he said. "I may only have succeeded in trapping both of us and our friends in this cave."

"What was that explosion?" asked the camerlengo.

"Unless I'm wrong, that was the Karik's way of saying good-bye and good luck," said J.E. sardonically.

"I think J.E. is correct," responded the monsignor. "That was the sound of the Karik blowing up the marabout and, in all probability, sealing us in here."

The two parties came together in the lights held by the newcomers.

"Cloe, perhaps some introductions are in order since we may be destined to die together," said Michael wryly.

"Yes, forgive me," said Cloe. "You have already met my colleague, Monsignor Albert Roques, and my son J.E. This is Father Sergio Canti, of the Vatican, along with our Swiss Guards." Cloe's eyes narrowed a bit as she thought about Michael's "monsignor" slip when he said good night to her in Tunis.

"I am Miguel, and this is my number one, Tomás, along with my soldiers," replied Miguel. "We have come for the Karik."

"The Karik?" asked Cloe, surprised this was not the rescue party Michael had initially suggested. "Why would you be after the Karik? How do you know him?"

"Cloe, this was the cause for my note to you and wanting to talk to you," said Michael. "I have reason to believe the Karik is implicated in the murder of my wife and children. I have chased him from Lyon to Tunis to here. I knew he was interested in the jars, and I knew you were also searching for them. This is why I was not completely truthful with you in Tunis."

"I see, Michael," said Cloe, turning directly to him in the low light. "It seems that my friends and I served as bait in your efforts to trap the Karik. I don't think I like the implications of that one bit."

"I'm sorry, Cloe," he responded. "That was all before I knew you."

"Be that as it may, this has to be taken up another time," Cloe whispered with a heavy heart. "We have to get out of here now." Cloe turned to her son and said, "J.E., what do we do now?"

"Well, at least Miguel and his soldiers are armed," said J.E. He turned to Miguel and explained, "We lost all our weapons in a plane crash we believe was engineered by the Karik."

"Yes, I would agree with your assumption that the Karik was behind the sabotage of the airplane," responded Miguel. "That's exactly the kind of thing the coward would do."

At that point, Miguel ordered his men to divide their weapons with Cloe's group. Some had rifles, and some had pistols, but now all were armed. It was surprising how this gesture improved morale and bonded the two groups together. Food and water was also shared from the packs of Miguel's people.

"Michael, I don't know what to say," said Cloe. "This is quite a gesture of trust."

"We are indebted to you, sir," said the monsignor.

"I think we can help each other, assuming we can somehow get out of here," replied Miguel.

They all sat in the corridor and refreshed themselves. Soon Cloe felt invigorated in spite of the circumstances. At least the Karik had moved on. *But to where?* Cloe wondered.

"Where is the Karik?" pressed Father Sergio, seemingly plucking the thought from Cloe's mind.

"Everything he said before he left tells me he is after the Sicarii. He must believe the Sicarii had something to do with the relics not being here," said Cloe.

"Could the Sicarii have moved them?" queried J.E.

"We can't know that one way or another for sure," said the monsignor, "but certainly, the Sicarii is one group with that knowledge and a strong motive to protect the contents of the cave."

"Are these the relics the Kolektor sought?" asked Miguel.

Cloe was stunned by Miguel's mention of the Kolektor, and her instincts told her there were other revelations to come. "Michael, you know of the Kolektor?" she asked.

"Cloe, the time for lies and deceit is over. I know of the Kolektor. I know who all of you are, and I know everything about the jars and Hakeldama," he replied softly.

"If you know all this, you must be here for the relics yourself," said Cloe, suddenly wary.

"Yes," said the monsignor, "what do you know of them?"

"I know nothing of the supposed contents of the cave, only that the Kolektor coveted them," responded Miguel. "That … and now the Karik pursues them. I'm the only one in this group who is not interested in the cave or the jars. I want the Karik."

"Yet here you are," said J.E. "Miguel, or whatever you call yourself, your actions give lie to your words. If you don't care about the relics, why are you here?"

Cloe saw that the tension was growing between the two groups. Nothing made sense. Men fingered weapons.

"Wait," Cloe yelled. "If you don't know anything about the relics and don't seek them, how did you even know they existed, and why would you care? Who told you about them?"

Michael looked at her and said, "My father told me about the relics and the cave."

CHAPTER 61

"Your father?" queried Cloe. She had no idea what was going on. Was his father someone from Thib's outfit from the El Guettar campaign? Thib had never mentioned someone else. Somehow, with Bobby Morrow dead, Cloe had believed Thib had never told anyone else about the cave.

"Was your father at El Guettar?" she asked.

"No, Cloe, you are on the wrong track completely," said Michael. "My father was not a soldier with your father. He was not a religious who knew what the monsignor's people know."

"Well, who the hell was he?" questioned J.E.

"His father was the Kolektor," said the monsignor. "Miguel is the son of the Kolektor, the man who tried to crucify us all at Hakeldama."

"No, no, nooo!" cried Cloe. "That can't be right. Michael … tell him."

All eyes were now on Miguel. Time passed as he considered his answer. Meanwhile, Cloe's heart sank, weighed down by the truth.

"How did you know, Albert, if I may call you that?" Miguel asked.

"Whether we are all going to be chums on a first-name basis remains to be seen," asserted J.E., a little defensively.

"I understand," said Miguel. "But I do wish for your friendship, and please call me Miguel, or Michael if you prefer." He turned back to the priest.

"I didn't know for sure," replied the monsignor, "but you eliminated most of the possibilities. If you didn't come to the knowledge of the cave through Thib, the Church, or us, that left only the Sicarii and the Kolektor. Years ago it was rumored he had a son, but it was said the child died as a youth."

Miguel nodded. "The man known as the Kolektor was my biological father. However, I never actually knew him. As a child, apparently for my own protection, I was sent off to South America, and all records of my existence vanished."

"So you *were* that child in the rumors," mused the monsignor.

"Yes, I grew up in Rio under a different name with Brazilian citizenship," he continued. "The family who raised me treated me as one of their own, but the Kolektor paid all the bills. After I had not seen or heard anything of him for close to thirty years, I began to think the Kolektor had died. My retainers looked into it after I matured and became a businessman, but they found nothing but dead ends. Eventually, I stopped thinking about it at all."

"I gather something happened to change all that," ventured Cloe.

"Yes," replied Miguel, pausing and seeming to struggle with the next part of the story. "One day out of the clear blue sky, I was in my office, and my personal cell rang. Very few people have that number. Cloe, I believe you are familiar with his voice."

Cloe shivered at the memory of the Kolektor's voice on the phone after he had taken Uncle Sonny. "I am," she said. "We all are."

"Then you can understand the shock I felt with the past reaching out to me like that," said Miguel. "There was no explanation for the thirty-year hiatus. He told me something had been discovered that might change the world. I don't know if he thought his search for the jar would interest me or might endanger me. But he told me what he knew and in a series of calls kept me abreast of the search. In retrospect, I know now he omitted a few details, mainly his murderous methodology and the kidnapping of your poor uncle."

"My God," said Cloe.

"I can only say how sorry I am that you have gone through such a terrible experience at the hands of a member of my family," said Michael.

"When did you talk to the Kolektor the last time?" asked J.E.

"On the night of Hakeldama," replied Miguel. "He said you had decided to share your work with him because of his expertise and resources. He told me everything he had learned from Dr. Lejeune."

"What did he hope to accomplish?" asked the monsignor. "Why did he contact you and tell you all this?"

"I cannot say," responded Miguel. "I had my life and family, and his passions were not my passions."

"Do you think this was his way of trying to make up to you for the lost years?" asked J.E.

"No, he had no such feelings as far as I could tell," said Miguel. "This was not about me at all. This was about his legacy."

"That makes all the sense in the world, considering who the Kolektor was," said Cloe. "The discovery of the jars and the journal was enormous. It might have changed everything, even to the point of bringing down the Catholic Church. Maybe this was something he just needed to be able to pass on to someone."

Cloe considered what she had just heard. Michael's phone call from the Kolektor after so many years was not unlike the call she had received from Uncle Sonny when Thib was murdered. There was a certain symmetry here that she could not deny. Michael seemed to be as much a victim of circumstances as she was.

"Michael, Miguel, or whatever your name is, I'll ask you one final time. Are you here for the cave? What do you want?" asked J.E.

"No, I couldn't care less about the cave. That was my father's passion. It is not mine," responded Miguel. "I don't really even know what he thought he would find. To me the cave is the location where I might find my real quarry, the Karik."

"To be clear, Michael, you have no interest in the cave or the jars?" pressed Cloe.

"No, the Karik killed my family," said Michael softly. "I have come to kill him."

CHAPTER 62

"You seek only revenge," said the monsignor sadly.

"No, I want justice!" replied Miguel heatedly. "The Karik is beyond the justice of any state. But he is not beyond my justice. It's very simple. He caused the deaths of my wife and my boys. He will die for that."

Cloe studied Michael carefully, but she could see no deceit in his words. He felt and meant what he said. She had known in her brief encounter with him that he had a mystery about him. Now, she knew it was an irretrievable sadness. Her long-lost mother and father came to her mind.

Just then a muffled cracking like the snapping of stone vertebrae reached them, followed quickly by another wave of debris and sand.

"What's that?" asked Father Sergio. "It seems to have come from the front of the cavern where the marabout was located."

"I'm not sure," said the monsignor, "but judging from that sound, the stone structure of the whole system of caves may have been compromised. The huge explosion set off by the Karik to destroy the marabout and to bury us may have damaged the roof of the large cavern we first entered from the trap door. If so, that cracking may foreshadow the collapse of the roof and walls. This whole thing could come down on top of us."

"We have to get out of here," Cloe said.

"But how?" asked Father Sergio. "The Karik blew up the only exit."

Cloe heard the crashing thud of what she took to be the roof and walls of the large cavern as it surrendered to the weight of the cascading forces created by the Karik. Again dirt and debris blew over them. Cloe could hardly breathe.

"Use the handkerchief," yelled the monsignor.

"Albert, do you have any ideas?" cried Cloe. "I can barely see anything in this dust."

"Back ... back into the area where Thib found the jar!" shouted the monsignor.

They grabbed what little they had and ran for their lives. Cloe put the handkerchief over her nose and mouth, but she could see little ahead of her.

They all arrived at the chamber where Thib had found the jar, but Cloe could hear the sequential failings of the cavern structures behind them. Soon, this part of the cave would also fail, and they would die under tons of rock.

"Cloe, here!" called the monsignor.

Cloe and the others ran to him in the corner of what she now thought of as Thib's room in the underground cavern. The calamitous collapse of the large cavern had put unbearable weight on the supporting walls and roofs of the smaller caves, causing each to fail in turn. It was as if a murderous line of million-ton stone dominoes had been tipped, and they were all rushing to fall on Cloe and her companions. Each time a closer cave failed, more and more dust and debris washed over them.

"Albert, what do we do?" cried Cloe.

The monsignor grabbed her, cupped his hand over her ear, and yelled into the rising crescendo, "This must be the place! That pile of debris over there has to be it."

"Yes," she screamed back. "This is Thib's chamber. We're going to die here!"

At that point the monsignor grabbed a shovel from the backpack of one of Miguel's men and scrambled up the pile of debris. Cloe watched as he began to vigorously dig into the ceiling. *He's lost his mind!* she thought.

Just then, J.E. ran by her with a shovel in his hand. He too attacked the ceiling above the heap of debris. The crashing cave-ins of the stone ceilings and walls of the chambers behind them were much closer now, perhaps only a cave or two away. Whatever was going to happen to them would be decided in seconds.

Cloe squinted at her son and the monsignor through the dirt and dust, realized what was happening, and turned to the others. "After them!" she screamed. "It must be where my father fell in. Dig with whatever you have. For God's sake, dig with your bare hands if you have to! It's the only way out!"

Cloe, Miguel, Father Sergio, and the Swiss ran up the rock pile like so many steps, and all attacked the roof of the chamber, some with rough tools but others with their hands. Tomás and the others dispersed the dirt and debris.

With a great blast, the chamber next to them succumbed to the destruction. They had to be right and fast, or they would die. There would be no do-overs. The walls around them began to shake like the vibrating floor of an old fun house in a carnival midway. They were coming down.

It's over, thought Cloe. Just then a strong arm enclosed her in a protective embrace. *J.E.?* But when Cloe turned, it was Michael.

"Here!" screamed the monsignor against the cacophony.

Cloe looked but could see nothing. Suddenly the monsignor disappeared. One second he was standing on the top of the debris stack, and the next he was gone. Michael half-pushed and half-carried her to where the monsignor had been.

"My God, it's a hole!" she cried as Michael handed her up to the monsignor.

In the starlight, Cloe could see she was in a low swale between two sand berms.

The monsignor yelled, "Run!" And Cloe ran like her life depended on it.

As she looked back over her shoulder, she saw several men catapult out of the cavity by the strength of the men below. It was obvious that there was a team working below to propel the ones yet to be saved out of danger. They all gathered with Cloe at her place of relative safety.

From the top of the berm where she had sought refuge, she turned and saw the monsignor reach down and grab Father Sergio's hands and haul him out of death's maw like a rag doll. The earth around the hole was collapsing, and geysers of dust were erupting from the sand around them. How many more could they save?

"J.E.!" Cloe screamed. Father Sergio stood his ground, and the two clerics grabbed the next pair of hands to fill the hole and yanked the person out. When Cloe saw it was J.E., she cried.

The monsignor yelled for the camerlengo to run, and he did. J.E. and the monsignor then pulled Miguel out of harm's way, and he ran toward Cloe. Now the portal itself had begun to settle as the cave below filled in. The monsignor and J.E. were instantly up to their knees in sand and sinking. They were on the edge of being sucked down.

Cloe knew they would not give up as long as there was anyone to be saved. She thought again about how much she loved these men. They might die trying, but they would save everyone they could. As the ceiling of the cave began its final collapse, one last pair of hands appeared in the hole. J.E. and the monsignor grabbed them and tugged for all they were worth, but they could not pull the man free. Michael and Father Sergio jumped up from their positions of safety and slid down the back of the berm into the sinkhole. All four of the men pulled until the man, one of the Swiss, was free. J.E. hoisted the exhausted man to his shoulder, and all ran for safety, as the sounds of the catastrophic final failure of the cavern behind them filled the air.

Cloe lay worn out on top of the berm. The settling had finally stopped, and everything was eerily silent. From the crashing and the exploding of rock pounding upon rock, now there was nothing, no sound.

Just as quickly as everything had become silent and stable, all the men jumped up, ran to the cave-in site, and began to dig, one or two with shovels and the rest with their hands.

J.E. looked up at Cloe with tears in his eyes and yelled, "We left men behind."

CHAPTER 63

Cloe looked down at the exhausted men still digging in the sinkhole. She knew it had been a long time. She was ashamed to admit she might have dozed a bit, as dog-tired as she had been. The excavation had spread out 360 degrees from the site of the original hole.

"J.E.," she called, "have you found anything?"

Her son looked up at her, clearly worn out, and said, "Mom, we can't even find the rock slide where we climbed out. They're all lost."

J.E.'s face was lined with worry, and he looked like he had aged while she slept. *He was truly beaten,* Cloe thought. She had never seen him succumb like this, not even under the clutches of the Kolektor or in the plane crash. Here, her son had lost men under his command, and he felt guilty for having allowed himself to be pulled out before them. But he and the monsignor had saved many who otherwise would have died. On the very site where Thib had lost a soldier in his charge, Bobby Morrow, J.E. had lost warriors he had led. She wondered if this would forever scar J.E. as it had Thib. Finally, the exhausted diggers slowly began to leave the excavation area and to climb the berm to her position.

"J.E., we would need an enormous excavator to dig our friends out, and then, after all this time, we would only find their bodies," said the monsignor, sensing the young man's reluctance to give up. "They are gone."

"What if they're trapped in an air pocket or something like that?" queried J.E. "We may still save them."

"They are gone," agreed Miguel. "The cave-in was so massive that there are hundreds of tons of rock and sand on top of what was

Thib's chamber and throughout the rest of the cavern. If I believed there was any hope, I would never give up."

"What do we do now?" asked Cloe.

The survivors had begun to salvage the gear they had been able to bring out of the cave. Cloe could see this mainly consisted of backpacks the men had been wearing at the time. Still, they had put together a little bivouac area and were building a small fire. A couple of the men had canteens, and in a little while Cloe could smell coffee.

J.E. stood up and looked about. "We lost one of the Swiss. Miguel, how many of your men?" Aside from Miguel and Tomás, the new arrivals' group was down to four.

"There are three men lost including your Swiss soldier," said Miguel sadly.

The monsignor stood, walked to the center of the survivors, and said, "I don't know the religious beliefs of you and your men, but I invite you to join us in a prayer for them and their families."

The monsignor knelt on the hard-packed sand and rock. As he crossed himself, all the others, to a man, knelt while the monsignor and Father Sergio led a prayer for the repose of the souls of their colleagues. Cloe noticed that Michael seemed a little uncomfortable with this at first, but then he joined in. After this, the two priests took small vestments from their interior pockets and administered the last rites to the fallen men.

Even after the impromptu service had concluded, the men and Cloe remained on their knees, each with their thoughts on their departed friends. Finally, Cloe stood, brushed herself off, and settled near the small fire.

"What the hell happened?" asked Cloe bitterly. "Where did the Karik come from? For that matter, Michael, how did you know we were here?"

"I have had men watching the Karik since he left Tunis a few days ago," responded Michael. "He seems to have expected you to come here. It was plain that whatever plans he had made to find the cave failed somehow. He was waiting for you to lead him to Thib's chamber."

"Michael, you used us as bait to find the Karik," reasserted Cloe, looking directly at him.

"No! My men only learned you were here when we heard a rumor in El Guettar, and then they spotted you up here. By that time, the Karik already knew you were here and was on his way," explained Miguel.

Cloe examined his face closely to see if he was telling the truth, and it seemed to her he was. Still, she was not quite sure Michael's story held together. Something about the timing didn't quite fit.

"As far as I know, the Karik still does not know my men and I are here," continued Miguel.

"He or his men must have seen you on the way here or in the tunnel when you entered the cavern," sneered J.E.

"No, my men and I followed after him and his men, and we were careful to hide our presence," replied Miguel. "When the Karik left you in the cave and exited, we hid in an offshoot tunnel and watched him and his men run by."

"Why didn't you take him out then? You had the weapons," questioned J.E. "This would have been finished."

"Our first priority was to make sure Cloe was—you all were—okay. We didn't know if you had been hurt or booby-trapped or if the Karik had left explosives on timers," said Miguel. "Perhaps that was an error, but there it is."

Cloe saw Tomás look hard at his boss. Something passed between them, but she could not tell what. She needed to talk to J.E. and Albert privately about Michael.

"The key point right now is, what we do from here on? How do we find the jars?" queried the monsignor.

Just then, a black-clad figure stepped into the firelight. "The best thing for you to do is go home. We will deal with the Karik, as we did with the Kolektor."

CHAPTER 64

Startled, Cloe dropped her coffee and snapped her eyes toward the figure. Several of the men began to rise. As she looked around, Cloe saw about a dozen similarly clad shapes materialize around them. All were garbed in black, and each wore a Bedouin-style head scarf that was wrapped to also cover her lower face. Cloe could see only their eyes.

Some of the men began to reach for weapons.

"Hold," yelled the leader. "We mean you no harm."

Cloe jumped up and said, "These are the Sicarii. They saved all of us from the Kolektor at Hakeldama."

"Yes," confirmed the monsignor, "without them we all would have been crucified. Let them speak."

Michael and the others backed off.

"We would have words with your leader," said the Sicarii who had first appeared.

All eyes turned toward Cloe. Although the monsignor might be their spiritual leader and J.E. was their undisputed military commander, no one doubted the Sicarii meant Cloe, who was the heart and soul of the group.

"What do you wish of me?" asked Cloe. "I owe you my life and the lives of my son, my uncle, and my friend. Whatever I can do to repay your courage and kindness will be done."

"Our camp is not far from here," replied the Sicarii leader. "We wish for you to attend us there."

"No, Mom, absolutely not," said J.E. as Cloe moved to go with the intruders. "It's too dangerous. You don't know what you are dealing with."

"Signorina, I have to agree with J.E.," said the monsignor. "We must stay together."

"Cloe, I have no say here, but I agree with J.E. and the monsignor," said Michael. "It's out of the question."

Cloe looked at Michael hard at first and then softened. *He doesn't know the Lejeune women*, she reminded herself. "Michael, nothing is out of the question to protect what we seek from the likes of the Karik," said Cloe kindly, smiling. "We're all soldiers to protect the jars. This is not possible without some risk."

"But ..." started J.E.

"No buts," responded Cloe. "These women are my friends. I'll be fine."

CHAPTER 65

"Sir, the entire complex of underground caves and caverns has been completely destroyed by our explosives," said the servant. "Doubtless, everyone who was in the cavern when it blew up has perished."

"Very good, Noosh," replied the Karik. "But I am concerned that we were unable to find the two sentries we left to guard our rear. What do you think happened to them?"

"Sir, it is possible the wretched dogs heard the explosions, felt the ground shake, and ran off in fear," said Noosh. "They are now afraid to return."

"Possibly," mused the Karik. "You don't suppose there is another group that we have yet to see?"

"As you say, we have had no sign of anyone else," replied the servant. "In spite of our watchfulness, there has been only the Lejeune group, and they are now all dead."

"Quite right!" said the Karik, smacking his left hand with his right fist. "The Kolektor has been avenged. His shameful death has been visited in spades upon those responsible. As I believe the Americans would say, I have done my duty."

"Yes, sir. No one could say otherwise," replied the servant.

The Karik slowly turned to him and asked, "Why would anyone say otherwise?"

The servant realized he had misspoken. "Sir, I only meant that you have gone beyond what loyalty and honor would demand of any man. You have gone the extra mile to avenge your predecessor," replied the servant, beginning to shake.

The Karik stared at the servant for a long moment and wondered, not for the first time, whether Noosh's tongue might not get his head chopped off at some point. Certainly, the Kolektor would not have put up with him all this time. Still, life was good. Noosh *was* growing into his role. The Karik felt that he too was beginning to understand what was necessary to master the Kolektor's enterprises. He had wondered originally whether it was in his nature to be able to do some of the harsh things that the Kolektor had required. It had been one thing to carry out such orders and another to originate them. Things were changing. He was changing. Perhaps he was even going to enjoy some of this now that the Lejeune woman was dead. Yes, he was beginning to see that what he had done was good.

***

As he relaxed on the roof of the home in which he was staying in El Guettar, all his enemies lay dead with tons of sand and stone in their faces. The next day they would start back toward Tunis. There, he and his men would resume the search for the jars. Eventually, they would find the right Sicarius, and she would tell them what he wanted to know. He would have what had been denied his master, the Kolektor. It was only a matter of time. He would have all the jars and the knowledge and riches they represented. Religions might rise or fall on his whim. Even the Kolektor had never possessed such things and such power.

He leaned back in his chair and surveyed his surroundings. Although it was very late, the view of the mountains in the moonlight was magnificent.

"Sir, we have some especially fine lamb and a wine I think you will appreciate," said the servant. "The lamb is seasoned with garlic and bitters and has been nicely roasted."

The Karik allowed himself to be served.

CHAPTER 66

The sun was rising over the edge of the mountain range. The red-orange early morning light reflected various colors on the rocks, from bright gold to deep purple. It had been hours since Cloe had gone into the night with the Sicarii.

Now, as she approached the camp in the distance, Cloe saw J.E. stand up and survey the horizon. As soon as he saw her, he began to run toward her. Progress was difficult because of the loose stone swag surface. Soon, though, he was there, sweeping her into his arms.

"Mom, I ..." he started, but one look at Cloe silenced him.

Cloe smiled tiredly at J.E., and together they began to walk back to the camp.

"What happened?" he managed.

"When we get back," she said.

By the time they reached the camp, the light was strong, and they needed to shield their eyes.

Cloe entered the bivouac area with J.E.'s help and sat down hard next to the campfire. She knew she must look a fright. Anyway, that's how she felt. The Swiss offered her coffee, which she gratefully sipped.

As she tried to collect herself, she thought back to the scene after she had arrived in the Sicarii camp.

"Dr. Lejeune, we are all that is left of the Sicarii," said the leader.

Cloe looked around and saw maybe fifteen to twenty souls. "But there must have been many more of you when your mission of encouraging and protecting Christian writings began," she replied.

"Yes, but over the years people have changed, and our commitment and discipline are difficult for modern women," said the leader. "This is all that is left. We are now mainly caretakers of the jars and their contents."

"Why are you revealing yourself to me in this manner?" asked Cloe.

"Our prior experience with you at Hakeldama and since has impressed us greatly. We have followed your actions with respect to the second jar and now on this quest to protect the jars and the cave," said the leader. "You have plainly been with us in spirit, and now we would have you as our sister."

Cloe was shocked. A two-thousand-year-old order of women dedicated to protecting Christian relics thought her worthy of joining their number. Cloe said the first thought that came to mind. "I have no daughter and probably will not have one. I would be a dead end for you."

The leader said, "We know this, but you have a fine son and may have grandchildren. You may not be the end; you may be the future."

"What must I do?" asked Cloe, knowing whatever it was, she would do it.

"We must teach you the fullness of our history. You must swear to keep our secrets, and you must dedicate yourself to the protection of the information in the jars."

As Cloe sipped her coffee, she reflected on the many things she had learned, astounding things. In the end, she had become Sicarius.

"Mom, what happened? Your hair?" pressed J.E., jolting Cloe from her reverie.

"What I can say is that I have spent the night with the Sicarii listening to their history and what they say has happened," responded Cloe wearily.

"But your hair has changed," said J.E. "There's more gray in it—much more."

"J.E., I'm sure it's just fatigue and the stress of the whole thing," said Cloe.

"What can you tell us?" asked the monsignor.

"I think much of it you know," replied Cloe. "You know the origins of the Sicarii, of their defeat by the Romans and their fostering of Christianity. You know of their link to Judas. We have learned that Irenaeus was persuaded by something he read to sponsor the Lejeune Manuscript, which represents the original Judas Gospel. They provided me with a lot more detail, but you have the gist."

"Yes, but what of the jars that were in Thib's cave? What do they know of them?" queried the monsignor.

"They have them," Cloe said simply.

Silence fell upon the group. The only sound was the crackling of the small fire in the center of the campsite.

The monsignor stood, turned toward the rising sun, and seemed to consider the situation. "Well, at least we know the jars are safe and have not fallen into the hands of the Karik," he said after a bit, with his typical understatement.

Cloe could not say why this struck her as funny after all they had been through searching for the jars, but she stifled a chuckle. Father Sergio laughed out loud. Soon they all were rolling with laughter at the monsignor's innocent remark. *Talk about the glass being half full*, thought Cloe.

The monsignor looked about as his colleagues belly-laughed at his apparent expense. He smiled and began to chuckle.

"Albert, please don't take offense. We needed a release," cried Cloe. "It's just one of those things that would never be funny under any other circumstance, but here and now what you said was beyond hilarious."

"Thank you," said Father Sergio, tears running from his eyes.

After a while, the laughter had run its course, during which the monsignor had certainly been a good sport. Quiet once again overtook the group.

"Now what?" asked J.E. "Where do we go from here?"

"Well, the Sicarii have the jars and have secreted them someplace they believe to be safe," said Cloe. "Should we just go back to Louisiana and continue the translation of the Lejeune Manuscript and the journal?"

"But the Karik is still out there, and the one thing he does know is that the Sicarii are the key to the location of the jars," observed J.E. "I think he will hunt them down until he finds one who will tell him what he wants to know."

"It's only a matter of time for someone as ruthless as the Karik seems to be," said Miguel, nodding in agreement. "The body count won't matter at all to him."

"I made all the same arguments to the Sicarii last night," responded Cloe. "Their point of view is that they have survived for nearly two thousand years, and they will survive the Karik. Indeed, they insist they will deal with him as they did the Kolektor. They don't want help from us and have urged us to go home. The jars are safe in a sacred place, according to them."

The monsignor seized on the words. "A sacred place?" he repeated.

"Cloe, did they actually say that, or did you simply surmise that?" questioned the camerlengo, picking up the thread. "This is very important."

Cloe thought about the night, and as tired as she was, she could not remember precisely. "I'm not sure," she said after a bit. "Why does this matter? The jars are somewhere safe."

"Perhaps it could be a clue to where the jars are located," observed Father Sergio.

Cloe thought about this, but she was exhausted. The hidden room at the Church of St. John would have been a safe and a sacred place, but it was no longer so. She was sure Vatican historians and other experts had, by now, been all over that chamber. Was anywhere really safe from the Karik?

"Michael, what will you do now?" asked Cloe.

Miguel seemed to ponder the question and then turned and faced her directly. As he spoke, his gaze quickly moved from neutral to fierce. "Cloe, I will pursue the Karik to the ends of the earth. He will pay for the evil he has wrought," he said. "My wife and sons were innocents. He had no regard for them. He and his organization must be exterminated."

"Miguel, revenge is not the way," said the monsignor. "You have had a terrible loss, but revenge is like a boomerang. It only comes back on its host."

"Father, I thought long and hard about that while I lay in the hospital convalescing from my injuries from the bombing," whispered Miguel. "I concluded that you are correct and revenge is not the path. It *is* self-destructive. However, can one stand by and witness evil without taking action?"

Cloe knew that the monsignor saw the paradox, and he visibly struggled with an answer. If an evil person wrongs you personally, is it revenge to seek to snuff out that evil? "We must all stand against evil wherever we find it," he said finally. "God gives us the strength to overcome it."

"I do not judge the Karik's heart, for that is God's job," replied Miguel. "But I judge his actions, and they are evil. He is beyond justice, as was his predecessor. We must find him and put an end to his ways. The lives of many people, including the Sicarii, depend on it."

Cloe stood up and turned to the group. "Michael is right," she said. "We must stop the Karik. The information that may be in the jars cannot fall into his hands. The pope has made that clear. The Karik will kill every Sicarius he finds until one of them tells him where they are. This cannot happen."

"Agreed," said the monsignor.

"Agreed," said J.E.

"Agreed," said Father Sergio, as the rest of the cohorts repeated the same.

Cloe looked at them and said, "Then it is settled. We continue to seek the jars to keep faith with the mission given us by the pope, but we stop the Karik at all costs."

CHAPTER 67

"Well, the Karik certainly has a substantial head start on us," said J.E., gazing at the disabled vehicles. "This won't help us catch up."

They had decamped, packing what little they had. Cloe was still exhausted but knew they had to move out. After a couple of hours of trekking, they had arrived at where they had left the Land Rover. What remained of Father Sergio's vehicle was there next to it.

"The Karik's men must have set the gasoline in the tanks on fire," observed the monsignor, looking at the burned-out vehicles. "Interesting that he would do that since he hardly would have expected any of us to survive and return to the cars."

"Belt and suspenders, perhaps," quipped the camerlengo.

"Just pure meanness to burn those cars," said J.E.

"All true," said the monsignor. "But burning the cars also destroyed any forensic evidence that was ever in them. This would delay the authorities' efforts to find out to whom the vehicles belonged and what might have happened to them. I see he has also taken the license plates."

"Okay, now what?" asked Cloe. "It's at least a six-hour drive back to El Guettar. It will take a lot longer to walk. Can we call some help?"

"I already have," said Michael, gesturing to his satellite phone in its belt holster.

Cloe heard a roar come up the valley and over the edge of the road bank to the south. She turned and saw a large helicopter feather out above the parking cul-de-sac. Slowly the machine settled into the niche where cars normally parked. Its skids made solid contact, and the turbine engine begin its deceleration. The rotors kicked up an enormous amount of dust, but this too quickly began to settle.

"Well, that's very impressive," observed Father Sergio. "I wondered how you got up here in the first place. Perhaps the Karik is not as far ahead of us as he thinks."

The pilot swung out of the left-hand seat, walked to the group, and saluted Miguel. "Hello, boss. Can we give you a lift?"

Miguel turned to Cloe and the others and said, "Lady and gentlemen, meet Sky. He can fly anything better, farther, and faster than any other man alive. He was a child pilot in Vietnam, then the Balkans, Iraq, et cetera."

Sky could have been forty-five, sixty-five, or any age in between. He was tall and had a weathered, tan face and almost-white hair. His dark arms were stringy but muscled. Sky had a mustache that Bill Cody in his day would have envied. Cloe thought the man looked like a walking, flying myth.

"Good morning, ma'am. At your service," said Sky with a bow.

Cloe smiled in spite of the fatigue and said, "Mr. Sky, we need a ride to El Guettar."

"Well, happy to oblige, ma'am, but if it's all the same to you, we'll go to Gafsa where the boss has his jet parked," said the pilot. "Then we'll go wherever the fuel load will take us that you may want to go. And if that's not enough, we'll stop and get some more go-juice."

Cloe's smile broadened, and she actually began to feel good in the halo of the man's optimism. "Tunis sounds pretty good right now," she said.

"Well, Tunis it is if the boss man says go," replied Sky.

Miguel looked around and then to the east, pointed to the sky, and said, "Go."

CHAPTER 68

Cloe could not remember the last time she had felt so good. Submerged to her chin in a full-size bath filled to the brim with hot water and soapy bubbles, she was in heaven. Michael had insisted on sending an ice bucket and very fine champagne to her room. She thought about whether she wished Michael was there. He had been very brave coming into the cave for her. On the other hand, she needed to talk to Albert and J.E. about Michael's story in the cave. Had he really come for her or for the Karik? Or had he come for the jars?

The helicopter had ferried them to Gafsa, where Michael's jet indeed was waiting. The ground crew had it serviced, and the copilot was warming the engines when they arrived. The group had transferred what little gear they had and then shot off the runway like a scalded dog. Sky did like a hot ride.

Cloe had slept a little on the way back, but mainly she watched and listened to J.E. and the monsignor discussing everything that had happened. They were debriefing each other as if they had been astronauts on a moon shot. She knew it would not take J.E. and the monsignor too long to figure out the Sicariis' plan. It was only a matter of time.

In the tub, she leaned back and took a long sip of the clean, crisp wine. Strangely, her thoughts shifted to her Uncle Sonny. He was her dad's only sibling and her only near relative. He had been through hell with the Kolektor, as they all had. But Uncle Sonny was ninety years old. She worried about him and said a silent prayer that the Swiss Guards who had been assigned to him were doing their job. She made up her mind to call him as soon as she could.

Cloe thought about the pope and his charge to her. The Karik must not find the cave with the jars, he had said. Well, he had found the cave but not the jars since it was empty. Cloe now questioned whether they had underestimated this Karik. He was plainly very clever and determined, and at times, he seemed to be more ruthless than the Kolektor himself.

Even so, the Sicarii had been ahead of everyone. Cloe guessed that the pope would be pleased that the Karik had not found the jars and their contents, at least not yet. Doubtless, by now the monsignor and Father Sergio had been in touch with the Vatican, and the pope knew what could be known. She hoped the amazing ops center under the Vatican had swung into action and was somehow tracking the Karik. Maybe it would all fall into place.

Realizing she was done, she popped the drain, rinsed off, and grabbed a full-length towel from the heated bar near the tub. The hotel was nothing if not full of detailed elegance. She dried off and sat in front of the mirror at the dressing table. The jet had brought them back to Tunis in less than two hours. The pilots had made reservations for them at the Les Berges Du Lac Hotel, where they had stayed on the way in country. They had no intel on the whereabouts of the Karik.

She had to meet her friends for drinks in a bit. Michael would be there. Her thoughts were all jumbled, and she felt on edge, a little like random lightning strikes were hitting near her. Was she doing the right thing?

***

Cloe put on the cocktail dress the concierge had purchased for her from the designer store in the hotel. The woman had excellent taste, and as Cloe sized herself up in the full-length mirror, she thought she looked pretty spectacular, the new grayer shade of her hair notwithstanding. The hotel's jewelry store had actually loaned her a few pieces for the evening. She was beginning to like Tunis.

Cloe joined her friends on the same terrace where she had met Michael. An orchestra was playing softly. The terrace overlooked the bay, and the light was beginning to fade. Here and there a star made its appearance in the growing darkness.

As she approached, they all jumped up, and Michael seated her.

The monsignor said, "Signorina, you look marvelous."

All nodded in approval, and Michael added, "Cloe, my compliments. How do you do this?"

Cloe looked around and saw they had all been to the hotel or area boutiques. J.E. had on a linen jacket with open collar. The two religious had once again found their traditional garb, although they had had to go outside the hotel to do so. Michael was splendid in a summer tux with white jacket. Cloe thought she and Michael were a bit overdressed for the time of day, but in the moment it was perfect.

Cloe reveled in the wonderful evening, her friends, and the gorgeous venue for just a bit. But then she got down to business. "I know you have checked your sources," she said finally. "What of the Karik?"

"Nothing," said the monsignor.

"Nothing," said Michael.

"Mom, as far as we can determine, he is not in Tunis. Where he has gone is a mystery," added J.E.

The group was silent for a moment while this information was digested. The monsignor leaned forward and looked directly at Cloe. "Cloe, you have not told us the details of your hours spent with the Sicarii," he said.

"As I have said, much of the time with them, I spent listening to their history, some of which they had related to me after Hakeldama. Also, they confirmed that it was one of their sisters who was captured by the Karik's thugs and who, they believe, drew a map of the cave's location. She must have been tortured and near death to give him any information at all. Still, in drawing the map, as we now know, she transposed key landmarks so that the Karik would never find the cave by himself," said Cloe.

"Such courage," whispered the monsignor.

"Yes, they are a strong, courageous band of women," replied Cloe.

"Where did they take the jars?" asked Father Sergio directly.

"They emptied the cave after their sister was tortured and killed. They could not take the chance that she had revealed the secret. But they would tell me nothing except that the jars were safe."

"If I remember correctly, you said they took the jars to a 'sacred place,'" said the camerlengo.

"Yes, that's what I remember they said, but they gave me no further information on where that might be," replied Cloe.

"A sacred place," considered the monsignor again.

"Why don't we order?" suggested Cloe. "I'm famished!"

A waiter materialized, distributed menus, and took drink requests. After a bit of discussion and consideration of the evening's specials, orders were placed, and the friends settled back into the ambience of the evening.

"Cloe ..." started the monsignor.

"Albert, can we have the rest of the evening without the Karik?" asked Cloe sharply. "I have told you what I know. Let's enjoy tonight."

"Yes, of course," replied the priest, surprised by her abruptness.

Michael stood and said, "Cloe, may I have this dance?"

"Michael, I'm terribly sorry, but Father Sergio has asked me for the first dance," Cloe replied, looking to the young cleric.

Smiling ear to ear, the Reverend Father Sergio Canti rose to his full height and circumnavigated the table to escort Cloe to the dance floor.

As they danced, Cloe said, "Father Sergio, you were very courageous in the cave, and without your insights, we never would have made it here. You've been a marvelous addition to our team. I shall make sure His Holiness knows. There's nothing further for you to prove."

Tears welled up in the young man's eyes. "This is so important to me and to my people, Dr. Lejeune," said the cleric. "My small village in Italy sacrificed so much to send me to seminary, and they have celebrated every achievement. When it became known I had a chance to possibly become a part of the pope's personal household, they all prayed daily for me. I must succeed on this mission."

"You have succeeded," emphasized Cloe. "Please let this burden fall from your shoulders. No one could have done better."

"It has been heavy at times, but it's not a burden; it's a privilege. My entire village succeeds because of me," concluded the cleric. "God has blessed me."

As the music ended and they walked back to the table, Cloe reflected on the two gems of the younger generation she was with and gave Father Sergio a great hug before sitting down, this time with tears in her eyes.

CHAPTER 69

"Michael, the dinner and dancing were wonderful," said Cloe as they walked together through the lobby of the hotel on the way to the elevators. The hotel was quiet, and the lights had been turned down for the night. The rest of the group had long since retired.

"Yes," he replied. "Cloe, I know we have not known each other very long, but I'm very happy."

They entered the elevator and went to Cloe's floor. Michael slipped his arm around Cloe's shoulder as they walked down the corridor to her room.

Too soon, she thought, they were at her door. They turned, looked at each other, and kissed softly. Cloe had not felt like this in twenty-five years. She felt like a teenager again. Was she in love?

"Michael, come in and have coffee or a nightcap," suggested Cloe.

She opened the door to her room, which had a seating area separate from the bedroom. Michael followed, and she turned to flick on the light switch. When she turned back to face Michael, he was looking over her shoulder into the room, an expression of horror on his face. As the door slammed behind them, she spun and saw several armed men coming at them.

"Run!" shouted Michael as he stepped by her, seeking to defend her from the first intruder.

But Cloe did not run. It was not in her to desert Michael. She slipped out of her heels and scooped one up to use as a weapon. She joined him at his shoulder and fought the way Thib had taught her on the river when she was young. She clawed, she kicked, she gouged—there were no rules except to survive. They both fought like the cornered animals they were.

Cloe expected to be shot since all the men had to do was step back and fire on them. Strangely, they did not.

Cloe and Michael had taken down two of the attackers with their bare hands and Cloe's stiletto, but numbers were against them. One of the thugs struck Michael with the butt of his pistol, and he went down hard. Then it was just Cloe against four of them. Still, she pointed the heel of the shoe at them and made to fight on.

"Hold," said a shadowy figure in the bedroom doorway.

Cloe looked up. It was the Karik. He had a pistol in his hand, and it was pointed squarely at Michael's chest. The pistol had a silencer on it and would scarcely make any noise if he fired.

"It is nothing to me, but if you want your friend alive, at least for the time being, come here and sit on the couch," said the Karik evenly.

Cloe glared at him but straightened her clothes, held her head up, and walked to the couch. As she sat, she was pleased to see the relief on the bleeding faces of most of the Karik's men. She smiled sweetly at them, but her thoughts were furious. This was not a killing mission, or she and Michael would now be dead. The Karik's men had them dead to rights with guns drawn when they entered the room. *No,* she thought, *this was something else.*

"Imagine my surprise," said the Karik, "when I returned by car to Tunis only to learn that you and your people had survived and were already here." He approached and sat lightly on the couch an arm's length away from her. "You will have to tell me how you survived my explosives," said the Karik. "They should have brought the whole cavern down."

"They did," she responded, "you dirty coward. You killed a number of our friends."

"Pity I did not get you all," replied the Karik. "How did you get out?"

Not seeing any reason to lie, Cloe said, "We went out the way Thib fell in decades ago. We dug through the ceiling above the cave-in that brought my father into the cave in the first place."

"Ingenious! My compliments on your escape," said the Karik cheerily. "But it seems that what was your good fortune has also turned into my good fortune."

Cloe studied the man. Unlike the Kolektor, who spoke little and then very directly, this man was full of riddles. He seemed to amuse himself by toying with people under his power and to be more enamored of himself than was his predecessor. The Kolektor was self-obsessed, but the Karik was eaten up with self-love, with narcissism. Cloe thought there might be an advantage in understanding this. He wanted something from her. She guessed she would soon find out.

"My dear, I think we have common cause in one thing," said the Karik. "We both seek the jars, do we not?"

Cloe ignored the intimacy and stared stonily at the man. She noticed what looked like a small tremor in his left hand.

"I search for the jars to vindicate my master," continued the Karik. "If I find them, I want them to be rigorously examined by the best scientific minds and the findings made public so all can know what's there. Do you not seek the same goal?"

Cloe laughed. She knew she should not have done so, but she couldn't help it. The man was such a lying fraud. He was terribly dangerous, but he did not frighten her the way the Kolektor had. The Kolektor was brilliant and chillingly scary, but the Karik was a power-mad brute who was little more than a blunt instrument. Essentially, it was Stalin versus Idi Amin. *Still,* she thought soberly, *the latter had done a lot of damage.*

"Karik," she finally replied, "we don't seek the same ends. If anything, we seek the opposite. You want the jars. My job is to prevent you from finding them. Thus far, that's worked out."

His face began to color. Cloe knew she might have a bit of an advantage because the Karik would be taken aback by the boldness of a woman talking to him like this. Even so, she could see he was fighting for self-control. Baiting him might be good to a point, but only to that point.

"Karik," she asked, seeking to divert the conversation, "may I see to my friend?"

He gestured with the barrel of the gun, and she went to Michael. She examined the head wound carefully. It had bled a good bit, but it seemed shallow. Even as she held his head, Michael began to come around.

The Karik watched this closely and said, "This man … he means something to you, yes?"

Cloe thought hard and knew she had to detach herself from Michael. "His name is Miguel. He's one of the pilots who flew us back. He was escorting me back to my room after dinner with my friends."

Cloe hoped the Karik's men had not been watching through the peephole in the door. They would have seen the kiss. From the men's reaction to her claim, or lack thereof, they apparently had not.

The Karik studied her closely, but she did not blink. She had been studied by his better, the Kolektor.

"You lie, I think," said the man uncertainly, his hand shaking again. "But no matter. I have plans for you and your colleague. Put on some clothes that are suitable for travel."

"Oh, and what might your plans be?" asked Cloe.

"This lucky accident of finding you here has saved me a great deal of bother," replied the Karik. "My plan had been to find one of the Sicarii and persuade her to tell me where the contents of the cave have been taken. If the first could not be persuaded, then perhaps the second or the tenth."

Cloe looked at him silently. Her anger rose as she thought of the poor Sicarii he would hurt and destroy in his lust for power.

"But here you are," continued the Karik, "associate of the Sicarii. Perhaps you can be convinced to tell me where the jars have been taken."

"I don't know," said Cloe. "But if I knew, I wouldn't tell you."

"You are so brave and strong and, certainly, game. You proved that tonight," countered the Karik, gazing directly at Cloe. "But I think you do know, and I know you will tell me everything."

CHAPTER 70

J.E. wandered into the gaily lit restaurant for breakfast. He looked around, blinked several times, and realized his eyes burned. His mouth was also very dry. It was midmorning and very late by his standards, but last night's celebration of their safe return to Tunis had caused him to sleep in. Still, he had a job to do, and he would do it.

"Good morning," said the monsignor, smiling. "J.E., you look like you could use a little more sleep."

J.E. yawned and said simply, "Yes."

Father Sergio joined them in the booth.

The waitress approached, and J.E. could say only one word. "Coffee."

"Make it two," said the equally sleepy camerlengo.

"J.E., where's your mother?" asked the monsignor. "She should have been here by now."

"I don't know. She and Miguel were still dancing when we all said good night."

Coffee was served and swilled down. Father Sergio began to perk up and looked hard at the monsignor, as if he was remembering something.

"Albert, this is not like Cloe," said Father Sergio. "She has overslept before, but usually, by this time we would have heard something from her."

Now J.E. looked up, his headache, dry mouth, and burning eyes forgotten. "I'll call her right now," he said, heading for the house phone.

He dialed her room number several times, always ending up with the hotel voice-mail system. He tried another number without any success. He shook his head, slammed the phone down, and turned back to the table.

"I'm headed to her room," J.E. told the others. "There is no answer in her room or Miguel's."

Worried, the monsignor threw some bills on the table and said, "Then we are all going with you."

A few minutes later, J.E. and the others stood outside Cloe's room tapping and then banging on the door. Heads were beginning to appear in doorways down the hall.

"Nothing," said Father Sergio. "What do we do?"

"Perhaps we can get a maid or someone to let us in," replied the monsignor.

J.E. knelt down in front of the door lock and gazed at it for a long moment. "Ha," he mumbled without explanation.

He took his wallet out and drew a small pick-like tool from it. He fiddled with the lock for a few seconds, and then they were in.

The three men strode into the room. The place was a wreck. Clearly, some kind of brawl had taken place. There were splashes of blood amid overturned chairs. "What in the world?" queried the camerlengo. "What happened here?"

"J.E., please go check out Miguel's room," said the monsignor. "We'll wait here."

Five minutes later, J.E. was back. "His room has not been used at all," said J.E. "His stuff is there, but no sign anyone slept there last night. Whatever went on, it happened here."

"All your mother's things seem to be here," said the monsignor.

"Wait a minute," said J.E. from the bedroom. "Here's the dress she had on last night. She changed clothes for some reason. Her cosmetics are all here. She would not have voluntarily left these things."

"But why?" asked Father Sergio. "Why would she change?"

"So she could travel?" asked the monsignor.

"She has been taken," surmised J.E., stressed and analytical at the same time.

"Taken?" whispered Father Sergio. "As in kidnapped?"

"Wait—maybe Miguel and Cloe are still out somewhere, having a good time," responded the monsignor.

"Maybe …" said J.E. "But if so, what happened to the room? What about the blood? What about the dress?"

J.E. began to study the room very carefully. He walked back and forth and then saw something in the foyer. He bent over and picked up a reddish object. He held it up for the others to see. The room was deadly quiet. Gazing at the object, he said, "Mom never would have left this behind except as a message to us."

The others looked and saw, without doubt, the old night-vision lens from Thib's flashlight that Cloe had found in the cave. This was the very thing that had convinced everyone that it actually was Thib's chamber in the cavern. Cloe had taken it from the cave and would not part with it.

"There's only one person with the resources and the motivation to take Cloe and Miguel," said the monsignor. "It has to be the Karik."

"But all our intel said he had not returned to Tunis," said Father Sergio.

"Yes, but that was earlier," responded J.E. "Suppose he came in after us. He must have driven from El Guettar."

"The young sir must be correct," replied the monsignor. "We flew back and were here before him. Thus, our intel failed because of the timing."

"All right, now what?" asked the camerlengo. "Do we go to the police?"

Just then the phone in the suite rang, jostling everyone's nerves. They all looked at the ringing phone as if it were a coiled, poisonous snake.

Finally, J.E. edged forward and picked up the receiver. He put it to his ear but said nothing. The phone popped and crackled, but no one spoke on the other end. J.E. looked at his mates and then back at the phone before asking angrily, "What the hell do you want?"

CHAPTER 71

"We'll get to what I want," said the Karik. "You may be interested in what I already have."

There was a pause on the line, but from the sounds it was clear the phone was being shifted around.

"J.E.?" said Cloe with a steady voice. "I'm fine. Michael's fine, but has a head wound from a gun butt. Just remember, we can take care of ourselves, and I love you."

"Mom …" said J.E. But before he could say more, he heard the sound of the phone being snatched from his mother and returned to the Karik. There was something else as well, though. J.E. thought the racket sounded like an aircraft in flight.

"Your mother is fine and will remain so as long as you and she do what I want," said the Karik.

"You are a lying, no-good lowlife. Stealing a woman—where's the honor in that?" responded J.E.

The line was quiet for a moment, but J.E. knew the Karik was still there. He could feel his presence. He could now also hear the muffled sound of jet engines. The Karik had made a mistake.

"Your insults will only further injure your mother when her time comes," said the Karik. "The best thing in her future was going to be a quick, merciful death. But you have condemned her to a long, suffering passing."

J.E. gripped the phone in a crushing grasp as the monsignor and Father Sergio anxiously looked on. He spoke directly but calmly into the mouthpiece. "Karik, the best thing for your future would be to release my mother and Miguel immediately. This would extend your life expectancy considerably. If you fail to do so, you will have forfeited your miserable existence."

"Bold threats from a powerless child," replied the Karik. "Hear this: You will not contact the authorities, or your mother will die. You will not seek to follow us, or your mother will die. You will return to the United States, or your mother will die. Have I been heard?"

J.E. was silent for a moment and then said, "Until we meet again, Karik." He hung up the phone and then looked at the monsignor and Father Sergio.

"How could you hang up on him like that, J.E.?" questioned the camerlengo. "Your mother's life is at risk!"

"I don't think so, at least not immediately," said the monsignor.

"That's right," said J.E. "I would never risk Mom's life—or Miguel's, for that matter. But the Karik took them for a reason. Until his goal is satisfied, she will not be killed."

"Well ... okay, why did he take them?" asked Father Sergio.

"As you know, we surmised the Karik's strategy would be to seek out the Sicarii and torture one of them to reveal the location of the jars," said the monsignor. "I believe he learned we were in Tunis and decided to short-cut his efforts."

"What are you saying?" continued the camerlengo. "He thinks Cloe knows where the jars have been secured?"

"Yes," said J.E., struggling. "He thinks she knows. He knows of her connection to the Sicarii from Hakeldama. He might torture her, but more likely, he will torture Miguel until she tells him where the jars are. If Mom knows anything, she's a lot more likely to talk if Miguel is tortured than if she is. She's tough, and the Karik may sense that Miguel is special to her. But he will not kill her intentionally until he's satisfied he knows everything she knows."

"Horrible!" asserted Father Sergio.

"We have a little time," said J.E., his shoulders slumping.

"I agree with J.E.," said the monsignor. "But the more important question is ... does she know?"

"How could she know where they are?" queried Father Sergio. "Only the Sicarii know."

J.E. and the monsignor only looked at him.

"Oh my God," Father Sergio whispered, everything crashing down on him. "She's one of them."

"Cloe identifies with the Sicarii," said the monsignor. "They are sisters. They saved her life and J.E.'s. Is it farfetched to believe that the Sicarii would feel similarly, that they would trust her with their secrets?"

"When you put it like that, no … it isn't," the camerlengo replied. "So what do we do?"

"Well, we need to figure out where they are going," said J.E. "We need someone who can track an airplane in the air. I'm almost certain the background noise was that of a jet in flight."

"Agreed," said the monsignor. "This requires the services of an airman extraordinaire."

They all looked at each other and said with almost one voice, "Sky!"

***

While J.E. went to find and coordinate with Miguel's pilot, Sky, the monsignor left to go to the hospital to check on Father Anton and the Swiss, who had been injured in the plane crash. When he arrived, he learned that Father Anton and all but one of the Swiss had been discharged from the hospital. Tracking them to their rooms in one of the hotels close to the hospital, the monsignor climbed the stairs to the second-floor room of Father Anton.

He knocked on the door and said, "Tony?"

Heavy footsteps approached from the other side of the door, which opened promptly.

"Hello, Albert," said Father Anton. "Where in the world have you been?"

"Tony, it's a long story. How are you?" asked the monsignor, examining his colleague.

"Come in and sit down," said Father Anton.

The monsignor watched as Father Anton sat. He seemed to be slow, without energy. *What had happened to the man's spirit?* the monsignor wondered.

"Albert, the hospital was difficult, and the loss of the other men ..." Father Anton faltered.

"Yes, Tony," said the monsignor. "I understand completely. You did everything that could be done."

They sat in silence for a bit.

"But, Tony, our mission is ongoing," said the monsignor. "We have survived yet another deadly contact with the Karik, but Dr. Lejeune has been kidnapped. We have much to do."

The monsignor watched as his friend reached deep and summoned what strength he had left.

"Okay, Albert, where do we start?" asked Father Anton, straightening his shoulders.

PART III

THE PLACE OF THE SKULL

They then took charge of Jesus, and carrying his own cross he went out of the city to the place of the skull or, as it was called in Hebrew, Golgotha where they crucified him … The place where Jesus was crucified was not far from the city …

—John 19:17–18, 20 (The Jerusalem Bible, 1966)

At the place where he had been crucified there was a garden, and in this garden a new tomb in which no one had yet been buried. Since it was the Jewish Day of Preparation and the tomb was near at hand, they laid Jesus there.

—John 19:41–42 (The Jerusalem Bible, 1966)

CHAPTER 72

An hour after the monsignor had found Father Anton and the surviving Swiss Guards, they were all gathered at the Les Burges Hotel. The monsignor looked around at the assembled group. J.E., Father Sergio, Father Anton, and Sky stared back at him. There were also four Swiss, Tomás, and his four surviving men. *Not a bad team*, the monsignor thought.

"Do you have news?" asked Tomás.

"Yes," said the monsignor. "Your boss has been captured by the Karik, as has Dr. Lejeune." He related the telephone call to them.

"So what will you do?" asked Tomás. "Are you going back to the States?"

J.E. stepped up and said, "No, we intend to find and rid the world of this toad who calls himself the Karik and get my mother and Miguel back safely."

There was only silence among the embattled and wounded men.

"I know you men have suffered greatly and have been wounded," said J.E. "But we fight for what is right. If the Karik finds the jars, he will pervert their meaning. He will use them to attack the Church. Now, he has my mother and your boss. They are dead unless we can find them."

While this hung in the air, the monsignor joined J.E. in studying the men to determine their able-bodied status. There were lots of healing cuts and bruises. The main physical injuries these men had incurred were inhalation and exposure injuries. The larger damage was internal. Still, they seemed to be game. Each had tuned up as well as he could with a trim, a shave, and fresh clothes. No one had any weapons.

"J.E., my men and I are in this to the finish," said Tomás. "We will find the boss."

Father Anton spoke for himself and the Swiss. "We may look like refugees from a hospital emergency department, but we are ready. We too will see this to the end."

The monsignor could see there was color back in the face of Father Anton. Gone were the low-energy, defeated look and motions. His eyes were clear, having refocused on his duties.

"So be it then," said J.E. "What do we know?"

Tomás turned to Sky, who said, "The Karik's jet was wheels up this morning about ten o'clock from the general aviation depot of the Tunis airport. My sources tell me a flight plan was filed, but shortly after takeoff, the plane dropped below radar, and its location and direction are unknown. This is not unusual in this part of the world."

"I have been in touch with the Vatican ops center," said Father Anton, "and they report the airplane was headed east at its last observation. The monks who run the center are studying what is known about the Karik to try to determine his tendencies and whether there are any identifiable places where he may go to ground. I'm sorry to say he will need time and privacy to work on Cloe and Miguel to get what he wants."

"Yes, he will go somewhere where he feels safe and can take his time," agreed the monsignor. "Tony, we need the best efforts of Father Emilio and the monks he leads. We need some intel, and we need it now."

"Okay, we are going to triangulate this thing for information purposes," said J.E. "I still have friends in intelligence who are deployed throughout the Mediterranean. I will put out an alert to them. Sky, get with your buddies in the commercial and private flying businesses. There must be thousands of private and commercial planes in the air in this area at any given time. We know the tail number of the Karik's plane from the flight plan. Your contacts can be our eyes. Finally, Monsignor and Father Anton, please coordinate with the Vatican on what they learn."

"A sound plan, J.E.," said the monsignor.

"Tomás, what resources do we have?" asked J.E.

"Well, we have the boss's jet, which is big enough to carry all of us," said Tomás. "Beyond that, we have only the backpacks, mainly with some camping gear, that we were able to carry out of the cave-in."

"I can get us another jet," said Sky. "Rentals are available at the airport. But we have no pilot."

Father Anton looked up and said, "I'm certified as a pilot. It goes with the territory."

"With two planes, we could cover a lot more territory since we could follow multiple leads that might take us to more than one place," observed the monsignor.

"Okay, Sky, you and Father Anton get the second plane. The rest of us, gather up what gear we do have and run your intel traps. You have four hours," said J.E. "In four hours, we will be wheels up, going somewhere to find my mother and Miguel."

CHAPTER 73

The Karik sat across from Cloe and Miguel in the executive jet high above the Mediterranean Sea. Two of his thugs stood nearby, weapons at the ready. Though some of the Karik's men were refreshing themselves, neither Cloe nor Michael had been offered food or drink. The Karik had been mostly quiet.

"Where are the jars?" the Karik suddenly asked.

"Only the Sicarii know that," Cloe responded quickly.

"I think you know," said her captor.

"Only the Sicarii know," she repeated.

"She does not know," interjected Miguel. "Leave her alone."

The Karik turned his attention to Miguel and said, "You are here only for the ride. If you meddle in this again, I will have your throat cut."

"Karik, do you know who I am?" he asked.

The Karik, diverted for the moment, studied Miguel carefully. "Certainly," he finally said. "You are the *dwnwuq*, the heir. You are the Kolektor's son, his only surviving relative."

"Yes … and you tried to kill me with a bomb blast but succeeded in killing my entire family instead," said Miguel softly. "Now you have stolen my father's wealth and my inheritance."

As Cloe watched and listened closely to this match of words, she wondered about the "wealth and inheritance" remark. Michael had previously denied any interest in such things.

"Knowing that will do you no good. When I learn what I seek, you will both die," said the Karik. "I don't care who you are. Dead will be dead."

"You know, Karik, the funny thing is I had not seen my father for decades before his death. He was merely an abstraction to me. His wealth is tainted, and I have said that I want nothing of it," said Miguel. "None of this was necessary."

"I have his wealth. I have everything. You will have nothing when I'm finished," retorted the Karik angrily.

"Yes, but you have much innocent blood on your hands for which you must answer," said Miguel. "And answer you will, I promise you."

CHAPTER 74

Four hours after their meeting, J.E. had his entire crew in the air to the northeast of Tunis. They had gathered their meager gear, and it was stowed aboard the lead jet, Miguel's big Citation. They had scored a second plane, a smaller Learjet, and Father Anton was flying it a thousand feet below, on their six.

J.E. had been able to buy two satellite phones with encryption capabilities at an electronics shop on the way to the airport. They would now have confidential communications both with each other and with their various intelligence sources. Although none of their sources had been able to give them anything on the Karik, they did have a destination: Rome.

"Everything we know suggests the Karik headed eastward," said the monsignor. "It could be due east, southeast, or northeast."

"Or it could be a head fake," said J.E.

The monsignor looked puzzled, but the young camerlengo interpreted. "A feint, Albert."

"Ah, perhaps, but remember, the Kolektor was rumored to have a safe house in the region where he grew up on the Turkish-Armenian border," said the monsignor.

So J.E. and the rest thought east was the correct direction. Stopping in Rome en route would not take too much time or put them too far afield. In Rome, they could resupply and, importantly, secure the weapons this mission would surely require.

"Monsignor, it feels funny going back to Rome for weapons, among other things," said J.E. "The Vatican is a holy institution invested in peace. We're seeking death-dealing guns and ammo. Isn't that inconsistent?"

"It might appear so at first, J.E., but the guns will only be used in self-defense," said the monsignor. "Even the pope's personal guard must be armed in this day and age. There are simply too many people out there who have no scruples about violence. Sometimes, evil has to be fought on evil's terms."

"Amazing," said J.E. "I still can't get used to the tactical capability of the Vatican."

"The Vatican is a sovereign state as well as the seat of Catholicism," replied the camerlengo. "It must adapt to the modern world as best it can."

The call light on the satellite phone flashed. J.E. picked it up and answered. "Monsignor, it's for you—the ops center."

The monsignor put his ear to the phone and listened intently. He then hit the speaker button and turned up the volume to maximum so that the conversation could just be heard over the engines.

"Albert, that's what we know now," said the voice. "We went back and studied the tapes of satellite observations for the time shortly after Hakeldama. We know one of the Kolektor's men got away from Jerusalem in the Kolektor's jet."

"That could be our man, Father Emilio," said the monsignor.

"The plane landed at a relatively small municipal airport in Turkey near the Turkish-Armenian border. I'll send the coordinates via cell phone," said the priest on the other end of the phone.

"Anything else?" asked the monsignor.

"No, that is it," said Father Emilio. "But I would add that the same plane has made that trip several times before, according to the tapes."

"Very good, Father," replied the monsignor. "Do you have anything on the Karik's lair?"

"Nothing on the Karik at all, but we believe the Kolektor had a place in the mountains on the border. We don't have a precise location, but it must be relatively close to this airport," said the priest.

"Thank you, Father. Please let me know if you find anything else," said the monsignor as he rang off.

J.E. looked around at the rest and said, "I think we now have our second destination."

***

A couple of hours later, Sky had landed the plane at Rome's Ciampino Airport, the closest to the Vatican. The Swiss Guard was there waiting with supplies and medics. Very shortly thereafter, Father Anton landed with his Swiss soldiers. A quick examination indicated that all the men were battle-ready although cut and bruised. Bandages were changed and antibiotics administered. As the jets were being refueled, supplies and weapons were transferred and stowed.

While all this was ongoing, J.E., Father Anton, Sky, and the monsignor conferred with Father Emilio, who had driven out to the airport with the Swiss.

"Our intel sources at the small airport in Turkey where we think the Karik may have gone report that someone important keeps a helicopter on alert at the airport. The man is rarely seen, but when he comes, the copter is ready and flies him off into the nearby mountains."

"Excellent, Father Emilio," said the monsignor. "That is our destination. Can you arrange for a helicopter to be available for our use?"

"I can, but given how these things work, you would be well advised to rent a car and drive into the mountains," the old monk responded. "There can't be too many places up there that would suit the Karik, and it's likely the Karik has spies at the airport who would report an extraordinary event like the rental of a helicopter."

"Quite right, Father," said the monsignor, considering the situation. "We will be slower by car, but we may preserve the element of surprise."

The jets were idling as the last of the supplies were loaded. The monsignor boarded the lead plane and turned to say thanks and good-bye to Father Emilio. He reached out and took the thin hand of the ops center leader.

"Albert," said the old warrior monk, clutching his hand with a fierce grip, "go get our friends."

CHAPTER 75

The plane had landed in the gathering evening, and they had been transferred to a waiting helicopter. After the gear was loaded, the helicopter had flown off toward the looming mountains, now almost purple in the dusk.

Not all the Karik's men had been able to go in the helicopter. Cloe had seen some loading into Range Rovers as they took off. Doubtless, those men were following by road.

As Cloe studied the Karik, who had largely kept to himself since the dustup with Michael, she reviewed her feelings about the fact that Michael was the son of the monster who had shot and almost killed her. His blood flowed in Michael's veins. Still, Michael had hardly known his father and seemed to completely repudiate him and his great wealth. Yet what did she really know about Michael?

The helicopter landed, and they were walked quickly into a large chalet-style house. Immediately, she and Michael were taken to a basement holding area. A steel-barred cell had been installed there. The Karik himself went off in another direction, into what looked to Cloe like living quarters.

The steel door clanked shut, the Karik's men retreated, and she and Michael were left in total darkness. It was such a heavy blackness that Cloe felt the physical weight of it. She moved toward where she had last seen Michael and whispered his name.

Though he had to be relatively near, the reply came back as if from a great distance. "I'm here, Cloe."

"Michael, what are we going to do?" asked Cloe.

"Well, we are in a lot of trouble," replied Michael. "We are in the lion's den. He wants what he thinks you know."

"Yes, he thinks I know where the Sicarii have taken the jars," said Cloe.

"Do you?"

Cloe was silent for several moments. "Only the Sicarii know," she finally responded. "Why would you ask me that?"

"Because if they think you care about what happens to me, they will use me to get to you," he responded. "I'd like to know that I'm part of a good cause."

"You know your cause, and it's different from mine," Cloe said. "I'm so sorry about your family. The man, this Karik, is a monster."

"At some point he will come for the information he wants. He will kill us both to get it," stated Michael flatly.

"Michael, I'm very scared, but I don't know anything," said Cloe. "What can I do?"

"Maybe there is some clue, something you know, without knowing its importance, that could help us," suggested Michael.

Now something was beginning to nibble at Cloe. Was Michael trying to get information out of her? Or was he just trying to find something to feed to the Karik to satisfy him for a while? She hated to think it, but was it possible that Michael's insistence about not caring about the jars and his father's wealth was an act? Was it possible he and the Karik were somehow in this together? No, she could not abide that. Every instinct told her no. Still …

"Michael, in your early years did you ever know the man who calls himself the Karik?" she probed.

Silence.

"Go to sleep, Cloe. You will need your rest," Michael finally whispered.

CHAPTER 76

The monsignor gazed out the small, hard port that passed for a window on the jet. They had left Rome and then Italy behind and were now headed east. J.E. was dozing opposite him. Most of the rest of the men were preparing in some way for battle, cleaning weapons, sharpening knives, or trying to get some last rest before … before what? Before they found the Karik, liberated his captives, and pulled the Kolektor's network out by its roots. *Never again*, he thought.

***

The monsignor started awake. He must have nodded off.

He looked at the radium dial on his watch. About two hours had elapsed since they departed Rome. They should be in the vicinity of the target. He looked out the window but could discern nothing in the darkness. Still the plane seemed to be descending.

J.E.'s eyes popped open, and he too looked around, assessing the situation. "Monsignor, where are we?" he asked.

"I'm not sure. I'll ask Sky," the monsignor responded, standing and moving toward the cockpit.

Before he could enter the cockpit, Tomás, who was seated a row or two ahead of them, grabbed him and said, "I think we approach the place my boss always talked about growing up before he was sent to Rio."

"Miguel? Miguel talked of this place?" asked the monsignor.

"Yes, he was only a child then, and he did not know where it was, but this must be it. He knew it was in the mountains in Turkey," responded Tomás. "He spoke of being with his father and the good times they had."

"I see," said the monsignor.

"But of course, he was only a small child," repeated Tomás.

The monsignor moved on into the cockpit, but he was back in a moment, plopping down across from J.E. "We are a few hundred miles from the area where the Karik's hideout may be located," said the monsignor. "We are about an hour out. I have asked Sky to take us down when we are close and fly along the mountains so we can see if we can spot the lights of the Karik's lair."

"All good, Albert," said J.E.

"Funny thing, J.E.," said the monsignor. "Tomás says Miguel remembers his childhood with the Kolektor here in Turkey."

"Yes?" replied J.E.

"Fondly," said the monsignor.

CHAPTER 77

The incredible brilliance of the lights flashed against Cloe's sleeping eyes. For a few moments she did not know where she was. Rough hands grabbed her and dragged her from the cell into the open area of the basement. Her hands were bound behind her back with wire. She was slapped into a hard wooden chair and surrounded by the Karik's thugs.

"What? What do you want?" she cried. "Where is Michael?"

For a while there was no answer. After a bit, the Karik and his servant, Noosh, joined the other hoodlums in the room.

"Well, Dr. Lejeune, now is the time for truth," said the Karik. "Where are the jars? I have no time for lies or delay. You put the Kolektor off with your endless stories, but I will not be fooled."

"Karik, I have told you—only the Sicarii know where they have been taken," she responded.

Noosh reached forward and backhanded Cloe across the face, almost knocking her from the chair. Cloe recoiled and tasted blood from her split lip. She stared straight ahead and said nothing. Generations of stubborn Lejeune genes locked into place, reinforcing her resolve. This murderer would get nothing from her.

The Karik looked at her expression, turned, and considered the situation. After a moment, he nodded at one of his henchmen, who flipped a nearby switch that lit a heretofore darkened corner of the basement.

Cloe gasped in shock at what she saw. A man, naked, had been bound with wire in what almost looked like a fetal position. He was hanging from a cable fixed to an overhead beam and attached to the wire binding him. He was slowly turning into the light. The metal bands of the wire wrapped him so tightly that Cloe wondered how the poor soul could breathe.

"Where are the jars?" asked the Karik patiently.

Cloe was silent, studying the bound man across the room. As he revolved, she could see his shoulder and then his face. Cloe screamed a terrible scream from the bottom of her soul as she recognized Michael. She felt hot and cold. Her heart rattled in her chest. She thought she might pass out.

"You worthless bastard!" she screeched at the Karik. "He knows nothing and has done nothing."

"Where are the jars?"

"Only the Sicarii know," Cloe said mechanically.

The Karik nodded at his retainer.

Whoosh. Cloe heard the sound of a fire lighting. She looked more carefully and saw that Michael had been suspended over a fire pit of some kind, this one lined with gas jets. The blue-orange flames began to lick upward. Michael started to struggle against the wire bindings, which only caused him to be more tightly constrained.

The room was becoming warmer. Cloe could now smell the pungent odor of burning hair. There was something else, but she could not force herself to think about Michael being burned alive. She heard Michael scream as the flames reached out to him.

"It is an old Armenian torture that we usually reserve for the Turks, but regardless, it is remarkably effective," said the Karik coolly. "Where are the jars?"

Cloe glanced at Michael and saw his skin beginning to turn a bright red, as if he had been in the sun way too long. The reek of burning hair and now flesh was pervasive. Michael screamed again.

"Tell them nothing, Cloe," cried Michael, hoarsely.

Cloe could hear the intense pain in his voice. How could she ever have suspected that Michael and the Karik were working together? Cloe was devastated that she had ever questioned Michael. But what could she do? There was nothing left to do but try to stay at the table. After the Karik finished with Michael, doubtless, the same fate awaited her. What would that gain?

"Karik," she said urgently, "I do not know where the jars have been taken, but I know a location, a certain place. Whether they are there or not, I can't say for sure. If you will take Michael down immediately, I will take you there."

"I do not believe you," said the Karik. "This is more of your trickery."

"No, the Sicarii were in the mountains when we got out of the cave. I spent some time in their camp. They talked of this place when they thought I was asleep," she responded. "The jars may be there, or it may be something else altogether. But it's all I have."

The Karik studied her very closely. She thought she might wilt under his gaze, but she summoned inner strength and stared resolutely back at him.

"Turn off the fire," he said. Immediately, his thugs cut the gas jets under Michael.

Cloe wondered how much damage had been done. Michael just hung there; he seemed to be unconscious.

"Come then," said the Karik.

"No, I want Michael down and given medical treatment," Cloe responded. "I'm not going anywhere without him."

"That was not part of our bargain, Dr. Lejeune," said the Karik. "We go. He stays. He is my insurance. If you have lied, his death will be most terrible."

"How do I know you won't kill him anyway?" Cloe demanded.

"How do I know you aren't just taking me on some wild-goose chase, hoping your friends will find you?" parried the Karik.

There it is, Cloe thought. She was making another deadly pact with a homicidal maniac. First the Kolektor and now this Karik. They had to trust each other to a point and look for opportunity.

"Very well, Karik," she replied after a bit. "I will take you to the location I know, but you will keep Michael safe and give him proper medical treatment."

"Done," said the Karik. "But if you fail, he dies, and you die. The only question will be whether I will bring you back here to watch."

CHAPTER 78

As they flew along the arched backbone of the mountainous ridge, J.E. stared out the window of the jet. They had seen a couple of faint patches of lights that could have signaled the Karik's hideout, but nothing that they had observed was sure. *How could anyone be sure from this height in the dark?* J.E. wondered.

Landing at the small airport in the early morning hours was its own challenge. The airport was uncontrolled at that time of night. Although there were basic red and blue lighted markers, there was no one to turn on the landing lights. Still, Sky and then Father Anton in the second plane somehow put the executive jets down on the main runway, and soon they were taxiing to the private terminal.

The important thing at present was a vehicle. This was a delicate operation because they needed transportation immediately, but they dared not do anything that would set the Turkish authorities after them.

Deplaning, J.E. looked about and saw several vans and trucks that either belonged to the airport or perhaps were rentals. As he studied them and considered his options, a truck made its way up the hill toward the airport. In a clashing of gears and squealing of brakes, it edged up to and stopped in front of the commissary.

J.E. realized after a moment that it was a milk truck making its morning delivery. He grinned and said, "Albert, I think our transportation problem has been solved."

A few minutes and a hundred American dollars later, the truck headed up the road into the mountains, belching thick blue smoke and loaded with all their men and gear, with J.E. riding shotgun. J.E.

had left Sky and one of the Swiss to refuel the planes and to make sure they were safe and ready to go when they needed them. The old milkman, an Armenian, spoke no English, but he knew the value of a dollar. Because he delivered milk in the area, he also knew the place where the helicopters from the airport went when they flew into the mountains. The monsignor spoke enough Armenian that he had been able to learn that vital piece of information.

Two hours later, they were staged outside the Karik's mountain lair. The Swiss were in tactical gear, including bulletproof armor and camouflage fatigues. Though supremely disciplined, they were nevertheless itching for a fight after the plane crash and the cave-in where their comrades had been lost.

"J.E., what do you think?" asked the monsignor.

Both J.E. and Father Anton had been observing the chalet-style house with their binoculars for several minutes. It was cool here in the mountains, but J.E. was sweating under his battle gear.

"There's not much activity," said J.E. finally. "I wonder if this is the right place."

"The milkman assures us that this is where the helicopters come," said Father Anton. "Our scouts report a helicopter pad to the rear, although there is no helicopter there now. This must be it."

"What about electronic defenses?" asked J.E. "Have we detected anything?"

"Nothing," said the Swiss soldier who was manning the portable computer with the field sensors. "Everything is cold and dark. No infrared, heat, or other defenses. There's just the standard household alarm system, but it has not been engaged. He must think himself safe because of the location. There were two heavily armed sentries, but our men have disabled them."

J.E. said, "Wait here. I'm going to move up and reconnoiter the situation."

J.E. swung away from the assembly and moved cautiously from tree to tree toward the semidark house. There didn't seem to be any movement within. He reached the side of the mountain retreat near where a wide porch wrapped around the entrance and one side. Mounting the steps and climbing to the deck, he peered inside through at first one and then several floor-to-ceiling windows. At last, he could see flickering lights from what appeared to be a room at the top of a staircase.

Father Anton and several of the Swiss now joined him on the porch.

"From the foyer window, the only sign of life I see is at the top of the stairs," he whispered. "It could be a television."

Father Anton looked up at the glittering light. J.E. tried the door knob, but it was firmly locked and probably bolted. He was not sure they could jimmy the door without whoever was inside hearing them. They needed to know exactly where Cloe was and what her situation was before attacking.

He signaled to Father Anton that he needed to reconnoiter the room where the light originated. He climbed up an ornamental facade to the second-floor roof and crept along the wooden shingles to the nearest window. It was a dormer-style window extruding from the roof on the top floor. Although the Swiss had machine pistols, J.E. was armed with his trusty .45 automatic. He moved quickly but very carefully. He studied the scene inside and then returned to the porch and the waiting troops.

"The window opens into the room at the top of the stairs," he said. "There are four men on one side of the room playing cards and watching TV. On the other side of the room, there is a bed with someone in it. I can't see who it is."

"That could be Dr. Lejeune," said Father Anton. "But if so, where's Miguel?"

"I don't know," whispered J.E. "It could be either one of them or neither of them."

They looked at each other as military men do. Both knew they had to act, but neither knew all that he would have to know to make sure no innocent was hurt. "We have to safeguard my mother and Miguel," said J.E.

"Agreed," replied Father Anton. "I'll put one of my men on the roof outside the window with a flash grenade. We will rig the front door with explosives. At the agreed time, my man will shatter the glass and throw the grenade through the window. We'll blow the door and rush the men inside. If we execute properly, they will have no chance."

"All good," said J.E. "Except I'll be on the roof with the flash grenade. After I throw it in, I'll follow and put myself between the bed and the men inside. When you get there, make sure your fire is to your left as you enter. I'll protect the right."

Father Anton looked carefully at J.E. "Agreed," he said finally, reluctant to put J.E. in danger.

They both looked at the luminescent dials of their watches, and J.E. called out, "Five minutes on my mark ... now."

As J.E. scrambled back up toward the roof, he saw the priest's men lining the door with explosives.

J.E. was now in position at the window. He examined the card-playing guards to his right. They were armed to the teeth. This had to go down just right. J.E. strained to see who might be in the bed to his left. It was large, with a canopy overhead. Whether because of mosquitoes or for privacy, it had a sheer drape around it. This made it hard to see who was inside. He knew when he went through the window, he would be exposed. There was nothing he could do about that but come up firing and hope the Swiss would be entering the door at that time to back him up.

J.E. watched as the seconds ticked down to the five-minute mark. He was not afraid. If anything, he was exhilarated. He had received the finest training the world could offer. He was ready.

The five-minute mark tolled, and J.E. heard the explosives blow the door below to hell. He gave a three-second count, thinking it would take Father Anton's men that long to head up the stairs. Just as the guards were rising from their chairs and reaching for their weapons, J.E. smashed the glass and pitched the flash grenade through the window. He jumped back around the dormer window frame to avoid the blast.

BLAM! Light and smoke blew out through the window. J.E. dove through what remained of the window, rolled, and came up in the firing position with his .45 aimed at the Karik's men. Smoke from the grenade filled the room, so it was hard to see. The guards had all been knocked to the floor. One seemed to be out cold, but the others were slowly getting up. They seemed to be moving in slow motion.

Suddenly, Father Anton and the Swiss burst through the bedroom door, weapons in the ready position. The guards were covered from two different potential fields of fire.

J.E. could not tell where the first shot came from, but immediately chaos erupted. J.E. and Father Anton's men poured fire into the hapless guards. J.E. heard a shot from his left pass his ear very closely, and then he was hit by a second shot. He went down hard against the wall near where the window had been. The world seemed filled with gunfire and smoke. He tried to get up, but then there was only blackness.

CHAPTER 79

"I'll tell you when we are in the air," said Cloe with determination.

They had taken the helicopter from the lair back to the airport. All the while, the Karik had pressured her to reveal their destination.

The Karik's jet was ready to go when they arrived to the faint, but rising, eastern light. The helicopter landed, and she was whisked onto the jet, but not before she caught a glimpse of Sky. He was in a shadow, leaning against a wall by the general aviation facility with a cigarette dangling from the corner of his mouth. He looked directly at her and nodded slightly.

Cloe knew there was nothing he could do against the heavily armed force that guarded the Karik. But where was J.E.? She guessed that Sky had been left behind to attend to the equipment while J.E. and the rest had gone after her and Michael. For the thousandth time since she had left the chalet, her heart hurt for the pain and torture to which Michael had been subjected. He had been so brave. She did not even know if he was alive.

Even now, she imagined J.E. and his forces were storming the Karik's hideout. He would find Michael, if he was alive, and free him. Then, J.E., the monsignor, and the Swiss would be after her. But, she worried, how would they find her? It would not be easy, but she knew J.E. would not give up. She smiled slightly as she considered the fate of this beast who called himself the Karik.

She was thrown into a seat on the plane, and immediately it began its taxi to the main runway. As they turned, she saw the second jet in line behind them. Doubtless, it was filled with the Karik's henchmen and their weapons. The plane paused at the end of the runway as its mighty engines wound up, the brakes locking the steel bird on the ground. Suddenly, the pilots released the tether, and the metal cylinder that could not possibly fly raced down the tarmac and leaped into the sky, its fiery signature trailing behind.

As the jet reached its cruising altitude, the Karik leaned toward Cloe, seated opposite him, and said, "Now! What is our destination?"

She looked at him with disdain and said only a single word: "Jerusalem."

CHAPTER 80

"J.E. … J.E.," called a voice that seemed a long distance away. Someone was lightly slapping his face and alternately washing it down with a rag soaked in cold water.

"What the …?" said J.E. haltingly. Finally, his eyes opened, and he looked up to see the monsignor, concern evident on his face.

"J.E.," said the monsignor with a gasp. "Are you all right?"

J.E. took inventory. He felt pretty terrible, so he wasn't sure. He should have felt a lot worse, though, if he had been gravely wounded or was dying. J.E. looked around and saw they had moved him from the wall near the window where he had fallen to one side of the bed. "What happened?" he asked.

"We're not sure," replied the monsignor. "When we broke in, someone fired, and the Swiss destroyed the Karik's thugs. We found you knocked out."

"Where's Mom? Is she here?" asked J.E., suddenly remembering the mission to rescue Cloe.

"No. She's not here. The Swiss are clearing the rest of the building, but it looks like she has been taken away," replied the monsignor.

"Who was in the bed?" asked J.E., trying to rise.

"Miguel. He seems to have been injured, perhaps tortured," said the priest. "We can't get much out of him at this point."

"I jumped through the window and had the drop on the Karik's men," said J.E. thoughtfully. "Then a shot was fired, and all hell broke loose. I remember one round missed me, but not by much. Then I was hit. That's all I can recall."

"As best we can tell, you were hit on your left side, but your body armor deflected it," recounted the monsignor.

"Yes," added Father Anton, joining the group. "But it banged off the armor, knocking you backward, and ricocheted against your helmet hard enough to ring your bell."

"You have not been wounded, but you probably have a slight concussion," concluded the monsignor.

"Where's Miguel now?" asked J.E., rolling off the bed and stumbling to his feet.

"He's getting medical treatment in the next bedroom," replied Father Anton. "He's been burned."

J.E. surveyed the scene, the Karik's men dead around the card table, and then he wobbled his way out of the room and down the hall into the next bedroom.

The Swiss medic was swabbing Miguel down with some salve. J.E. sat down and studied him. He appeared to be awake but certainly not alert. "Traumatized" was the best word J.E. could think of.

He turned to the medic and asked, "How is he? Can I talk to him?"

"He's in better shape than I would have expected after what apparently happened to him," said the medic. "Though painful, his injuries are not physically serious."

"Miguel, what can you tell me?" asked J.E.

Miguel looked up in obvious pain, but he stuffed it back and said, "They grabbed us in the hotel room. I walked your mother back to the room, and we went in for a drink." He paused, and J.E. was unsure whether he could continue. He was bent over and looked wretched. "We were overwhelmed by the Karik and his armed thugs," said Miguel. "I think they might have killed me then except for your mother's intervention. But because she did intervene, the Karik saw that I might mean something to Cloe. He saw his advantage."

"Go on," whispered J.E.

"They took us to the airport, and we flew here. Cloe and I were locked in a cell in the basement. In the night they came for us," said Miguel. "They tied me up with wire and suspended me over a fire pit.

Later they brought your mother in and, by torturing me, forced her to help them. I pleaded with her not to tell them anything."

J.E. looked up at the monsignor, who along with Father Sergio had followed him into the room, and gritted his teeth with anger.

Father Sergio stepped forward and said, "J.E., I'm so sorry. Somehow, if it's God's will, we will find your mother." The young camerlengo found himself riveted in the stares of his friends. J.E.'s Tchefuncte River–brown eyes and the monsignor's steel-gray orbs targeted him like lasers.

"We will find her," said J.E.

The monsignor turned to the assembled force of soldiers clustered in the doorway and ordered, "Bring all the bodies downstairs. Lay them, respectfully, on a funeral bier of the wooden furniture and then burn it … burn everything! Burn this God-cursed house to the ground."

CHAPTER 81

Cloe watched the Karik as they flew toward Jerusalem. He sat on one side of the posh wooden table on the executive jet and she on the other. Noosh had served him some refreshment. It seemed this morning his idea of an elegant snack was iced tea and a peanut butter and jelly sandwich. Cloe had laughed to herself when it was served. It was certainly a far cry from the Kolektor's favorite, caviar and toast points, served, of course, with a dry white or perhaps a frozen gin on the rocks. *The Kolektor must be spinning in his grave*, she thought. This was his successor?

He saw her disdain, smiled, and said, "Think what you like, but you will take me to what I want."

She knew that in some ways the Karik was but a pale imitation of the Kolektor, but he was very clever and as vicious, if not more so. She had to marvel at the man's single focus: the jars. He never lost that point of concentration. She had to keep her own counsel and look for opportunity to escape this monster. She felt the plane begin its descent, presumably into Jerusalem. It would not be long before the Karik would start pressing her for the destination.

Later, after the jet had landed, Cloe was led to the waiting van and seated in the second row in the rear. The Karik sat in the front seat. After their gear and the men had been transferred to their vehicles, the Karik turned around to her and said simply, "Where?"

Cloe had thought about her predicament, but no strategy had immediately manifested itself. She believed, but could not be entirely sure, that J.E. was following her. The problem was how he would possibly track her through the skies. "Gordon's Calvary," she said at last.

"Explain," responded the Karik immediately.

"I can't explain what I don't know," she replied. "All I can tell you is that I heard the Sicarii mention Gordon's Calvary. That's it."

"I know the place from our time in Jerusalem," the Karik said after a time. "It's outside the old city's walls but near Golgotha, supposedly the place where Jesus Christ was crucified."

"Yes. Gordon's Calvary and the Garden Tomb, as some call it, are places that came to public attention a little over a hundred years ago under interesting circumstances," said Cloe. "I have read about it in my work." Cloe caught herself discussing these things as with an old colleague rather than a murderous adversary. She would tell him no more.

After a period of silence, the Karik queried, "Dr. Lejeune? Have you lost interest in our scientific inquiry?"

"I have only agreed to take you to the place I heard the Sicarii discussing," she said. "Whatever the historical ramifications, they are irrelevant."

"You will do much more than that," replied the Karik, anger flashing and his voice rising. "You will do and say what I want, and you will tell me what I want to know. You will take me to the jars. Are we perfectly clear? Your friend Miguel is back at my mountain retreat under my power. Are we clear?"

Cloe felt like she had been slapped. She had no power. She was simply a pawn. Michael was the lever. The Karik would use him to get what he wanted from her, and then he would kill them both. Still, something the Karik had said had caught her attention. What was it? Cloe couldn't focus enough to figure it out. It was something important. It would come to her.

CHAPTER 82

Now seated on the jet, J.E. reflected on the past few hours. The Karik's hideout had been thoroughly searched and then burned. J.E. had every expectation that after the fire they had set, there would be nothing left but ashes. Evil, he felt, had been pushed back by the flames.

The jet rose, glistening in the morning sun, and in spite of the engine noise, J.E. heard the monsignor's satellite phone buzz.

"Hello," said the monsignor. After a bit the monsignor hung up and came over to him. "J.E., that was the ops center." The priest almost had to yell to be heard over the engines. "The Karik's plane popped up on radar a while ago. They are headed toward the Middle East."

"But what's their destination?" asked J.E.

"Unknown. It could be anywhere in the region," responded the monsignor.

"Did we find anything at the chalet to help us?" pressed J.E.

"Maybe," said Father Anton. "My men searched the cell in which we think Cloe and probably Miguel were held during the night. We found something, but we can't tell if Cloe left it or if it's just graffiti."

"What is it?" asked J.E. "We need something to go on."

"Well, we found the words 'Gordon's Cav' scratched on the wall behind the bunk," responded the priest. "It was where it could not be seen unless one was looking for it. The *v* was partially scratched out."

"Hmmm," mused the monsignor. "Gordon's Cav. What could that be? Or should we omit the *v* and just think of something that starts with 'Gordon's Ca'?"

"Well, one thing I know from my military history is there was a famous British general in the late 1900s who was something of a Mideast explorer—General Charles Gordon," ventured J.E. "Could 'Cav' be a reference to cavalry?"

J.E. looked around and saw that everyone was stumped, everyone except Father Sergio; he was chewing on something. "What is it, Serge?" he asked, raising his voice over the sound of the plane's engines.

"If I remember my religious history correctly, Gordon, a Protestant, was looking for an alternate burial site for Jesus," said the camerlengo.

"Yes, yes!" cried the monsignor. "The message was not 'Gordon's Cav' but 'Gordon's Calvary.' That's why Cloe scratched out the *v*. Gordon thought he discovered not just an alternate burial site but a different site for the crucifixion—in effect, a new and different Calvary."

"Right, Albert. It's called Gordon's Calvary, and the burial site is referred to as the Garden Tomb," said the young camerlengo.

"What do we know about it?" asked J.E.

"What we know comes straight from the Bible, largely from the Gospel of St. John," responded the monsignor. "Christ was crucified at a place called Golgotha and buried nearby in a newly hewn rock-cut tomb belonging to Joseph of Arimathaea, a pious man."

"The orthodox site of Jesus's burial is within the Church of the Holy Sepulchre," continued Father Sergio. "The place thought to be Golgotha, or Mount Calvary as it is sometimes described, is nearby."

"It was hardly a mountain even in those times," said the monsignor. "It was more of a large rock marking the place of executions. *Calvary* means 'skull' in ancient Latin. This is an equivalent for Golgotha, which means, to some, 'place of executions.'"

"Amazing, but if that's where Christ was crucified and buried, what's all this about an alternate Calvary?" queried J.E. "Surely, all this must have long since been settled."

"One would think so," said the monsignor, rubbing his hands together and warming to the details of the story. "However, it seems affairs in Jerusalem, particularly about religion, are never simple and are rarely completely settled. As layer upon layer of history is pulled back by modern science and even amateur exploration, a thing once thought to be fully known and sure may not be so or stay so."

"Oh, Albert, for goodness' sake, in point of fact there are issues—some would say problems—with the traditional site at the Church of the Holy Sepulchre," said the camerlengo impatiently.

"Sergio, you are correct," said the monsignor. "The site of the burial and nearby crucifixion of Christ at the place now marked by the Church of the Holy Sepulchre is plainly within the walls of even ancient Jerusalem. This is part of the problem. It is an undisputed fact that the Jews of that time did not permit a burial within the city except in the case of their kings. So unless the Jews were implicitly accepting Jesus as their king, he could not have been buried within the city walls. Thus, the argument goes that the Church of the Holy Sepulchre, which is located within the walls, is not the true burial place of Christ. This calls into question the whole location of the crucifixion."

J.E. looked around at Father Anton and the Swiss to see what their reaction might be to the suggestion that the burial site of Christ, thought to be known and revered for two thousand years, might be in doubt. He smiled to see that the warriors were all fast asleep, saving themselves for more practical challenges to come in the future.

"This is hard to figure," said J.E. "The Church of the Holy Sepulchre has marked Christ's traditional burial site for almost two thousand years. Yet you are telling me there's doubt about this."

"Yes," said the camerlengo. "But you have to know a little about how we got there. For the first three or four hundred years of church history, the best written evidence of the location of Calvary and the burial site was in the four Gospels. Variously, Matthew, Mark, Luke, and John chronicled that the crucifixion location was outside the walls of Jerusalem at a place known as Calvary. The burial site was in a garden near the place of the crucifixion. It was close to the city but near a road. Of course, everyone agrees that the tomb itself was that of Joseph of Arimathaea, newly hewn out of native rock. That's it. The exact location for the first several hundred years was handed down by oral tradition."

"Fascinating," said the monsignor. "In the time of Constantine, he marked the site with a church, a basilica. This was around the year 326. Since then, numerous churches erected to mark the spot have been burned or destroyed by invaders, and successor churches eventually rebuilt. This has not been a static situation."

"So what does Gordon's Calvary have to do with all this?" asked J.E.

"Well, late in the day, in the eighteenth century, people began to question the exact location of the burial site, in part due to the problem of Jewish law making it illegal for burials within the walls of the city," responded the monsignor. "There were other issues with the orthodox site, but this was the most important one."

"Later, General Gordon, in the nineteenth century and perhaps with more modern exploration techniques, posited a theory of the true Calvary being outside the city walls at the site now known as Gordon's Calvary, with the burial site at the Garden Tomb," said Father Sergio.

"Why would anyone believe that Gordon's Calvary was the true site after so many years of venerating the orthodox site at the Church of the Holy Sepulchre?" asked J.E.

"Well, as we have discussed, the Jewish tradition of not burying anyone but their kings within the city walls is a given fact that's very difficult to refute," replied the monsignor. "Lately, the exercise has turned to trying to identify exactly where the ancient walls at the time of Christ might have been located. The thought is that perhaps there is an even more ancient wall than is known today that might have left the Holy Sepulchre site outside."

"Has anything like that been discovered?" asked J.E.

"There's nothing satisfactory as of now," replied Father Sergio, speaking over the engines. "So we are left with a dilemma. The Gospels and Jewish tradition are clear that the site was outside the walls of the city, but the Holy Sepulchre is within the known walls. Either there was another wall or ..."

"Or what?" queried J.E., beginning to grow impatient and wondering how this could lead them to his mother.

"Or," said the camerlengo, "as we've been discussing, the site thought to be the very site of Christ's death and burial for two thousand years, and venerated as such, is not the correct location."

CHAPTER 83

In Jerusalem, the air was cool, and a light rain was coming off the mountains. All the Karik's men and their equipment were loaded in two large vans. Cloe heard the Karik discussing his options with Noosh. He wanted to leave his main body of men at the airport and go into the city with a smaller group to search Gordon's Calvary for clues of the jars. But he couldn't know whether the trail was a short one or a long one. Everything he knew suggested that this was only a way-stop and not the final destination. But where was the end point? Was it a mile away or a thousand miles? Therefore, not knowing, he had to take everybody and everything with him. Cloe realized this would slow him down.

In the van, Cloe gazed out the window as they sped through the Old City. She could not help but remember a similar journey months earlier when she was the captive of the Kolektor. *Where would this path end?* she wondered.

The Karik said, "Dr. Lejeune, in my time with my master, he talked occasionally of Gordon's Calvary. What do you know of this place?"

"Not much, Karik," she responded. "Some rubbish about an alternate site for the death and burial of Christ."

"Rubbish?" mused the Karik. "I wonder. There is so much under heaven and earth that is not known. We shall see."

Cloe thought about this response. Had she misjudged this man? There seemed more depth in his contemplation. As she watched, they pulled into the back parking lot of a modern bus station.

"What are we doing here?" she asked.

"We are near the place of Gordon's Calvary," responded Noosh.

These were the first words the servant had spoken directly to her, and she could sense his excitement at the moment. She wondered if Noosh might be a closet Christian. She studied him closely and thought he might be of Middle Eastern origin, perhaps Egyptian. Could he be a Coptic? She realized it was more likely that he was Armenian like most of the others in the Karik's employ, but many Armenians were also Christians.

As she exited the van and looked around, Cloe was almost paralyzed by the irony. Here she was in the back parking lot of a contemporary bus station searching for a site that might be the alternate location of a two-thousand-year-old crucifixion and burial.

"Karik, there must be some mistake," she said as one of the buses, belching smoke, pulled out loaded with travelers. "There's nothing here but asphalt and buses."

The Karik seemed to be caught up in the mystery and majesty of the moment, but he said nothing. He simply stared off in the distance at a rock cliff formation.

"Dr. Lejeune, what do you see there?" asked Noosh respectfully, pointing at the rock face.

Cloe turned and studied the rocks, and suddenly her breath was taken from her. "Oh my God!" she exclaimed.

"Yes," the Karik said matter-of-factly.

"It's ... a skull!" she said, looking at the gaunt openings of granite eye sockets and a gross aperture that appeared to be a stony mouth, all framed by the cliff face. In between, there was a rock slash of a nose. It was like looking at a puzzle whose disparate features suddenly come into focus.

"Golgotha!" cried Noosh.

CHAPTER 84

"The Karik's plane descended below our radar, but our satellites tell us it landed in Jerusalem," said the chief of the spy monks in the Vatican ops center on the other end of the satellite link, now on speaker with volume turned up fully.

"Father Emilio, we need to know anything you and your monks can tell us about Gordon's Calvary," said J.E.

"We have a good deal of historical information on General Gordon and his theory of finding an alternate Calvary," replied Father Emilio. "I'll relay what we have by e-mail link to your phones."

"Thank you, Reverend Father," responded the monsignor as they all made ready for landing.

J.E. gazed out the window and wondered what this all might bring. It seemed a little like he had been here before. *Was this in another hour or another lifetime?* he wondered. Surely, every soldier on the eve of battle had such introspections. But those musings were for philosophers, he realized. He was about duty, and he would perform his.

J.E. looked around and saw that the men were preparing for what might be ahead. Weapons had long since been cleaned and recleaned. Most were smaller weapons that could be concealed under their clothing. It had been decided, given the urban nature of the expected terrain, that the heavier weapons would be left in the airplanes. The men were now changing into local clothing that had been secured in Rome. Some were in Arab-style robes, others in slacks and jackets. Still others wore more touristy clothes—shorts, sandals, and the like. They planned to blend into whatever crowds they found.

"Monsignor, what about Father Anton and his contingent?" asked J.E. as he began to read the incoming information from the ops center on Gordon's Calvary. "What's their ETA?"

"They are not far behind us, and at my last contact with Father Anton, he figured to land about thirty minutes after us," responded the priest.

"Good, we'll get in and get things on the ground organized," said J.E.

"No need to worry about that," said the monsignor. "Father Emilio has called ahead to arrange for transportation and trusted local drivers who know the area very well. What are your orders?"

"We will leave Miguel with one of the Swiss Guards at the airport," said J.E. "When Father Anton and his men come in, leave one man with Miguel, and then have all our fighting men follow us."

"Good," responded the monsignor. "Our man can look after Miguel and make sure the airplanes are protected and are ready to go when we need them."

"Yes," responded J.E., once again assuming the mantle of command. "We'll go on ahead and establish an observation post at this Gordon's Calvary to determine the situation. When Father Anton and his men catch up, we'll be ready to take the necessary action, whatever that might be."

CHAPTER 85

Almost at once, Noosh rose, collected himself, and ordered some of his men to take up an unobtrusive defensive perimeter around them. The rest were directed to stay with the vehicles. There was no one else to be seen in this area just now because what tourists there were in this off-season seemed to be occupied elsewhere. Cloe, the Karik, and Noosh followed the cliff face westward. Cloe was able to get a perspective on the knoll, the cliff face of which was the rocky skull. It rounded off at the top, and there were shrines marking something, but she could not make out what.

"Some people believe this is the place of executions, also referred to as the place of stoning," said the Karik. "My master the Kolektor was intrigued by it and the work of General Charles Gordon here."

"I have heard of this," responded Cloe, pulled in by the collegial repartee. "Wasn't there something about the martyrdom of St. Stephen?"

"Yes, it is believed in many quarters that up there on the top of the hill is where Stephen was stoned," replied the Karik. "This area was clearly located outside the city's walls in Christ's time, and this place of executions could have been the location of the crucifixion. It would have been highly visible to travelers on the main northern road, and that, with the skull-like appearance of the rock face, would have acted as a powerful deterrent to criminal acts."

As they moved on and approached a smaller knoll, Cloe could see it had been excavated at some point. It had a rather flat facade with an open door gaping in the center. A smaller portal was fixed in the wall to the upper right of the door. *A niche along the front of the door could,* she thought, *have at one point housed a stone to be rolled across the doorway to close it.* Cloe hugged her arms across her chest. Even though the day had warmed up a bit, she felt cold chills and goose bumps up and down her arms.

"My God," she said. "Could this be it? Could this be the actual burial site of Christ?"

"I don't know or care right now, but this is where you said to go. This is Gordon's Calvary, and now here is the Garden Tomb," said the Karik. "If you want to see your friend again, get to work and find my jars."

The jars, thought Cloe. She had been so taken by the possibilities of this place, the jars had fled from her mind for a moment. One look at the tomb, though, told Cloe the jars could not be here. It was too public and seemed too small to hide what Thib had described seeing in the cave. The best they could hope for was some sort of clue to lead somewhere else. Another bread crumb from the Sicarii?

Cloe moved toward the entrance to the tomb, once again feeling almost in a daze over the enormity of what see was seeing. She might be tracing the very footsteps of Mary of Magdala on the morning of the resurrection. Cloe stumbled on the niche that at one time might have held the stone. Stooping to catch her balance, she looked into the mouth of the cave-like tomb. Although it was not artificially lit, the sunlight from the door and the window spilled into the tomb, illuminating it. It was clearly hewn from solid stone, as noted in St. Luke's Gospel. From where she was, she could see two chambers: a sort of anteroom that she knew from her work was called a "crying room" and then, off to the right, an interment niche in the burial chamber itself.

"My God," she said. "This may be the very spot on which Peter and the other disciple crouched to look into the tomb."

Cloe felt lightheaded but grabbed the edge of the rock-face door and slowly stood. As she did, she stepped into the antechamber. She turned right and went down two small steps into the death room. This space was about six feet by nine feet or slightly smaller. To the left was the burial niche she had seen from the door, and to the right were two smaller unfinished nooks. The head space of the larger niche had been hollowed out somewhat as if a man larger than the intended occupant had been laid there. The window admitted light into this room.

From behind, the Karik pushed into the death chamber. He looked around but said nothing.

Cloe let out a long breath, not realizing she had been holding it. She had the unabated feeling of being in an incredibly special place. As she studied the walls, she could just make out two faint but ornate crosses and sacred monograms carved or perhaps frescoed among the cross pieces. Cloe thought randomly of a tic-tac-toe game except with a cross with an upper bar and a center crosspiece interspersed with characters. She studied these very closely. One, the older one, she thought, had notations on it that she did not recognize at all. If there was something there, she could not understand it.

"What have you found?" pressed the Karik.

"Nothing," responded Cloe. "I thought this cross might be a clue, but if it is, I can't read it."

"Is there anything else?" queried the Karik, plainly disappointed and beginning to get angry.

"I see nothing but the crosses," she replied.

"Noosh, come photograph the two chambers," ordered the Karik. "Make sure you get good photos of the crosses."

Cloe saw that Noosh had come prepared with a small digital camera, and he proceeded to capture the rough-hewn chambers in detail, including the crosses.

As they were leaving the tomb, the Karik turned to her and, barely able to control himself, spewed, "You have failed me."

"I have done my best," said Cloe.

"Small words from a dead person," said the Karik.

CHAPTER 86

Cloe was thrown roughly into the van in the parking lot behind the bus terminal. The Karik, bitterly disappointed, had told Noosh to get them all back to the airport and to prepare for departure. She sat on the backseat thinking about the Karik and what might happen to her and to Michael. She was desperate to find some answer that could help her save Michael. She had been told she would know when she saw. She had seen, but she had not understood. Her thoughts turned to the crosses in the tomb. The first one was of no use to her; it was just "all Greek" to her, she mused.

"Greek!" she exclaimed. "It *is* Greek."

The Karik turned around in the front seat and stared coldly at her. "You have something?"

"Let me see the camera," she demanded.

Noosh looked at the Karik, who nodded slightly. "If this is another of your tricks …" threatened the Karik.

Noosh gave her the camera, and Cloe powered it up. She hit the memory function and studied the pictures of the crosses that Noosh had taken.

"It is Greek, or rather, a mix of Greek and ancient Phoenician," she said after a bit. "This cross is different from the other, older one. I have no clue what the notations on that cross might mean. This one, I may be able to decipher."

"What does it say?" pressed the Karik. "Tell me."

"The first thing I can see is that the cross is highly stylized and has two laterals on it," said Cloe, closely studying the picture. "Above the upper cross-piece are the Phoenician letters *yuhd* and *shin*. I have seen those before, first on my father's jar and then at the Church of St. Irenaeus at Lyon, France. They are roughly equivalent to the English letters *I* and *S*."

"But what does that mean?" asked the Karik, clearly becoming more frustrated.

"It's not 'IS' but rather 'SI,'" she stated. "It's the signature of the Sicarii."

The Karik smirked. "So this is a message or a clue from your sisters."

"So it seems," responded Cloe, studying the rest of the message. It was written above the transept that lay across the midpoint of the cross. "This part is in Greek, and because of the way it is laid out, it tells me it is of more modern origin than the writing on the other cross."

The Karik's burning eyes stared at her silently.

Cloe continued. "The rest of the message consists of a single letter and four numbers. In English, the best equivalents would be the letter *S* and the numbers 1, 2, 5, and another 2."

"What in the world could that mean?" ruminated the Karik, half to himself.

Cloe hated to give him the information, but she had little choice. Unless J.E. had found and freed Michael, he was still the Karik's captive and under his control. She could not take the chance. She had to play for time and hope somehow J.E. could find her or she could escape.

"Karik, I think sequenced properly, the message reads '1S522,'" said Cloe. "But it could be '1S252' or some other permutation of the last three numbers. Does that mean anything to you?"

"I have no idea," said the Karik defensively. "You are the expert. You tell me what it means."

"What we need is a computer to run all the possible variations and to make some sense of it," said Cloe, "a supercomputer."

***

By the time they reached the airport hangar, Cloe had convinced the Karik that she had to have access to a major research computer to figure out the mystery in any reasonable period of time.

"Karik, I need to contact my colleagues at the university in Louisiana in the United States," said Cloe, knowing the capabilities of "Mike," the supercomputer at LSU. "If their supercomputer cannot solve this puzzle, no one can."

Fifteen minutes later, from the guest phone at the general aviation hangar, she was on the line with Dr. Harrell, the dean of the College of Arts and Sciences at LSU. The Karik was listening to every word, with his gun pointed at Cloe's temple.

"Dr. Harrell, I'm working on something and have gotten stumped," said Cloe, hating that she had to lie to her colleague. "It's part of my work on the translation."

"Sure, Dr. Lejeune. How can we help?" asked the scientist.

"I need to use Mike for help on a very obscure reference," said Cloe.

Five minutes later, the call was transferred to the lab, and a technician had the supercomputer on line and ready to go.

Cloe gave the search parameters to the tech. She included the background that she knew for context. She asked that Dr. Harrell have the results e-mailed to her phone, which the Karik had taken from her hotel room. After a bit of catching up, Cloe rang off and awaited the information. The Karik paced up and down in the lounge, holding Cloe's phone in his hand.

Three minutes later, Cloe's phone beeped, and the screen lit up. The Karik opened the message, filled with numerous entries from the computer, peered at it briefly, and then handed it to Cloe.

After a bit, she looked up and said, "The supercomputer thinks the reference is 1S225, and it most likely refers to a section of the Old Testament of the Bible. Mike thinks it means something in the fifth line of the twenty-second chapter of the first book of Samuel."

"First book of Samuel?" the Karik said, almost laughing. "What does that have to do with anything?"

"Perhaps it's just the way the Sicarii have of communicating their secrets," suggested Cloe, even though she knew the clue was outside the New Testament pattern the Sicarii always used. "Here's the quotation from the Bible that Mike has sent along for us."

Cloe studied the small screen and read aloud: "But the prophet Gad said to David, 'Do not stay in the stronghold; go and make your way into the land of Judah.' So David went away and came to the forest of Hereth."

CHAPTER 87

The monsignor's satellite phone rang as they were nearing their destination of Gordon's Calvary. As they entered the parking lot behind the bus station, he lifted the receiver and listened.

"Hello, Albert," said Father Emilio over the long distance.

"Yes, Father Emilio," said the monsignor. "I cannot speak now. We have arrived at the tomb."

"Albert, I have an urgent call from the United States from someone named Dr. Ransome Harrell at a university in Louisiana," said the old monk. "What shall I do?"

"I know this man. He helped us open the original jar that Thib brought back from Tunisia," responded the monsignor. "How did he get to you?"

"He called whatever number you gave him, apparently very insistent on talking to you, and eventually, he was routed to me," said Father Emilio.

"Oh yes, I gave him my private number," said the monsignor.

"What is it?" asked J.E. as he watched the men begin to deploy to set up the observation post. "Father Anton and his men have landed and are on the way. We have to move."

"Hold … J.E., this might be important," said the monsignor. "I can't think why Dr. Harrell would be urgently calling unless it has something to do with your mother, but how could that be?" Turning back to the satellite phone and hitting the speaker button, the monsignor said, "Father, please put the doctor through."

A snap of static later, a voice said, "Hello … hello?"

"Dr. Harrell, this is Monsignor Roques," said the priest.

"Hello, Monsignor," said the faraway voice. "Albert, I just had the strangest contact. Is Dr. Lejeune ... Cloe ... with you?"

The monsignor wondered how much he should tell the doctor. They had all been through a lot with the Kolektor, but was there any possibility he could not be trusted?

Deciding quickly, the monsignor said, "Doctor, we are on a mission from the highest possible authority on this earth and in the course of too many things to tell you much now, but Cloe has been taken by the Kolektor's organization, headed now by a man called the Karik. If you have anything that could possibly help us, this would be a good time to pass it on."

The line was silent for a time, and then the voice of Dr. Harrell came through, hesitantly at first and then with strength. "Albert, Cloe just called me saying she needed access to Mike the supercomputer for some work she is doing on the translation. We transferred the call to the lab, and she gave the tech the search parameters."

"I see," whispered the monsignor, not actually seeing at all.

"Well, I do not want to overstep my bounds, but Mike automatically locates the source of such remote inquiries," said the doctor. "And there is no doubt Cloe that Cloe was not in Madisonville working on the translation when she called, as she implied."

"Hello, Dr. Harrell, this is J.E.," said the young soldier. "Where is she?"

"She is in Jerusalem," responded the scientist. "I can e-mail you the latitude and longitude coordinates, if you wish."

"Yes, by all means," responded the cleric. "But what made you call me, Doctor?"

"That's the thing, Albert—not only is she half a world away from where she's supposed to be, but her inquiry makes it plain she is not working on the translation," responded Dr. Harrell. "Her translation work has everything to do with the New Testament and nothing at all to do with the first book of Samuel from the Old Testament, which is what her inquiry led to."

The monsignor and J.E. looked at each other, but neither had any answer. Why would Cloe have to consult a computer on a question answered by something in the first book of Samuel? That was ancient, back in the historical books of the Bible.

"All the clues the Sicarii have left have been from the New Testament," said Father Sergio. "I don't see what Cloe could be doing."

"True enough," said J.E. "But Mom knows Dr. Harrell very well, and I think she would have expected him to contact us under these odd circumstances."

"Yes, yes!" exclaimed the monsignor. "She would certainly expect Dr. Harrell to do just what he has done. She knew he would pass on the information to us."

"Dr. Harrell, what does Mike say the likely result of the search means?" asked J.E.

"There is no result on that, just the verse that Mike believes the letter and numbers refer to," answered the academician. "I have sent it to your cell phones."

There was silence in the van while all searched their cell phones and then studied the verse from 1 Samuel 22:5.

The monsignor looked up and yelled, "J.E., let's get our people loaded immediately. Contact Father Anton and get everyone back to the airport as soon as possible. There's no time to lose."

CHAPTER 88

Noosh hurriedly entered the small common area in the general aviation terminal, and Cloe saw him whisper something in the Karik's ear. In response, the Karik quietly issued orders to him, and Noosh quickly exited the terminal. Something was plainly up, she realized.

The Karik turned to her and said, "We must depart immediately."

"Why? What's going on?" Cloe asked. "We don't even know where we are going."

The Karik grabbed her by the arm and began to walk her out of the terminal. She thought about struggling, but she knew that if she did, the other people in the terminal might be in danger. The Karik did not seem to care about collateral damage. There was nothing to do but go along and play out the hand.

Outside on the tarmac, the planes were preparing for departure. She entered the first jet and walked to her usual seat. Glancing toward the rear of the plane, she saw a body behind the last seat. The clothes were familiar. Rushing to him, she looked down on a man who was bound hand and foot.

"Michael, Michael," she cried.

Slowly his beautiful eyes opened. "Cloe, they came into the hangar where one of the Swiss and I were hiding. The soldier fought bravely, but the Karik's thugs beat him senseless and tied me up."

"But how did you get here?" Cloe asked.

"Your son and his friends rescued me from the Karik's chalet," replied Michael. "They followed you and brought me here."

"Are you hurt?" she asked, lifting his head, anger beginning to well up in her.

"No, only bruised and in some pain still from the burning. I will be fine," he said.

One of the Karik's men roughly grabbed her and began to wrestle her back to her seat. She was thrown into the seat and buckled into it. She was furious but helpless.

The Karik smiled that irritating smile of his, like the cat that caught the canary. "Well, it seems I once again have my full complement of guests," he said.

***

The Karik's men had loaded the jets, and both were now in the air, climbing out of Jerusalem's airspace. The pilot had asked for a destination so that he could program the jet's computers, but there was none as of yet.

"Dr. Lejeune, what is the answer to the riddle?" asked the Karik acidly.

Cloe had been studying the verse from 1 Samuel, but although she had an idea where the clue might take them, she was certainly not sure. "I will have nothing to offer you as long as Michael is tied up in the back of this plane," responded Cloe, regretting the words as soon as they came out of her mouth.

"Noosh, I think it is a very good idea to bring Dr. Lejeune's friend up here. Untie his feet but leave his hands shackled," commanded the Karik. "We will see what he has to say."

Once Michael had been untied and seated on the sofa seat across the aisle from Cloe and the Karik, Cloe looked at him and smiled slightly. *Michael had been through a great deal,* she thought.

"Now your friend is here," said the Karik. "Where are my jars?"

"Tell him nothing, Cloe," stated Michael bravely. "He's going to kill us as soon as he has what he wants. Don't help him."

Cloe was sorely torn. She knew Michael was right about the Karik's intentions, but she felt J.E. and the others were probably after them. She didn't know if they were a day behind them or an hour or a minute. In dealing with these thugs, it was like with the Kolektor;

she had to draw things out and look for her chance. With Michael here, she felt stronger, better equipped to do just that.

"Why do you force me to my darker side, Dr. Lejeune?" asked the Karik. He nodded to Noosh, who walked to Michael's couch and drew a handgun with a silencer on it. He aimed it at Michael's left knee and awaited orders.

"Cloe, it's a bluff—they would never fire a weapon on a pressurized airplane such as this," said Michael. "The bullet might pierce the skin of the plane, causing it to lose pressure and crash."

The Karik laughed. "This is a special pistol. It is a .22-caliber with a singular, light load … very unlikely to harm the aircraft but quite painful at close range. It will also not cause death unless fired directly into your eye or ear."

Cloe cringed. She knew this ruthless bastard would shoot Michael until she told him what she thought. There was nothing she could do. So Cloe told the Karik all she knew about the verse from 1 Samuel. As he listened to her speak, he carefully studied a map of the area. The jet was now over the Mediterranean.

Finally, the Karik signaled Noosh, who holstered the pistol and approached. "Noosh, turn the plane around and tell the pilot to make for Bar Yehuda Airfield as fast as possible."

PART IV

THE STRONGHOLD

Charge once more, then, be dumb!
Let the victors, when they come,
When the forts of folly fall,
Find thy body by the wall.
—Matthew Arnold, "The Last Word"

CHAPTER 89

As the vans sped through the streets of Jerusalem headed back to the airport, J.E. asked the monsignor, "Albert, what is it? What do you know?" J.E. had learned to trust the judgment of this strange cleric, but there were tactical issues and plans to be laid for whatever was ahead.

"The irony of it is spectacular," said the monsignor. "I just don't see how they could have done it."

"Do what?" pressed J.E.

"J.E., do you remember the verse from 1 Samuel?" asked the monsignor.

"Certainly, I have it right here on my phone," responded the young soldier.

"What words jump out at you from that verse?" queried the cleric.

Father Sergio leaned back and said, "Gad? David?"

"No, those are names, not places where the jars might have been taken," answered J.E.

"Right you are, young sir. You are on the correct track!" exclaimed the monsignor.

"That leaves only the land of Judah and the forest of Hereth," mused J.E. "The land of Judah may be a reference to Judea. I can't see keeping the jars in a forest."

"Judea is not specific enough, and I agree about the forest," added Father Sergio.

"What's left then?" asked J.E. "That's all the proper references in the verse."

"Is it?" questioned the monsignor.

"No, that's not all. There's a reference to a 'stronghold,' an unnamed fortress where the verse says, 'Do not stay in the stronghold,'" whispered J.E.

"A stronghold … where better to keep the jars?" asked Father Sergio. "But what stronghold? What could it be?"

"There's only one place it could be," said J.E. "It's the mightiest stronghold ever conceived by men of the time. We studied it in military history. It's the one thought to have been impregnable."

"Yes," said the monsignor.

"Masada," said J.E. "Masada, where it all began for the Sicarii. The jars have been taken to Masada."

***

"Sir, the planes appear to have been sabotaged," the Swiss soldier reported to J.E. "Father Anton advises that the wiring has been tampered with, and the planes are not safe to fly."

"Doubtless the work of the Karik and his thugs," J.E. said to the monsignor as he approached.

"I have more bad news, J.E. The Swiss report that Miguel is gone, and the man we left with him has been badly beaten. He needs a hospital," said the monsignor.

J.E. turned and gazed at the airplanes, now useless to them. He should have left more men here to guard them and to take care of Miguel. On the other hand, if there had been a firefight here, Cloe and the others might have been killed.

"Father, have one of the Swiss take our injured soldier for medical treatment. He is to remain with him until we return. Give him some cash and a cover story like a motorcycle crash to cover the trail," said J.E.

"Yes, certainly," said the monsignor, turning to one of the Swiss Guards and providing the necessary instructions.

"J.E., from this we know the Karik was here," said Father Sergio. "Here and gone."

"Yes, if the information we have is correct, he and Cloe have been to Gordon's Calvary, and they probably know what we know," said J.E.

J.E. and the two priests huddled with Tomás in a circle on the tarmac while Father Anton and Sky examined the damage to the planes.

"I think we can surmise that Cloe found a clue in the tomb, which is why she called Dr. Harrell," said the monsignor. "She must have expected him to pass the information on to us and that we would figure out that the jars have been taken to Masada."

"Now we have to assume the Karik and his captives are on their way there," said J.E.

"Cloe may not have told him what she learned in the tomb, or if she did, the Karik may not have been able to decipher the clue," suggested the young camerlengo.

"Possibly, but they have gone somewhere, and I think with the recapture of Miguel, the Karik will once again think he has a bargaining chip," responded the monsignor. "Cloe will want to keep the information from the Karik, but if he threatens or tortures Miguel as he did in Armenia, she will tell him to save Miguel."

"Yes, that, and she will believe we have received and understood this clue and will be coming to help," said J.E. "But the Karik is ahead of us now, and we have no planes."

"J.E., shouldn't we call in the authorities?" queried the young camerlengo.

"Father," said the monsignor, "as soon as I was advised that the planes had been sabotaged, I called the ops center, and we will have a helicopter here in about forty minutes. Masada is only fifty to sixty miles from here. If we contact the authorities, we will be dealing with the Israeli Army and the Mossad, their secret service. By the time we answer all their questions and they mobilize, it will be hours and too late."

"Besides," added J.E., "the Vatican does not want a diplomatic incident. We have had the access here and elsewhere because of our Vatican diplomatic credentials. This is something we must take care of."

"What's our approach?" asked the monsignor.

"The three of us, along with Tomás and his men, will take one of the vans, and we will immediately leave for Masada by ground. We should be there in an hour or so. Father Anton and the Swiss will follow by air if and when the helicopter shows up," said J.E.

The four men looked at each other, absorbing what might lie ahead.

Finally, Tomás said, "My men and I are with you. We will find and rescue the boss and your mother."

CHAPTER 90

Cloe watched the sun setting in the west as the Karik's planes landed at Bar Yehuda. The airfield was really a glorified strip of asphalt in the desert near Masada, which itself was located in the Judean Mountains along the shores of the Dead Sea. Landing, the planes taxied to a rough hangar and terminal. Noosh was out quickly, seeking ground transportation to Masada. A few minutes later, in the gathering darkness, a fair-sized truck had been secured, and all the men and equipment had been transferred.

"Karik, how far is it to Masada?" asked Cloe.

"Not far," answered the Karik absently.

Cloe studied the man carefully. He had a greasy sheen to his complexion, and his eyes seemed almost glazed in anticipation. It was apparent he thought his prize, the jars, were within his reach.

As they traveled up the rural road to the mountain stronghold, she reviewed what she knew about Masada. It had been a mountain fortress from the ancient days as early as when young David hid from King Saul. Located near the Dead Sea, Masada itself was a plateau surrounded by deep gorges. Some points of the stronghold were near one thousand feet high, and the plateau on the top of the mountain contained an area of about twenty-three acres, about the size of a small ranch in the United States.

The Sicarii had told her that the Jews were persecuted by the Romans during the time of Christ, and eventually, they rebelled. The Romans gathered in force to put down the Jewish rebellion, sacked Jerusalem, and destroyed the Temple in AD 70. A little under a thousand Sicarii men, women, and children fled to Masada to take refuge from the Romans.

Cloe knew the Sicarii had been Judean freedom fighters dedicated to the overthrow of the Romans by any means. They had earned particular enmity of the ruling authorities as a result of their strategy of using short knives to assassinate leaders in public places. In essence, they were first-century terrorists using knives instead of explosives. But her Sicarii sisters had been clear: the Romans were occupiers of their land, and although their forefathers had used assassination as a political weapon, they had not caused collateral civilian casualties, like modern terrorists. Cloe had wondered when she heard this if it was just a form of rationalization.

Still, the history of Masada was one of the most amazing and fascinating stories she had ever heard. It was adopted by Herod the Great in about 24 BC as his winter palace and fortress. He thought he might need an invincible redoubt in the event of a Jewish rebellion. The entire top of the plateau was encircled by a wall about eighteen feet high and twelve feet thick. Battle towers were constructed at numerous intervals, some as high as seventy-five feet.

Cloe thought that this was not even the most impressive part of Herod's work. He built a palace on the northern end of the mountain on three separate levels that had to be considered an ancient marvel with its hot-water baths, storage vaults, and other grand accommodations. Of course, there were barracks for his military and palatial housing for his guests. All in all, with proper provisions, a community the size of a small city in ancient times could maintain itself on Masada for years without privation. Even the soil was fertile enough for crops.

Cloe was shaken from her reverie by the excitement of the Karik and his men. "That's it," said the Karik, pointing to a huge shape in the distance.

Cloe looked at Michael and then in the direction the Karik pointed, but she saw only a darker shade of black against the nightfall. As she studied the enormous object in the desert, it began to form a silhouette. The shape was magnificent and ominous at the same time. She could not see a single light on the mountain.

"Noosh, how long before we reach the foot of the Path of the Serpent?" queried the Karik. Masada had been one of the Kolektor's keenest interests in Judea.

"Only a few minutes, Karik," replied the servant. "It is known as the Snake Path because of its winding nature. It is one of only three ways up to the fortress."

Cloe had heard of this. In the ancient times of Masada, the Snake or Serpent Path was the only access to the summit. Because of the difficult climb and its winding way, it was easily defended by very few men with bows and arrows. When the Romans laid siege to Masada, they were unable to reach the stronghold by the Snake Path. The defenders, Sicarii bowmen, were deadly in striking the Romans each time they tried an assault.

The truck slowed and eventually came to a halt in the darkness. The truck's rear gate was lowered, and the Karik's men unloaded. As they assembled, the Karik and Noosh conferred, and Cloe watched the soldiers. They had a remarkable array of equipment, including rifles, machine guns, and what looked like mortars or RPGs. She and Michael were told to stand outside the truck.

Noosh separated the men into two groups. The first was ordered back into the truck. After a bit of grumbling, they obliged, obviously disappointed at the apparent lack of opportunity for action.

Noosh then gave instructions to the leaders of the other group, who had automatic weapons and large spotlights to illuminate the path. "You will take the Snake Path to the walls of the fortress and attack from there."

The Karik and Noosh then jumped into the truck, dragging Cloe and Michael with them.

"Hurry," said Noosh to the driver. "To the west, around the base of the mountain."

The driver fired the engine and raced toward what would have been the setting sun if it had not been completely dark. Cloe glanced behind them to see whether there was a moon tonight but saw only darkness.

"Michael," she whispered. "Where are we going?"

He rolled toward her and said softly, "I don't know. Perhaps we are to be taken into the desert while the raiding party assaults Masada and recovers the jars."

Cloe considered this and was chilled to the bone. Could this be the end? "Where are we going?" Cloe asked the Karik. "I thought we were going to the top of Masada."

The Karik reached back and slapped her hard across the bridge of her nose, drawing both blood and tears. "Shut up," he said. "The finish is near."

CHAPTER 91

J.E., the monsignor, and Father Sergio bounced in the van as it sped in near-darkness over the rural road outside of Jerusalem, headed for Masada. In the rear of the van, Tomás and his men worked on their weapons, cleaning the guns and sharpening the knives. It had always been so with military men. Someone would provide the objective, but their job was to be ready.

"J.E., we can be at Masada in less than an hour," observed the monsignor. "What are our plans?"

"Albert, you are asking me the question that has defeated armies for thousands of years," mused J.E. "Masada was thought in ancient times to be impregnable. You are asking how we assault the unassailable fortress."

"But the Romans defeated the Sicarii, so there must be a way in," responded Father Sergio.

"The Romans never militarily defeated the Sicarii," stated the monsignor. "Roman engineers defeated the Sicarii, not Roman soldiers."

"It's the most astounding assault of anything I have ever heard," said J.E. "We studied it in a military tactics course. After the Romans sacked Jerusalem in about AD 70, the remaining rebels, largely consisting of about one thousand Sicarii men, women, and children, retreated to Masada. Raiding nearby villages, Elazar bin Yair, the leader of the rebels, accumulated enough grain, animals, and supplies at Masada to last years. Herod had assured there would be plentiful water in cisterns and military weapons for an army. They thought they would outlast the Romans and that eventually the Romans would give up and go away."

"Well, it did not work out that way," said the monsignor, picking up where J.E. left off. "The Romans tried several assaults, but at that time there was only one winding path up to the plateau, and once one got to the top, one was greeted with high, thick walls and watchtowers teeming with rebel fighters. It was either that or try to assault the top over bare rock and cliffs. No army could do that."

"Attempts to ascend the Serpent Path proved futile, and many Roman soldiers were killed," said J.E. "The Romans then settled back into a siege posture. They built a wall circumnavigating the entire mountain and set up multiple camps for the soldiers. This was to prevent the Sicarii from sneaking out, from escaping. We are talking about several miles of wall and campsites. This had to deliver a frightful message to the Sicarii that the Romans were very determined, and death would be the only escape."

"Astonishing," said Father Sergio.

"What came next is the really astounding part of all this," said J.E. "Rather than simply lay siege and try to wait them out as the Sicarii had expected, the Romans brought in thousands of slaves, including many Jews, and on the west side of Masada began to build an enormous ramp." J.E. paused, contemplating the enormity of what the Romans had accomplished. He studied the wide eyes of Father Sergio and knew he and the monsignor were equally amazed.

"A ramp? Why?" queried the young camerlengo.

"Two thousand years ago, the Romans built the equivalent of an interstate highway right up the rock face and walls of Masada," said the monsignor.

"It was thousands of tons of rock and dirt," added J.E. "It was wide and deep, leading directly up to the wall on the lowest side of the plateau. Once this had been built, the Romans brought up their siege machines to pound the wall until it had been breached. There was little the Sicarii could do with bows, arrows, and lances against the monster war machines."

Tomás, who had been listening to this colloquy for the last few minutes, asked, "What happened? The Romans must have won a great battle."

"Sadly, from a number of points of view, there was no great victory and, in fact, no final battle at all," responded the monsignor. "The Sicarii, virtually the last man, woman, and child, died by their own hands, robbing the Romans of any battle glory and of the opportunity for numerous captives."

"History tells us that the Sicarii soldiers killed their own families and then drew straws, picking ten among the survivors to finish the business," said J.E. "These ten slew the rest of the soldiers, and then only the ten remained. They chose one, and that one killed the other nine, who gladly submitted to the blade to join their kin. The last fell on his own sword after setting fire to the place. There was not much for the Romans to recover. Seven survivors hid in one of the cisterns and lived to tell the tale."

Silence overtook the men huddled in the van speeding toward Masada as they contemplated the history of the fortress. How could a few men hope to do in one night what it had taken thousands of Romans and their slaves years to do?

Breaking the quiet among the group, the driver yelled back that they were about twenty minutes out from the eastern side of Masada. J.E. gazed out the window and observed that it was now fully dark. Even so, in front of them he saw that the black brute that was Masada had obliterated the stars.

CHAPTER 92

As they rounded the base of Masada, the Karik and his men were focused on the mountain and their plans, paying little attention to Cloe and Michael.

"We seem to be headed to the west side of the fortress," Michael observed quietly.

"Secure your night-vision equipment," Noosh ordered the armed men. "Make sure the batteries are fully charged and bring spares."

Cloe knew they were ready for whatever plan the Karik had devised. As she watched, several of the men assembled sniper rifles. "Hmmm," Cloe mused, "sniper rifles and night-vision goggles."

"Some sort of stealth attack," said Michael. "But on what? The main body of the Karik's men is assaulting the stronghold from the east side."

"Can there be another target?" considered Cloe. "Oh my God! The ramp, the ramp—that's got to be it."

CHAPTER 93

"There are now only three ways up to the fortress," said J.E. "The first is the Snake Path we have discussed. The second is a modern access route, a cable car that takes tourists to the top. The final path is the ancient ramp the Romans built in their first-century siege. The first two are on the east side, and the ramp is on the west."

"Exactly," said the monsignor. "What's our best approach? I think we have to assume the Sicarii are already on the mountain guarding the jars. That's a huge advantage for them, and I'm not sure, in the dark, they could distinguish us from the Karik's men."

"Without Cloe with us, they might not care that we aren't the Karik's men," observed the camerlengo. "They might consider any band of men to be enemies bent on taking their treasures."

"Good point, Serge," said J.E. "Let's make sure our men are very careful around the Sicarii." J.E. stared alternately at his map and out the window into the blackness. After a bit of time, he said, "Driver, make for the cable car." A few minutes later, J.E. stood at the foot of the building housing the line of cable cars leading to the summit. He gazed intently up at Masada. He could see a line of lights ascending the Snake Path. *The Karik must be going up that way,* he thought.

"How long to the old ramp?" he asked the driver.

"No more than twenty minutes, sir," responded the man.

"Tomás," said J.E. "Leave one of your best men here. In thirty minutes he is to break into the cable car building, energize the electricity, and start the string of cars up the mountain. Understood?"

"Certainly," replied Tomás.

J.E. could hear Tomás giving the orders as he directed everyone else to the van. Soon, they were all off at breakneck speed around the base of the mountain.

In the van, J.E. glanced at the monsignor, who was watching him, slightly smiling. "Do you think that will fool them?" he asked at last.

"Fool who?" responded J.E. innocently.

"The Sicarii, of course," responded the monsignor.

J.E. looked at the monster mountain through the window for a moment and then finally turned to the monsignor and said, "The Sicarii? What makes you think I'm trying to fool them?"

CHAPTER 94

Now outside the truck, Cloe could see a bright field of stars on one side and on the other nothing but blackness. The Karik's men had donned their night-vision goggles, and she was now being pushed along in the dark. "What is happening? Where are we going?" she asked.

Again, this earned her a backhand across the bridge of her nose. Stinging from tears and pain, she glared at the Karik but kept silent.

He chuckled and pointed toward the summit high above them. She and Michael were pushed and half-dragged up the great rock-and-stone ramp that the Romans had used two millennia earlier to successfully pierce Masada. The climb was very rough because the path had deteriorated over the generations. In some places, parts of the ramp had fallen through or washed out completely. Still, they made progress, and the walls of the stronghold seemed to grow in size as they climbed.

The long slog was disturbed by a slight whirring sound. Cloe recognized this as the Karik's satellite phone, now set on vibrate mode.

The group paused to catch their breath as the Karik answered the phone and listened intently. "Ha!" he said softly, and then he terminated the call. To Noosh he whispered, "The fools are trying to take the cable cars to the top."

Cloe heard this clearly and said, "Who? Who is taking the cable cars?"

Before she could blink, one of the thugs had grabbed her, slammed his hand over her mouth, and put a pistol to her temple.

The Karik came very near and said so quietly she could barely hear, "It seems your would-be rescuers have joined the party. My men will have a bit of a surprise for them."

Cloe's eyes bulged, but she could say nothing because of the strength of the man holding her mouth closed.

The Karik leaned in again and whispered, "If you say another word, I will have your friend thrown off the edge of the ramp into the valley below."

Cloe nodded her assent, eyes filled with tears and hatred.

Now about halfway up the stony incline toward the walled plateau, Cloe could see some detail silhouetted against the night sky. There was a great gap in the defensive wall above her. This must be where the Roman war machines had successfully breached the perimeter. Cloe thought about what it must have been like on that day so long ago. The Roman soldiers would have been queued up behind the battering rams and the wooden shelters that protected them from the arrows of the Sicarii. They were more than ready for a fight, having been on this siege for so long. Swords would have been drawn, and Roman archers would have been pouring fire onto the battlements above. As the wall began to crumble under the slamming blows of the ram, some of the soldiers and certainly their leaders would have been wondering why there was no answering fire from Sicarii archers and no sign of anyone on the walls.

But as Cloe knew, there had been none of that because by that time, almost all the Sicarii had been put to death by their own kin. Surely, the Romans must have been suspicious of some trick. Even as the wall fell and they rushed into the interior of the fortress, they would have done so cautiously. As they moved forward toward Herod's palace, they would have been enveloped by thick smoke from the burning stores that had been set afire by the last of the Sicarii. The defenders wanted nothing useful to be left for the Romans. Perhaps on the wall of Herod's palace itself, they may have found the last Sicarius, maybe Elazar bin Yair himself, hanging on the point of his own sword.

Cloe shook herself from ancient Masada as the Armenians began to spread out and assume battle positions. She and Michael were pulled down behind a series of large stones that at one time might have made up a part of the wall.

Noosh handed each of them a pair of goggles and whispered to them to put them on. "We don't want anyone falling and making noise from here on," he said very quietly. He then made a sign to some of his retainers on the perimeter of the ramp. Cloe watched through the goggles as they moved cautiously toward the gap in the wall. Not only were the lenses able to collect what little ambient light there was and greatly amplify it, but there was an infrared aspect to them as well. The soldiers were a little brighter than everything else around them because of their heat signatures.

Slowly, the Karik's armed men crept up in the way that soldiers and police have to cover each other in places where they expect to be attacked. Finally, they achieved the wall and went into the stronghold. For a while, Cloe could neither see nor hear anything from the scouting party. Eventually, one of them came back to the breach in the wall and signaled that the coast was clear.

The rest of the party ascended the last few paces into the walled fortress. Noosh then gave orders to spread out in battle formation and to head for the place where the Snake Path entered the plateau on the east side. To do this they traveled to the southeast, taking cover among the ruins of numerous small palaces and garrisons. Cloe thought the Karik must be planning to meet his comrades coming up the Snake Path.

She whispered to Michael, "They seem to be looking for the rest of their soldiers so as to put together the largest force."

"Yes," he said quietly. "Perhaps with all his men he will try to overwhelm the Sicarii."

"But why did he split them up in the first place?" asked Cloe.

Not far from the wall on the eastern side above the Snake Path, the Karik's thugs stooped and found shelter behind stone ruins. Noosh issued orders in Armenian to the mercenaries. Cloe could see they were modifying their weaponry. Where they had previously carried close-quarters weapons, they were now unslinging long rifles with huge telescopic sights on them. She realized these must have a sight capacity similar to the night-vision goggles they now wore.

"What are they doing?" Cloe quietly asked Michael. As she watched, six of the men aimed the sniper rifles toward the east wall where the Snake Path ascended.

She looked at where they were aiming and saw a dozen or more figures highlighted in the night lenses, apparently hunkered down behind the east wall.

"Oh my God, the Sicarii," she hissed. "The Karik has laid an ambush for them. They have been watching his men ascend the Snake Path with lights ablaze. That group is nothing but a diversion."

The Karik, who was nearby and who had heard her whisper, merely chuckled. As Cloe looked for them, she could discern more of the ghostly figures along the wall further to the north.

All of the Sicarii must be here, she thought as she counted the fluorescent silhouettes. *They mean to put an end to the Karik here on Masada. Everything has been committed.*

In the distance from that same direction came the clanking of the cable car. Its noise became louder as it ascended toward the plateau. Cloe could see the halo of the lights on the car, which was now just below the rim of the wall. As she glanced back at the snipers, she saw they were clearly ready, having acquired their targets.

"Michael, we have to do something!" she whispered urgently.

"Sit down and shut up," he replied.

CHAPTER 95

As J.E. and his cohorts rounded the base of the mountain, the ancient ramp loomed ahead of them. Thousands of tons of rock and dirt had been hauled by slave hands to make the new path up the back side of Masada. *Surely*, he thought, *this must be one of the engineering marvels of the ancient world.* "Hold up at the foot of the ramp," ordered J.E., noting the other vehicle parked nearby.

As the van glided to a halt, Tomás and his men organized their equipment. They had picked up night-vision gear in Rome during their stop for supplies and weapons.

J.E. turned to Tomás and said, "Have one of your men check the truck. Break into it if you must."

As the team assembled outside the vehicle, J.E. quickly reviewed what they had. There were only eight of them, including the two priests and Tomás. The Karik's force was twice, maybe three times, their size. Still, it was a game bunch. Even Father Sergio had donned a vest and picked up a Benelli semiautomatic pistol. J.E. listened as the monsignor gave the young camerlengo a crash course on loading, aiming, and firing the weapon.

"Albert, you are amazing," said J.E. "Is there no end to your expertise?"

"Not expertise," retorted the monsignor, smiling. "Experience."

The rest grabbed weapons of choice, resulting in most men carrying close-quarters pistols or automatic arms plus longer-range rifles. It would have been better to specialize, with some men ready for short-range contact and others outfitted as snipers, but they did not have the manpower. Everyone had to double up.

"J.E., the truck was unguarded and unlocked, and my men have searched it," said Tomás. "According to the paperwork, it's an airport rental from a local airport. There are rucksacks in the back with equipment and weapons that I don't think hikers would carry. I think we have to assume at least a part of the Karik's force may have come this way."

"What's our plan, J.E.?" queried Father Sergio.

"Well, from what we could see from the other side, the Karik's men are also assaulting Masada up the Snake Path. They were pretty apparent going up, so the Sicarii will be waiting for them," said J.E., scratching his chin. "Now we may have some part of his force on this side ahead of us on the ramp. It's good that we know, but it doesn't change our mission, which is to get Mom and Miguel back, which, right now, means getting up the ramp as rapidly as possible and supporting the Sicarii when they get into it with the Karik. We have to assume he has a lot of firepower to come up both ways, and we don't know what the Sicarii have."

"Do you have any idea where the jars might be secreted?" asked J.E., turning to the monsignor.

"Based on the history and geography of this place, there are a lot of possible hiding places, including the ruins of barracks and storehouses in or near Herod's palace that could all be used," responded the monsignor. "The palace is on the northern point of the mountain. The palace complex was built on three separate elevations, with Herod's personal palace on the top. If I have to pick a place to start looking, that's where I would go."

"There are also dry cisterns and underground caves," said Father Sergio. "The jars might be there as well."

"True enough, Father," said the monsignor. "But my instincts tell me we will find what we are looking for at Herod's palace."

J.E. looked up the ramp illuminated by the miracle of his low-light goggles and said, "Tomás, take the point and move us up the incline."

At that, Tomás half-walked and half-trotted toward the base of the long stone road up to Masada. They silently climbed toward whatever fate had been ordained for them.

CHAPTER 96

Cloe looked up into Michael's face in shock. She did not see the man who had captured her affections. Instead, she saw the bestial image of her last contact with the Kolektor. In the green, low-light glow of the goggles, evil seemed to emerge.

"Michael ..." she said.

"I'm sorry, Cloe, but you have to be quiet and wait for our opportunity," he whispered, smiling gently.

Cloe looked at him again but saw only Michael. What had just passed? Had she seen what she thought she had seen, or was Michael only as on-edge as she was? She was exhausted. "Michael, I didn't mean to add to the problem," said Cloe softly. "But the Karik is laying a trap for the Sicarii, my son, and my friends. We have to do something."

Just then an enormous explosion erupted from the area of the cable car line. The radiance was blinding with the low-light glasses. Cloe ducked down behind the stone wall, tore the goggles off, and rubbed her eyes. Pieces of steel and plastic from the large car rained down on the whole area. It was apparent that the cable car had taken an explosive round or had hit a booby trap and had been blown to smithereens. Not only that, but the cable had been severed, and the rest of the line could be heard crashing, clanging, and falling into the valley a thousand feet below. There could be no survivors.

"Oh my God," whispered Cloe. "J.E., the monsignor, and all the rest. The Karik said they were coming up via the cable system."

"Cloe, I'm so sorry," replied Michael softly.

"Noooo," cried Cloe softly. As she turned with tears in her eyes, she was struck wickedly with something very hard, and she knew only darkness.

CHAPTER 97

Cloe was not sure she had been truly unconscious because she had continued to have some sense of what was happening around her. Or had she been dreaming? In any event, she felt she had only been down for a few seconds. As she opened her eyes, the pain flashed brightly. Her head ached like hell. She looked around carefully and found that she could see but could not hear any sound except the roar of a fire burning somewhere in front of her. *The cable cars*, she remembered. *Oh my God.*

As she looked around, she discovered she was alone at the rear of the group of stones behind which she and Michael had first taken shelter. Michael was gone! She groped in the darkness and soon found the night-vision glasses. She raised them to her eyes, and as she wrapped the strap around the back of her head, she felt the sticky ooze from the wound she had suffered. She glanced down at her hand and saw the bright warm signature of blood now cooling and turning black at the edges. Someone had slugged her with something hard, a gun butt or rock.

In spite of the pain and her distress, she rose up and saw the Kolektor's men a few paces ahead of her. They must have thought her either dead or out cold. As she watched, Noosh gave a silent signal, and the sniper weapons fired. A crescendo of light, heat, and noise blasted across the plateau.

Cloe's eyes turned to the eastern wall where the Sicarii had awaited the Karik's men in ambush and saw them falling from their positions, shot in the back by the Karik's assassins. Even as Cloe watched, the heat signature of each Sicarius began to dim as her now lifeless body lost heat.

A second terrible fusillade was fired by the snipers. Weaponless, Cloe knew she could not help her sisters. But she gritted her teeth and resolved that they would not go unavenged.

As the second volley rang in her ears, she darted off to the north. Clotile Lejeune of Madisonville, Louisiana, might be an ancient languages professor. She might be a lot of things, but now, first and foremost, she was Sicarius. She had been saved by them at Hakeldama, and somehow, she would save the last of them.

As Cloe ran toward Herod's palace on the northern point of Masada, she could hear screams and sporadic gunfire as the wounded were administered the coup de grâce. Her heart was torn apart for the lost and dying. How could it have come to this? The Sicarii had miscalculated terribly.

Anger welled up in her breast. She could feel the birth of her kinship with Elazar bin Yair and the ancient Sicarii who would not be taken by the Romans. Cloe knew she would do what had to be done.

She continued running in a northerly direction, but she was suddenly knocked down by a man running toward the fight on the east wall. She rolled quickly to her feet and faced the assailant. She then dropped to her knees, crying.

"J.E.," she whispered.

CHAPTER 98

"They are all dead," said Noosh. "Our plan has been completely successful."

The Karik surveyed the battle scene through the night-vision goggles.

"The Sicarii are all dead, and the friends of Dr. Lejeune have met the same fate on the cable cars," said Noosh. "The field of battle is ours."

A few of the nearest fighting men had begun to assemble around their leader. Most were still out in the rocks finishing the Sicarii. The smell of gun smoke and death permeated the air.

"Men!" cried the Karik. "There is no time to lose. We must push aside our fatigue and move forward to Herod's palace to find the thing we have fought for. The jars, the jars. They are there. We must have them. I must have them."

CHAPTER 99

"Oh my God, J.E., how can it be?" pressed Cloe. "What? How? Where have you come from?"

"Mom, we are here now. Everything will be all right," said J.E., grabbing his mother and lifting her up in a fierce hug.

The monsignor ran up and joined the reunion. "Thank God, Cloe, you are all right," he said. "Where is Miguel?"

"I don't know," she responded. "He may be dead. The Karik's men ambushed the Sicarii on the east side where the Snake Path comes up. Just before the attack began, someone knocked me out. Michael had been with me, but when I awoke, he was gone. I'm afraid he may have been killed."

Cloe looked around at the group and then continued. "Time is of the essence here. I do want to hear everything about how you got here. But we can talk later, and there are some things you should know now about the Karik and the strength of his force." She filled them in on the number of the Karik's troops and his weaponry.

All the men had queued up to hear the odds they were facing. Their faces now turned to J.E. Cloe knew the way of fighting men. Highly trained in their skills, they were confident as long as leadership was present. Many a battle had been lost by brave men who were routed because of the failure of their leaders. Similarly, bold leadership had won conflicts against overwhelming odds.

"We go to Herod's palace on the northern end of the mountain," said J.E. "This is the likely hiding place of the jars and the most easily defended area of the plateau."

"J.E.," said Tomás, "we have your mother. We should consider the odds and leave by the old ramp before we are cut off."

"No!" said Cloe, preempting any other response. "We will help any of the Sicarii who may have survived. We will find the jars and prevent the Karik from getting them. We all agreed we would put an end to the Karik."

"Cloe, perhaps Tomás is correct," said Father Sergio. "We can only do so much."

The monsignor drew himself up to his full height and turned and faced them. "We don't have much time, but it is imperative that the Karik not recover possession of the jars and the knowledge that might be contained within them," he said. "We don't know what's in them, but we know they are thousands of years old. Many have died both in the past and here tonight to protect that knowledge from those who would pervert and distort it such as the Karik. I say if this is the place I must die to make a stand for my faith, then so be it."

There was silence as the group absorbed the monsignor's words.

"As you say, it is your faith and your decision to die for it," responded Tomás. "As for me and my men, our mission was to find our boss and Dr. Lejeune. We have Dr. Lejeune, and she says the boss is likely dead. Our operation here is complete, and we will depart for the ramp. We will fight another day."

J.E. hung his head in weariness and defeat, but he knew Tomás had made his decision. He could not disrespect a man who had fought bravely at every turn but now was done.

"Tomás, go with God," said the monsignor. "We are better for having been with you."

CHAPTER 100

Cloe watched briefly as Tomás and his men departed for the old Roman ramp. Now there were only the four of them, J.E., Father Sergio, the monsignor, and herself. *Hardly an elite fighting force,* she thought.

They moved quietly but quickly to the north, seeking Herod's palace. Before long they came to the outer walls, now in ruins. Rapidly, they moved through the storehouses of the upper regions of the palace. The night-vision goggles were a great help and precluded their discovery since they were not using flashlights. They checked the cisterns, caves, and other areas where the jars might be stashed but came up empty.

"We have found nothing here," said the monsignor. "The Karik cannot be far behind us. We may be better off setting a defensive position."

"I think you are correct, Albert," responded J.E. "But we will need to split up. Mom, you have to go on and search the rest of the palace for the jars. There are two more levels, and the jars could be at either. If necessary, you must destroy them."

"J.E., I could not destroy relics of such age and importance," Cloe said at once.

"If the three of us cannot hold the Karik's men here, would you let them fall into his hands?" asked J.E.

Cloe was silent as she contemplated the enormity of the choice. Her entire life's work was all about preserving and translating such texts as they might find in the jars—a treasure trove of ancient writings. Yet could she countenance this material coming into the possession of the Karik? He would twist the information and misuse it for his own selfish purposes, at best. By destroying the jars, she would be keeping her promise to the pope. "J.E., I understand what must be done," said Cloe sadly.

"Here, take this lighter and matches. We will hold as long as we can."

She looked at them and realized this was a suicide mission. The Karik had four or five times their number, plus long-range rifles with those scopes she had seen take out the Sicarii.

"Mom, we will do the best we can, but the odds are sobering," said J.E. "If it were not critical to protect the jars, we would have gone with Tomás. He did leave us additional weapons and cartridges and some explosives. We have sniper rifles too, but the Karik will eventually triangulate us and overrun our position."

"The young sir is quite correct," said the monsignor. "But suppose we plan our defense with that in mind?"

"Ah, Albert, I definitely like the way you think," replied J.E., smiling.

"What are your orders, J.E.?" asked the monsignor. "We need a battle plan for all times. This is certainly the place for such inspiration."

J.E. turned and surveyed the ground before them, including the remnants of the old exterior walls outlining the outer perimeter of Masada from Herod's days. "There's enough rubble around the walls that the Karik and his men can't sneak up on us from the outside and use the perimeter walls for cover," he observed. "They will have to approach from the inside of the fortress walls.

"Albert, here on the north end of Masada, the plateau narrows considerably. This will force the Karik to come at us inside of the perimeter walls through a rather narrow approach. The only good cover in the area is the ruins of the commander's barracks a few hundred yards to the south," continued J.E.

"Quite so," said the monsignor. "Once they leave the barracks, they will be in the open."

"How do you and Serge feel about that?" asked J.E. "You are priests. If we are successful, we will kill many people tonight."

The monsignor seemed to study the question and to struggle with it. Finally he said, "The Karik will give us no choice. As long as we stand between him and the jars, he will kill us all if we do not defend ourselves. Even priests are entitled to preserve themselves and what they believe in. We will fight to protect ourselves, Cloe, and you."

The young camerlengo was quiet for a moment and then said simply, "Yes."

"We need to position ourselves so the area between the palace walls and the walls of the old barracks becomes a killing field for us," said J.E. "Albert, take a sniper rifle and go to the eastern end of the palace wall and set your sniper nest there."

"What about me?" asked the young camerlengo.

"Serge, you go to the western end of the wall. You must be aware that there is a short wall there, and they may try to flank us on your side," said J.E. "I'll stay right here in the middle."

"But, J.E., that's the most dangerous place," said Father Sergio.

"Not to worry, Serge," responded J.E. "I've been trained for this. I'll do my piece, and then we'll all fall back to the inner walls of the palace right on the point."

"How will we know to coordinate our fire? That will be essential," observed the monsignor. "We have to fire together and then fall back together to have any chance."

"My mom will take our short-range automatic weapons and ammo to the inner wall. I have an idea how I want to set the four Claymore mines that Tomás left," said J.E. "As to communications, we will use this." J.E. pulled a flashlight out of his tunic.

"But that will give you away," said Cloe.

"Not if I use this," replied J.E., and with respect he produced Thib's old low-light red lens that had lit the way for Thib and Bobby Morrow in the cave of jars so long ago.

Cloe watched as he screwed the lens into his flashlight. When he was finished, he flicked it on, and it gave a muted red glow.

"I will hold this aloft when the Karik's men have entered the killing field outside the wall. Count five seconds and open fire," said J.E. "Make your shots count. Our lives depend on bringing down the odds against us. When I think we have gotten as much gain as we can, or when they have regrouped and are on to us, I will wave the light in a circle above my head. This means fall back to the inner wall. Have your path marked in your mind and make haste."

"What about the mines? Where will you put them?" asked the monsignor.

"As we retreat to the inner walls, I will set up a couple of them in the corridors the Karik may use to follow us, and the rest will go just inside the last covered position the Karik's men could use for shelter before crossing the open ground to the inner walls where we will be," said J.E.

"So whoever is left after the killing field and the mines will have to cross this area, and we will use our short-range weapons on them. I think I get it," said Father Sergio.

"Right, Serge, but remember that in battle, after the first shot is fired, all plans can go out the window," said J.E. "Stay disciplined and stay to the plan, and we have a chance."

As they prepared to split up to take on their separate tasks, the monsignor knelt on the dusty surface and bowed his head. J.E. noticed first and joined him. The others followed.

CHAPTER 101

The Karik fumed at the delay. His men were still scattered up and down the various rock formations and broken walls they had used to hide behind during the assault on the Sicarii. Once the firing had begun and the Sicarii were obviously being overwhelmed, the Karik's thugs had charged the mostly wounded women. Although they were game fighters, they were not disciplined soldiers. They had taken souvenirs, body parts and hair. The Karik had blanched and felt nauseous at the sight, and his doubts had returned. Once again the Karik had wondered whether he was really up to this. Briefly, he had wished he were back at the chalet. The sound of Noosh yelling, trying to form the men up to go north to the palace, had brought him back to the jars.

"How long before we can go after what we came for?" pressed the Karik, his mouth dry.

"In just a few minutes, Karik," said Noosh. "I will have them together shortly. I should send scouts forward to make sure the way is clear."

"Rubbish," cried the Karik in frustration and anger. "There is no one here but us and Dr. Lejeune. The Sicarii are all dead. Make haste. I want the jars."

At that point, one of the Karik's men pushed Miguel into the circle where Noosh and the Karik stood.

"What shall we do with him?" asked Noosh.

"He is mine," said the Karik. "Bind his hands tightly, and I'll take him with me. I'll let him see the painful death of his friend, Dr. Lejeune. Then I'll put him out of his misery."

"Karik, the men report the Lejeune woman is not where we left her," said Noosh.

"Damn that pesky woman!" exclaimed the Karik. "She can't have gotten far. Tie his hands and find her."

Noosh saw to it that Miguel's hands were bound. The captive man hung his head and seemed to have little fight left in him.

It took fully thirty minutes for Noosh to round up all the Karik's men and get them briefed and prepared. At last, Noosh reported, "Karik, we are ready. What are your orders?"

"We advance toward Herod's palace on the northern face. That's where the jars must be hidden," replied the Karik. "Search everywhere. Anyone who comes across Dr. Lejeune, bring her to me immediately."

"As you wish, sir, but we will have to cross open ground once we get past the commander's barracks," said Noosh. "I think scouts are in order."

"Noosh, we are alone. Only Dr. Lejeune is here," said the Karik. "But we have made enough noise that there may be others here shortly. We need to find the jars and get out."

"Very well, Karik," replied Noosh, leading his men to the north.

CHAPTER 102

Cloe struggled under the weight of the close-quarters weapons and ammo, but she made it to the inner wall of the palace. After tucking a .45 automatic in her belt near the small of her back, she put the other guns and ammunition behind the inner wall and turned to the north. There, she saw only blackness, with a background of distant cold stars. She was gazing over the edge of the highest promenade of the upper palace. Beyond this point there was only empty space. The next level of the palace was several stories below.

***

J.E. studied the nighttime landscape below him through the low-light lenses. The view was all white but painted with a soft green glow. He heard them before he actually saw them. The Karik's men were making no pretense of stealth. They clearly did not expect any further opposition. J.E. smiled in spite of himself.

He glanced to the east and saw the monsignor watching the incomers. A quick glance to the west told him Father Sergio was ready as well. He worried the most about Serge. The monsignor had a certain militaristic air about him, but Serge was more like Father Al—a parish priest. How would he do in a fight?

J.E. watched as the Karik's troops trod across no man's land with their weapons slung over their shoulders. When most or all of them were in the open, he lit the flashlight and waved it aloft.

Five seconds later, J.E. opened up on the soldiers in the kill zone. His fire was like a wave cutting the force in two. Several of the

Karik's men went down. The assailants divided, some going east and some going west away from the withering fire. Weapons had been unslung and now were returning J.E.'s volleys with a vengeance. They were pouring it on J.E.'s position, which they had soon located.

J.E. hid behind his cover and listened for fire from the monsignor and Father Sergio. He heard nothing. J.E. was the only person shooting at the Karik's men. Now they were zeroed in on him.

J.E. peered out from his redoubt and saw that the opposition had formed up and were now rushing his position. Someone threw a grenade, but it fell short. If they were able to advance a little more, their grenades would be on target. J.E. rose up and squeezed off a few more rounds. Though a couple more of the thugs went down, the return fire was murderous. There was nothing J.E. could do but duck down and hope his friends would join the battle. He had known the priests would be conflicted about killing anybody, including the Karik's henchmen, but he hadn't expected them to do nothing.

"Albert, I'm in a bad way here, and I need help!" yelled J.E. to the east.

Just as he finished his plea, a wicked fusillade opened up from both the east and the west. The killing field was joined. J.E. raised his rifle and fired into the rushing mass. *Thank God*, he thought.

The Karik's men had been beaten back. They turned and ran like scalded dogs. Tracers from the bullets of J.E., the monsignor, and Father Sergio followed them back to the commander's barracks, where they took cover.

Then there was silence, the profound silence that is left in the wake of taking life. Surveying the field, J.E. could see they had inflicted major damage. Probably a third of the Karik's force had been killed or knocked out of the fight by their wounds. This meant that whereas it had been five or six to one, it was now only three or four to one. Progress.

There was suddenly a deadly whooshing sound that J.E. had heard many times before but could hardly believe here.

"RPG!" he screamed. "Down!" He immediately saw that the explosive had been aimed at his position but fired high. It passed over

J.E. and was still going out into the valley below. He recognized this as a sign of inexperience with these rifle-propelled grenades. Firing high was a very common error, for which he thanked God once more.

Still, the Karik's men would soon have their measure. J.E. took out the flashlight with Thib's red lens on it and waved it over his head in a circular motion.

Ten seconds later, another RPG was launched and landed exactly in the monsignor's location. The wall he had been positioned behind blew up, laying waste to the entire area. J.E. could only hope the monsignor and Serge had gotten the signal. Now more grenades were coming in. *Time to move!* he decided. He emptied the magazine of his weapon, spraying the hiding places of the Karik's troops. Then J.E. threw the sniper rifle over his shoulder and ran like a madman.

As he crossed the open area that led to the inner wall, he was joined on the one side by the lithe figure of the monsignor and on the other by the roly-poly silhouette of the camerlengo. Both were very welcome sights.

CHAPTER 103

Cloe had heard the battle sounds as she searched for the jars. At one point, they had become so intense that she wanted to put her hands over her ears, lie down, and curl up into a ball. But as long as her son and friends were fighting to give her time to search, she would search.

She had been completely through the second level and had found nothing. Now she descended to the third and final level. If the jars were not here, they were probably not at Masada. But how could that be? The Sicarii themselves were here, supposedly defending them, and were now most likely all dead. Had they planned for this possibility and not told her? If the jars weren't here, where could they be?

***

The monsignor and Father Sergio ran on ahead to the inner wall while J.E. stopped at the nearest cover from there to set the Claymores. As he glimpsed his compatriots, J.E. noted that Serge seemed to be limping a bit. Well, he was clearly out of shape.

J.E. turned to the task of setting the booby traps. He had to move quickly because the enemy was close behind. The low walls were about thirty to forty yards from the inner ramparts of the palace. This had probably once been one of the many storehouses that had serviced the fortress. Now roofless, it was only a series of stone-and-rock partitions. Although it would be good cover, J.E.'s plans would make his adversaries hiding here very uncomfortable.

He quickly took in the area and set a mine at each end of the last row of old stones before the open area leading to the inner palace. He looked toward his pursuers and set the timers for fifteen minutes. He then used his last two mines in the two lanes that looked like they might be used as access corridors by the Karik. These he set with trip wires. If the Karik came that way or tried to retreat from the Claymores at the forward wall, he would find nothing but fiery hell.

Having done what he could, J.E. ran for all he was worth toward the inner wall. Sporadic fire overshot him as he dove behind the covering wall. "Okay," he yelled, "set up the same as before."

Then he jerked up, now noticing that the monsignor was kneeling over Father Sergio. "Albert, what is it?" he cried.

"Father Sergio has been hit," said the monsignor. "I don't think he knew it himself until we collapsed here, but they got him in the leg, and there is arterial bleeding."

"Noooo!" shouted J.E., now watching his friend's leg pumping blood. "Albert, we have a kit. Do what you can, and I'll hold the Karik off. Hurry!"

J.E. took the medical kit from his pack and tossed it to the monsignor. He then leaped to the wall and surveyed the area. It was quiet and empty. But in the silence he could hear the telltale clang and clink of men getting into position. He looked at the timer on his watch and saw it would be ten minutes still before the mines would go off.

BLAM! A huge blast erupted as one of the corridor mines was tripped. This backlit the Karik's forces for a moment, and J.E. got a pretty good look at their deployment. J.E. was unsure whether the poor SOB who had tripped the Claymore was lucky or unlucky.

"How is he?" J.E. called back to the monsignor.

"Not good, but I think I've slowed the bleeding. I have it pretty tightly wrapped," responded the monsignor. "He needs a doctor now."

As J.E. peered over the rock wall, the Karik's men let go with a great fusillade of fire. The rocks around J.E. were blasted, and the air was filled with dust and grit. He hunkered down but still checked to see if they were coming.

As the gunfire slacked a bit, he turned, feeling a presence at his arm. There was his mother, crouched down with her .45 aimed at the Karik's forces.

"Mom, what are you doing here?" he yelled over the noise of the sporadic firing.

"The jars aren't here," said Cloe. "I have searched all three levels, and there's nothing."

"But you must have missed something," replied J.E. "All the clues lead here."

"I have looked everywhere there is to look in and near Herod's palace … in the storehouses, the caves, and the cisterns," she said. "The low-light glasses made it easier and quicker than I would have thought. Unless, somehow, the jars are buried, they are not here."

J.E. took this in. "Mom, Serge is badly wounded," he said solemnly. "Can you see what you can do to help? I need Albert on the line if we are to defend our position."

"Sure, J.E.," she said, turning toward the priest. Then Cloe turned back and said, "I want to see an end to the Karik, but if Serge needs medical treatment and if there are no jars here, we need to rethink what we are doing … Let's just get out of here."

"We're trapped against the northern side of the fortress," he replied. "No matter how we go, we would have to pass the Karik. I doubt we would get a get-out-of-jail-free card from him."

"But there's nothing here," she said. "There's nothing to defend or to fight for."

"I think the Karik would feel otherwise," responded J.E. "We're fighting now for our lives."

CHAPTER 104

"No jars?" queried the monsignor. Cloe had gone back to help Father Sergio, and the monsignor had come up to man a fighting position.

"No jars," agreed J.E.

"So Masada and all the clues were never about the jars," mused the monsignor. "What does that mean?"

"It means it was always a trap," responded J.E. "In the mountains when she came back from their camp, Mom said the Sicarii would deal once and for all with this devil, the Karik, and his organization. I remember her saying we were not invited. Of course, the kidnapping changed all that. The Sicarii laid a clever trap."

"Clever, indeed, with your mother in the center with just enough information to convince the Karik to come here," replied the monsignor. "The only thing they did not count on was the ruthlessness of the Karik and his weaponry. Now they are all dead, caught in their own trap."

"True, but they must have considered that a possibility since the jars were apparently never here, or if they were, they were moved again," observed J.E. "Belt and suspenders."

Just then Cloe appeared at the wall.

"How's Serge?" asked J.E.

"We've got the blood loss slowed but not stopped. He needs a doctor and a hospital now," she said urgently.

"The only way out from this end of Masada is to fight our way out. We are outgunned four or five to one," said J.E. "We need a miracle."

J.E. had been watching the no man's land between the Karik's position and the inner wall. Now he straightened and peered down at them. "They are coming," he said simply, glancing at his watch. "We still have two minutes before the forward Claymores go off. Albert, let's spray their positions with fire and see if we can back them down a bit."

"Okay … I'll go east and try to get a cross fire going," responded the monsignor.

"Remember, they will target your position with their RPGs. Don't stay in the same place for long," said J.E.

The monsignor responded with a sardonic smile and said, "With God's help, we will get out of this thing yet."

The priest turned and ran up the wall to the east, and J.E. looked at his watch: one minute. He could see the thugs edging their way out from behind the wall and then jumping back. They were working up their nerve now, but eventually, they would come.

J.E. leveled his AR-15 and sprayed the Karik's position with high-velocity .223 rifle slugs. Immediately, his assault was answered by a great volley of return fire. He and Cloe dove down behind the wall as far as they could get. They could hear the screams of the charging men coming for the inner wall.

At almost the same time came the sound of the monsignor opening up with his AK-47, the heavy slugs making a *womp, womp* sound when they hit dirt, stone, or flesh.

J.E. and Cloe looked out and saw that the men who had charged were conflicted. The monsignor's fire had them in a cross fire, but the Karik was screaming to charge. J.E. lifted his rifle with a new clip and added to the melee. Some of the men dove for cover, and some went back to the wall they had only just left.

At that point, the two Claymores exploded and lit up the night. Men screamed and cried in the aftermath of the explosions. If only he had had more mines, he might have been able to lay them out properly and finish it right here, J.E. thought. But with just the two last mines, planting them the way he had was the only thing he could do. It was not the most lethal use of the explosives because only the men on the ends of the trench formed by the walls would be hit. Still, it was a start.

Whoosh. Following the now familiar sound of the RPGs, the wall near where the monsignor had been positioned exploded in flame. J.E. grabbed Cloe and ran about ten yards to the west and then dove for cover. No sooner had he done that than the place where they had been positioned also exploded in flames.

They looked out and saw that the Karik's men were once again running across the no man's land below. J.E. emptied another clip on them and shouted to the monsignor, "Fall back!"

As Cloe ran to Father Sergio and J.E. followed, the sound of the monsignor's AK pounding the oncoming forces filled the air.

The three of them converged on Father Sergio. The monsignor and J.E. grabbed him under his arms and carried him down the stairs to the next level of the palace. He was not fully conscious.

"What do we do now, J.E.?" asked the monsignor.

"From now on, we improvise. We watch our ammo, and we lay in wait for the Karik's soldiers, guerilla fashion," responded J.E. "We have to sting them to the point they give up, or we have to annihilate them. One by one, we get them all. That's it."

"All right, they have to come down these steps along the outer edge of the cliff face unless they have some way of rappelling down from above," said the monsignor. "Take Father Sergio to the last level below. He is likely to be safer there. I'll guard these steps and hold them off."

"Albert, we have to hold them here. The next level is little more than a terrace overlooking a thousand-foot drop," said J.E. "It's indefensible."

The monsignor looked at him seriously and said, "I know."

CHAPTER 105

Cloe and J.E. frog-walked Father Sergio down to the lower terrace and put him in a sheltered place under a stone outcropping where he could not be seen or shot at from above. Cloe turned and looked out into space dimly lit in the moonless night and wondered what would happen to them if they were trapped here. There was no further retreat and no place to go. She shivered at the thought in the gathering coolness of the mountain air.

Cloe and J.E. bent over Father Sergio and briefly loosened the bandages binding his wounds so that he would not completely lose circulation. The blood began to once again pump from the bullet hole. Clearly, an artery had been damaged or, God forbid, severed.

As J.E. turned to rise, Cloe saw the injured man's hand reach out and grab her son's leg. "J.E.," whispered Father Sergio.

Ducking back down, J.E. looked at his friend. "Yes, Serge," he replied. Cloe silently watched, tears in her eyes.

"Thanks, J.E., for everything. Please tell His Holiness I did my best," said the priest, struggling to get out the words.

"Tell him yourself," said J.E. with a smile. "You're not going anywhere."

"You'll be fine, as soon as we get out of here and get you to a hospital," echoed Cloe.

"I'm sorry to be such a burden," whispered the young camerlengo wearily.

Cloe and J.E. looked at each other, and after a moment of silence, it seemed Father Sergio had passed out from his wounds. But he surprised them.

"J.E., leave me a weapon. I can still try to fight," said the priest gamely. "I will make my village proud."

J.E. placed a pistol next to him just as the priest did lose consciousness. *God help us*, Cloe prayed.

As they finished securing the young camerlengo, Cloe heard shots from above. Hustling back to the second level, she and J.E. found the monsignor hunkered down behind good cover, watching the steps. He had not fired his weapon.

"They are just trying to goad us into revealing our position," said the monsignor quietly. "Pay that no mind."

"I can hear them scrambling above us," whispered Cloe.

"They are looking for some other route down, but if I know the Roman engineers who built this place, there is no other way down … just the steps," said J.E. "I suspect they are also carefully searching for more mines. We did some damage a little while ago with them."

"What do you think the odds are now, J.E.?" asked the monsignor.

"Well, based on what I could see just before we moved back, I think they are down to about one-third of their original strength … maybe six or seven left," said J.E. softly. "Not bad for a day's work, but they still have plenty enough to do the job."

Just then Cloe heard a loud clunk and a rolling sound.

"Grenade!" hissed J.E. "Down!"

BLAM! With the explosive report from the grenade, Cloe and the others were showered with bits and pieces of stone and dust.

Cloe started to speak.

"Quiet," J.E. whispered in her ear. "They don't know where we are. They are dropping the grenades at random, hoping to hit us or scare us out."

Then came the clunk of two more of the explosives, which rolled to the center of the plaza and detonated. These were actually farther away than the first grenade, so no real damage was done.

"It's working. I'm scared to death," cried Cloe.

"They will be coming down the steps in a minute," said J.E. "Be ready."

After a couple more grenades, the automatic fire opened up from above.

"Here they come," cautioned the monsignor.

Several men pounded down the stairs firing wildly, hoping to get lucky or at least to keep them down. J.E. and the monsignor opened up with their weapons, and Cloe could hear the AK rattle above the fray. Ricochets, rocks, and stone particles flew everywhere. At least one of the men was hit before the others held up and retreated. Still, the Karik's men had succeeded in locating their position.

"We've got to go," J.E. said hoarsely. "They know our position, so we can't stay here; the grenades are going to start coming again very soon."

"There's no other cover on this level," replied the monsignor. "We will have to go down."

"But the lower terrace is nothing but a death trap," said Cloe. "There is little cover and no escape."

"Have faith, Cloe," said the monsignor. "God has not led us all this way to abandon us in our moment of greatest need."

She looked at the monsignor and smiled. "Then I hope he has a few extra angels he can send."

CHAPTER 106

Noosh looked at the Karik, who was exhorting the men to get down the stairs at any cost. Plainly, he was willing to lead them from behind.

"Sir, we have plenty of grenades," Noosh said to the Karik. "Are we not better conserving the men, now that we know where Dr. Lejeune and her friends are? We can drop explosives on them until we get them, they give up, or move lower."

"Yes, yes," replied the Karik restively. "Let it be so."

"In effect, our strategy will be to herd them to the last terrace below, from which there is no escape," offered Noosh.

"Yes, there I will have my revenge and the jars too," said the Karik, "for surely that is where they are hidden."

Noosh gave the order, and his men began dropping the pint-size bombs on the very area where they now knew J.E. and his forces were located.

The Karik laughed as the explosives blew up.

CHAPTER 107

In the hiatus after the firefight and before the grenade assault began again in earnest, J.E., Cloe, and the monsignor bolted for the steps along the side of the cliff leading to the lowest area of the palace. If any of them had questioned the decision to retreat, the explosions that rang out above just after they left convinced them they would now be dead had they stayed.

Although Cloe knew they had escaped one death trap, she recognized that it was a temporary reprieve unless something fundamentally changed. There was just nowhere to go. They were still outnumbered by the Karik at least two or three to one, and he had the high ground. "J.E., we are in a bad way here," she said. "What do we do?"

Her son turned and surveyed the plaza, only a low wall separating it from eternity below and the surrounding rocks. The place was maybe thirty to forty feet across, ringed by the low wall on three sides and perched atop a rocky point. The cold night wind blew briskly over them as it had cooled others here for thousands of years. The only access was the way they had come, a rocky staircase that swung out over the edge of the mountain. At one time, J.E. knew, there had been access by means of an internal corridor, but the stone walls had long since collapsed, blocking the way.

"The old corridor provides some shelter and enough rock and overhang that it will be difficult to drop grenades directly on us," said J.E. "This will be where we make our stand."

"Let's get Father Sergio in there and get ready," said the monsignor.

As they hunkered down, Cloe noted that from their shelter, they could not see all of the steps down from the upper level. The Karik's men would be almost all the way down before they could get a good shot. If the assailants could rush down in force throwing grenades and shooting, they might overwhelm them.

Seeming to read her mind, J.E. said, "Don't worry about the blind spot. The Karik's men don't know about it, and there are not so many of them to try to rush us. They will drop their grenades and try to lure us out into a firefight."

No sooner had J.E. spoken than the first explosive hit the terrace, rolled, and exploded. Shrapnel and debris showered their position, but the grenade was not near enough to do any damage to them. Several more followed, blasting away a part of the retaining wall overlooking the thousand-foot drop.

Cloe stared at the opening, which led only to oblivion. Waves of gooseflesh assaulted her arms as she huddled from the wind, the cold, and the fear.

Just as suddenly as the grenades had ended, automatic weapon fire began. But the bullets merely ricocheted off the rock floor and walls. After a few moments, there was silence.

"Dr. Lejeune," called a voice from above.

"J.E., what should I do?" she asked.

"Why not answer him?" asked the monsignor. "We might learn something. What do we have to lose?"

Cloe looked at J.E., who nodded and said, "Draw it out."

"Yes?" she yelled.

"Dr. Lejeune, it seems we have a situation," shouted the Karik. "You cannot leave, but I cannot get at you without exposing my men."

"That works just fine for me," Cloe responded. "Come on down and let us show you some American hospitality with my two friends, Smith and Wesson."

J.E. smiled, and the monsignor chuckled.

"I offer you a deal," screamed the Karik, clearly frustrated. "I only want the jars. You and your friends can leave. Just give me what I want."

"Karik, I have a deal for you," said Cloe loudly. "You and your men get off my mountain, and I won't destroy the jars right where they sit. We have rigged them with explosives. My first job was to recover the relics, but my second was to keep you from getting them. It would be a damn shame, but I can still accomplish my mission by blowing them up."

The monsignor was gazing at her with new respect. J.E. smiled with pride.

At first there was a deep silence, and then in answer to her offer, a terrible fusillade of grenades, RPGs, and automatic-weapons fire ignited the night. It was the loudest and most dangerous display of firepower yet, but still it did nothing but push Cloe and friends a little deeper into the corridor.

"Okay, be ready," said J.E. "This may be when they rush us."

As J.E. crept out a bit to get an angle on the steps, another terrible blast of firepower came from above, but it was markedly different from the previous one. It did not seem to be aimed at them, and it seemed to have a more distant origin.

"What the hell was that?" exclaimed J.E.

CHAPTER 108

J.E. crawled back from the mouth of the portal in which they were hiding and said, "Something is happening up there."

"What is it, J.E.?" queried Cloe.

As they struggled to hear what was happening above, the shooting from the Karik's soldiers increased to what sounded like a desperate cacophony of gunfire, but it was clearly not aimed at them. Soon after this started, it became apparent that someone else was returning the Karik's fire. While Cloe and her cohorts huddled in the corridor, a war was going on upstairs. Grenades and RPGs blasted amid the rifle fire. Men screamed and cried. Suddenly, there was a terrible silence.

"Get ready," said J.E. "Somebody won. We may be the prize."

In the still of the night, they could hear the whimpering of a man or two, probably wounded. Two single pistol shots rang out.

"My God," said J.E. "They're shooting the wounded."

Cloe saw J.E. and the monsignor ready their weapons, checking the ammo clips and cocking them. The group could hear footsteps and men shuffling around over them.

"Dr. Lejeune!" someone shouted from above. "Hold your fire. We are coming down."

She looked at J.E. and the monsignor, but they were as baffled as she. Who was coming down? "What do we do?" she asked the others.

"We blow the hell out of whoever comes down those steps," responded J.E. "We do not want to be at the mercy of anyone who shoots helpless men, whether it be the Karik or whoever else is up there."

Cloe could now hear footsteps on the top of the stairs leading to this level. They all went to the front of the corridor, but they could see only the very bottom few steps of the staircase. Time seemed suspended as the men advanced down the steps. Cloe could see shoes and now trousers and robes on the stairs. In a minute they would be on them, or J.E. would have blown them off the stairs into the valley below.

Cloe dropped to her stomach on the cold stone floor and looked up and then moved quickly back. "Hold up. Don't shoot," whispered Cloe.

"J.E.!" yelled a man not yet visible.

"I know that voice," said J.E.

Now the man at the front of the line was fully visible, but he had his hands up and was without any weapons.

"J.E.!" the other man shouted again. "It's Tomás."

CHAPTER 109

Relief flooded over Cloe like a tsunami. Tomás! Where had he been? Where had he come from?

J.E. edged toward the front of the corridor. "Tomás," he yelled, "what's going on?"

"My men and I have captured the famous Karik," replied Tomás. "We bring you a prisoner."

In a moment, all of the men were down on the terrace, with the Karik, one of his men, and Miguel leading the way. Tomás and two of his men followed, covering the Karik's group very carefully with their weapons. The Karik seemed beaten but unharmed. Head hung low and shoulders slumped, he trudged across the terrace.

On seeing Michael, alive, Cloe's heart lifted. "Michael," she called.

J.E. ran to Tomás and hugged him. "Tomás, you are a sight for us. We were in a very tight spot," said J.E.

"It's great to see you, Tomás," added the monsignor. "We thought you had left by the ramp."

"I did," replied Tomás. "But when we began to hear shooting and grenades from the north end of the mountain, we realized the Karik had to be after you. Moreover, since he and his forces had gone to the north, we could not be trapped by them. We could always have retreated to the ramp. We knew this was our chance, so we decided to come back. It seems we have also found the boss, Miguel."

"Tomás, it is so good to see you and your men," said Cloe, joining the group. Cloe could scarcely believe that somehow they had been delivered from the Karik's forces.

"We saw the fight at the inner wall of the highest level of the palace," Tomás continued. "That was very well done, and you cut the odds considerably. But we could not help since the Karik was well covered from behind, and it looked like you might be booby-trapping the area."

"Yes, I set out all the Claymores you left us, but I think all but maybe one have been tripped or timed out," responded J.E.

"We did not know that, so we had to look for our best opportunity," said Tomás.

Cloe looked at Michael and focused on the fact that he was somehow still alive. She was moving toward Michael to embrace him when Tomás addressed him.

"It's good to see you alive, boss," said Tomás.

"Thanks, Tomás," said Miguel, apparently overwhelmed. "We didn't have time to talk above, but you have put me right where I want to be."

"Here's your old .45," replied Tomás. "It was in your room in Tunis. I have carried it all this distance in hopes of presenting it to you in this very way."

Miguel took the weapon, looked it over, and then checked the magazine and jacked a round into the chamber. He then eased the hammer and tucked the automatic into his belt.

"I feel whole again," said Miguel seriously.

Cloe studied Michael carefully, thinking that was a strange thing to say. Tomás turned away from his boss and continued his story.

"We saw you hold the second level briefly, but the explosives were too much. When you ran to the terrace on the third level and the Karik took the second stage, we knew our chance had come. They were so intent on you, they did not even post a man to guard their rear," observed Tomás.

"I gather you had good cover and high ground and were able to fire down on the Karik," said the monsignor.

"Yes, to make the story short, we blasted them until they threw up their hands and quit," said Tomás with a smile.

"But, Tomás, shooting the wounded?" questioned J.E.

"That was the Karik, not us. He shot his own wounded men and then threw down his pistol," replied Tomás, spitting. "Coward!"

The Karik snickered but said nothing.

"Well, we have him now, and he will pay for his crimes," said J.E. "Thank God it's over."

CHAPTER 110

Cloe wasn't sure it was over. She looked at the figures on the terrace and was filled with an inexplicable foreboding. Something was missing, or she had missed something. All she knew was that the atmosphere crackled with a terrible expectation.

Without warning, Miguel turned snake-quick, drew the automatic from his waistband, and shot Tomás in the back. Cloe watched with horror the puzzled look on Tomás's face as he fell first to his knees clutching his chest and then face first to the hard tiles on the terrace. He did not move again.

Cloe screamed and looked over at Tomás's men, expecting them to return fire. But Miguel shot the two of them dead as they stood processing the situation. Tomás and both of his men were down, dead. Miguel had the only drawn gun. J.E. made a move to pull out his.

"Hold!" shouted Miguel as he pointed the weapon at J.E. and the monsignor. Then he swung it toward Cloe. "If you make one move, I will shoot Cloe."

Cloe looked around and at her colleagues and saw Michael had them stymied. His gun was pointed dead at her. His face was the same one she had seen when he told her to shut up and sit down. He was his father's son. "Michael?" she asked.

He looked at her, but there was no vestige of the man she had danced with in Tunis or the man she had kissed. How could she have been such a fool?

The Karik turned to Miguel, bowed deeply, and said, "Master, it is so good to have you with us again."

Reality came crashing down on Cloe as she realized Michael had always been his father's son and had probably conspired with or directed the Karik in everything he had done.

The Karik and his one remaining thug disarmed Cloe, J.E., and the monsignor. Now guns were pointed at them from three directions.

"Where are my jars?" queried Miguel.

"Michael, consider what you are doing. How could you follow your father's footsteps when his organization, under the auspices of this man the Karik, killed your entire family?" pleaded Cloe.

"Oh, that," said Miguel with a smile. "Well, I was tired of the woman, but the boys were a mistake." Miguel continued, his voice now rising and cracking a bit, betraying his emotion. "They went running back to the car for something after I triggered the bomb. I hated to lose them."

Cloe was stunned. Michael had killed his family? "Why?" was all she could say.

"A simple calculation, really," he replied, now back in control. "If my wife were blown up apparently by my father's organization, you would believe anything I said about not being a part of it. It gave me credibility. As I have said, the children were unintended collateral damage."

"But, Michael, the Karik tortured you at the Armenian hideout," responded Cloe. "I saw you tortured with my own eyes."

"There was never any torture at the chalet. It was a circus trick to fool you. My skin had been coated with fire-retardant chemicals. I got nothing worse than a bit of sunburn," said Michael, laughing. "The rest was just acting the part. You fell for the whole thing!"

Cloe crumpled to her knees. She had never been so appalled and humiliated in her life. She thought she had seen evil in the Kolektor, but this was so far beyond what he had done as to be inconceivable. As she leaned over, her gut clenched, and she thought she might vomit. J.E. started toward her, but the Karik pointed his gun at him and told him to back up.

Miguel laughed again. "You were so easy."

Cloe hesitated but found she was no longer humiliated. Now she was just appalled and beginning to get angry. She raised her head and looked directly at Michael. "Why me, you SOB?" she hissed.

"Because you were always the key to the jars," he answered. "You were our best lead. You had been with the Sicarii, and they trusted you. I figured that you would lead me to my heritage … to the jars."

"But you tried to kill me in New Orleans," Cloe said.

"Not at all," Michael said. "We were very careful, but we had to jolt you out of your comfort zone, translating the materials from the first jars. I needed you looking for the cave."

"You planned this whole thing, didn't you?" Cloe yelled. "Everything—the chance meeting in Tunis, your supposed torture in Armenia, and your capture by the Karik. It all led here."

"True," said Michael. "But you weren't exactly Miss Innocent, were you? I may have fooled you, but you led the Karik here through the Sicarii's misdirection and mysterious clues. They intended to put him down. Now they are all dead. Do you deny it?"

"The Karik is evil and a threat to the treasure of knowledge the Sicarii have safeguarded for millennia," Cloe said unapologetically. "But you controlled the Karik and everything else. You are the real evil."

Cloe could hear the Karik snickering in the shadows, and she knew she was correct. Michael, "the boss," had been behind everything.

Michael smiled and asked, "Where are the jars?"

"There are none here," Cloe responded flatly, as Michael's announcement that the Sicarii were all dead began to sink in. "You have failed even with all your evil efforts. The Sicarii have outsmarted you, and now you say they are all dead. No one alive knows where the jars are."

"You must know," said the Karik. "You led us here."

"They could be anywhere in the world," responded Cloe. "I just followed the clues the Sicarii gave me. Like everyone else, I thought the jars would be here."

Michael walked over to where the seriously wounded Father Sergio was lying and put his gun to the young camerlengo's head. The priest did not stir. Cloe cringed, fearing where this might go.

"Where are the jars?" he yelled.

"I don't know, and you have wiped out everyone who might know! You have succeeded in doing what the Romans could not do in the first century and what time has been unable to accomplish," she replied hoarsely. "The Sicarii are now no more, and with the last of them died all their secrets."

"I wager there is one last Sicarius ... you!" Michael yelled at her. "This man's death will be on your head."

"I don't know!" she screamed, but the scream was drowned out by a gunshot.

Cloe gawked down at Serge, who had opened his eyes and rolled slightly, freeing the gun beneath him, and fired at Michael. The shot missed Michael but hit the last of the Karik's men, knocking him flat. The man now writhed in agony from a wound in the groin area.

Michael had jumped back as the priest aimed his weapon, and he now fired two shots into Father Sergio from point-blank range. The terrible sound of the impact of those terminal shots hung in the air. Cloe watched Sergio drop the gun and go limp. She heard his last rasp of breath as he exhaled for the final time. He smiled at her as he died. Cloe screamed again and wobbled on her feet.

J.E. and the monsignor visibly struggled against the urge to leap forward at the man who had killed their friend.

Cloe collapsed and fainted.

CHAPTER 111

Cloe lay on the cold stone of the terrace and began to hear sounds and sense people around her. She did not want to wake up. She wanted to stay unconscious forever, until there was no more pain. But as she remembered what had happened to Father Sergio, her eyes jerked open. The demon, Michael, was squatting next to her, waiting for her to come around.

"Ah," he said, "while you were napping, we all changed positions in anticipation of playing a new game."

Cloe sat up and looked around. The monsignor and J.E. were now standing on the precipice at the edge of the terrace where the wall had been blown out. She almost swooned again but held on. There was nothing behind J.E. and Albert but a thousand-foot drop. The wind had picked up, and the two of them swayed in the gusts.

"For God's sake, Michael!" she cried.

"God has nothing to do with this, and they will certainly fall or be shot if you don't tell me where the jars are," replied Michael.

"I don't know where they are; if I did, I would tell you," she pleaded.

"I don't believe you," he said. "Which will it be, your friend or your son?"

"She doesn't know, you scum-sucking pissant!" yelled J.E.

The monsignor was fingering the beads of the rosary attached to his tunic. "Michael," he said, not unkindly, "this is a final chance to change your ways. Can you hear God calling to you?"

"I hear nothing but the wind and your death song," said the son of the Kolektor.

"Every man has a last chance to turn aside from evil. Even Judas had his chance," said the monsignor. "Turn aside!"

"How did that work with my father, priest?" spat Michael. "But you have helped make up my mind as to who should go first. Step out, Father, and let's test your God."

"Michael, testing God is a bad idea, as your father learned in his last moments," said the monsignor. "My God will catch me in the next world. Who will catch you?"

"Step out, priest!" screamed Michael, taunting the priest.

"No! Wait," said Cloe.

"Have you remembered what I want to know?" asked Michael.

"I ..." Cloe faltered.

Michael turned and fired a shot just over the monsignor's head. Albert took a small involuntary step toward the abyss and teetered on the brink.

Then without warning, a helicopter shot straight up from below the edge of the cliff face like a hot ember climbing a stone chimney, and the prop wash blew J.E. and the monsignor away from death's door. Sideways to the terrace, the helicopter hovered, and the Swiss sharpshooters shot the Karik's remaining henchman, who had regained his feet, holding his crotch in one hand and his gun in the other. Another shot rang out, hitting the Karik squarely in the chest. He grabbed the front of his robe, now soaked in blood, and gazed at them with a confused look.

The monsignor yelled, "It's Father Anton and the Swiss!"

As Cloe, J.E., and the monsignor lay on the stones looking up, the Karik stumbled, spun around, dazed and in pain, and tumbled off the terrace into oblivion. His terminal screams could be heard even over the sound of the helicopter. They were the black screams of horror from a soulless man.

Cloe looked at Michael and saw panic in his eyes. He turned and ran up the stairs to the next level. The helicopter steadied itself over the terrace, and three of the Swiss rappelled down to the group's aid. Then the helicopter flared off after Michael.

J.E. jumped up, grabbed the dead thug's pistol, checked the clip, and ran up the stairs after the Kolektor's heir.

"J.E.!" screamed Cloe.

CHAPTER 112

Father Anton turned on the helicopter's searchlight and scanned the middle and top levels of the palace for the man who had run. Although there was lots of ground cover, there was nowhere to hide from the air.

Meanwhile, J.E. ran up the first set of stairs and stopped at the top to test whether Michael was waiting for him. Sure enough, a slug banged off the stone near enough to his face that the dust blinded him for a moment.

J.E. shook it off, fired a shot in the general direction of where Michael had been, and ran after him. As he did, the helicopter roared over him, almost close enough to touch. J.E. saw that Father Anton had activated the searchlight and was taking up station south of the top level of the palace, near the old commander's barracks. Michael could not get by Father Anton without being seen. Even now, the rest of the Swiss were coming down ropes to further block his escape.

J.E. rose, stood behind a storage house wall, and yelled, "It's over, Michael! There's no place to go. You are trapped. Everyone else is dead."

"That's what you think, soldier boy!" screamed Michael, rising up from his hiding spot and raising his weapon.

J.E. ducked as a shot hit the wall in front of him. But he had seen where Michael was. J.E. circled around through several corridors that had, at one time, interconnected the storage houses. He figured he was roughly abreast of Michael's position. J.E. could see the lights of the Swiss coming toward Michael from the rear. Father Anton flew over and then did a one-eighty. He too had spotted Michael. J.E.

aimed his pistol when he had Michael in his sights, but he could not bring himself to take the certain death shot. The man was helpless.

Stepping behind a nearby doorway, he shouted, "Give it up, Michael. You are surrounded. Your rotten day is done."

Another shot rang out, and J.E. saw Michael bolt for the commander's barracks just outside the palace walls. As he ran, Michael snapped off a shot at the hovering helicopter. J.E. heard the bullet ricochet off the metal skin, and the aircraft then roared off to the east, its engine shrieking. Cautiously, J.E. peeked around the edge of the stone archway serving as his cover and saw Michael running flat-out up one of the corridors that traversed the barracks.

"Michael," yelled J.E., "stop! The Claymores!"

BLAM! The mighty explosion from the midst of the barracks blew dust, stone, and sand everywhere, showering J.E., who had run after Michael. J.E. lowered his weapon, turned back toward his mom and the others, and shuffled heavily away from the blast site. He had no doubt what he would find there.

CHAPTER 113

Father Anton landed the helicopter and received a huge bear hug from J.E. when he jumped down.

"Thank God, Tony," J.E. said as they walked back toward his mother and the others. Glancing around, he could see the Swiss taking up a defensive position in case there were stragglers from the Karik's force.

***

When the group was reunited, there were hugs and tears all around. The monsignor had just finished administering the last rites to his friend and colleague, Father Sergio. Even in her happiness at being saved, Cloe cried for Serge. Two of the Swiss put together a field stretcher and with a quiet dignity lifted Father Sergio's body onto it. They then started up the stairs to the helicopter.

"He will be taken back to Rome and buried with full honors," said the monsignor. "He certainly was a hero here."

His words caused Cloe to cry even harder for her friend. J.E. and the monsignor were also shaken and deeply saddened. The monsignor, on one knee, looked up at Cloe with tears in his eyes. J.E. comforted his mother as best he could.

J.E. turned to Father Anton and asked, "Tony, where have you been, and where did you come from?"

"When you left the airport in Jerusalem, we waited for a helicopter," he replied. "Our cohorts in the Vatican ops center scrounged one up for us, but it took a while. Finally, it came, and we immediately took off for Masada."

"But how did you know where we were, and how did you find us when you did?" asked Cloe.

"We knew J.E. had gone to Masada. When we arrived in the vicinity, we saw the cable car had been blown up, so we stood off to reconnoiter," responded the cleric. "This particular bird has infrared radar and some other toys that allowed us to get the lay of the land. We could see that one group was being pushed inexorably down the face of the palace to the third level. We assumed that was you because we couldn't think of why you would do that to the Karik. The rest was just a matter of timing."

"Well, your timing was excellent," said the monsignor. "We owe our lives to you—that and the destruction of the Kolektor's empire."

"J.E. … is it finally over?" asked Cloe.

"I think so," said J.E. thoughtfully. "We know the Kolektor is dead. The only thing that held his organization together was the Karik, who was the Kolektor's servant and number one, Dadash. And that was only possible because Michael, the Kolektor's son and heir, collaborated with him and probably directed him. And Michael is gone now too. You must have heard the explosion a few minutes ago. Michael, trying desperately to escape, tripped the last Claymore I had set in the barracks' corridors."

"Ironic that the man who sought to use the deaths of his family in a bomb blast to further his efforts to possess the jars should die here at Masada in an explosion," whispered Cloe. "Is it over?"

"Yes," said the monsignor. "Michael, the Karik, and all their men are dead. Even the field general, Noosh, has been accounted for. It is over."

"We thought that in Jerusalem after Hakeldama," Cloe mused. "How can we be sure?"

CHAPTER 114

Cloe had been back in Madisonville working on the journal translation for several weeks. It was going pretty well. The most interesting thing she had discovered so far was an obscure reference to the end of times in a dialogue between Jesus and someone she had not yet been able to identify. She thought it might be St. John.

Did this relate to the destruction of Jerusalem or something else? She was not sure. She had asked the monsignor to meet her in New Orleans to review the text and to discuss it. She needed the religious context.

As she drove across the causeway toward New Orleans, she thought about her last trip and all that had transpired. She had finally begun to sleep better. Right after returning to Louisiana, she had had nightmares about Father Sergio's death and then about J.E. and the monsignor being pushed off the side of the mountain. Cloe had awoken in the Water Street house sweating and with bedclothes in knots on many nights. Today was better. She still hurt for Serge though.

The plan was to meet the monsignor at the Criollo restaurant and to have lunch. As Cloe drove toward the hotel, she felt a sense of déjà vu, but she knew this was nothing like the last time because there was no Karik and no Kolektor organization to present a threat. At least she told herself so.

As she strode into Criollo's, she greeted Marco, who always had a hug for her. He led her to the table where the monsignor was waiting. He jumped up and hugged her warmly.

"Hello, Cloe," he said. "You look marvelous. Clearly, life in Madisonville on the river agrees with you."

"Thanks, Albert," she replied. "It's good to see you as well."

They sat and enjoyed a glass of wine in a familiar silence.

"Where's J.E.?" asked the monsignor.

"He's back on active duty in the Middle East," said Cloe. "I'm not sure just where because of his intelligence job."

"Well," said the monsignor, "he's had a world of experience in that area."

Cloe laughed and felt that the ice had been broken. Each brought the other up to date on everything that had happened since Masada, including the services for Father Sergio, which Cloe had been too ill to attend.

"The pope himself led the funeral procession to Serge's small village, where he was buried. Such a thing has never happened. The pride and happiness of those poor people was amazing even in their sorrow for Father Sergio."

"I understand, Albert," said Cloe. "I just wish I could have been there."

They discussed her dilemma regarding the passage from the journal. The monsignor was extremely intrigued and offered some excellent insights on what it might mean.

"Albert, I have an appointment to look at some old books up at the library at St. Mary's Church in the old Ursuline Convent," said Cloe. "Come with me."

The priest seemed to think it over and said, "I'd love to. It's a beautiful spring day, and walking this wonderful meal off would be a joyful task, but I have something to ask before we go."

Cloe tensed as she remembered the last time the monsignor had had something to ask of her in this very room. "What is it, Albert?" she inquired hesitantly.

"Were you the stalking horse sent by the Sicarii to lure the Karik to the trap at Masada, as Michael declared at the end?" he asked directly.

355

"No," Cloe responded with equal frankness. "No one knew who would be taken by the Karik in his search for information on the location of the jars. It might have been any of us. We were all given the same bits of information. The way it worked out, it just happened to be me. Only the leader of the Sicarii knew everything."

"I see," said the monsignor. "I think I would have liked to have known the leader."

"Yes," agreed Cloe.

They left the hotel through the parking lobby, the same one near where the bomb had been planted in Cloe's car. It seemed so long ago. They crossed over to Chartres and strolled up toward the Ursuline Convent.

"I was supposed to visit the library the last time we were in New Orleans, but you know what happened to interrupt that trip," said Cloe, drawing in the sights and sounds of Jackson Square as they passed through it.

"You know, there is some connection between St. Mary's Church and France," stated the monsignor. "The founder of the Order of St. Ursula was born in Dijon, not far from Lyon. The order had facilities not only in Europe but also in Africa. Old records have been stored at the library for many, many years. Heaven only knows what you may find there."

"Well, we'll know shortly," said Cloe as they climbed the steps to the little souvenir shop that served as the entrance to the courtyard for the convent.

Soon they were greeted by the librarian, who led them into the building that housed the library. Cloe knew the library was on the second floor of the building, which seemed to stretch almost across the entire city block.

"You know, this library, because of its great age and fragility, is closed to the public," said the librarian, pausing at the foot of a beautiful circular staircase that was roped off to restrict access. "However, we are pleased to make exceptions for such a noted scholar as Dr. Lejeune and a Vatican representative." She removed the velvet rope and gestured that they should proceed upstairs.

As they rounded the curve in the stairs, she called out, "Take your time, and if you need any help, please call me. By the way, your shipment arrived some time ago, and we have stored it upstairs in the rear of the library. It was quite a challenge."

"Shipment?" questioned Cloe as they entered the large upper floor that seemed filled with old books and papers. While Cloe stopped to examine a paper that had caught her eye, the monsignor strolled through the library.

"Cloe, come quickly!" he suddenly shouted.

Cloe nearly ran to the rear of the library because of the urgency in the monsignor's voice. She rounded the last bookshelf and stopped in her tracks.

"Oh my God!" she cried, gazing over what appeared to be a veritable sea of ancient oil jars.